EMPIRE'S PASSING

Marian L Thorpe

Arboretum Press

EMPIRE'S PASSING

Arboretum Press
Guelph, ON, Canada

www.arboretumpress.com

ISBN (print): 978-1-990711-06-0
ISBN (e-book): 978-1-990711-05-3

Cover Design by Anthony O'Brien
www.bookcoverdesign.store

~

Epigraphs

Part I: from *Morte d'Arthur* by Alfred, Lord Tennyson. Public Domain
Part II: from *Lays of Ancient Rome,* by Thomas Babington Macauley, Public Domain
Part III: from *Ulysses,* by Alfred, Lord Tennyson. Public Domain
Part IV: from *Eclogae,* by Vergil. Public Domain

Dedicated to the memory of my brother.
Christopher John Thorpe
1954 – 2019

A map, the character list, and the vocabulary lists are found at the end
of the story.

Prologue

~Colm~

I HAVE SNATCHED AN HOUR'S SLEEP, grief and exhaustion overcoming me. But outside the tent men are readying for battle; not something that can be done quietly. I lie on my cot, gathering strength for the day. Preparing myself for the lives I must try to save, and the ones I will lose. There will be more of the second.

My mother's letter lies on the table beside the wine flask. I must, today, put it from my mind, concentrate only on the wounded and dying men. When night gives way to the first light of dawn, the battle will start. A battle, the Emperor of the East has told me, he has little chance of winning. It will be an ending. The power of the world will shift when this empire of a thousand years is finally defeated.

What will this mean for my family, for the small province, far in the west, where my sister is *Principe*? My father's last letter spoke of an alliance among the western countries, trade and marriages creating some stability. But I am a physician first, and my duty is here, today. I cannot think beyond that.

I start to do an inventory in my mind of the tools I will need, the vinegar and honey for the wounds, the extract of poppy to dull pain. We haven't enough; half-doses will be all we can give.

I push the blanket off and sit up. Time to wash, to eat a little, drink. Outside, commands are shouted. I hear Bjørn's voice, which means Alekos is readying himself for battle. The Emperor and the commander of his personal guard are never far apart.

"Colm?" The tent flap is pushed aside. Alekos bends to enter. "No, don't stand. I have only a minute, and something to ask of you."

"What is it?" They were with me last night, both Bjørn and Alekos, for a while. Good friends, saying a farewell on the eve of battle. I hadn't expected to see the Emperor again. In the faint light, I can't read his face.

He pulls up the stool, sits. Dressed for battle, armoured. "You are to go back to Casil, to the palace." He hesitates, rare for the decisive Emperor. "And then, if you will, take my wife and children to safety in the west."

"You need me here." There will be so many wounded today. Perhaps even Alekos himself.

"You are one doctor among many," he says bluntly, "but you are more than that. Who but a prince can I entrust my Empress and my heirs to? This is not an order, Colm, only a request. But who you are matters." His face softens. "Tell my wife I have loved her. Tell the children the same. Will you do this for me, my friend?"

"My work," I say, "is to save lives."

"You will be. Three very important lives. My son and heir is one of them. He is only six, Colm."

Bjørn ducks into the tent. "It is time, Alekos."

The three princes, we are sometimes called by the men. I'd tried to dissuade it, did not allow myself to be called anything but my name in the hospital tents.

Two of us will die today, almost certainly. So might I; the victors may not care I am a physician. But there is a fourth prince, a child. How do I balance his life, all it means, against the men I might save?

"Colm?" Alekos is standing now, waiting. "I will not order it. I ask as a friend." He adds something that under other circumstances might have made me smile.

Do not argue over what a good man is. Be one. Catilius, and among my father's last spoken words to me.

"Is there a horse for me?" Men will die because I am not here, but a child, and all he will represent, might live.

"Yes. Saddled and waiting, with food and water in its saddlebags. Take only what you must, and go. Before you can be stopped." Alekos is brisk now, the commander. He turns to go, turns back. "Thank you." There is no time for anything else, and even if there was, there are no words,

I look at Bjørn, and back at Alekos. A memory surfaces. There are words. "Go with the god," I tell my friends. When the tent flap settles back into place, I begin to pack.

Part I

The old order changeth, yielding place to new.
Tennyson

Morte d'Arthur

Chapter 1

~Gwenna~

"THE EMPEROR NEEDS AN ANSWER." Talyn glanced at my mother, sitting further along the table. She had papers in front of her, troop records, but her eyes were unfocused. "General, your thoughts?"

The use of her military rank brought my mother's attention back to the room. "There are troops we can send," she said. "Construction will slow, or cease, on roads and in towns. As it will with half the Casilani cohorts gone, of course."

"Half for now," Talyn said. "Should we be sending any Ésparian soldiers, if in another month or two the rest of the Casilani are ordered home?" An important question, one I had been wrestling with for some time. Morning light brightened the room, the air still chilly. I'd had the shutters opened anyhow: it was easier to think in fresh air, I found, even if the day was grey and damp.

"Some will want to go," I said.

"Some are already asking," Talyn concurred. "Just as I am told there are those among their troops who want no part of Casil's war, who see themselves as Ésparian, after thirty years here."

"Perhaps we should ask for volunteers?" My mother's voice was flat, disinterested. She picked up one list, glanced at it, put it down again.

"The request is a courtesy," I reminded my generals. "Alekos could have ordered our troops sent, instead of making the personal plea." One would have been the act of an Emperor; one was the request of an equal. He had treated me with this consideration since I had declined to marry him, twelve years past. I could, in theory, refuse to send troops at all.

Whether purposely or by habit, my mother had taken her usual chair at this council table, leaving one between me and her. Today, with difficult decisions to make, its emptiness hammered at my heart. I should have chosen to sit at the other end, made a new configuration. Or used my workroom at the fort. I wasn't ready for this yet.

I stood to pace the room, the mosaic floor warm under my indoor shoes. Movement helped me think. What were the implications of sending Ésparian troops? What might happen, were our defensive forces reduced?

Very little, were Casil victorious against their enemy. But the order to the governor had come with grave news. The Boranoi had made a treaty with an invader from their northeast, the Kidari, and together they had swept west. Casil's client kingdom of Trakïya had joined them, shifting their allegiance, followed quickly by the provinces of Odïrya and Qipërta.

I sat again, at the other end of the table, resting my elbows on its polished surface. My generals shifted to face me. "Can we ask for volunteers, tentatively? See who is interested?"

"Just troops, or officers too?" Talyn asked.

"Both," I said, reluctantly. But I did not have to allow everyone who volunteered to be part of the deployment.

"The Casilani fleet may not wait." My mother sounded a little more animated. "Ships are already sailing from the Eastern Fort. A rider came this morning."

"Then we will send our own," I said. "Talyn, will you ask Dern to attend tomorrow, with a list of what ships we can spare? I will not rush into anything."

I could do this. I could look at the numbers of ships and soldiers and arms, and decide who and what to send, calculate the effects on production and construction and labour within Ésparias. But that was far from the only consideration. If Casil fell—I winced inside at the thought—if it no longer needed the metals and grain, cloth and dried fish and other goods we, as a royal province, had provided for them— what happened then?

I should have a plan. All the work my parents, and I, and others, had done for the last thirty years had been to respond to exactly this situation. But that Casil could fall in only a few months had not been part of our thinking. No reports—from the palace to our governor, in letters from my brother, serving as a physician somewhere with Casil's army, or even in the secret messages from Druisius's informants—had suggested such a sudden defeat was imminent.

And perhaps, if I'd still had the support and advice of my father, I could have responded rapidly and decisively to the terrible news. But I didn't. The messenger who had brought the news of Casil's plight had arrived just ten days after my father had died.

His death hadn't been sudden, or unexpected, and he'd done his best over his last winter to prepare me for the decisions that would be mine to make. His confidence in me had never wavered. But I needed advice, and my mother was not, right now, capable of the extended analysis needed. Talyn knew Ésparias and its people, but not the relationships and politics of the northern countries. Sorley did, but grief still held him in a net of near-despair.

The voices of gardeners drifted in through an open window, along with the sharp scent of sap. I listened for a moment, wishing I too only had to decide which branches of the vines to prune. Not that I would know. The wry thought brought me back to myself. There was only one person I could turn to for advice. I would have to ask him to come to me, but I had reasons—two, just now—that no one would question. One was the raising of the memorial stone for my father. The other was, quite simply, that he hadn't seen our son, Gwyllar, in nearly half a year.

"While we wait for the information on ships and volunteers," I said, "I'll send a message to Dun Ceànnar. Ruar's thoughts will help me decide."

~

"Will you go?"

The skin beneath Sorley's eyes looked bruised. He'd been tuning a *ladhar* when I came in. Now he reached up to hang it on the wall, his back to me. "If you want."

"The *Teannasach* is coming for the memorial, yes? So why are you sending Sorley to him now?" I turned at Druise's voice. He stood in the doorway. He must have been in the next room.

"I need Ruar's advice, and I want to give him time to think about it on the journey."

Druise chewed at his lip before nodding. "But you send me too." It wasn't quite a request.

"For what reason?" I guessed why Druise wanted to accompany Sorley, our unspoken but shared concern for his partner. We both knew how lost he was, how disoriented—and in the steep and sodden hills of Linrathe, negligence could be dangerous. Even on a road he'd ridden a hundred times.

Twelve years earlier, Ruar had sent Sorley to Ésparias to oversee the teaching of music and poetry in our new schools, so that he wasn't separated from Druise or my father. But regardless of his official role, he was a *scáeli* first. And *scáeli'en*, by Linrathe's tradition, travelled alone and unguarded, although they could join an individual or a party travelling on the same road. I would need a reason to send Druisius to Dun Ceànnar, one fitting his position and rank.

"How can I send you? It would be too obvious that I'm asking for a political discussion."

"All can see there will be problems, once the Casilani leave. That is no secret. You send the letter with me. Sorley can visit Linrathe whenever he likes. He needs no reason."

I didn't want Druise to go north; I didn't want to be without him and his pragmatic advice. But did my selfish wants outweigh what Sorley needed?

"I can talk to Ruar about the larger concerns, yes?" Druise argued. "Who else can do that?"

My mother and Talyn and Lynthe could, I thought. I couldn't send my mother, or Talyn; I needed them here. Lynthe wasn't possible. She disliked Ruar too intensely.

Still, I hesitated. Something beyond my wishes might make sending Druisius equally impossible, something I couldn't discuss in Sorley's presence. Perhaps Druise saw it on my face, because he turned to Sorley. "I have someone to see, amané. But I will be back soon."

Sorley was still standing, a distant, slightly puzzled look on his face, as if he'd just remembered something. As I watched him, a faint smile touched his lips. The thought of going to Dun Ceànnar? He blinked at Druise's words. "Yes. I'm teaching, anyhow."

"I'll walk with you," I said to Druise. We crossed a corner of the inner courtyard of the villa without speaking, the splash of water and the chirp of sparrows the only sounds. Druise, I noticed, was rubbing his left arm, where Decanius had stabbed him a dozen years past. It ached sometimes, he'd said this past winter, adding, 'I am getting old, yes?'

He was, something I really didn't want to think about. He was only a few years younger than my father had been, and both his hair and the stubble of his beard before he shaved were almost entirely grey. I'd noticed bruises on his arms and legs recently, too, as if he'd taken too many hits in sword practice. Walking beside me now, he seemed steady enough, his usual strong self.

My father had been my teacher in the arts of diplomacy and argument and in the subtleties of thought and language my position required, but it had been Druise who had carried me on his shoulders, held me on my first pony, and taught me to swim. He'd sworn an oath to me before I was even born, and I had no doubt of his love or his loyalty. But he'd made a different promise first, and it was that which concerned me.

When, in my first days of being *Principe*, my father had told me of Druisius's dual allegiances, I'd been shocked. "He's betrayed us?" I'd asked. "Is that why Eudekia accused you of treason?"

"Teaching treason," he'd corrected. "And no. Eudekia is an intelligent woman, and shrewd. She drew her conclusions based on what she and I sometimes discussed in our letters, and, I believe, on what she would have done in my place; perhaps even on what her father taught her. Druisius's work for her was simply to keep us safe. As he has done now for over eighteen years. What he has reported back to her, and you can be assured this is all, Gwenna, are threats he has identified and dealt with."

"Like Decanius."

"Among others. Knowing what I do now, I suspect strongly Eudekia sent a letter to Casyn, and perhaps even to Ruar as a client ruler, asking them to remove me—us—from Ésparias, and Decanius's easy reach, when you were a baby. Quintus, his uncle, was too powerful in the politics of Casil and the palace for her to recall Decanius quickly from the procurator's position. But in retrospect, I see her hand in my appointment as *Comiádh*, and in the governor sending Decanius south."

"Because Druise told her he frustrated an assassination attempt on you?"

"Yes. But he has told her nothing of our other plans. There his loyalty is to us. The risk to our safety that arises from that is our own doing, and outside what Druisius sees as his responsibility to Eudekia. But . . ." He'd glanced back over his shoulder then. We had been on the deck of the ship taking us home from Casil, the splash of oars and the creak of boards enough to obscure our words, and no one had been near.

"But?"

"Whatever awaits you in Ésparias, whatever opposition there is to your leadership—that Druisius will report to the Empress. And he will deal with threats however he feels he must, something he has long experience in."

~

I blinked in the coolness of the arched gallery that separated the courtyard from the interior rooms, thinking of how I'd shivered, inwardly, at that last sentence. The man who had killed Decanius in front of me hadn't been the Druisius I knew. But the passage of time and the lessons of leadership had allowed me to first accept and then welcome the realities of his protection. I was, almost certainly, alive because of Druise, and the promise he had made both to the Empress and in his oath of loyalty to Ésparias. Only my father and I had known of Druisius's service to Eudekia. Not my mother, and not Sorley, by Druise's request. Now it was only me.

I'd left my workroom door open. I kept my papers locked away, and, anyhow, there were guards everywhere. Druise waited for me to sit before he did, the extent of his private adherence to any protocol. I didn't bother with preliminaries. "What will you tell the Empress?"

He shrugged. "Nothing."

Nothing? "Why not?"

"The Emperor is at war, yes? A war that goes badly. Her interest is elsewhere."

He was right, I realized. Eudekia would not care what happened to me, here in this little province about to be abandoned by the Eastern Empire for the second time. Her bond had been with my father. More than friendship and less than love, I had thought, seeing them together in Casil, the spark of intellect and physical attraction strong between them. Now he was dead, and her son was leading his army with little chance of victory. Her concern would be for Alekos.

The room blurred, tears welling. For my father, for the Emperor, who was my friend; for the grey in Druise's hair and for the gulf between Lynthe and myself; for Sorley's pain and my mother's. All the things I could not fix, could not change . . .

"Kitten." Druise leant forward across the desk to lay a hand on mine.

I grasped it, my knuckles white with tension, and swallowed, hard. "I don't know how to do this."

"This?"

"Any of it. All of it." Not without my father to advise me.

"What would Cillian say?" Druise disengaged his hand, gently. I sat straighter, wiping my eyes quickly.

"To look for the greatest good for Ésparias."

"Then you do that, yes?" He stood, even though I hadn't moved. "I will take the letter to Ruar, and make Sorley come with me. He needs his hills and streams and sheep. He should have stayed when we buried Cillian at the *Ti'ach*. I told him so."

But you would not have stayed with him, I thought, and he could not face being alone. "He needed his family, too," I said.

"But maybe not this one." Druise stood. "If I am to go north, there are orders to be given to the guard. I may go?"

"Of course." I gave permission without thought, startled by what Druise had just said. "Leave the door open."

I sat, not reaching for paper and pen. On the day of my father's burial at the *Ti'ach*, deep snow had lain still under the trees. A step or two away, the first white *eirlysa* were just unfolding on my sister's grave. My mother had planted them a dozen years past, the year we'd returned from Casil, coming back to the *Ti'ach* to gather belongings and say goodbye. Lianë's sudden death had been the first time I'd ever seen my mother weep, her grief at her youngest, unexpected child's death intense and debilitating.

I'd expected a worse reaction when my father died. They had loved each other in a way I still didn't comprehend. But she'd remained strong: mourning him, yes, but she'd been the one giving comfort, more than taking it. When the ceremony was over, and my mother stayed to watch the men of the *Ti'ach* return the soil to the grave, Sorley had stood beside her, sharing this last duty of love. It wasn't tradition, but she would never have denied him. He had been shaking, I remembered, my mother's hand on his back perhaps the only thing keeping him upright.

Maybe not this family. We were not the only people whom Sorley loved, or who loved him. I'd seen his face when his brother, unlooked for, had arrived halfway through the gathering of friends who'd come to offer comfort and memories, to honour my father and to eat and drink and sing. There was always music in Linrathe, whether for celebration or mourning. By chance, I'd been looking at Sorley when his brother had entered the hall. He'd stood absolutely still for a heartbeat before he strode towards the door and into Roghan's enveloping embrace. I'd averted my eyes then, before the sight could shatter my own control, but not before I'd seen Roghan's daughter Lairís slipping her arms around both her uncle and her father.

Had Roghan suggested Sorley go back with him to Gundarstorp, to grieve with his blood family around him, to take comfort in the unchanged landscape and rhythms of his first home? Druise seemed to think that was what Sorley needed, and shouldn't he know?

As if you know what Lynthe needs, or even wants. Tears pricked again, this time from frustration. The distance between my *quincala* and me, a distance that had first arisen when I'd chosen to bear a child, was returning. During the weeks of my father's illness and in the aftermath of his death, Lynthe had been my support. She'd held me as I wept, listened to my fears, counselled me into sense when I'd wanted him buried here at Wall's End. I'd thought our previous problems were over. But it was becoming obvious they weren't.

Maybe we'd been apart too much these last few years, I thought. Maybe I'd been too distracted by motherhood. If I told her she couldn't lead Ésparian troops east, I wasn't sure what she'd do.

I took a deep breath. I didn't have time for Sorley's despair or Lynthe's attitude. I needed to plan, to weigh the consequences of choices, to consider the difficulty and the price of each possible course. I reached for the pen and paper.

Chapter 2

~Lena~

"I'LL WALK BACK WITH YOU," I told Talyn, gathering my records. Outside, thick clouds dulled the light. But all the world seemed dulled to me, so maybe it was brighter than I thought. It didn't matter.

After a few steps, Talyn said, "Inviting Ruar here will cause problems."

"I know," I said. I did, but I couldn't get involved. This disagreement was between my daughter and her partner. Lynthe wouldn't like Ruar's presence. I didn't understand her jealousy; Gwenna didn't love him. They were friends, and her choice of the *Teannasach* to father her child had made political sense. But even if Gwenna's feelings for him were stronger than friendship, what did it matter? It hadn't, for Cillian and Sorley and me.

But Sorley and I were friends, close friends, and I'd known how much he loved Cillian long before they became lovers. It had always been the three of us. For all my love and desperation, I hadn't been able to call Cillian back from the threshold of death thirty years past. Sorley had. That he couldn't, this time, was part of his anguish. Even though Cillian had told Sorley what he had known was the truth. "Play for me," he'd said. "The music is a balm. But the god does not allow a third return."

The third decides. Two sets of scars on Cillian's back, one from childhood, one from the Taiva. He shouldn't have survived either. Music had called him back to life twice: first his grandmother's cradle songs, then Sorley's. With the memory arose the tiny thread of anger I tried my best to ignore. Regardless of what Cillian—or I—had said, Sorley had wanted to try. And deep inside, I had wanted him to. I felt the prick of tears, blinked. I knew the anger, directed as much at myself as at Sorley, was senseless. It would pass, in time.

"Lynthe thinks we should send troops. And she wants to lead them," Talyn said.

"Lynthe?" A shock penetrated the invisible wall that seemed to separate me from the rest of the world. "Leave Gwenna? Now?"

"She's restless. She always has been," Talyn said. "And I think she feels the need to do something that's not in Gwenna's shadow."

"She has no experience of war," I said.

"Who now among us has?" Talyn countered. "No-one under fifty." We'd been at peace for over thirty years. "I expect any troops we send will be under the command of a Casilani officer."

She was probably right. "Gwenna has to approve the officers."

Talyn stopped, turning to face me. "And if she forbids Lynthe to go? What will that do to their relationship?"

I had always been restless too. When that restlessness had grown too great for my solitary rides around the *Ti'ach*'s lands to contain, I'd gone to Han to buy horses, or once or twice to Tirvan to visit my sister. Cillian had never demurred, never tried to convince me not to go. Here at Wall's End, my little boat had been enough, the hours I spent sailing sufficient to settle my mind for a while.

Sailing. It wasn't raining, and it was only mid-morning. "Will you take these back to my office?" I asked Talyn, handing her the bundle of records.

"Of course." I saw the concern on her face. "Are you—not well, Lena?"

She was the senior general, and she'd loved Cillian too, as a cousin and friend. She worried for me, I knew. "I want to go sailing," I said. "A day on the water will help, I think." Space and silence, and no need to be strong or a support for others.

Her face cleared. "A good idea. Do I need to ask your adjutant to cancel any meetings?"

"No. I had nothing but desk work today."

I went back to the villa to change into clothes more appropriate for a chilly day on the water. Our—my—rooms were in the southwest range of the building, its terraces overlooking the sea and catching the afternoon sun. Cillian had died on the terrace outside our bedroom, falling asleep in his chair and never waking. Quietly and painlessly, I'd written to Colm. I wondered where our son was, and when, or if, he'd received my letter.

I changed and found my thin gloves in a chest. Then I walked out onto the terrace. The air smelled of freshly turned earth, and the faint odour of cooking from the kitchens. Sometimes I felt Cillian's presence here still, as I did throughout our private rooms. His body was buried at the *Ti'ach* beside our daughter Lianë, but that made no difference. "I'm going sailing," I told him. "I need to think."

Music drifted through the open doors, barely audible above the splash of the courtyard fountain. A *ladhar*, but not played with Sorley's skill. He must be teaching. Good. An excuse not to see him, to say what I was doing. Someone—someone other than Cillian's shade—should know, though, although the idea rankled. I was tired of people and responsibility. I'd tell someone on duty at the harbour. That would suffice.

At the jetty I prepared *Tystie* for the water. Paddling her out, I realized I'd forgotten to bring food. It didn't worry me. Free of the sheltering harbour arms, I raised the sail and caught the breeze. A line of darker cloud lay at the junction of sea and sky, but it would be hours before the wind and waves would reflect the coming weather. I had time.

Beyond the scrutiny of eyes on land, well away from the fishing boats, I let the sail down. Drifting on the gentle sea, the waves rocked me like loving arms. The knot inside loosened. Out here, in the space and solitude of the sea, I had no need to pretend. The tears began slowly, the first sobs half-choked back. *If you do not grieve, Lena, you will break.* My mother's words, from so very long ago.

I howled my anger and loss to the sky and water, sobbed until my gut hurt and my breath came in gasps, until there were no tears left to wet my face and my throat was raw. In all the long weeks since Cillian's death, I hadn't given in to grief like this before. Not even in the emptiness of our wide bed.

I slumped against the side of the little boat. I'd held Gwenna as she sobbed, and Sorley too. Only Druise's tears had been as controlled as mine, at least that I'd seen. Even when I'd argued with my daughter over where Cillian was to be buried, I'd only allowed cold anger. At the graveside, with Sorley's voice cracking as he sang the parting song, I'd willed myself to stay dry-eyed, even as I rang the bell, the three notes echoed by plucked strings on Sorley's *ladhar*: one for loss, one for love, one for forgiveness.

The boat and my mind drifted. Images, memories, thoughts passed through my mind. The quiet moments of the last few months, when it was clear to us all Cillian was dying: music, words, his voice, comforting and counselling. His hand on my hair. Then further back, past our years at Wall's End, past even our years at the *Ti'ach*, to the time it had been only the two of us, first in the mountains and then later the plain, our survival dependent on each other. Lovers by then, but not admitting love, until a night by an unexpected lake, water in a desert, a cobalt sky studded with stars above us.

Never again. I sat up. *Tystie* had moved with the tide and breeze, and I could no longer see land. The distant clouds had blown closer, and the wind had picked up, making the slap of waves louder, the rock of the boat more pronounced. Gulls wheeled and screamed above me. I wasn't worried; I could find my way back. *Or not*, my mind said. *Or not. Hoist the sail, catch the wind again, and sail into the storm. The sea is a gentle death, it's said. Cold and dark, but only briefly. Not on and on.*

Would the seas of this world take me to the river Cillian had spoken of? The flowing water he had heard, before the god sent him back?

Käresta, no. Cillian's voice was as real as if he stood beside me. *No.*

"Cillian?" I said aloud. No answer. But a sense of his presence for a moment, disorienting here on *Tystie*. He'd never sailed with me, except for our desperate flight from Fritjof.

I stood, my legs trembling, to raise the sail. Then I turned the little boat and let the wind take me back to Wall's End.

~

I changed out of my outdoor clothes, ran first my fingers and then a comb through my salt-stiffened hair, and washed my face and hands and arms. Then, as I knew I should, as I knew Cillian would have, I went to our daughter.

I found her in her workroom, writing. "Your message to Ruar?" I asked, sitting across from her.

"I've written that. Druise is taking it."

"Druise?"

She explained. "It might be good for Sorley, don't you think?"

"Yes." The idea was a relief. I was worried about Sorley, but frustrated with him, too. I understood that he mourned, that sorrow had him in its icy grip. But it was I who slept alone now, in a bed too wide and too empty. He did not. I hated my thoughts, but regardless of what Cillian's beloved Catilius proclaimed, I couldn't control or ignore them. I wasn't quite rational, and I knew it. Hearing Cillian's voice today just confirmed that. "I'd been wondering if we should find Lairís, have her return to Wall's End."

Sorley's niece had learned all she could at the *Ti'ach na Barì* from Eithnë, its *scáeli* and Lady. Sorley, knowing her talent, had suggested she come to him for some additional instruction. Lairís had arrived last autumn, just when the physicians had told us Cillian had little time left. "I won't intrude," she'd said then. "You don't need a stranger around just now." She'd gone to travel around Ésparias, gathering songs, part of the requirements to become a *scáeli*. Like her father, Lairís had come to Cillian's burial to support Sorley, but she'd made the journey on her own.

"Maybe," Gwenna said. "Or maybe just leave him to himself. We all have our ways to grieve; *Athàir* told me that, when I was worried about Druise's drinking when Lianë died."

"Taking the message to Ruar might be good for Druise, too," I said. His grief wasn't expressed openly, but that didn't make it less painful. Being away from Wall's End might help them both. I'd sensed a distance recently between Druise and his partner, both mourning a man they'd loved, if differently. Maybe they were as unable to help each other as Sorley and I were just now.

"What are you working on?" I asked, wanting to change the direction of my thoughts.

"I'm thinking about how trade might work, with the Casilani gone. We won't need Linrathe's timber, or not as much."

"We'll need more of their wood and charcoal, unless the weather improves," I noted. We'd endured months of cold and wet since the autumn two years past, when, we had been told, a mountain had exploded in the north of Varsland, filling the air with ash. Ever-present clouds obscured the sun, and it rained five days out of seven. The grain harvest that first year had been almost complete, thankfully, because last year's had been poor across all of Linrathe and most of Ésparias. Only the south had been spared. The provision of food for Ésparias's army was part of my responsibilities, although civilian staff did most of it. I read reports.

"It can't stay like this another year," Gwenna said. "We won't need most of Varsland's fish, or the furs. We'll have to renegotiate those agreements, but we need to keep something in place with them."

"When I was a girl," I said, "we traded for almost nothing, except spices from Leste. Linrathe was our enemy, and Varsland unknown."

"And there will be some who will say we should return to that," my daughter said, an edge to her voice. "But we can't. We have agreements and obligations now, and whatever the future holds depends on those alliances."

"If we are not to fall back into enmity."

Gwenna put her pen down. "I am sure—for now—of Linrathe."

For now? But she was still speaking.

"Varsland, though, worries me. What will happen to their trade with the east, if Casil falls? They have grown used to the luxuries and wealth that has brought, whether they chose the river route east or indirect dealings through Linrathe's trading port."

"If Casil's enemy takes the city, they may well continue that trade, even expand it," I suggested. I had to try to be dispassionate, as if we were not speaking of a city and people known to me.

"They might. Bryngyl might distance himself from Bjørn, to keep that market." That the King of Varsland's brother led the Emperor Alekos's personal guard was not something that would be ignored by a victorious invader. "But it's not just Varsland, is it?" Gwenna said. "How many men from Sorham use that trading route too?"

I understood now. Sorham, sometimes belonging to Linrathe, sometimes to Varsland, its people always poised between loyalties.

"Ruar has been *Teannasach* for thirty years," I said. "He must have thought of this." Rain began to patter on the roof. The room had grown darker, too, although I hadn't noticed.

"His oldest son Daragh has almost complete oversight of the trading port at Abher Tabha now," Gwenna said. "He had a good grasp of trade even at twelve, when he came with Ruar to watch our border negotiations. He'll understand the implications of losing the Casilani market." Gwenna stood to light the lamp hanging over her desk. The air was growing colder.

"Then you need to involve him in the talks. Ask Ruar to bring him to the memorial." The stone being carved in Cillian's memory would be dedicated soon, to stand beside his father's and his uncle's. Gwenna had insisted on it, when I hadn't allowed Cillian to be buried anywhere but the *Ti'ach*. We'd exchanged angry words then, emotion running high in us both. It had been Druise's quiet reason that had made her capitulate. Honouring her father here as if he'd been *Princip* was her compromise.

Regardless of the solemnity of the occasion, it was also an opportunity for discussion: private family discussion, without a Casilani presence. I'd never asked Gwenna if she'd considered that benefit in choosing Ruar as the father of her heir, but it wouldn't have surprised me.

My daughter began to say something. But her eyes went to the open doorway behind me, and she stiffened, just slightly. I turned to see why. Lynthe's voice told me. "What are you asking Ruar for now?"

She was in uniform. I was not. The question—or its tone—as a response to my suggestion bordered on insolent. But my brief stab of irritation wasn't enough to rouse me to action; I simply couldn't find the interest. Lynthe had heard Ruar's name; the context had been ignored.

Disagreements were normal, I told myself. Cillian and I hadn't always been on good terms. I remembered stalking out in anger, leaving Sorley to explain. At least Gwenna never asked me to mediate between her and her partner.

"I am not asking him *for* anything." Gwenna was trying to be calm, but I heard the tightness in her voice. "It was suggested that Daragh should also attend the memorial, so that I can hear his views on how the withdrawal of the Casilani might affect trade in Varsland and Sorham."

I stood, my chair scraping on the flagstones of the floor. "And that," I said, "is all I can contribute to an analysis of trade." It was almost true, and as good an excuse as any to leave. "Major, see me in the morning, please."

"General."

I should hear her thoughts on the troops that might be sent east. Really, I should ride to the Eastern Fort, to discuss the situation with Finn, the general commanding. What was the feeling among our troops about supporting Casil in this war?

It had been too long since Gwenna had spent much time in the south; before Gwyllar's birth, she'd divided her time between Wall's End and the Eastern Fort, a *Principe* making her presence and interest known throughout her land. But first the baby, and then her father, had meant her recent visits had been short, and she had refused to go at all over the last winter. She'd sent Lynthe instead, as her representative, and, I thought privately, a way to relieve the tension between them.

A pang of a different grief gripped me. Gwenna and Lynthe had been happy together, their quick minds and different approaches—Lynthe's almost always the military one, Gwenna's the diplomatic—leading to argument, but not at a personal level. Discussions, sometimes with me or Cillian present, had become heated—but quickly set aside to go riding, or to the senior commons with friends, or simply to be together. Until Gwyllar.

Although that was unfair: Lynthe, while not a natural mother, was affectionate enough to Gwenna's son. It wasn't the child; it was his father, and the political and personal ties that brought Gwenna and Ruar together that Lynthe resented.

Perhaps I should suggest Lynthe be sent south again; whatever her issues with my daughter, she could be relied upon to gather and report information both analytically and dispassionately. It would save me a journey I didn't want to make, and it would give Gwenna some breathing space. After the memorial, I thought.

I closed the door to Gwenna's workroom and stood, indecisive. To my right was our—my—wing: a sitting room and two bedrooms, one Apulo's; Cillian's classroom and library, his treatment room and our private baths. To my left, Sorley and Druise's wing, and across the courtyard, Gwenna and Lynthe's. The public rooms and Gwenna's office were contained in the north wing, completing the four sides of the villa. It had taken almost two years to build after our return to Ésparias, but Gwenna had refused to supplant Faolyn's widow Siusàn and her two children from what had been the *Princip*'s villa. There were rooms enough at the fort, she'd said.

I chose a seat under the portico, remembering the worries of those first years. The opposition to Gwenna's leadership—a girl, too young, brought up in Linrathe—that she had countered with calm words and sensible decisions, and a few ruthless punishments for the ringleaders. And, I knew, a few more, made without her prior knowledge or approval, throats cut at night in alleys and lonely tracks, apparent robberies. Deaths that reminded me of one at Wall's End after the assassination attempt on Cillian, when Gwenna was a baby. I'd had my suspicions then about who was responsible, and I had them still. I would never ask. Wasn't it better, sometimes, not to know?

In private, there had been tears of frustration and fear in those years, and not only from Gwenna. It had been a time of transition for us all: I, trying to find a direction for my life in the demands and discipline of the army; Cillian adjusting to teaching less, his principal role now as Gwenna's advisor; Sorley gone on Linrathe's business for long weeks. Only Druise had appeared to adapt to the new structure of our lives easily. I thought perhaps the return to Wall's End was a relief for him, freedom from the restrictions of life in Linrathe.

But the rebellious element had been subdued, Gwenna grew in confidence in her role, and as time passed I found a degree of peace with my youngest child's death. I did my job, largely administrative, accepted, reluctantly, my promotion to a rank that was appropriate for the *Principe*'s advisor, and bought my sailboat. Cillian and Sorley taught the cadets and the junior officers: history and diplomacy from Cillian; music and poetry from Sorley. Books came from Casil, and boxes of carefully packed, exquisite glass, and sometimes a strange instrument that had made its way to Casil from the eastern trade routes. And letters: Eudekia's to Cillian; Alekos's to Gwenna; Colm's to me and his father. Even Druise had letters from his brother. In exchange for Ésparias's grain and salt, metals and timber, fine wool and dried fish, the ships brought us oil and wine, spices and linen, and every year more people, coming to find work or land. One had been a mosaicist, with his books of patterns showing scenes from the ancient poems of Heræcria. Cillian had been delighted, and the floor of the principal reception room of the villa now told a story to those with the eyes and education to see.

"You are smiling." I looked up at Apulo's quiet words.

"Was I?" I motioned to him to sit. "A good memory."

"They lighten grief." He touched my hand, briefly. "Is there anything I can do for you, Lena?"

I shook my head. "No. I went sailing today, so I'm sore, but the baths will be enough." I'd accepted his offer of massage some years earlier, when the deskwork began to take a toll on my neck and shoulders. His fingers were strong, and skilled, and completely impersonal. I glanced at him. He looked, I thought, tired, and his tunic was damp. "Were you at the infirmary?"

"Yes. They appreciate my help."

"You don't have to work," I said, not for the first time.

He gave me a look. "No more than you do." He'd been Cillian's personal aide for thirty years, never taking a day off. His life had been changed by Cillian's death in ways even I couldn't fully comprehend.

We sat in silence for a while, watching the rain splashing on the stones of the courtyard. Sparrows huddled under the roof. Apulo spoke, suddenly. "I had thought to go east," he said. "To find Colm, and offer my services to him, to his patients."

"But not now." Colm was not in Casil, but somewhere beyond it, a battlefield physician as his teacher Gnaius had once been. Where surgery advances, Gnaius had told us. My fear for my son was constant, pushed back behind my duties into that hollow, echoing place inside me.

"No."

I understood. Apulo had no skills useful to a surgeon attempting to save lives; his expertise was in mitigating the damage done when healing had begun. He'd lessened Cillian's pain and kept him mobile for three decades. At the fort's infirmary, he was working on wrenched shoulders and knees or the weakness that followed broken bones: even in peacetime, there were always accidents on the training ground or on patrol.

"But." His voice was uncharacteristically hesitant: Apulo had dropped unnecessary deference after his first few years with us. "I told Cillian this, when we spoke of what I might do."

That they'd had those conversations came as no surprise. Neither man would have refused to face what they both knew was approaching. "And?"

"He asked me that if I did, would I take his ring to Colm."

Chapter 3

~Gwenna~

RAIN LASHED AT THE VILLA THE AFTERNOON Druise and Sorley returned. I'd had to close even the shutters that faced the courtyard, so fierce was the wind. Druise's cloak still dripped as he stood at the door to my workroom. "Sorley has taken Ruar and his son to the baths. But the *Teannasach* said he would come to see Gwyllar next."

"In my rooms," I told him. "Not here." By visiting his son before anything else, other than getting clean and warm, Ruar could bypass the usual protocols attached to the *Teannasach* of Linrathe's visit to Ésparias. I'd better warn Lynthe, though.

"How is Sorley?" I asked, before Druise could leave. "And sit down." The brazier was lit, and the room reasonably warm.

"He has started to write a song. It will help." He didn't sit.

"This is hard for you."

He shrugged. "It is hard for all of us, yes?"

I didn't press him. He wouldn't say more: only once had he revealed any of his inner thoughts about Sorley and my father to me. *You see the four of us, Kitten; you think we are solid, like the four walls of a building that stands square. But it is not so. The wall that is Sorley leans more heavily on the wall that is your father, and his wall leans more heavily on your mother's. My wall leans on no one.'*

I hadn't believed that when I was eighteen, and I didn't believe it now. I had a much better sense of how close the friendship between my father and Druise had been, and an inkling of how Druise dealt with the emotions he wouldn't admit openly. Lynthe had heard the rumours from her soldiers, and told me. I refused to think of what that meant in his life with Sorley. I refused to think of it at all: it was not for me to know. I loved Druise, and he loved us. That was what mattered.

Right now, I couldn't let any of it distract me: the future of Ésparias could not wait for private grief. "What do you think of Daragh?"

"In Casil we would call him the harbourmaster, yes? He knows the captains and the ships, who will argue, who will try to falsify weights. And the price of everything."

Most people would have thought his tone neutral. "But?"

"He thinks about what benefits his country, yes? In the agreements with Casil, a portion of each trade made goes to Linrathe."

Agreements made when I was a baby. Linrathe's trade with Ésparias was mostly through land routes; the sea trade was for Casil. They and Varsland had had the sea-going ships needed, and we'd never seen a reason to expand our own fleet to include merchant ships. Some privately owned small boats moved goods between coastal villages, but even that had declined as more roads had been built in Ésparias. A mistake?

If so, it was my error. Both Michan, the officer who had trained me and been my first senior trade envoy, and later Muire, who held the post now, had agreed, but the responsibility was mine. Something to think about. I brought my attention back to Druise. Unusually, he had a hand on the doorframe, supporting himself.

"Thank you, Druise," I said. "Now go to the baths yourself. You look like you need them."

"I can come and see the little Bear later?" His name for my sturdy, dark-haired son.

"You'd better," I said. "He's been asking for you."

~

I'd wondered if Daragh would be uncomfortable with me, the mother of his illegitimate—by Linrathe's laws—half-brother, but if he was, he didn't show it. Gwyllar didn't remember his father; not surprising, for a child barely three, but Ruar had him happily sitting on his lap within a few minutes. His head was bent to his son, listening to his almost-coherent story about his pony, an elderly animal that had tolerated a generation of excited youngsters' drumming heels and hands tugging at its mane.

Daragh had commented good-naturedly on Gwyllar's resemblance to Ruar, but he showed little real interest. And why should he? Gwyllar was twenty years younger, and no rival to the leadership of Linrathe. The two half-brothers might, one day, be leaders together of their respective lands, but that was, I trusted, long years in the future.

I thought Daragh looked more like his mother, blue eyed, with hair the brown of winter beech leaves. His face in repose fell into a pleasant expression, but also an alert one: a man used to paying attention. He'd expressed his sympathies to me both gracefully and in fluent Casilan.

When Gwyllar began to fuss I rang for his nursemaid, her appearance acting as an apparent natural end to our gathering—but one I had orchestrated. "Come and see our Casilani glass," Sorley suggested to Daragh. "If any of its quality ever escapes my notice and actually makes it to Linrathe, I can tell you what it's worth."

"And I will tell you what I would pay for it in Casil," Druise added with a grin. "Which is less." There was no polite way for Daragh to refuse. I stood to accept his hand in farewell. He followed them from the room. I turned to Ruar.

He smiled, his blue eyes crinkling. "Hello, Gwenna." He opened his arms. I went into them, feeling the strength in his embrace, and the momentary sense of safety, of relief.

"Ruar." We didn't kiss.

"How are you, *leannan*?"

"I'm—all right. Coping. I must."

"I know. Gwyllar is a credit to you. So confident, and happy."

"He's stopped asking for his grandfather," I said. "I wish he'd known him longer, at least to have his first *xache* lessons." The child-sized pieces that I'd learned the game with, the only thing my father had from his mother's family, were safe in a chest. I'd start teaching Gwyllar when the shorter days of winter kept us indoors.

We sat again, opposite each other. The brazier was lit, and the room warm, but the atmosphere of quiet comfort had as much to do with the man across from me as the heating system. "You want my advice," he said. "Unofficially."

"And officially," I said. "We will have to meet with the procurator. There are demands for more grain and salt to be sent east, and Muire tells me I should be concerned about the grain supplies." I paused. I might know Ruar intimately, but this was not a moment for emotion. "But separately from that, I—we—must plan for Casil's fall. To make the western alliance into something real, and not just an understanding among a few."

"For all we have worked towards this since I was first *Teannasach*," he said, "I never really believed this day would come. Is Casil's defeat certain?"

"It is—probable. I think this is why Alekos did not order Ésparian troops to Casil."

"Because you might need them here?"

"Yes. His mother knew—guessed—the plans. She called it 'a contingency plan for the day the Eastern Empire fails,' and chose not to see it as sedition. I am sure she would have told Alekos, although he has never spoken of it in his letters."

Ruar nodded. "Cillian told me of that conversation. And if Alekos is of like mind, then not stripping Ésparias of its soldiers is the response of an honourable Emperor."

I didn't have time to dance around the point. "An honourable Emperor, but also a friend. One who believes I may well have a need to defend my land. Remember who commands his personal guard."

Ruar's chair creaked as he leant forward. "You think Varsland could be a threat again? Are you thinking of food shortages?"

"I wasn't," I said, narrowing my eyes at his words. "I was wondering what happens to the guard, those who survive, if Casil falls? If Alekos is dead? Whether he is killed in battle or not, I cannot imagine the Boranoi and this new ally of theirs allowing him to live."

"Nor Bjørn," Ruar said thoughtfully. "But the soldiers of the guard, perhaps. If they leave Casilani lands."

"If they return home," I said, "perhaps they will be tired of war, and ready to settle to farming and fishing. Or perhaps they will be angry, and looking for a way to regain their pride."

Ruar ran a hand over his chin. "Men who have spent so long together, with one purpose—they will not settle easily. And after these last two years, farming is unlikely to be a tempting choice."

"Then you agree? I must consider this?" As I spoke, I heard the door open. I swore, silently. I'd forgotten to send the message to Lynthe, alerting her to Ruar's arrival.

"Consider what?" She tossed her wet cloak onto a stool before giving Ruar a curt nod. "*Teannasach.*"

"Major." He stood, offering a hand. She accepted it, if briefly.

"What were you discussing?" Lynthe asked, dropping into a chair. She pushed damp hair off her face. Lynthe hated being wet; it wasn't going to help her mood.

"Change first, *käresta*," I suggested.

"I'm all right. Is this a meeting of parents, or of allies?"

"Are we not both?" Ruar said mildly. He hadn't taken his seat again. "I dine with the procurator tonight, and I believe we meet tomorrow, Gwenna, regarding the changed demands from Casil?"

"We do. Mid-morning."

"I'll see you then. Good night, Gwenna, Major." He held up a hand to stop me from rising.

Lynthe waited until the door was closed. "Why was he here?"

"To see Gwyllar. And I wanted his thoughts on a few things, privately."

"What things?"

I sighed. "Lynthe, you know Casil is in real danger; that is no secret. We were speaking of what might happen if they are defeated." My irritation was rising. "Of whether Varsland is a threat, in those circumstances."

"Why do you think they would be?"

My irritation vanished, to be replaced by a profound tiredness. "A feeling." I explained, summarizing what I'd told Ruar. Lynthe listened without interrupting, a frown deepening.

"But those men wouldn't have their king's approval," she said. "Surely?"

"While Bryngyl might not support them publicly, perhaps he would privately. Varsland has no real ties to Ésparias, beyond trade." *I do not trust them*, the Empress Eudekia had said to me once.

"But they do to Linrathe," Lynthe said. 'What if Ruar's been biding his time all these years? When Casil's troops leave, wouldn't it be a perfect time for Linrathe and Varsland to invade?"

"How can you suggest that?" Anger tightened my throat, making my voice hoarse. "He's Gwyllar's father. He wouldn't put him in danger." Did she hate Ruar this much?

"He wouldn't have to. Think, Gwenna: it would be easy to take Gwyllar to Linrathe. It's only a matter of crossing the Wall."

"You can't believe this," I said.

"Did I say I did? But you're worrying about Varsland based on nothing but a feeling." Her voice was reasonable, measured. "Wouldn't your father have told you to examine every possibility?"

He would have. She was right. My father had trusted Ruar completely, but still, as at least an intellectual exercise, he'd have played this out.

Lynthe smiled apologetically. "I'm just trying to make you think beyond your assumptions, Gwenna. Don't be angry."

I took a deep breath. "Why didn't you raise this when I chose Ruar to be the father of my heir?"

The placatory smile vanished. "I did. But you just dismissed my concerns. All your family approved of Ruar, so my thoughts didn't matter."

She had, it was true. And I had dismissed her apprehension. 'Ruar is an ally,' I remembered saying, 'and there will be no question of him wanting control or influence over the child.'

"I'm sorry," I said. "But I believed then that you were wrong about this, and I still do. There is no threat from Linrathe." It was unthinkable.

"Your father always favoured Linrathe," she said. "His real country. And so have you, brought up there like you were. But what if you're wrong?"

My stomach clenched. I'd been taunted by the same accusations against my father when I'd come to Wall's End at twelve. Sorley had helped me deal with them, and I'd thought in my years as *Principe* I'd put the doubt and distrust to rest. To hear the same accusations from the woman I loved—

"There are others in the army who think as I do," she said, her voice goading. "Ask my mother, if not yours. Who, by the way, has ordered me to the Eastern Fort, to find out what Finn thinks about sending soldiers to support Casil, and to see what the governor will reveal. I leave after the memorial." She had turned very cold. "At least you told me about this potential threat from Varsland, because that will have to be considered in our planning. Or were you going to let us waste the time and effort, and then veto whatever we decided?"

"No." It wasn't a lie. Not entirely. "We need a plan. But—" Honesty was needed now, to appease her and mend at least a little of the hurt. "I don't want you to lead the troops, if we send them."

"I wouldn't be. They'd be commanded by some Casilani. I don't have battlefield experience." She laughed, a bitter sound. "That seems to be the judgement. Not enough experience to lead troops in a war; not enough experience to advise you. Will I even get a mention, when the histories are written?" She hauled herself to her feet. "I'm going to the baths. Are you coming?"

"It's Gwyllar's supper time." I tried to be there for that as often as I could.

"Fine. I'll find someone to keep me company. Don't expect me early."

I was late: Gwyllar had nearly finished his meal. When he was done, and his hands and face washed, I took him by the hand. "Let's go see your grandmother," I suggested.

"Yeth!" He tugged his hand from mine and was off running. I didn't try to stop him; he'd come to no harm within the villa, except perhaps a skinned knee if he tripped. On my parents'—my mother's—side of the villa, the doors were closed; she'd have the braziers lit, even though the furnaces were fueled. I hope the steward had ordered more wood and charcoal to keep the villa heated properly.

I knocked, heard my mother bid me enter, and opened the door. The room glowed with lamplight. She was seated at her desk, writing; seeing me, she closed her journal. "Gwenna. What a horrible day." She held out her arms to Gwyllar.

"In more ways than one." My son gave his grandmother a kiss, then went straight to the box of toys she kept for him. He took out the carved farm animals and began to arrange them on the floor. They would keep him occupied for some time, I hoped.

"There is wine warming by the brazier." I poured a cup; it tasted of honey and spices. "What's wrong?" my mother asked.

I slumped into a chair. "Lynthe. She's angry because I didn't tell her I was worried about Varsland."

My mother picked up the pen she'd been writing with, turning it over in her fingers, her eyes distant. Then she put it down and faced me. "Almost every disagreement I had with your father was about exactly that. He would keep things from me, thinking he was protecting me. Your intentions may be good, Gwenna, but Lynthe feels excluded and ignored, I would guess. I know I did."

I remembered my mother's palpable anger at my father during our travel to Casil. She'd been mourning Lianë, and later, when our lives had settled again and I'd had time to think about it, I'd thought the episode an anomaly, fuelled by grief. But my father had been keeping a secret on that journey: his fear he would be charged with treason in Casil. Had my mother realized that, as I had?

Even if she had, this wasn't the same. "There's more to this," I admitted.

"What has Lynthe done?"

I told her what Lynthe had said today her accusation of Ruar, and her allegation of my father's favouring of Linrathe. My mother listened, her face tightening.

"I suppose it was too much to hope that rumour had been put to rest," she said, when I'd finished. "But for Lynthe to believe it . . ." She exhaled, frustration evident.

"And then to accuse Ruar of having designs on Ésparias," I added. "She said you knew of that, too."

My mother laced her fingers together. "There is always talk. Your father trusted Ruar implicitly. So does Sorley." Did that mean she didn't? "Why didn't you tell her your concerns about Varsland?"

"I wanted Ruar's thoughts first; he's closer to them. But she felt it meant I didn't value her opinion." I sighed. "In hindsight, I should not have made it a private conversation, but a discussion at council."

"More can be revealed in a private talk, especially when there is a tie beyond politics."

"The tie that she hates," I said.

"That is between you as partners," my mother said. "A personal matter. But you need to consider how to deal with the distrust; that has ramifications beyond your private life." She rubbed her eyes, absently. "When Sorley left Wall's End when you were a baby, because he could not deal with what Cillian had done for his sake, I was furious with him. I nearly hated him, for a time. But I never once thought he would betray your father. Can you say the same for Lynthe?"

I tried to say yes, but the word wouldn't come. A year past, I wouldn't have hesitated. But today wasn't the first disagreement we'd had over my leadership. Oh, Lynthe, I thought. What has happened to us?

My mother regarded me calmly. Sadly. "What will you do?"

The tone—almost the one my father would have used—jolted me back into dispassion. "Isn't there a larger question to be answered first?" I asked. "Do we have an obligation to Casil to send troops?"

"Your father would have said so. A royal province has protections and perquisites that come directly from the throne, but those benefits have a price. But you must weigh that obligation against your responsibility to Ésparias."

Uncertainty flooded through me again. "That's what Druise said. That *Athàir* would have told me to do what is best for Ésparias."

"As you must." My mother put out a hand to touch my arm. "Gwenna. I know it is difficult, but yours is the directing mind now. The decisions are yours. But—" Her eyes grew distant. "When your father and I met Turlo and Sorley on the river, when Turlo told us of Varsland's invasion, Cillian wanted to return home, to fight. Even though he had no skill with weapons beyond the bow. Turlo prevented it, for which I was glad. But later, when we had come home, there was no question of us both taking part in the war, in different ways, as much as we were each afraid for the other. You must allow Lynthe to do what she believes she should."

"Mat'a." Gwyllar pulled at my sleeve. A well-timed interruption; I needed to think about what my mother had just said.

I knew that stance. "He needs the latrine," I said, getting up. "May I?"

"Of course."

Gwyllar fussed as I refastened garments and washed my hands and his. He was tired, ready to sleep. I bade my mother good night, and carried him to our rooms and his nursemaid. Lynthe, as I had expected, wasn't back.

I poured a little more wine, watering it well. Wrapping a shawl around my shoulders, I went out into the courtyard. The rain had stopped. Overhead clouds almost obscured a waxing moon. No stars shone.

What was best for Ésparias. Not what was best for me, or for Lynthe, or even for our relationship. Before I was born, my father and a now-dead general had negotiated a treaty with Casil for a chance to save our land. My mother had signed that treaty, on behalf of the women's villages. Because it had been best for her country.

Movement near the fountain caught my eye: one of the villa's cats, out hunting. I called it, softly. It turned its head, regarded me, and continued on its way. I'd have liked to cuddle it, feel it purring against me, but cats did what cats wanted.

To do nothing may also be injustice. Catilius. I knew, deep inside, that I did have an obligation to Casil. I would send those who volunteered. To prevent Lynthe from being one of them was within my rights as *Principe*, but it too would be an injustice. Not just to her, but perhaps to Ésparias as well.

The terrible responsibility of love. Sorley had used those words once. He hadn't told me the weight of those responsibilities; I wouldn't have understood, at fourteen. I did now.

I was *Principe*, however, with all its attendant obligations. And so I would wait to hear the thoughts of all my generals before I told Lynthe she could go.

Chapter 4

"THE ARMY STILL NEEDS TO BE FED and clothed, whether they are here or in the east," Daragh pointed out. Across the conference table, his father stayed silent. I glanced at my senior trade envoy, offering him the opportunity to respond. Daragh was correct. The immediate demands of the army and officials in Ésparias had benefited both Ésparias and Linrathe over the years. Grain and fish, wool for tunics and cloaks, leather for sandals and belts and harness—all these needed to be produced here, not imported. The Empire, the governor had told me more than a decade previously, needed its provinces and client states to add to its coffers, not drain them.

"Of course," Muire said. "But already what is available both to send and to bring back is diminishing. We have seen little oil, and its price has more than doubled; the same with wine. I hear of vineyards uprooted in favour of grain to feed not just the army, but Casil itself, now two of its eastern provinces have declared for the Boranoi."

Odïrya had been the latest to change allegiance, its neighbour, the client kingdom of Trakïya, already allied with the Boranoi. Odïrya's fertile river valleys and plain had been a significant source of grain for the Casilani, as had Trakïya. When the old Boranoi king had died, the uneasy peace with Casil had failed. Bolstered by Eudekia's marriage to the Boranoi heir, Hathus, it had barely survived Hathus's death nine years previously, but somehow the old king had kept his people in check. His successor, a younger, legitimized son, had consolidated his claim to the throne by taking advantage of their simmering resentment and suspicions. He would avenge his brother, he had vowed, and destroy Casil and her Emperors forever.

Until just over three years ago, that vengeance had been little but posturing and words, kept in check by diplomacy and bribes—money, it appeared, that the Boranoi had quietly spent on weapons and a greatly increased army. The border skirmishes became fiercer, longer, involving more troops, but still Casil's army had kept them contained.

Until a new threat had arisen, the Kidari, from a land north of the provinces that bordered the eastern end of the Nivéan Sea. The Boranoi king had quickly allied himself to them, creating the greatest threat to Casil and its empire it had faced in hundreds of years. A threat, the procurator had told me, quietly and privately, there was little chance of Casil suppressing.

Daragh listened, his eyes narrowing as he took in Muire's explanation. "This will cause unrest," he said finally. "Both in Linrathe and Varsland. You are talking of the collapse of markets that have made some men rich and supported many more. Even if I think only of Abher Tabha, the trading harbour, if fewer ships arrive many men who load and unload them will be out of work, and the barrel-makers and rope-makers and many others will have less demand for their products and less money to spend, at a time when grain prices are rising. Hunger is possible. But what can we do to alleviate this? Procurator, what do you suggest?"

"That is beyond my responsibility," Oriacus replied. "Except to say this, which perhaps I should not. If Casil's withdrawal is complete, then so are our taxes and tariffs, and all other levies we currently collect."

"For the first time in generations," Ruar said, "Linrathe will be making no payments to another country. Not Varsland, not Casil. Our own taxes can decrease, and we could subsidize grain, if needed."

"As well," Daragh said, with a nod to his father, acknowledging the point, "the Casilani rule that stops the Varsland ships at Abher Tabha no longer holds."

"But Ésparias may choose to maintain it, with our agreement," Ruar warned. "A later conversation."

"One I recommend you have," the procurator said. The skin beneath his eyes sagged. So did his shoulders. A man both distraught and exhausted. Was the news from Casil worse than I had been told?

"Bryngyl may have his own thoughts on that." Daragh's gaze was levelled on his father.

"I expect him to," I said. "He will be invited to a discussion at the appropriate time." But not one with Oriacus present, or any Casilani.

"What we need now is a thorough evaluation of the flow of trade and the current and future markets. How much of Varsland's smoked fish goes to Ésparian markets—and does that market still exist if our population drops by a third? By half? Will they want our fruit, if grain prices increase?" Muire spoke to Daragh directly. "The same for all exports and imports, whether from Varsland or Linrathe. I understand you are best placed to make that analysis."

"I suppose I am," he said.

"Then can we leave that to the two of you?" I asked. Trade was important, enormously so, but it was not my only concern. The other was not for Daragh's ears, though.

"You may, *Principe*." Muire gave me a smile. I'd always liked him, from when we'd been students together, and briefly lovers one summer. A good friend. How much, I wondered, would I need to share with him in the coming weeks? "Daragh, shall we go to my office?"

Oriacus excused himself too, leaving me alone with Ruar. "The procurator was surprisingly honest," he said.

"He was. It worries me." I stretched, glancing at the lightly clouded sky beyond the high windows. "Let's go for a walk." After days of rain, I'd welcome the fresh air, and I needed to talk to Ruar privately.

"Can we bring Gwyllar?" The question surprised me, pleasantly. I wanted our son to know his father, but Ruar was being more attentive than I'd expected.

We found him in the courtyard, 'helping' a gardener under the watchful eye of his nursemaid. She scooped him up to wash his hands in the fountain before handing him over. "Shall I come with you?"

I told her no. She could have an hour on her own. I spent as much time with Gwyllar as I could: before my morning's tasks; sometimes at the midday meal; always in the later afternoon. It had been the pattern of my childhood, and while my parents had been as occupied with work as I was, I'd never felt neglected. I wanted the same security for my son.

We walked out along the gravelled path that ran beside the gardens. Bees hummed, attracted by the flowers on the mint. A blackbird sang from the peak of the villa's roof. Gwyllar ran ahead of us, happy to be out of the confines of the villa.

"He's becoming a boy," Ruar said. I understood what he meant. In the last weeks, Gwyllar had lost much of his baby roundness, his torso and limbs lengthening.

"I know. He should begin lessons soon." The thought brought a sharp pang of loss. I'd expected my father to be his first teacher, as he'd been mine. "I'll have to find a tutor for him."

"Someone from a *Ti'ach*?"

"Yes. I want him to be taught as I was. To learn to think, not just to recite facts."

"Even at mealtimes," Ruar said. "Did Cillian ever stop being the *Comiádh*?"

I smiled too at the memory. "Rarely." But even beyond the classroom, the learning had never felt forced. He'd used my own curiosity—and Colm's—to foster and encourage discovery. Could I find someone who could do the same for Gwyllar?

Another thing to think about, but not why I wanted to talk to Ruar. Where the path branched ahead of us, Gwyllar chose the one leading to the stables. He paused, looking back at us. "Go on," I called. He scampered ahead.

I wanted to take advantage of these few minutes alone. "Varsland," I said. "How do we bring them closer, without a marriage alliance with Ésparias?"

"There will be another with Linrathe," he reminded me. Bryngyl's daughter was promised to Daragh, but there would be few years yet before they could wed. A king's daughter to the *Teannasach*'s presumed heir: a good match, adding to the strong links between the two countries, links that went back centuries. "But," Ruar continued, "why is a marriage alliance with Ésparias not possible, Gwenna?"

"Eudekia forbade it. I've told you that before."

"You also told me your reply."

I have no intention of, and no interest in, a marriage alliance with Varsland, I had said to the Empress of the East. I'd been eighteen, newly *Principe*. Then I'd qualified my assertion. *Not for myself. I will not rule out other avenues.*

Nor should you, Eudekia had replied. *They are better as an ally.*

Ruar didn't wait for me to speak. "At Cillian's burial, Roghan brought me a message. Bryngyl is interested in Siusàn's daughter as a possible bride for his heir."

"I thought the prince—Trygve, isn't it?—was betrothed?" We'd been informed of that through the usual channels last autumn.

"He was, to Earl Vidar's oldest daughter. But she died over the winter. A cut that festered, and then killed her."

"Poor girl." A horrible death for anyone. "Why did they approach you, not me?"

"Because Siusàn and Flynsà reside at Dun Ceànnar, and in the ways of Varsland, with her father dead, I, as her mother's brother, am who should be approached."

Ruar's sister had returned to Dun Ceànnar with her daughter when her son Constyn had entered the cadets. She'd wanted Flynsà to experience life in Linrathe, she'd said, and how could I argue? My father had wanted the same for me. They'd been at my father's burial, but I'd had little chance to speak with them, beyond accepting condolences. Flynsà, at twelve, was a quiet, alert girl. "Isn't she starting at a *Ti'ach* this autumn?"

"The *Ti'ach na Kúsi,* the same as her mother, although it was Asgaill's school then. But that is of little matter. The betrothal is the bond. The marriage can wait."

"Flynsà is Ésparian. She may have other thoughts." Or other tastes. I was arguing against myself, because once I had let myself consider it, I'd seen the benefit immediately. The heir to Varsland, married to a princess of Ésparias. A match similar to the one I'd once proposed for myself, when I was fourteen.

"Gwenna. You asked how to strengthen the alliance with Varsland. This is one way. Do we have a choice free of politics? I am not Gwyllar's father because we are in love." He spoke lightly, but the truth was there. I had made a political decision, and so, I supposed, had he. But I had made it for myself, not for a cousin of barely twelve.

A question I should have asked earlier pushed itself forward. "What did you reply to Bryngyl?"

"That it was not I who should be approached, but you. I gave a letter to Roghan immediately; he will have delivered it by now."

"Why didn't you tell me then?"

"At your father's burial? It wasn't the time, *leannan*. I knew I would see you again before Varsland made any move."

I couldn't argue with that, and yet Ruar's action rankled. But would it have, had Lynthe not made her accusation?

"You could have written to me," I said.

"I could have," he said mildly. "But I thought a conversation would be better. I have another thought. Would your brother make a marriage into Varsland, were he here?"

"Colm? I don't even know if he's alive." I hoped he was; prayed, sometimes, to a nebulous deity I didn't really believe in. The statue of the huntress had been brought from the *Ti'ach* to Ésparias, and now stood in the courtyard of the villa. I still touched her for luck, or in supplication, sometimes.

"No Casilani marriage, or partnership?"

"Not that I'm aware of." I hadn't seen him since he was fourteen. He'd sworn then never to marry, or to father children, the pain of Lianë's death too great. But he was twenty-five now, and time and distance may well have changed his mind. "But what suitable match in Varsland is there for a prince of Ésparias?"

"If an earl's daughter was suitable for the heir to Varsland, surely it would be for Colm?" Ruar said. "It is what my Helvi was, after all."

"One of Bryngyl's regents' daughters," I countered. "Not quite the same." There had been something about Colm, perhaps just the detachment of a mind already focused on medicine, that had made me wonder if his vow to remain unmarried and childless had come almost naturally to him. Nor did I think it was men who interested him. But perhaps he'd just been slow to mature; still, he'd never wanted to be a prince, and unless he'd changed, he'd baulk—or outright refuse—to be part of our plans.

"Mat'a!" Our son, impatient, ran back to us. He tugged at my hand. "I wan' see G'uaga'." He couldn't quite say Gruagach, the pony's name. Ruar bent to lift his son up.

"We will," he told Gwyllar. "Look. There he is."

Ruar pointed. The stablegirl, seeing us approaching, had saddled the shaggy animal and led it out into the yard. "Shall I take him, my lady?" she asked.

Ruar settled Gwyllar into the deep seat of the saddle. "Sit up," the stablegirl said firmly. "Like I showed you. Good." She led the pony away, Gwyllar's hands holding the pommel.

We watched Gwyllar on the pony. A strand of hair, caught by a gentle breeze, brushed across my face. I repinned it. The air smelled, not unpleasantly, of manure. The stablegirl circled back to us. "He's ready for a slow trot, I believe. Shall I call for someone to steady him? If you agree, my lady."

"I'll do it," Ruar said. The stablegirl managed not to show her surprise. Ruar put a hand low on Gwyllar's back, his fingers spread. Slowly Gruagach was urged into a gentle trot. Gwyllar's eyes widened for a moment. Ruar spoke to him, and Gwyllar's apprehension turned to fierce concentration.

I wondered if Ruar had done this for his older sons. Probably, given the ease with which he was supporting Gwyllar now. It had been Druise's hand on my back at the *Ti'ach*, the memory surprising to me now, given how much he had once disliked riding. But he'd come to it late; it wasn't a skill learned by merchant's sons in Casil.

Merchant's son, and a merchant's brother. What had Marius told him in his last letter? I should have asked. My thoughts were too scattered. I needed to see all the moves on this gameboard, all the threats and all the plays I could make. So many aspects to consider. And I needed to tell Ruar what Lynthe had said.

But, I told myself, not now, not in the morning breeze, watching my son learning to ride with his father's help. This was a moment to savour, a memory to hold—whatever the future brought. I wouldn't let Lynthe's suspicions spoil it.

Chapter 5

~Lena~

GWENNA HAD ASKED TO MEET in the early afternoon. I forced myself to go to the senior commons first, for the midday meal. The cadet who served as my errand-boy or girl had been sent to bring me food far too often. As much as I craved solitude, I couldn't avoid my responsibilities.

I found a seat, gave my order—soup and bread, nothing more—to the steward. Lynthe, he told me when I asked, wasn't here. I swore, silently. I'd wanted to review what I expected her to learn at the Eastern Fort; it was half the reason I'd come. In this public setting, she would maintain the military protocols better than she managed in private meetings. I wondered if she'd be less on edge, when—if—Gwenna told her she could join the troops leaving to fight for Casil.

In the sleepless hours of the night, I'd had a strange thought: Lynthe's simmering anger reminded me of Cillian when I'd first met him, his barely controlled resentment of my land, its people, even me. To the extent that the *Teannasach* of the time, Ruar's father Donnalch, had reprimanded him, swiftly and publicly, for his attitude. I had, I remembered with a twisting pain, not liked the man I now grieved so deeply for at all.

Any more than I liked Lynthe right now. But was jealousy of Ruar enough to cause her to behave as she was? Cillian's anger, at the heart of it, had been at himself, for the parallels he'd seen between his then-unknown father's apparent desertion of his mother, and his own choices—both personal and political—regarding Sorley. But if there was more behind Lynthe's behaviour, I didn't know what it was.

A woman came into the commons: not Lynthe, but Garia, Talyn's adjutant. I waved her over. She took the other chair at the small table. "General?"

"I won't keep you. But is everything ready for tomorrow?" Talyn had given Garia the task of overseeing the preparations for Cillian's memorial.

"It is. The stone is in place, and shrouded." She reviewed the order of the day: Gwenna would speak, and Oriacus, in place of the absent governor. "I have only one question: who is to lay the wreath?"

The wreath would be of ivy, its dark evergreen leaves standing in for laurel, the traditional Casilani recognition of eminence for both poets and soldiers. Cillian had been both, but he would have rejected any acknowledgement of his military role. I considered Garia's question. Sorley, as one poet's tribute to another? But Cillian's skill with words had gone beyond both poetry and prose; the treaties he had negotiated with his quiet, incisive persuasiveness should also be honoured. I thought about the words I had allowed to be carved on the marble, and the public man they represented.

"The *Principe*," I said.

"And do you have a preference as to who holds it during the ceremony? That is an honour in itself."

My gut gave me the answer immediately. "Druisius."

Garia nodded. "That was all that was left undecided. Did you have other questions, General?"

"No. Thank you, Major. Please join your friends now."

The steward had brought my food while we spoke. I spooned up the soup, and ate the bread, newly made and spread with fresh butter. It could have been stale and the butter rancid, for all I cared.

The door to the meeting room stood open, allowing in air. Gwenna glanced up from the papers in front of her to smile at me. The room felt different, and not just from the spill of brighter light through the high windows. Only when I began to take my seat did I realize. Cillian's chair, with its higher, cushioned back, and the small stool on which he'd rested his bad leg, were gone.

I controlled my expression. Gwenna had her reasons, and I understood them. But I was glad of the distraction of the other advisors' entrances: Talyn and Dern, followed by Lynthe.

"We have three concerns to discuss this afternoon," Gwenna began, after everyone was seated. "Firstly, are we to send troops to support Casil? If we assume we are, then the Commander of the Fleet must advise us on how many ships and crews we can spare. Then how do we adequately garrison our coastal forts, and maintain the patrols, with soldiers and ships sent east?"

"Is there a need to garrison or patrol?" Lynthe asked. Her tone was just slightly challenging. "We do not know the full extent of the Casilani withdrawal, nor what General Finn might advise."

"Oriacus is a worried man," Gwenna said.

"But the Emperor only requested our troops, he didn't order them."

"I doubt that reflects the seriousness of the situation Alekos finds himself in, Major." Gwenna turned to Dern. "Commander, your thoughts? How many ships could we safely spare?"

"I question the need to send troops at all to a futile war," Dern said. "But that is not my decision, although I would prefer better intelligence. Could Oriacus—or the governor—be convinced to share more information, *Principe*?"

"I can try," Gwenna said. "In the meantime, your analysis?"

"A quarter of our ships. No more."

Almost exactly what Casil had sent to help Gwenna's grandfather win the war against Varsland, three decades past. They had sent more, later, but those had been crafts meant to ferry men and supplies to Ésparias, not warships. Traders, too, bringing us wine and olives and oil, and taking grain and metals back to Casil. The ships that patrolled the coast and guarded the forts and ports, crewed by competent soldiers, were largely ours.

Two small lines appeared between my daughter's eyes as she made the calculations. "What if I asked only for volunteers?"

Dern's eyebrows—as grey now as his hair—rose. "I cannot answer that, *Principe*. Are you asking for ships to enter into whatever use Casil might put them to, or simply to transport troops and return?"

Two very different propositions, and without truly knowing how the war went, difficult to answer. I glanced at Talyn. She was leaning forward with one hand on her chin, listening.

"There is a risk that even ships sent only to transport troops could be caught in battle, if there is enemy advancement towards Casil." Gwenna spoke crisply, her mind made up. "I cannot ask anything different of our sailors than of our soldiers, so both officers and crew must be volunteers at this time."

"And if that is not feasible?"

"Then if Casil wants our troops, they must find space for them on their ships," Talyn said. "Is your mind made up, *Principe*? You will send volunteers? Because if that is so, then the procurator must be told."

"Commander, you will discover if there are sufficient volunteers to send ships. But as a contingency, General, please meet with Oriacus."

"If we do send ships," I said, "what of our coastal defences?"

"What of them?" Lynthe tapped one fist against the tabletop. "Have we any reason to think Varsland is a threat, beyond the *Principe*'s vague mistrust?"

"The *Teannasach* concurs," Gwenna said. "There is a risk. He believes they will eye the spice trade with Leste, and see no reason to be confined to the northern trading port. We spoke of this yesterday."

I'd seen them together the previous afternoon, walking back from the stables deep in conversation, Gwyllar on his father's shoulders. I'd thought then from their expressions they hadn't been discussing their son. "That could be negoti—"

Lynthe cut me off. "Another discussion with the *Teannasach*, and alone? Surely your advisors should be part of those talks, *Principe*? So that we are both all informed and have had a chance to question his judgement and influence? Or was this conversation after a private meeting? An intimate one?"

Gwenna, when truly, deeply angry, became cold and precise. As she did now. "You are," she said, her lips thin and her voice low, "beyond disrespectful, Major. To the general who was speaking, and to your *Principe*. You are dismissed from this meeting."

Lynthe's chair scraped along the stones of the floor. She stood, every muscle taut. For a moment, I thought she might speak, but she simply turned on her heel and left. Beside me, I heard Talyn's intake of breath. I felt—nothing, as if I were watching a badly staged play. But no. That wasn't right. I did feel something: contempt, for the player who had handled the scene so badly.

Gwenna swallowed, audibly, but her voice held no tremor when she spoke. "Commander, my apologies. A domestic matter that had no place in this discussion."

"Emotions run high when the future is uncertain," Dern said.

Or they did the opposite, I thought, barely stirring a sludge of weariness.

"Commander? Can you apply that thought to Leste?" Gwenna's question pulled my attention back to the table. "Will Casil's withdrawal lead to discontent and, perhaps, to an attempt to ally themselves with Varsland?"

"Two trading nations joining together? I don't know why Leste would see an advantage. They are part of Ésparias now, after all."

Eight years earlier, Casil had recalled their governor, putting in place a procurator instead, one who reported to Ésparias's governor. To the shock of many Casilani officials, the Emperor had appointed the parting governor's Ésparian liaison to the post. 'I am confident in his skills, and in his position of trust among the people of Leste,' Alekos had written. A position hard-won, after what so many on Leste must have seen as betrayal. But in his years with the governor, Garth had convinced them of his commitment to the island through his advocacy and willingness to listen. A marriage into the merchant families of Leste hadn't hurt his cause, either.

"For the glory they think was once theirs," Talyn said. "Stories of jewelled catboats and the riches of trade are powerful, Dern."

"A reminder that they are more than a province of Casil, that they have a history of their own—and without that, what are they?" Gwenna's words sounded like a recitation, a quote from something I didn't recognize.

"Garth has made no indication of any unrest," Dern argued.

"Because it has been like the dissatisfaction among our own people," Gwenna said. "Much of the time it is no more than words spoken quietly over ale or wine, late at night. But sometimes those voices are louder, and catch the attention of others. This may well be one of those times."

"In Ésparias, as well as Leste," Talyn said. "I am hearing rumours, but we need more intelligence."

"Druise hasn't said anything," I pointed out.

Talyn glanced at me, her face impassive. "He hasn't," she said, but there was no reassurance in her tone.

"The man I'd recommend to be sent to Leste is at the Eastern Fort," Dern said. "Is a messenger riding south?"

"There was," I said, pushing my worry at Talyn's words aside. "And there still must be. But the assignment will need to change."

Our discussion went on for another hour: where Ésparian troops, whether land forces or naval, must be redeployed—the Casilani garrisons on Leste, the Eastern Fort, the trading port—and, as a contingency against the loss of senior officers to the volunteer force sent to Casil, which junior ones were ready for promotion.

"Thank you, Commander," Gwenna said, after that list was recorded. "I think we are done for the day. I will ask my generals to stay; there is one more matter for us to deal with."

"*Principe*. Generals. I'll prepare the message to go south." Dern stood, his lean body barely thickened by age, his blue eyes bright in a face still tanned, although he'd rarely be at sea now. Something twinged inside me, something I couldn't put a name to.

When I looked at my daughter again her face had hardened. "General Talyn. You have been briefed on Major Lynthe's actions and accusations?" She was setting the tone: this was not a personal matter.

"I have," Talyn said. Lynthe had been under my command since we had returned to Casil. It had been my responsibility to have that difficult conversation with Talyn about her daughter. She hadn't seemed surprised.

Gwenna turned to me. "You were sending the major south, General?"

"I was."

"Can you still?"

Had I heard her correctly? "I should not," I said. "The task carries significant responsibility and trust. Lynthe should be given neither now."

"Is there a way?" Behind the brief words, I heard the strain, the cracks in Gwenna's control. "I can't decide what to do when she's confronting me every day."

"I suppose—"

"There is a way." Talyn interrupted. "We could send Garia, with Lynthe as her assistant."

Talyn's adjutant had the rank for the assignment—but she was both younger than Lynthe, and two years junior in her promotion to major. It would, indeed, be a strong message.

"Can you spare Garia?"

"I'll manage."

I considered. If Gwenna wanted Lynthe sent away, then Talyn's solution was both simple and appropriate, and better than mine. Which was to go myself. I had no real desire to be in Lynthe's company for so long, and it would signal little consequence to her behaviour.

Still, I hesitated. Being away from Wall's End had suddenly felt desirable. I wanted movement, the physical demands of riding or sailing, of swordplay or archery. I had always dealt with grief this way: Maya's desertion, the slaughter and rape of so many of Ésparias's women by the Marai. My own assault. Even with Lianë's death, I had found little peace until I had left Casil with Junia.

"General?"

"Yes," I said. "I agree. Gwenna, does this suit you?"

"Will it delay her going? She was meant to leave the day after tomorrow."

"I can brief Garia today," Talyn said.

Gwenna rubbed her lips. "Can she stand up to Lynthe? If she—"

"Tries to pull rank? Your mother will make it clear to her that she must not, and that there will be reports on the assignment that will become part of her record. But I do wonder about the governor, and if he will be as open with Garia as he would be with Lynthe. He has confidence in her, after all the times she's been your representative in the south."

Gwenna frowned, thinking. "I can send a letter, of course, instructing him that Garia too has my complete confidence. But she is still unknown to him." Her face cleared. "But he knows Muire well. I'll ask him to go too."

"May I make one other suggestion?" Talyn asked. "Send my grandson to assist Muire. I know Constyn is barely fourteen, but he is part of our family, and of an age where that should be acknowledged in some of his duties."

I saw the doubt on Gwenna's face. "Your father," I said, "thought Constyn had the makings of a diplomat. This might be a good introduction for him."

"It's not that," my daughter said. "I knew his opinion of Constyn. So does Lynthe. She has asked me—" She took a deep breath. "She wants me to appoint Constyn as heir after Gwyllar. She started to suggest this after *Athàir* commented on Constyn's suitability for diplomatic training last year."

"As a sop to those who believe you should never have been *Principe*?" Talyn said, frowning.

"Perhaps. But I think it's more so I don't feel the need to have another child."

"With Ruar, or with anyone?"

"With anyone." Gwenna's voice was flat.

"Gwenna," Talyn said, "are you sure that's all it is? Because there is an heir after Gwyllar: your brother."

A vague unease trickled along my spine. Was this what was driving Lynthe? Ambition for her nephew? She was close to her brother's son, acting as his guardian after his mother and sister had returned to Linrathe.

"By Eudekia's decree, yes." A trace of frustration coloured Gwenna's words. "But you know he wouldn't want it, and are we—will we be—bound by the rules she imposed, if Casil falls?"

The question was a good one. In all our planning, had we ever considered it? "Did you speak to your father about this?" I asked.

"No. By the time I realized Lynthe was serious—" She shook her head. "I didn't want to trouble him."

How much had we all kept from Cillian in those last weeks? I had been deeply glad that Eudekia's last letter had arrived after his death: it would, I was sure, contain her analysis of the war, its likelihood of ending the Eastern Empire. He would have spent his last days planning, advising Gwenna, devising responses to every potential situation that he could foresee, rather than with his books and writing and Sorley's music.

"Emperors used to be elected here," Talyn said quietly.

"And Linrathe's leaders come from within one family, but they decide who among them is best suited," I added. "Daragh, even though he is Ruar's oldest son, is the presumptive heir only."

We fell silent. Did anything bind us to Casil's idea of succession? The question hung heavily in the air of the room.

"If Casil falls," I said, finally, reluctantly, "then I think it is ours to decide. Yours, Gwenna, as *Principe*."

"A Casilani title."

"You are still the last Emperor's granddaughter. And," I added, "it isn't a Casilani title, not really. Your father suggested it. No other province of the Eastern Empire uses it. Cillian told me once it is very old, from Casil's distant past."

Gwenna nodded absently. "Nothing can be changed as long as Casil stands, and they have not fallen yet. The war could still be won." Her expression caught at my heart. She looked so much like her father, the night we had decided we could not choose to keep our children from the succession to Ésparias's leadership. Had we had any concept of the burden we would impose upon our daughter?

"You have decisions to make that need careful weighing," Talyn said. "Is there more we can do to help? If not, I had best see Garia."

"And I had better deal with Lynthe," I said, standing. "You will send word to Muire, so I can brief him?"

"Of course. Ask the cadet to come in, will you?"

"Take the *Principe*'s message," I told the cadet waiting in the hall. "Then find Major Lynthe, and send her to me at the fort."

Talyn and I took a few steps down the corridor before I spoke again. "Why have we heard nothing from Druisius about this talk about Constyn?" His net of informants should have made him aware.

"It implies," Talyn answered, "that Lynthe has kept her idea of Constyn as the next heir to herself. It could be nothing more than a ploy to keep Gwenna from having a second child."

"If she were just arguing against Ruar as the father," I said, "it would make more sense, given Lynthe's antipathy to him. But if we consider too the idea that Linrathe is overly influential?"

Talyn grimaced. "There is a pattern there. Lynthe is playing on old memories and fears. Gwenna is refusing to see it, and frankly, that surprises me. She is usually so analytical."

"I think that's why she wants Lynthe gone from Wall's End," I said. "To give her the space to make that analysis." I studied Talyn, seeing the fatigue. Her dark hair was streaked with grey, and the lines around her mouth and eyes had deepened this past winter. "I'm surprised you can be this dispassionate about your daughter."

"I gave birth to her," she said. "But I didn't bring her up, not past her first few years. My sister did, and then the cadet schools. We've never been close. But, you know, if she'd been born a man a generation ago, how different would she be from Callan? Impulsive, and now, it appears, ambitious, even if she's using Constyn as a surrogate for that ambition."

Almost my thoughts. "Is it wise to send him south with her? He looks to her for guidance, doesn't he?"

"But also to me, both as a general and his grandmother. I'll have him dine with me tonight, with the excuse of preparing him for the ceremony tomorrow, and do some probing. He respected Cillian immensely. I can't see him being part of this."

"You'll let Gwenna know your opinion?"

"Of course." She touched my shoulder. "If Druisius did disregard something he perhaps should not have, is that surprising? Should we expect him to be at his best just now?"

"Maybe not. I know I haven't been."

"I think you are doing very well. All of you."

"Perhaps after tomorrow life will be—" I couldn't say easier. "Clearer."

"Perhaps," she said.

I took the coastal path back to Wall's End. The sun was westering behind clouds again, although the rain had stopped for now. Seabirds glided, stiff-winged, their high, constant cries echoing off the cliffs. At the harbour below, ships were being prepared to sail.

Should the delegation to the Eastern Fort ride or sail? I thought about this as I walked: a distraction, but also a decision that needed to be made. The road was good, the inns appropriately spaced, and fresh horses could be had at every stop. The long ride—a week or so now, with the new roads—would be hard on Constyn, if Gwenna chose to send him. And on Muire, I reflected, who was more used to a chair than a horse, now, but sea travel meant confining an angry Lynthe to a ship, with little to expend the energy of anger on. Riding was the better choice.

I wished I were closer to Lynthe; my daughter's partner should be a friend. But the formalities of our professional relationship had always stood between us. There was fault on my side, I knew, my deep discomfort with almost all Ésparian women—Talyn was an exception—and Lynthe, too, had seemed more comfortable with Cillian and Druise. I'd never tried to strengthen the relationship, and now it was far too late.

I'd been in my office some time before Lynthe was announced. I did not offer her a chair. She stood at attention before me, but behind the formal posture I sensed the simmering rage. I regarded her, not speaking. After my recent regretful thoughts, my anger, threatening my own composure, surprised me.

"Your behaviour today should shame you," I said finally, my words tight and clipped. "Whatever your personal disagreements with the *Principe*, they are not to be aired in an advisory meeting. You have forced me to reassess your suitability for the assignment I had given you." In the same tone, I told her what had been decided. "I expect you to model exemplary conduct, Major. If the reports are otherwise, expect a demotion in rank."

"General."

I dismissed her. On my desk were several reports waiting for my attention, but what energy I had had was gone. I looked at them with no interest at all. Did the repairs needed at one fort or another matter? Probably. I picked up the one on the top of the pile and began to read.

I stopped working when the fading light meant a lamp was needed. I'd got almost nothing done, but my neck ached, and my eyes were as dry as they'd been on the wide plain east of the Durrains. The hollow in the pit of my stomach was probably hunger: the body needed fuel, even if food held no interest.

I tidied my desk. I could eat at the fort or walk back to the villa. The latter, I decided: the walk would loosen my muscles. I bade the door guard good night, refused an escort, and stepped out into the dusk. No stars glimmered, and the breeze off the sea was cold.

Soft footsteps made me turn. "Lena," Druise said. "We should talk, yes? About who goes south."

How did he know? Maybe Gwenna had told him. "You cannot," I said, "send guards with two officers who began their careers as bodyguards."

"Maybe not." He fell into step beside me. "But I have soldiers in the guard ready for new assignments. Some go to the Eastern Fort. I can send them now."

He wasn't asking permission; he didn't need to. The guard was his responsibility—and a source of much of his information, I was sure. I'd asked, once, careful to do so when we were both off duty. 'You think?' he'd replied, with a grin. I'd laughed, and hadn't probed further. Cillian, I thought, would have known.

"What will you tell them?"

He shrugged. "Some, nothing. One, more. But they are to ride fast, to learn the route." In the half-light, I saw him look at me. "Why the road? They will stop at many inns. Many people to complain to, yes?"

A valid concern. "Anything but her best behaviour will see Lynthe demoted. She will know Garia is watching." And Muire.

"And my man." I glanced at Druise, then decided not to ask. If the guard in his confidence—it would be the junior officer in charge, no doubt—asked questions over ale after a long ride, questions that goaded Lynthe into rash statements, it would give us answers. Surely, I thought, Lynthe's loyalty to Gwenna, her love for her, would supersede her anger? That was what Cillian would have thought; love and responsibility inseparable for him. And forgiveness.

But would Sorley have always agreed? The question gave me pause. Cillian's behaviour towards him in the years before I'd known them hadn't looked like love or responsibility, but a rejection. Even though behind that apparent rejection—one that had hurt Cillian as much as it had Sorley—had been fear. Not for himself, but for Sorley.

What would your lot have been? Cillian had asked Sorley, when he had finally told him why he had kept them apart. *Disinheritance and shame. You were newly a man; I was ten years adult. The fault was mine.*

But what could Lynthe be afraid of, to make her treat Gwenna this way?

"She is stupid," Druise said, interrupting my thoughts. "Lynthe. To have a child, there must be a father. Ruar is a good man."

"And he is only a friend," I said.

"Even if he was more, what of it?" Somewhere, a blackbird's night song rose and fell. "People do not control who they love. There is space for many."

"Perhaps, though—" I tried to concentrate on Druise's words. "Perhaps that is better understood when life has been precarious. When there has been great loss, so we know how precious both life and love are."

"Or when the gods give another chance, yes?"

I shivered. From the cold breeze, or Druise's words? So many second chances in our lives. We were nearly at the villa. "Have you eaten?" I asked. I wouldn't ask him about the rumours he hadn't reported. Not yet.

"No. Come to our rooms. Sorley has new music for tomorrow."

I glanced east, to where no stars shone. "He'll have to play in the rain, I'm afraid."

Chapter 6

~Gwenna~

CLOUDS HUNG LOW OVER THE HILLS, the air damp on our faces and hands. I had said my words, and the procurator his. Sorley had played his elegy, his music somehow both sad and stirring. The block of stone stood on its plinth, words carved on its face: Cillian, Major of the Third, Prince of Ésparias, diplomat and teacher. Nothing more: this was not a family gravestone, and my mother had refused to allow any likeness or adornment, save the suggestion of scrolls along the base of the stone.

The dedication had felt paradoxical, as if it had needed to happen before our lives could continue; at the same time, there'd been a sense of distance, an acknowledgement of something already in the past. Even Sorley's eyes had stayed dry. He'd been calmer and more controlled since his return from Linrathe. Beside me, Lynthe shifted a little. Please don't be impatient, I thought—and then I felt her hand on my back. Steadying me. Supporting. A rush of gratitude warmed me, the sensation welcome. The day belonged to winter, not early summer, and the fine mist was seeping through our required robes of mourning.

I had one last thing to do. I pushed back the folds of dark cloth that covered my hair, to see better, and caught Druise's eye: he'd been watching for my signal. He came forward with the ivy wreath, wordlessly handing it to me. I knelt to place it against the stone. The dark green leaves shone, even on this dull day.

Then I began the walk back to the villa, with my family behind me and the assembled men and women following. The Casilani procurator and officers of both armies were in attendance. The reception rooms of the villa would be crowded, and unless the clouds suddenly cleared, the courtyard not a place to spill out into. But the furnaces had been stoked, so the rooms would be warm.

~

With a cup of wine in my hand, I made my way from group to group, listening to stories of my father, memories of the public man, appropriate for the day. I caught glimpses, in the busy room, of my mother doing the same, and Sorley and Druisius; even Lynthe was playing her role with fair grace, although she disliked crowds. She'd been angry last night, but at my mother, not me, and my offer to massage her shoulders had quickly turned to lovemaking. Good lovemaking, I remembered.

My face ached with the effort of smiling, and between the warmth of the room and the crowd my head was beginning to hurt. I excused myself from the officer I had been listening to, a story of one of my father's lectures, to slip outside. The mist had cleared. Behind the clouds, the moon was a blurred half-circle.

I couldn't sit: the benches were wet. I took a breath, and another. Tomorrow Lynthe would leave, for three weeks or more. Even after last night, the thought relieved me. I had too much to consider, too much that involved her. I needed distance, to think clearly.

I walked across the courtyard. The portico on Sorley and Druise's side of the villa sheltered several chairs. They were, as I'd hoped, dry. The sound of voices was quieter here. I'd give myself five minutes.

Maybe I should make Constyn the heir after Gwyllar. Or maybe I should wait, see which boy was the most appropriate, the way Linrathe did. Colm and I were supposed to have been able to choose whether we wanted to be considered for succession to the leadership of Ésparias. Eudekia's decree and Faolyn's untimely death had changed that, and my life.

I had cousins at Han, on the grasslands, who were as royal as me or Colm or Lynthe, if descent from the Emperor Callan and his brother meant anything. But their mother, Talyn's sister, had made a different choice, and removed her children from the succession. They raised and trained horses for the army, and grazed cattle for hides and meat, as those who called Han home had done for generations. Did they ever regret their mother's decision?

And what if Gwyllar wanted to do something else, the way Colm had? It had been clear since he was ten that medicine was my brother's passion. He'd been free to follow his dreams: I was the heir. It wasn't as if I disliked the games of diplomacy, the thrust and parry of ideas and thought. Words could be as precise and cutting as a blade. But would it be what my son was suited for?

A steady pulse had begun in my left temple, tiny lights sparkling like miniature fireflies just at the edge of my vision. I groaned, inwardly. Not now. Please, not now. "Guard," I said, quietly.

"*Principe*?" I'd known someone would answer. Solitude was a fancy, for me.

"Find Apulo and bring him to me, please. At once."

The guard was quick, and Apulo came prepared. He would have guessed what I needed from the urgency of my request. I drank the infusion of ginger and willow bark and whatever else was in it, slightly sweetened. I might keep it down, and if I did, it would ease the worst of the symptoms.

Apulo crouched in front of me, holding the flask. "Enough?"

I nodded. "For now. Have some placed in my room, will you? And would you ask my mother to come to me?"

"I will make more, and leave you this. Stay here, in the dark and quiet." He left as quietly as he'd come. I closed my eyes, trying to concentrate on the gentle splash of the fountain.

"Gwenna?"

"*Mathàir*. Will you make my excuses to everyone?" I sat very still, willing the nausea to subside.

"Should I help you to your bed first?"

"Not yet. I'll go when I can."

She didn't fuss. "Send if you need me," was all she said.

After some time the pounding in my head lessened a little, and my stomach settled. I stood, carefully, and without moving my head or my eyes any more than I needed to, I made my way to my bedroom. Another flask of the infusion sat on my bedside table, as Apulo had promised.

I drank a bit more. Then I undressed, leaving my clothes where they dropped—I wasn't going to bend to pick them up—and got carefully into the bed. I'd tasted valerian in this second infusion. It would make me sleep, and with a little luck I'd wake in the morning feeling well.

But when I woke it wasn't morning, but the depth of night. Lynthe, holding a lamp, looked down at me. I closed my eyes against the light. The headache still lingered. "What time is it?" I murmured.

"Late. Did you ask Ruar to stay?"

"Stay?" I sat up, the pulsing ache deepening. "What are you talking about?"

"Daragh told me he goes home tomorrow, but his father is staying at Wall's End. For some private time with you, I assume?"

"No. I didn't know anything about this."

"Why should I believe you?" Her tone made my head throb.

"Lynthe. Can't this wait?" I pleaded. "'I'm feeling sick."

"So am I. At least when I think of you with Ruar," she spat.

"Then don't think about it." I wasn't of a mind to be diplomatic. "This is stupid, Lynthe. I didn't ask Ruar to stay, and I haven't decided about a second child."

"But you're still thinking about it. And if you decide yes, Ruar will be the father again, right?"

A wave of dizziness swept through me. "Yes. You know why. Both why I chose Ruar, and why I think I should have a second child."

"Because children die. Like your baby sister did."

"Yes."

"Like my brother did. But I'm not *Principe*. You are."

"Because Eudekia decreed it. You know this, Lynthe. And my children after me."

"And what if Gwyllar died now?" Her voice was ice, or a steel blade. "Because he could, couldn't he? So easily. Then who would inherit?"

Had she just threatened my son? Bile rose in my throat, sour and burning. "Get out," I said. "Now. Or I will call the guard."

"You didn't think I'd stay here with you, did you?" she said. "I'm going."

Gwyllar was guarded—but no guard would keep Lynthe from him. Not without being told to. Heart pounding, ignoring the cold sweat of nausea, I ran out into the corridor. No sign of Lynthe. Gwyllar's nursery was at the end of the wing, if I turned left.

"*Principe*?" My guard sounded puzzled.

"Which way did the major go?"

The guard pointed. Relief made me put my hand out, to steady myself against the wall.

"Do you need help, *Principe*?"

"No. Only a bad headache. They make me dizzy." I tried to smile for her. "I just forgot to tell the major something. "

"Don't get chilled," my door guard said. My feet were bare, and I was wearing only a sleeping shift.

"No," I murmured, turning. A shawl and slippers quickly found, I tried not to visibly hurry to Gwyllar's nursery. I wasn't going to alarm the guards, unless there was need—and I couldn't bring myself to believe what I'd heard. I must have misunderstood. But some deep instinct told me I hadn't.

Gwyllar slept, a thumb in his mouth. I had slipped into the room as quietly as I could, pantomiming silence to the guard, but still his nursemaid woke. "My lady?' she whispered.

"I just wanted to see him," I whispered back. "I'll sit with him a while. Go back to sleep."

I moved a chair close to his cot. The nursemaid brought me a blanket and arranged it around my shoulders. I touched Gwyllar's hand, and without waking he curled his fingers around mine. A hot, fierce love rose in my throat, and a fiercer vow. No-one would hurt my son. Whether she had meant to or not, Lynthe had forced a choice, and a consequence.

~

"Has the major left?" I'd lingered in the nursery as long as I'd dared. There'd already be talk; while I did occasionally come to sit with my son while he slept, I'd never spent the night in a chair beside him.

"Yes, *Principe*," the guard answered. "Just after dawn."

I'd decided on my course of action this morning, watching Gwyllar eat his porridge. I couldn't burden my mother with this, or Talyn, for different reasons. Only one person could advise me now.

I washed before dressing in outdoor clothes. No trace of the sick headache remained—I would have to remember to thank Apulo—but tension knotted my shoulders and neck. Tying my hair back, I opened the corridor door. "Find Major Druisius," I told the ever-present cadet. "Ask him to meet me at the stables."

Outside a fine mist lay over the land. Small puddles like pools of lead lay in depressions on the flagstones, and drops of water hung like pearls along cobwebs and at the end of leaves. The guard fell in step with me, a pace behind; I'd dismiss her once Druise had joined me.

I didn't have to wait long, and he didn't question why I wanted him to ride with me. We rode in silence until we were on the higher land, well away from the fort. I reined my mare in, looking down at Wall's End and the sea, shrouded in the light fog.

"What is it?" Druise asked.

My throat closed. I shook my head.

"Kitten?"

"I think—" I swallowed, tried again. "I think Lynthe threatened Gwyllar."

Druise swore. "Tell me."

I repeated her words. "She's been angry for weeks," I added. "Questioning who my heir should be, even why Constyn isn't *Princip*. All the things that were said when Faolyn died."

"I know."

Of course he did. Druise knew everything. "You didn't tell me?"

"I thought maybe it is just a way to speak her worry for you, yes? Now Cillian is gone, and all the responsibility is yours."

Could fear for me be at the heart of her anger? It might explain it: the weight of leadership, the risk of childbirth . . . Could it be true? "Then why threaten Gwyllar?"

"The words alone are not a threat, yes? Just a possibility."

"But her voice—" I shook my head. "I have no doubt, Druise."

He nodded, his jaw tight. "What do you want me to do, *Principe*?"

Principe. Not Kitten. The decision was mine. "Who else has she said this to? Who agrees with her? They will bear watching." Clarity was returning, out here on this height of land. "Increase Gwyllar's guard, immediately."

"Do I tell the others?"

"No."

He gave me a look. "I can't," I said. My mare tossed her head, snorting; she could feel my distress. I soothed her. "She is my *quincala*, Druise. How do I tell my mother or hers what she's done? And as you said, it's not a direct threat, and only my word against hers as to her tone."

He clicked his tongue. "You have three weeks, a month. Then she will be back from the south. You must choose a course before that."

Another decision to make, among so many. Not just my country's future now. *What is best for Ésparias.* And she had threatened my son.

"I will. Just give me a little time." Somewhere above the heath, mist or no mist, a skylark sang. A thought struck. "What if she stirs up trouble in the south, or at the inns?"

Druise's teeth flashed. "I will know."

"Who—?" I stopped myself. "Don't tell me."

He grinned again, this time with amusement. "You think I would?"

I half smiled. "Not really. Thank you, Druise."

"My job." He chewed at a lip. "Gwyllar's guard—we will say the new ones are in training, yes? Guarding a nursemaid and child is not like other assignments."

It would serve. "As long as they like horses," I said. "He's obsessed with the pony just now." I took another look at the fort below us, and the Wall disappearing into the fog. There were riders on the road that paralleled it: Daragh and his party, I guessed. I couldn't blame him for leaving; he'd told us what he could, and he had work to get back to.

Was that the only reason for his urgent departure? *Daragh told me,* Lynthe had said. What had they been discussing?

I'd been present when a prince of Varsland had offered, through my father, a sword to the young Emperor of the East, the beautiful, deadly weapon carrying an unspoken message. Had Lynthe done the opposite, and with her words extended an intangible blade to Daragh?

I touched the eagle incised into the ring on my right hand. If Casil fell, I thought, I should have another made, with Ésparias's horse, not Casil's eagle. The movement made my mare swing her head. I turned her back towards the track, my mind already moving to the possibilities I must consider, and the decisions that were mine to make.

Chapter 7

~Lena~

THE RING, HEAVY ON MY PALM, barely reflected the lamplight. Unworn, its silver had grown dull. I'd thought it might make me feel something beyond the numbness that had pervaded me since the memorial. Shouldn't I be angry at Cillian for not telling me he'd wanted Colm to have the ring? Maybe. What did it matter? I couldn't ask him why. He was dead, gone beyond hearing, beyond my anger or my love. Nor did I need an imagined voice answering my question, reminding me of my precarious sanity.

Outside the open window an owl called. It was very late. Sleep hadn't come; it frequently didn't, now. I couldn't send the ring to Colm; I didn't know where he was, or even if he was alive. It would have to wait. I put it back in the box and picked up the *li'ítho* bracelet. Taking it from Cillian's body had needed all the control I'd had. Even that memory was just—flat. But at least I knew what he'd wanted me to do with it.

Maybe today I could. What was stopping me? I had no quarrel with Cillian's request: it was what I would have done even if he hadn't asked. I'd told him that. The bonds of love and responsibility symbolized by the *li'ítho* had never been just between us. The bracelet belonged on Sorley's wrist. In another world, in another life, it might have always been his.

I let the entwined silver strands slide back into the box before I stood. Only coals now in the brazier, and the room had cooled. I would close the shutters and try to sleep. The words and numbers on the reports I had to read barely held my attention, without adding the impairment of another wakeful night.

The moon, full or nearly so, was sinking over the sea, barely visible through the persistent cloud. When had I last seen stars arching above the world at night? Did I even want to, for the memories they would bring?

The pounding of a horse's hooves on the road that passed the villa caught my attention. Ridden at speed, and at night? Whoever rode to Wall's End was bringing news that could not wait.

But as I stood, irresolute—would I be needed?—the sound grew closer. The rider had turned off the military road and was coming to the villa. The news that couldn't wait was for the *Principe.*

I reached the gate to hear the rider arguing with the guards. His lathered horse stood, head drooping, sides heaving, and the soldier who'd dismounted looked little better. "The *Principe* must be woken," he was saying.

"On whose authority?" the senior guard asked.

"The Major Druisius's."

"You can tell me," I said, stepping forward. "Guard, get someone to see to the lieutenant's horse. Ferand, come with me."

"General. The *Principe*—"

"I will wake her."

Apulo waited for us at the doors to the villa. Always a light sleeper, rousing easily whenever Cillian had needed him, he would have heard the commotion at the gates. "The lieutenant needs food and drink," I told him. "The conference room. I will wake the *Principe*"—I glanced at Ferand— "and the major."

But not in that order. Partly because I wanted to speak to Druisius first, and partly because I didn't know if Gwenna slept alone.

I'd always liked Ruar, from the time we'd both been declared hostages to the first truce between our countries. He'd been twelve then; two years later, he'd fought, Sorley at his side, against the Marai, our common enemy. In the discussions of the past two weeks, making plans for almost every possible outcome of Casil's withdrawal, he'd been calm and thoughtful, the wisdom of thirty years of leadership clear. But for all he was an ally, and Gwyllar's father, caution, perhaps higher now I knew what was being said, told me that whatever this urgent information was, he shouldn't be among the first to hear it.

Druise answered my knock at his door, wearing only a loosely belted robe. "Lena? What is wrong?"

"Ferand is here, demanding to see Gwenna."

Even in the moonlight I could see his cheeks grow slack with surprise. "A minute, yes? Let me dress." From the bedroom, Sorley called Druise's name. A moment later he too appeared in the sitting room, carrying a lamp.

"What's happening?"

"Something. Lena will tell you." Druise brushed past Sorley.

"Lena?" Sorley rubbed his eyes. "What time is it?"

"Two hours to dawn, maybe," I said. "The guard officer Druise sent to watch Lynthe is here, with urgent news. That's all I know."

"It must be important, if he rode at night."

"I've done it. With a full moon, it's easier." Sorley was right, though. Riding at night meant relying largely on your horse's vision, and riding at speed at night was always risky. I looked over Sorley's shoulder. "Druise. What were Ferand's orders?"

"To listen. To what Lynthe said to Constyn, and to people at the inns. To ask about what she said to them."

"And at the Eastern Fort?" Druise's guards, like their Casilani counterparts, were not part of the army; he'd argued, successfully, for their separation. Armies could turn against their officers, or even their leader: it had happened in Casil. His men and women guarded the residences of officials and dignitaries and patrolled the cities—large towns, here in Ésparias—that had grown around the forts. Their unofficial role, at least for some, was to gather and relay information for the *Principe's* spymaster, Druise's real reason for wanting an independent guard, no matter how persuasive his other arguments.

"The same. But also to find out what is said about the war, yes?"

So this might be about the war, and not Lynthe. "I sent Ferand to the conference room," I said. "Meet us there in five minutes. I'll wake Gwenna."

"What should I do?" Sorley asked.

I glanced at Druise. "Is Gwenna alone?"

"Maybe not."

"Then—" I turned to Sorley. "Ruar can't be present, but he may need to hear the news soon. Tell him what you know."

By now the household was aware of the messenger. The guard at Gwenna's door didn't ask, of course, but neither did she show surprise when I rapped on my daughter's door. I knocked twice, the pattern telling Gwenna who it was. She answered quickly, her dark hair loose on her shoulders.

"*Mathàir?*"

"There is a messenger," I told her. "You must come." I saw her involuntary glance back at the bedroom. "Sorley will brief Ruar."

She nodded. "I'll meet you there."

~

In the conference room Ferand's lank, matted hair and mud-splashed clothes told of his long hours in the saddle. "When did you leave the Eastern Fort?" I asked.

"Nearly three days ago."

Which meant he had been riding almost constantly, sleeping only for an hour or two and taking a fresh horse at every inn, and their strongest and fastest at that. Pain stabbed my gut, fear made physical. Druise sat, outwardly unperturbed.

Gwenna joined us, dressed in a plain tunic with her hair tied back, the working *Principe*. She signalled to the lieutenant not to stand. "The news?"

"*Principe*." Ferand's voice shook, but whether from nervousness or fatigue I couldn't tell. "The Major Lynthe took passage on a Casilani ship sailing east three mornings ago. And—" He paused, licking dry lips.

"And?" Gwenna demanded.

"She took the prince Constyn with her."

Gwenna's hands covered her mouth, as if to repress a cry. It was Druise who spoke. "You sent someone after them?"

"Yes, Major. On a later ship, the same day."

"Who?" Ferand told him. I didn't recognize the name.

"What orders?"

"Only to follow and observe."

"General Finn approved that?" I asked. Finn had the authority to have her brought back. Why hadn't he used it?

"She told him it was by your directive, *Principe*."

Finn had believed that? But Lynthe had been Gwenna's representative in the south. Why would he doubt her?

"And showed him a forged document, yes?"

"I believe so, Major."

Gwenna still had not spoken, but she sat with a straight back and a distant look I knew: thinking, analysing.

"Lieutenant, my thanks," she said, focusing on him. "You have made both intelligent decisions and a courageous ride. You have eaten, I believe? A bed will be found for you here at the villa, and the baths are yours to use. Apulo is waiting for you in the corridor. I need not tell you this information is for no other ears."

"*Principe*." He stood, unsteadily, one hand on the tabletop. "There is a letter, too. It is in my saddlebags; I forgot it."

"Apulo can fetch it," Druise said. "Tell him I asked, yes?"

A letter from whom? We'd find out soon enough; no reason to detain the exhausted lieutenant any longer. The door closed quietly. Gwenna buried her face in her hands. "Why?" she whispered.

"To declare Constyn the rightful *Princip*, and she his regent," Druise said.

Gwenna looked up, frowning. "Alekos would not support that."

"But the victors might, yes? So I think she has heard rumours of Casil's fall."

"But you have not?"

"If the news reached the Eastern Fort this week? Maybe it is in the letter Ferand brought."

"No fast messenger has come for the procurator," I said.

"Maybe today, and maybe by ship, yes?" Druise shrugged. "We will learn soon. But even if it is only rumour, she must be stopped. She knows too much."

"If Casil has fallen, or its fall inevitable, what does it matter?" Gwenna asked. "Eudekia knew what we planned. I am sure Alekos does too. They are leaving us to our own governance; are we not free to make what alliances we can, for our own survival?"

"Perhaps that is what Lynthe is thinking: to make the alliance with the new power in Casil? Could she see it as benefiting Ésparias? An impulsive decision?" I finished the thought. "Meant to show herself to us—to you, Gwenna—as a diplomat and leader?"

It was just possible. Lynthe had heard the stories: Cillian's apparently spontaneous claim to Ésparian citizenship, saving his—and my—life; my own disregard of orders at the Taiva, which had won a battle and a war. And a treaty I had signed, with no authority at all.

At the head of the table, Gwenna turned to Druise. He made a tiny, negative gesture. Her expression told me she agreed. What did Druise know that I didn't? A different pain pricked, a weary sense that I was failing Gwenna, both as her mother and as the *Principe*'s advisor. "What do we do?" I asked.

Before either Druise or Gwenna could answer, Apulo returned. He handed Gwenna a sealed letter and withdrew. She broke the seal, reading quickly, lines of concern deepening between her eyes. "This is from someone in the governor's household, reporting on what they have overheard."

"The steward," Druise said.

The governor's staff were Casilani. How had Druise suborned such a senior man? A question for another time. Gwenna finished the letter and looked up.

"What does it say?" I asked.

"The rest of the troops are to be recalled. But not only that. Every Casilani man under sixty and over fourteen. Even the landholders."

Druise snorted. "Many will not go. It is unenforceable, if their troops are gone."

"But—" Gwenna held up a hand for silence. "He also reports that no such order appears to have been given in Beria."

The implications of this penetrated even my clouded mind. It spoke of dissension at the highest level, a disagreement between the Emperor and his *dignitasi*. Beria was a procuratorial province, not a royal one, its administration managed by the imperial fiscarius. The Emperor could conscript men in his royal province of Ésparias. He could not, in Beria, without the Assembly's agreement.

"*Mathàir*, did you send a messenger for Talyn?" Gwenna asked.

I hadn't. I hadn't even thought of it.

"I did, yes?" Druise, doing what I should have.

"When she gets here, please fetch Sorley and Ruar. We must deal with Lynthe's actions first, regardless of this other news. I will tell Talyn what Lynthe has done, but I want them at the table."

"Isn't this a military matter, Gwenna?" I reminded her. "For us to deal with?"

"There something I want them both to hear, and to debate." She straightened, resting her hands on the table, palms cupped. "I was taught to evaluate every possible move of my opponents, and the minds behind the play. There may be one mind we have not considered at all."

Chapter 8

~Gwenna~

"GWENNA, NO!" SORLEY STOOD, as if the defence he felt compelled to make needed to be physical. But it was Ruar who put a hand on his arm.

"Hear the *Principe* out." He didn't look angry, or even confused. Perhaps saddened, or maybe that was just my imagination. We had made love not many hours before. Now I had suggested his oldest son might be guilty of something close to treason.

"Before Lynthe—" I stopped. Did everyone need to know Lynthe had threatened my son? Yes, I decided. "The night before she left, Lynthe made a barely veiled threat against Gwyllar's life," I held up a hand against the sounds of shock, Talyn's gasp the loudest of all. "But before she did, she told me she had been speaking to Daragh. Who is marrying Bryngyl's oldest daughter, and whose mother—"

"Was from Varsland too." Ruar's voice held no expression.

"Helvi would weep in her grave, could she hear this," Sorley growled.

"I mean no disrespect for Helvi," I said. "But her origins may change how Daragh sees himself."

Light was beginning to filter through the shutters, the room caught between the grey of dawn and the amber of lamplight. Talyn sat with her hands over her face. Apulo had brought food and drink, but it sat untouched.

"He is worried about trade, yes? The supply of grain." Druise took everyone's attention. "It is his job. I spoke to him a little, about ships and harbours and markets. How trade happens across the Nivéan Sea. He was interested."

"Would you trust him?" An unexpected question from Ruar.

Druise shrugged. "As much as I trust my nephews. They are merchants, yes? Even now they will be planning how to introduce themselves to the victors, if the Emperor loses the war. But they are not wrong. Lives must go on, and ways to make a living, too."

"Pragmatic as always, Druise," my mother murmured, her first words.

"But even so," Talyn said, looking up, "what could Daragh have said to Lynthe, to make her do what she's done?"

"Likely nothing," Sorley said grimly. "Gwenna is reading too much into a conversation. If Lynthe has been hiding her desire for Constyn to be *Princip* from us all, maybe she's just seen an opportunity for that to happen, and taken it."

"Hiding it for all these years?" my mother asked. "I doubt it. I think Cillian's death precipitated this, reminding Lynthe that if Eudekia had not decreed that you, Gwenna, were the heir, Constyn would indeed be *Princip*."

Talyn looked up, the lines on her face deeper than ever. "If Cillian said to Lynthe what he said to me, it is more than that. He told me"—she licked her lips—"that had the succession not been changed, Constyn would have been a fine *Princip* after Faolyn. And Lynthe loved her brother very much, for all she pretended to treat him with disrespect."

I remembered Lynthe's tears in Casil, and how we had almost overlooked her grief for her brother in the tumult of events that had followed, both there and here. Was this a recent resolve to see Constyn as *Princip*, as my mother had suggested? Or a long-standing conviction? Could Lynthe really have hidden a jealousy and an ambition this deep from me?

Why not? It was just one more secret in a family so very good at them.

No one spoke, each of us around the table caught up in our own thoughts and memories. Ruar broke the reverie first. "I will have to return to Linrathe," he said, without anger, but also without warmth. "There may be information waiting for me, and I must speak to Daragh, of course."

"Ruar?" It would be best to be honest. I took a deep breath. "Lynthe made a similar accusation against you: that you have hidden your desire to conquer Ésparias, biding your time, for many years. I did not, and do not, believe it, but now I must wonder if she had twisted her own designs into what she charged you with."

"And made you wonder if she approached Daragh, to support her plan," Ruar murmured, expressionless.

"I hope, very much, that I am wrong about why they spoke."

"As am I." The tiniest of smiles touched his lips. "You were well taught, weren't you? Your father would be proud of you." I couldn't tell if this was forgiveness or mockery. I looked away, blinking.

"Her plan?" Sorley's eyes narrowed. "What am I missing?"

"An alliance, yes?" Druise answered, before I could. "But not the one Cillian planned. Still Ésparias and Linrathe, but Constyn and Daragh, not Gwenna and Ruar. And Varsland, and maybe more, now she has taken the boy east."

I wasn't the only one who shivered at Druise's words. And Lynthe knew almost every facet of my father's plan. Currency to trade to the Boranoi and Kidari?

Sorley was still frowning, his eyes on his *Teannasach*. "There is information waiting for you. Regarding Varsland?"

"Regarding Varsland. Roghan's arrival at Cillian's burial was—fortuitous." He grimaced. "Forgive me. But I must take advantage of chance meetings when requests cannot be trusted to a letter."

"You sent him to Bryngyl?"

"I did," Ruar said. "For several reasons. But without knowing, then, how extreme the danger is for Casil."

"Or for us." My mother ran a hand through her hair. My father's gesture. "I wish we knew what Lynthe was thinking. And what is truly happening in Casil. The conscription of Casilani citizens is unprecedented, surely?"

"It is not done," Druise said. "Armies are trained and paid. Why take inexperienced men from here, so far away? It makes no sense."

"It implies great need," I said. But I agreed with Druise: what good were inexperienced men? The landholders themselves and their sons would have some skill with sword and bow, as befitted their status, but their workers? There was something more at play here, but I couldn't work out what. My mind wasn't functioning properly, still shocked over what Lynthe had done.

"Ask yourself this: why not from Beria too?" my mother said, but Druise spoke at the same time.

"I will go east," he said. "To find out what is happening, and to find Lynthe, yes?"

A gasp from Sorley. "No. Druise, no."

"No," my mother said firmly. "Druisius, thank you, but no. You are needed here. I will go."

Chapter 9

~Lena~

"YOU CAN'T!" MY DAUGHTER SAID.

But I could, and I was going to. The reasons had come together like the pieces on a *xache* board as the game reached its conclusion, all leading to one end.

"Why not? Someone needs to go after Lynthe and Constyn, someone of rank. Someone needs to find out what is happening in Casil." I spoke as the general, calmly. I would have access to the palace, I thought, as long as Eudekia were still alive.

"Gwenna needs you here." Sorley. "Cillian would have told you that."

I turned to face him, still the general, every movement controlled. But this was Sorley whose puzzled gaze I met, and surely he must understand? "Cillian," I said, "would have been the first to tell me to go."

"And leave your daughter?"

"Yes."

"How could you?" Disbelief coloured Sorley's voice. "How could you even think of it?"

"Because someone who will be welcomed at the palace must go. I am more use to Gwenna there than here."

"I don't agree, *Mathàir*," my daughter said. I turned to her.

"Then listen," I said. "I cannot give you advice for a future I can't see, a future that is . . ." The control crumbled. I wanted to weep. Sorley, I thought, you must know. I reached for a way to explain. "I can't think, or reason. Nothing makes sense. I stare at papers for hours because the words and numbers are a jumble. There is only . . ." Tears I couldn't hold back clogged my throat. "Darkness."

"Cillian would never have left Gwenna alone with all she has to face, and he would have expected the same of you," Sorley said. Anger threaded his voice now.

"No," I said, swallowing my tears, speaking what I knew was truth. "He never bound me, Sorley. The bracelet I wear is not a falcon's jess."

"He gave up the *Ti'ach*, being *Comiádh,* all he had ever wanted, to be Gwenna's advisor. And you think he'd just say, yes, leave?" Part of my mind—a detached, uncaring part—noticed the heat of Sorley's anger reddening his cheeks, but his knuckles shining white.

"Stop!" Druise said. "Thirty years together, and now you fight over who knew him best? I agree. Lena should go."

"But—" Gwenna began.

"You are capable, *Principe*," Druise said, matter-of-factly. "You will still have the general Talyn, and Muire, yes? And me."

"Who else has the rank and authority to stop Lynthe?" Talyn, attempting to bring logic to the argument.

"A more senior major. Or you," Sorley snapped.

"You baulked at Druisius going, and he is a senior major and has the authority, if the *Principe* chooses. Now you suggest sending me to a city I don't know, and to an Empress I have never met, to convince her, if she would even deign to see me, of Lynthe's betrayal? When both Druisius and Lena are known to her? Which makes more sense? Not," she added, "that an Ésparian military decision is any of your business, Sorley of Linrathe."

Sorley made a derisive, dismissive noise. His eyes on me were as hard as the pebbles of a shingle beach. "You told me once that leaving was unforgivable. Remember that, Lena."

"Perhaps not unforgiveable," Gwenna said. "But certainly too dangerous. Casil may have fallen. I forbid you to go, General."

My tears had gone, replaced by a cold clarity. "Then," I said, "I resign, *Principe*." I unpinned my insignia of rank, letting it drop to the table. "I will go as a civilian, to do what Cillian did ask. I will take his ring to Colm."

A discordant scrape and the crash of a falling chair shattered the silence that followed my words. Sorley was on his feet. "I cannot believe this." He shook Druise's restraining hand loose. "Everything we've done, everything he worked for—it's all at stake, and you are just walking away? As if all he was are those words on his memorial, and now that's in place—" He shook his head, his face working.

I could see his pain. I even understood his anger, distantly. But I knew what I had to do, and why, and Sorley was so very wrong.

"Sorley." Ruar laid a hand on his shoulder. "Come with me, *mo charaidh.*"

I thought he'd refuse. But he let his *Teannasach* escort him from the room, his shoulders high and rigid. No one spoke. I picked up my officer's insignia. "I am going, Gwenna." I kept my voice level, calm. "Is it as your representative?"

"I suppose. But why, *Mathàir*? Why are you doing this?" She sounded fourteen again, confused and hurt by what she could not understand. I thought of a lake on an endless plain, the infinite dome of the sky, the countless stars in its depth. Of the man who had been so much more than the words on his memorial, and what we had found in each other in that space and silence.

"To mourn, yes?" Druise said, as gently as I'd ever hear him speak. "Let your mother go, Kitten."

Chapter 10

~Gwenna~

"I DON'T UNDERSTAND," I said to Druise. We were alone; Talyn had gone with my mother a few minutes earlier.

"What she said." He leant back in his chair, regarding me. "Nothing makes sense. She does not know how to live without your father, but she must find out."

"And she has to leave me, with all that is happening, to discover this?" I wasn't angry, quite, but frustrated and confused, like Gwyllar when the cat he chased after eluded him. And like Gwyllar, I wanted to scream my feelings to the world. At least, part of me did.

"Yes. You listen now, Gwenna." Druise never called me by my name, unless he had something very serious to say. "You are twenty-nine. Not a child. Maybe you need this. To make you rely on yourself, not your advisors." He chewed at his lip, a habit when he was thinking. "Cillian was concerned, yes?"

"Concerned?"

"That you depended on him too much. Who was leading Ésparias, him or you?"

"I made the decisions." He'd never said anything about this to me.

"But how often without his advice?"

Rarely. It was true; I'd talked over almost everything with him. "I wasn't ready," I said.

"Once. But not later. We argued about this, Cillian and me."

"Did you?" The idea was strange.

"Not the first time. Even in Casil, when I was his guard. Then it was about your mother, but the same fault."

"What fault?" Other than working too hard—and hadn't my mother said he'd been impulsive, earlier in his life?—I didn't think of my father as having faults. I knew he'd made mistakes, and that there were things he regretted: Sorley had made me see that, the summer I'd been fourteen. But he'd learned from those. They weren't faults.

"His vow to your mother, and to you. He promised shelter, but a shelter is for storms, yes? Not for the rains of every day." He grinned. "Or no work would get done here or in Linrathe, yes?"

Everyday rains I could cope with. I wished I had my father's shelter in this storm of events. I reached for something to distance myself from the futility of that thought. "What did he promise you, Druise?" I'd wondered before, but I'd never had the temerity to ask. Not that I expected an answer, but maybe he'd distract me with some joke.

"Me? Nothing."

I tried again. "Why did you come west?"

"A chance, yes? A new life."

Why had he wanted one? But I'd probed enough. "Or at least a wetter one," I said, which elicited a chuckle. I smiled back. We talked a bit more, about inconsequential things, until I heard Druise's stomach rumble. "Go and eat," I told him.

But when he'd left, I rose to pace the room, remembering my mother leaving us in Casil to ride north with Junia. When she'd returned, she'd been calmer. In that time away she'd made a choice: she would return to Wall's End and the army. It had been Faolyn's death and my elevation to *Principe* that had brought all my family back to Ésparias. Without that, would my father have stayed at the *Ti'ach* with Sorley?

If she'd been willing to leave my father to find a way to live after Lianë's death, then should I be surprised she'd leave me—us, because Sorley and Druisius mattered too—now? I shivered, and crossed my arms to rub my shoulders. I wasn't really cold, not on the outside.

You are twenty-nine. Maybe you need this. Blunt words, but that was Druise. To me, and to any of us. Was he right?

Hadn't Lynthe said the same to me, that I relied too much on my father and my older advisors? If I'd listened to her, shared more with her, asked for her advice first, would she have turned against me?

What was past could not be changed. What mattered was what I did now. Perhaps I did need to rely less on my advisors, but I still needed allies and friends. I could do nothing about Lynthe. My mother was a different matter—and so was Ruar.

~

A guard dogged my footsteps, but she kept her distance, allowing me to think on my walk to the fort. Cadets practiced horsemanship on the training field outside the walls; I'd been one of them, once. The gates in the south wall stood open, guards standing both at the walls and overhead in the watchtowers. It must be, I thought, an intensely boring assignment.

I was letting my mind wander, something I could not afford to do. If Ruar was angry—and he had every right to be—I would need every tactic of diplomacy I had to attempt to repair at least the political relationship between us.

Ruar's guard—his own, not one of ours—blocked my way at the door to his room, in the residence that was nominally Talyn's as the general commanding Wall's End. "The *Teannasach* is not to be disturbed, *Principe*."

"Is he alone?" I would be polite, unless I needed to be otherwise.

"Yes, *Principe*."

"Then please tell him the *Principe* of Ésparias is here, and wishes counsel with the *Teannasach*." Clarity was needed: this man knew where Ruar had slept for the past weeks. Clarity for me, too.

The guard, thankfully, did as I asked. A moment later he opened the door again. "Enter."

I went in—alone—and closed the door. Ruar was at his desk, a letter half-written in front of him. To whom?

"*Principe*?" Neutrally, although with a faint irritation. At being disturbed, or that I was here at all?

"*Teannasach*." I had set the tone with my instructions to the guard. "I wish no misunderstanding between us."

"There is none." He gestured to a chair. "Linrathe's history with Varsland is not Ésparias's, and so we view them differently. They have been enemies, but they have also been allies, both now and in the past. Daragh would be a wise choice to approach, if someone wished to negotiate with Varsland privately."

"I understand. I have been considering my own views about Varsland."

Ruar tilted his chin. "And?"

"I don't trust them. You know that. But why?" I tried a smile. "You once suggested to Sorley that I marry Bryngyl, I believe. I thought, at fourteen, that was a sensible solution."

Just a flicker of reaction, I decided. "Did Sorley tell you that?"

"No. I had come to the same conclusion, and suggested it to Sorley. He disagreed."

"Wise man," Ruar said.

"Eudekia didn't trust them either," I said. "Her caution has undoubtedly influenced my views. But even more than her distrust, I find it difficult to ignore what happened here when Fritjof invaded."

"I can understand that." He reached for a wine jug, holding it up in an unspoken question. I nodded.

Holding the cup he poured for me, I continued. "We spoke about the Emperor's guard, what those who remain might do if they come home. Surely Sorley has told you what Bjørn said, when he asked my father to take his sword—and the offer of more—to Alekos?"

"Both Sorley and your father told me of his concern for the restless young men of Varsland," Ruar said. "I have been giving that some thought since you voiced your earlier concern."

"Have you?" I said, with unplanned asperity. "And were you going to share those thoughts with me?"

Ruar laughed, suddenly my friend again as well as the *Teannasach*. He indicated the letter in front of him. "I was. In writing, to give you time to consider and spend your initial anger elsewhere."

"Anger at what?"

"A possibility. But listen first, if you will. You asked if Helvi being from Varsland changed how Daragh sees himself, and perhaps his loyalties. Turn the question around. Does it change how Varsland sees him?"

"As a man who can be influenced?" I said, realizing. *Would you trust him?* Ruar had asked Druise.

"Exactly. A man who speaks their language as a cradle tongue, who knows the songs and stories, who has cousins among the captains and the landholders whose goods are bought and sold. A man who is marrying their king's daughter. So I must leave immediately, to catch my son and ask some hard questions. I want Varsland to control Linrathe after my death no more than you would wish that for Ésparias."

"I'm sorry," I said.

"Don't be." He smiled at me. "I am almost certain of his loyalty. I think I would have heard, were there anything to know, but—" His smile disappeared. "You thought the same of Lynthe."

I nodded. I didn't want to talk about Lynthe, especially not to Ruar. "You need to leave. I understand. But before you do, what is the idea that will make me angry?"

He hesitated. "Gwenna, it something you will have to consider, something that might meet a need for both Ésparias and Varsland."

"Then tell me," I said.

~

I cradled the wine cup, forcing myself not to speak, to analyze Ruar's words, not just react with the revulsion I felt. Be the *Principe*, I told myself. Remember your training.

Ruar finished speaking. He cocked an eyebrow, waiting for me to speak. "But it was ruled out, when Earl Vidar came to suggest a marriage between me and Bryngyl."

"Circumstances have changed."

"My father is dead, and that promise was made to him. Is that part of the changed circumstances?"

"It might be. But the other reason is real, Gwenna. Ask Sorley how Gundarstorp's harvest was last year, if you doubt me."

"Did you speak of this to my father?" It was the first thing I needed to know.

"No. One bad harvest means little. But we are well into spring now, and fields are too wet to plant or seeds lie rotting in the soil. Grain will mould in storage, too, if the weather does not improve." His mouth twisted. "And the further north you go, the worse the weather is. You must think about it, Gwenna."

"I can see I must," I said. But how could I?

Ruar nodded. "I never asked Cillian—I always meant to, but somehow I never found the right moment—did he ever tell you where his idea of a western alliance came from?" His tone was conversational, curious.

"From what he knew of alliances among Heræcrian states, I thought. He certainly used those as comparisons, sometimes."

"I wonder." He rubbed his chin. "Gwenna, I was still young when my father was killed. But he'd taken me to the negotiations between himself and Callan at the White Fort, to forge the truce between our countries. I heard what he argued for, not just for that temporary truce but for the permanent peace he hoped would emerge."

"And?"

"One of his hopes was for free movement—in either direction—of people across the border. The gates of the Wall standing open."

"And you think my father took the idea from him? From a man who never trusted him because his father was an Ésparian soldier, and his mother therefore traitor to Linrathe?" I shook my head vehemently. "He wasn't even at those negotiations."

"No. But he had been a *toscaire* for many years, and he likely knew Donnalch's views. And he was there in my father's last days at Fritjof's hall. What might have been said, once Donnalch knew he would not leave there alive?"

"You never asked him?"

"Once, when I was a student at the *Ti'ach*. But after he told me that one of my father's last thoughts was for my safety—" He smiled. "I have no doubt that that was true. I also have little doubt that Cillian purposely directed my thoughts away from my intended direction. Perhaps he thought me too young still for the regrets of a man facing the abrupt end of his life and the potential destruction of his country."

"Which you reunited in the aftermath of war," I said, "by planning and compromise. You are suggesting that the same on my part now can turn aside a possible war. But it is a very great compromise, Ruar."

"Is it greater than the one your parents made with Casil?" His eyes, as blue as a summer sky, met mine. "Our fathers are dead. It has not been my task to blindly follow Donnalch's dreams. Nor is it yours to follow Cillian's. Be courageous, Gwenna."

"I'll think about it." I finished my wine and stood. "Now you should leave, so you can reach at least the north road today."

"Yes. Before Daragh hears from someone else"—he flashed a grin— "of impunities taken with regard to his loyalties. And mine."

"I didn't question your loyalties. Lynthe did. I didn't tell you, because, well—" I stopped. "Aren't similar things said about me in Linrathe?"

"Similar things, yes." He was serious again, almost grim. "I'm not concerned with that, Gwenna. But your question about Daragh—I think Sorley heard an accusation, not a question that any sensible leader would ask."

I stared at him. Sorley? But he wouldn't— "Are you serious?"

"He is angry and grieving, Gwenna. And for all I love and respect him, I am not sure he can be trusted not to do something rash right now. His loyalty to Linrathe runs very deep. I told him I had understood your worries, that I had taken no offense. I think he will do nothing. But I am not sure, and so I must reach Daragh before any potential message from Sorley can."

The thought that Sorley might speak against me was horrifying. It must have shown, because Ruar stood, offering his arms. I went into them, needing the strength and comfort. He kissed my forehead. "I feel as if I am living through an earthquake," I said into his shoulder. All the foundations of my life crumbling."

"I remember that feeling," he said.

I sniffed back the threatening tears, and tried a smile. "And you were only fourteen. I should be ashamed of myself, at my age."

"Thirteen, when it all started, and terrified, although I tried my best not to show it. And then my uncle Liam, my regent in my first years as *Teannasach,* put almost every obstacle he could think of in my way, objecting to every decision I wished to make. I had to learn to make him think my ideas were his. You, at least, have been well-advised."

I kissed his cheek, slightly rough. "Thank you."

His hand cupped the back of my head, drawing me to him. His kiss was gentle enough, but not the kiss of farewell of a friend. "Thank you," he murmured, "for the honour of these past nights, *leannan.*"

A twinge, not quite of desire but of its memory and its fulfilment, made me smile. "I could say the same. Ride safely, Ruar."

~

A different group of cadets, somewhat older, were practicing horse archery on the training field now. I stopped to watch them, remembering the intense focus needed to maintain balance and loose an arrow at exactly the right time. There'd been no room for other thoughts. I'd been better with a thrown secca, but I was—or had been—useful enough with the bow.

I'd killed a man once with my knife, a Marai man pursuing a fleeing captive woman into Sorham. That, I mused, hadn't helped my distrust of them. But it went deeper than that. I knew what had happened to the women of Ésparias—Linrathe, too, but there it hadn't been the same purposeful, planned act of war. My own cousin Teárdh was Marai-fathered, his mother raped but her life spared. Young and fertile, she'd been useful. My grandmother, after the men had finished with her, had not been allowed to live.

I shuddered. How could I even think about what Ruar had suggested? But it might prevent a possible repeat of that horror—except that without a half-mad king to order such atrocities, would it really come to that? Then, unbidden and unwanted, the creeping doubt: was there an advantage to Linrathe in this suggestion?

I felt suddenly as if I were in the *Arénas* at Casil at the height of the games, thousands of voices shouting, trumpets blaring, men and animals screaming. I'd wanted to put my hands over my ears then, but these sounds were in my head. I turned away from the training field. I knew what I needed. I glanced at the sun. I had my records to write, and my hour with Gwyllar, but there was time.

~

My bodyguard was almost certainly cursing me. I crouched a bit more in the saddle, raising my hands on either side of my horse's neck. He leapt the stream without hesitation, pounding up the track toward the hill's summit. He slowed of his own accord at the top, and I pulled him up, swinging round to see where my guard was. Not far behind. I urged the gelding back into a trot, heading east.

Grouse scattered, running downhill. Overhead a buzzard turned in wide circles. The narrow, uneven track I followed along the ridge had been made by sheep, and needed all my attention. It was time I turned back, but even the thought of Gwyllar expecting me didn't make me less reluctant to do so.

Ahead, a wider stream, fast and turbulent, crossed the ridge. The sheep track continued, but an alternate path paralleled the stream— almost a waterfall—down to the lower moorland. I reined the gelding in. I could turn back, or I could take the descending track. My horse was surefooted. I turned him to the left, downhill.

My bodyguard called to me, but I ignored her. I loosened the reins and leant back in the saddle, letting the horse choose his path. The hill broadened out not too far below, but this first steep slope was tricky.

The gelding slipped once, his hindquarters tucking in. I'd kicked the stirrups free, to be ready if he did fall, but he regained his balance, snorting a little. A few steps further, and we were on more level ground. I patted his damp neck, breathing hard with exhilaration.

"My lady!" my bodyguard rebuked, arriving a minute later.

"It's easy from here on," I said. I dismounted, leading the gelding to the stream to let him drink. A dipper slipped from a rock into the water. I watched it swim under the surface, then bob up to another rock with something in its beak, white breast gleaming.

"Ready?" I asked my guard. We rode at a walk down the gentle slope, scattering the sheep and lambs. I raised a hand to the shepherd. My brief respite from responsibility was over.

Chapter 11

~Lena~

A LONG PATH OF GOLDEN LIGHT led across the sea to the westering sun. The flagstones of the terrace held the day's warmth, even if the offshore breeze was cool. Talyn had left perhaps half an hour before. We'd spent most of the afternoon deciding who would take responsibility for the tasks and troops I was leaving behind.

Apulo, back from the infirmary, came out to the terrace. "Is there anything you want, Lena?"

"No," I said. "Bring another cup and join me." His company was restful, in a way no one else's was. I couldn't quite define why.

When he'd settled in a chair with his wine, I said, "I'm going east, to Casil, to judge the severity of the war before we commit to more than volunteer troops. I hope I can also find Colm. I'll take Cillian's ring."

"This is a military assignment?"

It was, I supposed. Even if I had given it to myself. "Yes."

"You will not be travelling alone, then?"

I'd argued with Talyn about this. "Two guards," she'd said. "At least."

I'd refused. "When Callan sent Turlo east," I'd said, "he went alone. So will I." In fact, Callan had not sent Turlo alone, but the red-headed general had sent his companion back. That my father had obeyed had puzzled me for years, but I thought I understood now. Turlo had been grieving, not just for a war almost certainly lost, but for the death of his beloved Arey, mother of his children, at the hands of the Marai. He'd needed to deal with his grief and anger on his own, and Galen had accepted that.

Talyn had given me a long, assessing look. "At least you know where you're going. And the language."

"I plan to," I said to Apulo now.

"Would I be of any help to you?"

"Apulo, no. You already told me you don't want to go back to Casil."
He meant well, I knew. But I didn't want even him with me.

He smiled, briefly. "In truth, I don't. But I felt I should offer."

"Thank you." I put my wine down and sat a little straighter. "There is
something you could do here, if you would."

"Anything."

"Cillian's *li'itho* bracelet. Will you give it to Sorley, after I leave?"

I saw the flicker of—surprise?—in his eyes. He took a moment to
answer, but his voice was firm. "I spoke in haste. I won't do that, Lena."

"Why not?"

He took a mouthful of wine, no doubt giving himself time to compose
his thoughts. "If I understand its significance, what it stands for, then it
can only come from you. If I—or anyone else—were to give it to Sorley
instead, what would that say to him?"

Shame suffused me again. I had just tried to avoid doing the one thing
Cillian had asked of me, the last affirmation of love and trust. How could
I have even thought to have Apulo do it in my stead? *Cillian, kärestan,
forgive me.*

"I'm sorry," I muttered, angry tears pricking at my eyes. "I shouldn't
have asked."

"You are not yourself," he said gently. "Are you sure I shouldn't
accompany you to Casil?"

Talyn had asked me something similar, not surprisingly. I'd admitted
my confusion in the council meeting—and given in to tears in a public
setting. Seventeen years at the *Ti'ach* had trained me to show nothing
more than mild disapproval or amusement except privately, and I'd
thought I still had that control. Did they all think me slightly mad?
Maybe I was.

"I'm sure. I'll be all right, Apulo. I just need to get away from here." I
swept my hand in a half-circle. "From these walls, and the busyness, and
words on paper with no meaning."

He nodded. "You always did, every so often." He paused, and when he
spoke again his words were softer, reflective. "So did Sorley."

It was true. I'd thought, for Sorley, it was the pull of home, his deep attachment to Gundarstorp and his brother taking him back to its hills and moors and seacoast every few years. But he'd gone off on other journeys, sometimes alone, sometimes with Druisius finding a reason to be riding the same way, to gather songs and music within Ésparias.

"You," I said, realizing, "are the only one of us who never—" What words could I use, without sounding disloyal? "Had a respite." From the brilliant man whom I—we—had loved deeply, but who had never been easy. His melancholy had been well-hidden from the public world, and, I thought, from his children. But not from me, or Sorley and Druise—or from Apulo.

"It was not so hard for me," Apulo said. "Sometimes, yes, I had to insist he do his exercises, or walk. But mostly in the bad times he was just silent, and so I would be too, or I would sing. But there was always a formality between us, a politeness. It was different for you and Sorley, and in another way, for Druisius."

It would never be hard for any of us again, not in that way. A different burden to carry now, if one could be said to carry emptiness. The sun sank lower, its golden path changing to copper on a pewter sea. Fishing boats returning to Berge were silhouettes against the sky.

"*Mathàir?*"

"Gwenna." I turned in my chair.

"I knocked. The door was open, and I thought you might be out here."

"Sit," I said. Apulo rose.

"I will leave you. Would you like wine, Gwenna?"

"Please. But water it." She smiled at him, and took the chair he'd vacated. We sat in silence, looking at the sea, until Apulo had brought the wine. Gwenna took a sip. "When are you going?"

"As soon as there's a ship, either one of ours or a trader on its way to the Eastern Fort."

"I thought you might ride," my daughter said. "Perhaps stop at Tirvan on the way south."

"I thought about it." While I'd been to visit my sister a few times, I'd never been comfortable in my home village. The women had been friendly enough, but there had always been a distance. It was, after all, my name on the treaty that had changed, without consultation, so much about our land and its traditional way of life. Without consultation, and without authority.

I wasn't going to try to explain this to Gwenna. Kira and the other women had made her welcome, both when she'd spent a summer there as a young girl, and when she'd been sent to calculate taxes in her brief time in that role. "Kira would be too attentive," I said instead. "She would mean well, but her way of giving comfort is not what I need. Nor do I want the expressions of sympathy that would inevitably be made at the inns. I am better sailing."

"Who is taking on your responsibilities here?" A *Principe's* question. I told her what Talyn and I had discussed; Reif, my adjutant, would shoulder the majority of my work—a task, that if he did it well, would be rewarded by promotion. He'd be assigned an assistant, and Talyn would take one or two of my duties as well.

"Then Reif also takes your place on the advisory council." Not a question, I noted. "When Garia returns, I'm appointing her, too."

"Both are appropriate," I agreed. "Did you consider Dern as well?"

"I did, but he is away so often."

A valid point. "This leaves you with only one advisor with experience of war," I said. We had lost so many, officers and soldiers both, fighting the Marai. I stared out at the sea, thinking. "Gulian? Farry? Or Glynn?" She'd been my cohort-second at the Taiva, a competent, decisive woman from Torrey. She'd returned south after our victory, but to the Eastern Fort, not her village.

"I'll consider them. But I know Reif and Garia, and Muire, whom I will also appoint. I trust them, and—" A thread of uncertainty crept into her voice. "I will have to explain the idea of the western alliance to them, sooner or later. Lynthe always said more of our generation should know, and she was right about that, wasn't she?"

"I think she was." We had thought Gwenna and Lynthe and Colm were enough, until Faolyn's children were of an age to know. But our son had never come home, and Constyn and Flynsà were too young.

Gwenna rubbed her eyes. "What was your thought about Beria? We never returned to that question."

"That Alekos commands in a royal province, but not a procuratorial one."

She nodded. "I had the same realization. And if the Assembly will not conscript men from their provinces, it implies the Emperor has lost their confidence."

"And by extension the city, the families who look to the *dignitasi* for patronage?"

She winced. "Surely Druise would know that?"

"Things are happening so quickly. Either messengers or letters could be lost."

"Which is why I don't want you to go." Fear again, in my daughter's voice. "We have heard nothing from the Empress or Colm in reply to your letters. Shouldn't we have, by now?"

I counted weeks silently. "Not yet. I wrote to Colm first, but I have no real idea of where he is. The letter may take some time to find him. I sent the Empress's message on a later ship." I'd wanted to tell Colm myself, not have him hear of this father's death from the palace or a rumour in the city, but that hadn't been the only reason I'd delayed.

"*Mathàir*, please reconsider?" Gwenna asked. "You sound to me as if you are again thinking as clearly as you always have, and Druisius—"

"No!" I took a breath, to calm myself. "Sorley needs Druise. And I am— coping, just now. But tomorrow, or in an hour, everything will be fogged again, mired, and I will be no use to you at all. I can do this task, this reconnaissance and reporting, but I can't be here at Wall's End, in these rooms, day after day." I softened my voice, feeling the warring pains inside me. "I know you are grieving too, Gwenna, both for your father and for Lynthe. Grieving and angry. And perhaps I am selfish, but I can't help you carry your grief, or Sorley or Druise or Apulo theirs, with nothing to do but sit and think and analyse. I need to move, to train or sail or ride. It's how I deal with loss. It always has been." Since Maya, my roiling emotions clamped down by the need to learn the sword and the knife, to become someone capable of killing.

There was hurt in my daughter's eyes, but she didn't argue. "Sorley is angry with you," she said.

"I know." A different pain. I'd thought he would understand. Druisius did.

"*Mathàir*?" Gwenna was standing, preparing to leave. She looked down at me. "I have another task for you, then. Bring Colm home."

If I found him. "He might refuse."

"Then tell him his *Principe* orders it. He cannot ignore that if it comes from you. I want my brother at my side."

~

The sea had swallowed the sun. The clouds still glowed, faintly. If I stayed on the terrace, I would get cold, and I had things to do. Reluctantly I went inside. One lamp burned on a table. I picked it up; I'd need it. No lamp would have been lit in Cillian's study.

I opened the door, the scent of books and ink, overlaid by damp, strong in the closed room. Another door led to his treatment room. I'd rarely come here; these rooms had been space for Cillian and Sorley. But the box I wanted sat on a shelf.

I took the key from its drawer and unlocked the box. I sat at the desk, looking at the letters—nearly thirty years of them, only the last unopened. I'd never read them. Cillian had read parts of them to me, or to us, but he had kept most of his correspondence with Eudekia to himself.

That private aspect to their relationship had made writing to her difficult. I'd guessed Cillian had told her he was dying; I knew he'd told Colm, in his last letter to his son, not to expect another. But I still hadn't known what to say to Eudekia, to find the tone that acknowledged she too would mourn Cillian without presuming I knew her true feelings. Perhaps she had only thought him a friend, an equal with whom she could spar with words and argument. Perhaps he had thought only the same of her. I doubted both assumptions.

I picked up the last letter, the one that had arrived after his death. *Should I open it?* It wasn't just a question for me. But here, in the room where Cillian had spent so much of his last decade, I felt no presence.

This had always been a place for the parts of his life that didn't include me: his time with Sorley, his letters to Eudekia.

Thirty years of correspondence, thirty years of history—because whatever else the letters in this box contained, what Cillian had read to us was often commentary on the political situation in Casil and its provinces. Her last letter might give me, and Gwenna, insight into what was unfolding.

But it also might contain a farewell, and with it, memories and regrets, and maybe more. I wasn't ready to read those words, even if they might provide a reason for Eudekia to see me. I would tell Gwenna where the unopened letter was, and leave the decision to her.

Chapter 12

~Gwenna~

MY MOTHER'S SHIP WOULD LEAVE ON the morning's tide. It wasn't an auspicious start, the cold wind blowing rain across the deck of the ship and the dock. I'd wrapped myself in a winter cloak, and still I shivered.

Druise had come to see her leave too. Sorley hadn't. "Do not expect him," Druise said, when I asked, quietly. His tone told me not to probe further. I didn't really want to. This disagreement was between my mother and Sorley. No need for me to be involved.

She would meet with both Finn and the governor before continuing east, my mother said, and, yes, a summary of those meetings would be sent to me. "Give them to the head of the guard there," Druise said. "He can be trusted, yes? No one else."

The captain had been hovering. Now he approached, telling her it was time to board or they would miss the tide. She gave me a hug. "You do understand?" she murmured, for my ears alone.

"Yes," I said. It was almost true.

"Your father's last letter from Eudekia is in the box in his study, with the others. I haven't read it. You may wish to."

I nodded. "Be careful, *Mathàir*."

"Go with the god, Lena," Druise said. The soldier's farewell. "And come home, yes?"

She almost smiled, but it was distant, as if at a memory. "If I can. I'm coming, Captain," she added, in a different tone.

We watched the ship pass through the arms of the harbour into the rougher water beyond, my mother still standing on deck, regardless of the weather. Looking small, somehow, even in her own heavy cloak. *If I can?* Hers was not a journey without danger, for anyone, and she was both not young and travelling alone. Why had I allowed it?

I shivered. Druise glanced at me. "The gods decide, yes?" he said. "We need to talk."

"What about?"

"Things I have heard. If we stay here, no one can listen."

Sometimes Druise's caution amused me. Not today, in the cold breeze and heavy rain. But we had a reason to stand here, to watch the ship move south, and it was certain no one could overhear us.

"Well?"

"I have had messages, yes? From the south. About Lynthe."

"And?"

"She has support. Enough we should be concerned."

"What sort of support?"

"For Constyn, when he turns eighteen, yes? There is talk you should give him the title then."

"Abdicate?"

"Yes. And more."

"Well, tell me." I brushed water from my face, the cloak's hood insufficient to keep the blown rain off.

"A council is suggested. To guide you, but really to tell you what to do."

"I have one." Not to tell me what to do, though. To present ideas and counterarguments.

"But not who they want, yes? Not old men."

"Who are they suggesting?" Listen calmly, I told myself. Consider what is best for Ésparias.

"Generals and officials. Finn. And Dern too. Maybe even Leste's procurator, although" —Druise grinned— "they would not suggest him, if they knew what his son does for me."

"His son?" But I understood. "He is one of your informants?"

"He is head of the guard at the Eastern Fort. A good man, Valle. One you can rely on, yes?"

I could no longer make out figures on the deck of the ship; the vessel was picking up speed with the wind. "Can we go in now?" I asked. Druise was bare-headed, although he had worn his cloak. We began to walk towards the long flight of steps that led up to the fort. "How long have you known this?"

"A day."

"Did you tell my mother?"

"No." He gave me a sideways look. "She does not need more confusion. There is a complication."

The stairs were guarded, both at the bottom and the top. Druise fell silent. I preceded him up the steps, glad of the handrail in the wet. At the level of the fort, I turned. Druise was further behind than I had expected. Had he stopped for a word with the lower guard? I'd hurried, wanting to be out of the rain.

I watched him speak to the upper guard, a commiseration over duty in such foul weather. I'd only smiled at the man as I passed. I waited until Druise was beside me again. "What complication?"

He just shook his head. "Are you all right?" I asked. Did I hear a rasping in his breath? He coughed, bending, his hands on his knees. "Druise?"

A flashed grin. "Swallowed a fly." He straightened. "The fort, yes? Then I will tell you."

~

At the commanders' residence, I sent for towels, a brazier, and warmed wine, to be sent to the room I used there. It was early in the day for wine, even warmed and sweetened, but I thought Druise needed it. He was still coughing occasionally, and his face was drawn. I wasn't sure I believed his story about the fly.

It took a little time to arrive, by which time we were drier and getting warm. The steward brought bread, too, and the usual oil and salt and olives. I'd had breakfast, but I wasn't going to turn down fresh bread. Druise ignored the food, but he took a deep drink of his wine.

"You know who Maya is, yes?" he asked.

"Maya? My mother's first partner, at Tirvan?"

"She is headwoman of Tain village now." Tain was in the south, against the Durrains. Isolated and lonely once, one of the new Casilani-built roads ran close to it now. Much, I had understood, to the villagers' disapproval, because Tain was one of a very few villages that kept to the traditions of Partition: had, in fact, been founded by women who had chosen banishment from their home villages rather than defend their land against invasion. I closed my eyes against the obvious thought, hoping I was wrong. "Some of the call for me to abdicate in favour of Constyn comes from Tain."

"Yes. And more. If Casil does not rule here, she says Constyn should not be *Princip*, but Emperor again."

I laughed. I couldn't help it. "But even when Ésparias had an emperor, the title wasn't hereditary, and it would have never gone to an eighteen-year-old."

"But she is stirring up memories, yes? Like men in Casil who speak of the glories of the first Emperors there. As if they were better than the ones they know."

"Do people think the past was simpler?" It hadn't been; I knew that.

"Some do. And some want nothing to change."

"Things can change too quickly," I said, "or too much changes at one time."

He shrugged. "That is life, yes? The Casilani here would agree with you." He reached for a piece of bread, holding it between his fingers but not eating.

"What are you hearing?" I'd had other intelligence, but I wanted to know if Druise had heard anything different.

"Anger. Casil does not conscript men, especially not of their class. They do not understand why they must go to fight, and Ésparian troops stay behind."

The same as I had been told. "Should I send more troops?"

He took a bite of the bread, chewing and swallowing before answering. "How much grain is in the storehouses?"

"Grain? I don't know, exactly. We sent more east this spring. Why?"

"Go see Sorley. He will explain." He grinned. "I know about selling grain. He knows about growing it."

~

"It's simple," Sorley said to my question. "Who is going to harvest it, and prepare the ground and plant next year's grain crops, if the Casilani estate workers are gone?"

He'd not exactly been welcoming at first, but when I told him why I'd come I'd seen him visibly relax. The rooms he shared with Druise were warm and dry, braziers burning as well as the hypocaust heating. to keep their collection of instruments from being damaged by damp. On the shelves of their sitting room, glass bowls and jugs, most in the blues and greens they seemed to favour, glinted in the warm light of lamps. Sorley had been tuning a *ladhar*, getting ready for a lesson, when I'd knocked on his door.

Regardless of his status as a *scáeli* and his work for Ruar and my father, Sorley had never lost his connection with farming. The few times I'd seen him with his brother, Gundarstorp's crops and livestock were always discussed, and he'd managed the *Ti'ach's* lands for all the years we'd lived there. Had he missed that, here at Wall's End?

"The women aren't," I said.

"They are not Ésparian women," he answered. "Some can no doubt handle a scythe or a threshing flail, but generally they do lighter work. It will be a struggle, especially on the larger estates, even the ones that have Ésparian workers."

"But don't they also hire more workers from the villages, especially at harvest?" I'd remained standing, knowing his student would be here at any moment. Sorley was sorting through a cabinet, looking, I assumed, for the music he wanted his pupil to play.

"It won't be enough. Harvest needs many hands, from a few weeks after midsummer right through to the first frosts, and the villages have their own crops to gather."

A bit more than half the distance between the Wall and the southern ocean, the highlands of the north stopped abruptly, the hills and moorland ending at a steep escarpment. Below that divide was grassland, bisected by the Taiva. The grasslands curved up under the Durrains to the north and east, to the villages of Han and Rigg, but the western plains had been nearly uninhabited before the Casilani had arrived. Now they were divided into large estates, some of the grassland turned to fields of grains and pulses where the Taiva's waters were diverted for irrigation; some providing grazing for herds of cattle and horses.

These vast areas of unhusbanded land—not just the grasslands, but the warmer soils close to the southern coast, so well suited to growing fruit—had been an attractive proposition for some among Casil's *dignitasi*: younger sons, men retiring early from administrative positions. They had brought wives and workers, and it was the grain and other crops they grew that meant we had enough to send what Casil demanded of us each year, and a surplus to trade with Varsland and Leste.

"It might not matter, as there are fewer people to feed now," Sorley said, "except this weather worries me. Wheat does not like wet fields." He turned from the cabinet, a roll of vellum in his hands. "You don't need a hungry country on top of everything else, Gwenna."

Twice now. Ruar and Sorley. I didn't need a third mention, the old belief, to make me see the truth. The hungry country I should worry about wasn't my own. It was Varsland.

Part II

To every man upon this earth, death cometh soon or late.
Macauley

Lays of Ancient Rome

Chapter 13

~Lena~

I SHOULDERED MY PACK, the bow strapped to it, clipped the quiver to my belt, and offered the captain of the trader that had brought me here my hand. "Miqurios be with you," he said. "The inn is straight up the main road, at the north gate."

"My thanks." He nodded, but his eyes were already on the amphorae his men were loading. Olives, I guessed, or maybe wine; Beria supplied Casil with both. He didn't go that far east, he'd told me when I'd asked; only to Sylana, his home. On this voyage he'd come across the Nivéan Sea, bringing dates and figs from Cyrenis to Ésparias, so he hadn't any recent news. But he doubted it was good, from all he'd heard.

Thirty years ago, there hadn't even been a village here. Passage through the archipelago of islands that were the southern reaches of the Durrains was well-marked now, both on charts and by lighthouses and emblazons on the rocks, but in heavy weather it was still fraught with tension. The town—Occida—and its harbour served both as a place to recover from a difficult passage, or for ships, naval or traders, to wait out wind and storm. Its primary purpose, however, was as a port to ship the fruit and grain grown now in the foothills and on the plain. A good road linked the estates of the Casilani families who owned these farms, and made transport of the produce easy. I would ride the road north, officially taking a letter to a cousin of the governor. My real task was to look for the presence of Casilani soldiers, listen at the inns to what was said about the war—and watch for any sign of Lynthe and Constyn. Probably she would go straight to Casil, but I couldn't assume that.

Pallius, Ésparias's governor, had been told only that I was going in pursuit of Lynthe. The imperial messenger's seal had been his idea, and a good one. Not just because it would entitle me to both a decent horse and a fairly decent bed at the inns, but because imperial messengers were armed. I would have had my secca regardless, but now I also carried a short, powerful bow.

No one would know Lena, General of Ésparias, was here. I'd chosen a trader for passage because there was no chance I could travel on either an Ésparian or Casilani ship without someone recognizing me. I'd enjoyed being anonymous, just another piece of cargo. It almost made me feel free.

~

The town had a familiar feel; like their forts, the Casilani tended to use the same plan for all their settlements, adapting them as needed to the terrain. I followed the wide road through a market area, and then into a public square. People went about their business, buying and selling, gossiping, running errands or returning, late in the afternoon, from visits. Dust puffed beneath my feet. Here in the lee of the mountains, the spring had been dry.

No one gave me a second glance. Messengers were common here in Beria, and while only Ésparias tended to use women as imperial messengers, some came and went from Casil too, in the dowager Empress's employ. Since Decanius's plot to gain the throne for his own family had been exposed, Eudekia had relied on the mounted archers for protection and more. That Junia, their commander, was a friend of Druisius's had not escaped my notice. She was also a friend of mine.

I found the post inn on the right side of the road, its stable block shaded by the town wall. The man at the door glanced at my messenger's badge, nodded, and gestured me in. I blinked in the dimmer light of the large room. As my eyes adjusted, the figures painted on the walls became clear, men and women reclining under trellised grapes and fruit trees, drinking wine or eating while birds sang above them. A suggestion of Casilani luxury in this distant outpost of the empire.

Several men—merchants, I guessed—drank wine at a table in one corner. They looked my way. "Narma!" one called. "You've got a customer."

The innkeeper—a stocky woman of my age—appeared from another room. I greeted her, holding out my badge. "A bed for one night, please," I said, "and a horse. I'm travelling north."

"The bed, yes," Narma said. "The horse, no."

"You would deny an imperial messenger a post horse?" I'd met enough men and women bringing letters from the palace over the years to be able to copy their tone of both confidence and entitlement. But so had the innkeeper.

She shrugged. Dropping her voice, she said, "You must know what's happening. If there isn't an Empire, who is going to pay me for it?"

"It isn't your horse," I said.

"But it is my grain and hay."

"For which you are paid, and handsomely." I might need the intervention of the god of travellers and paths, at that.

"Not these last months." She eyed me. "Let's talk somewhere else."

I followed her into a small room, holding a desk and shelves lined with ledgers. Her office. "Pay me what's owed for its keep, and you can have the horse."

"Just the horse's keep? Not mine?"

"Yours too. But that's only one night."

I had money. I also had no intention of revealing the contents of my purse to anyone.

Narma laughed at my hesitation. "You haven't been paid either, have you? So no horse. I'll allow you the bed and food."

"Show me your records," I said. Beside each expense attributed to an imperial messenger would be his or her seal; the records were kept in duplicate, one set sent to the fiscarius's office for repayment quarterly. Narma would not yet have been paid for the last two months, but nor should she expect to be.

"You have no authority to ask that," Narma said.

"You'd rather I stopped to see the fiscarius here? The letter I carry is from the governor of Ésparias."

With a roll of her eyes and a huff of breath, Narma pulled a ledger from the shelf. I scanned the pages carefully. The seals appeared legitimate, the same three or four appearing in what looked like a reasonable rotation, and as I had expected her last repayment had occurred when it should. "These are up to date," I pointed out.

"Yes," she admitted—what else could she say? "But with all that's happening, I'm doubting I'll be paid when it's time."

"But you'd still give me a bed and meals?" I raised my eyebrows, hoping the look I gave her wasn't judgemental, but inviting.

"Well . . . " Narma hesitated, weighing her words. She gave me an apologetic—or was it conspiratorial?—smile. "I'll sell the best horses if I'm not paid. They'll more than cover what you'll cost me."

Conspiratorial was what I'd hoped for. I lowered my voice. "Horses?"

"Three."

"Who would you sell them to?"

"The Casilani estates. They're always looking for good horses."

"Imperial post horses?"

"Who is going to care, if the barbarians take Casil?" She closed the record book. "Are you going to run to the fiscarius now?"

I grinned at her. "Sell two, give me the third, and I'll swear to all the gods of Casil I knew nothing of your plans, should anyone ask."

She grinned back. "I thought so. You had that look about you. I keep the two best."

I considered. "The one I get has decent tack, and isn't in need of shoeing?"

"Both."

"And your best wine tonight?"

"What else?"

~

One of the inn-girls showed me to my room. It was clean, the bedclothes scented with some herb I didn't recognize. I'd asked for hot water to be brought, rather than go out to the public baths. I was nearly shaking with what I would claim was exhaustion, were it noticed.

How had I just managed that exchange with the innkeeper? I hadn't recognized myself, even while I spoke the words, made each necessary move in the game. I'd never bargained like that—but I knew who did. I chuckled to myself, surprised that I hadn't added Druise's characteristic 'yes?' to any of my statements. I'd even adopted his laconic speech. I sat on the bed, still laughing a little, but aware too of an inner tremor that wasn't amusement. A laugh became a gasp, then a sob. I dropped onto the bed, burying my face in the pillow, and let the sudden waves of fear and loss sweep over me.

Almost every journey I'd ever taken, including the one that had begun my exile, had been accompanied by a sense of adventure, of exploration and anticipation. Even a few weeks away from the *Ti'ach*, travelling to Han to buy horses, had meant feeling free, unconstrained by responsibility. I'd felt that on the trader. I'd hoped it would continue, that even so few weeks after Cillian's death, I might find excitement, or at least relief, in travel.

But the sense of freedom had slipped away, leaving only trepidation. I was, I reluctantly admitted to myself, frightened of what lay ahead of me. Being alone and unknown no longer felt comfortable.

I rolled over, staring at the rafters of the room. My cheeks, where the tears dried, began to itch. I brushed the damp saltiness away. *You've done this before*, I reminded myself.

But never alone, came my answering thought. *Not for more than a day or two. And you didn't even know how to handle an innkeeper who wanted to cheat you.*

An unfair thought. Yes, I'd sounded more like Druisius than myself. But the innkeeper believed I was an imperial messenger, and I'd acted like I thought one might. Hadn't I learned my role as Lady of the *Ti'ach* from watching Dagney, and later the expectations—and manner—of a general from Talyn?

I had wanted to be alone, to travel unguided, as I must, through the labyrinth of grief. The way shifted and reformed for each person, and no one could lead me through it. I would not be the same when I finally emerged from its dark and twisting paths, full of false waymarkers and obstructions. But until I had, until I knew who I would be after my time in its maze, I could borrow the strength and skill of others. I imagined Druise's grin when I told him what I'd done tonight. He'd approve, I thought.

And I, käresta, I heard in my mind. Cillian's voice, gentle, loving. It should have been reassuring. Instead, I shivered. He was dead. Was I going mad?

~

Dinner, served in the common room, was a bean stew, interestingly spiced, and a chewy bread. Half-way through the bowl, I realized I was enjoying the food. And the wine was very good. For several minutes, the pleasure of eating had occupied me as it had not since Cillian's death. I put my spoon down, blinking. The pervading sadness was still there, but its intensity had eased. A waymarker, and not a false one, on the path through this particular pain?

I finished the stew, filled my cup again, and looked around. The merchants who had been meeting here earlier had gone, but others had taken their place. A group of youths diced at another table. At my seat under a window, I was too far away to hear any real conversation, beyond the shouts of the dice players.

The common room of the Four-Ways Inn, eating alone, watching dice players. I had a task from Casyn, to listen to what was being said about changing opinions in my land, and to plant an idea when I felt it safe to do so. A craft of secrecy, I'd called it.

A loud oath from one of the boys brought me back to myself. I grinned at his dramatic despair and glanced at the merchants. One had turned to look at the players; as he swung back to his companions, our eyes met. He beckoned me over.

I picked up the wine jug and my cup, and crossed the room. "Lena," I said, holding out my hand. My messenger's badge spoke for itself.

The one who had beckoned me slid to make room on the bench. "Duante," he said. The other men introduced themselves. "We haven't seen you before."

"I haven't been here before. My travels have always been between Casil and Ésparias." Which wasn't a lie.

"Ah." I thought I heard new respect in his voice. "One of the old Empress's messengers? What are you doing here, then? If you can say," he added, quickly.

Let them assume; it would be safer. "A favour for Ésparias's governor," I said. "A message to a cousin north of here. A few days out of my way, nothing more."

"And you're in no hurry to return to Casil, I'd guess," one of the other men said. "How bad is it?"

I thought, quickly. Of course they would expect me to give them news. "I don't know. I've been in Ésparias over the winter. I fell ill, too ill for the captain to allow me to sail. I know what the recent orders have been, but—" I shrugged. "That's all." I swallowed some wine. "What's being said here?"

"The Emperor stands to lose the war, without more troops." That agreed with Narma's fears.

"The regiments here have been recalled too?"

"Yes. What there were, and they're mostly engineering regiments." As they were in Ésparias. "Probably not relishing the idea of actual fighting. Half'll desert, is my guess."

The common room was filling up, pairs and groups of men. Most seemed to know each other, and one merchant from our table excused himself to join another group. Business, going on as usual. From the corner of my eye, I saw the innkeeper stop to speak to the dicing boys. They'd been getting louder. She'd be warning them, I guessed.

"What about local troops?" Was I asking too many questions? I didn't think so; these men seemed eager to talk about what was happening.

"There really aren't any. A few cohorts attached to the Casilani regiments." Duante cocked his chin. "You didn't know that?"

"You're fucking cheating!" The words were loud, and slightly slurred, and followed by the sharp sound of dice flung against the flagged floor. I stood without thinking, my hand going to the secca on my belt. Duante put a hand on my arm.

"Don't concern yourself. Narma will deal with it."

He was right. Narma was out from behind the counter, scooping the scattered dice off the floor and dropping them into a pocket.

"That's it," she snapped. "Out. Now, or I won't have you back, and your fathers will know why."

I sat again. "Who are they?" I asked.

"Estate owners' sons," Duarte said, without interest. "You went for your knife rather quickly there. Not like most messengers I've met."

I swore to myself. Messengers were meant to stay out of trouble, unless it directly threatened them. The messages they carried took priority. "Old habits," I said. "I used to be a bodyguard."

The youngsters muttered apologies to Narma, who waited, arms crossed. The door opened. Another youth stepped over the threshold—and stopped. "Oh," he said.

"Not tonight." Narma gestured with a thumb. "And take these idiots with you."

"Can we have the dice back?" The question from one of the boys was asked meekly enough. The innkeeper didn't grace it with an answer.

"Come on," the newcomer said. "The Goose won't be full. Cenko will give us a table."

"Cenko," Narma said clearly, "is a fool. Don't come back here until you can behave in a decent inn. Rielo, see they get that lesson, will you?"

Her last words were addressed to the second man at the door. He was older than the others, and his bearing that of a soldier, or a guard. He caught my eye, frowning, and I realized I'd been staring. I looked away quickly. He was likely used to being stared at, with hair that red.

Red hair wasn't uncommon across the empire: Eudekia was proof of that. But hers was—or had been—the golden-red of copper. This man's was flame red, a colour I'd seen on only a few people. On Turlo, and his son and grandson.

"Lena?" Duante wanted my attention.

"Yes?"

"Who are you taking the letter to? Because if one of those young idiots is his son, you could save yourself a trip."

"I'm not sure I'd trust it to any of them."

Another of the men laughed. "Probably wise. Students aren't the most reliable of messengers."

"Students?"

"They attend the academy here to learn the things the *dignitasi* think important. How to make speeches, and argue, and how battles were won. But they're heading home soon, back to their fathers' estates for the summer."

So there had been no demand here for the Casilani landowners and their sons to defend Casil. Had that message simply not reached Beria yet, or had it never been sent, the Assembly not agreeing to conscript in the provinces they controlled?

The boys—they appeared to me to be sixteen or seventeen—were taking their time in leaving, finishing drinks and gathering belongings. Most of the other patrons ignored them; one or two watched with indulgence or irritation. The red-headed man strode up to their table. "It is time to go," he said, in perfect and unaccented Casilan. "Now, if you plan for Narma to ever let you drink here again."

The boys obeyed immediately. "Sorry, Rielo," one said. He shooed them out, gave an apologetic, wry smile to the room, a nod to Narma, and closed the door behind him.

"He has those boys cowed," I said, chuckling. "Who is he? A tutor?"

"Rielo? He's with the procurator's son. Supposed to keep him out of trouble, and mostly he does."

"Unusual hair colour, for a Casilani." I hoped these men had never been to Casil.

"He's local. Brought up on one of the estates, though. He has a reputation with both his fists and a sword. The youngsters respect him. They'd better, or he'll knock their heads together."

"Useful man," I said. "I have an early start, so I'll wish you good night now. Thank you for the company."

~

I slid the lock into place—even an imperial post inn wasn't necessarily safe—and dropped down onto the bed. Rielo looked to be in his late twenties. Turlo and Galen had disappeared the year Gwenna had been born; we'd always assumed they'd tried to cross the Durrains too late in the year, and died in the trying. Was it possible they'd made it?

I was, I told myself, assuming far too much from the colour of a man's hair. I'd known others with the same bright red: Catriona, a student at the *Ti'ach*, and Kyan, the woodworker from my home village. Rielo wasn't Turlo's son; that was nothing but wishful thinking. I was letting memories overlay the present, blurring it into shapes I'd known. Shapes I'd known, and loved, and missed.

If Turlo had made it across the mountains, could he still be alive? It was just feasible. Should I track Rielo down, ask him who his father was? What reason would I give for the question? *You look like someone I once knew.*

I'd done that before. Twice, in fact. Both times my recognition of a familial likeness had saved a life, Garth immediately, Cillian later. But it hadn't just been Garth's life or Cillian's that had changed because I'd seen someone else's face under theirs. Mine had too.

With that thought came a yearning for what I'd so briefly felt on the boat, a yearning so strong it nearly made me moan. A desire for a future free of all responsibility and the pain of love and loss; not a hunger for adventure, but a desire to escape, to leave all the choices to fate, free of duty or blame.

The third decides. Maybe I should ask this question. If Rielo was Turlo's son, what path might I be setting my feet on? The lamplight didn't reach the rafters. I stared up into the darkness, feeling the longing ebb away, like waves on a tidal beach. For a moment my mind was as undisturbed as washed sands, but from beneath the surface the buried thoughts began to reemerge. Free of duty. Free of blame.

Oh, Sorley.

No. I would not think of him. I had work to do, and I had begun it badly, unprepared for the role I had taken on. Duarte and his friends might already suspect I was not what I claimed. I needed a better story. Until sleep overtook me, I would think about that instead.

Chapter 14

THE THIRD-BEST POST HORSE wasn't bad at all. I'd half expected the innkeeper to substitute a poorer animal, but the dark bay gelding that awaited me was sound of leg, neither too fat nor too thin, and with a bright, intelligent eye. The tack, too, was in good shape. I let the horse smell me, murmuring to him as I stroked his neck. "What's his name?" I asked the stableboy.

"Gallus." He grinned. "You'll know why when you hear him whinny."

I gave the boy a coin and mounted. Gallus stood quietly while the stirrup straps were adjusted, and responded to the reins right away. The day, here in the lee of the mountains, was sunny, and promising to be hot. In the bright dawn, last night's fears seemed foolish.

Beyond the city gate the road ran north, straight and wide and shaped to drain into the ditches on either side, although today they were dry. I wondered when it had rained last. Water for the city itself flowed along a high aqueduct from some mountain source, and the fields on either side of the road were bisected by channels that diverted the flow from the rivers that ran down from the hills. Herons and boys fished along some of the channels, and swallows snatched insects from above streams and greening fields.

I rode slowly, not wanting to bring attention to myself. Unless the message was urgent, imperial messengers travelled at a steady pace, easy on themselves and their horses. I had another reason, too. Young men everywhere—especially those out drinking and dicing—were not early risers, and I had a question for the first I encountered.

Wagons passed me, heading into the city with vegetables and eggs, chickens strung upside down by their feet or clucking inside wicker cages. A few had tethered goats trotting behind, swollen udders telling me they would be milked once they reached the market. Out in the fields, men and women bent to pick vegetables or hoed the crop. Beside every few fields a child sat beside a pile of bags, flicking stones at any dog that came too close. Guarding the field workers' food, I surmised.

Hands were raised in greeting, but no one stopped me to ask my business. I hadn't expected they would. The sun rose higher, and the day grew hotter. After a couple of hours, I stopped to rest Gallus and stretch my legs at a watering station shaded by a grove of trees. Like the ones I'd first seen, riding south from Tirvan in my search for Maya, it had two levels: the lower for the horses to drink from, the upper, where the piped water entered, for people.

Already I felt the burn of the sun. I had neglected to bring a hat, and Ésparias' wet, cold spring meant I was still pale. I'd buy one somewhere, as much to shade my eyes as anything. Between the glare of the light and the dust, they stung. The cold water I splashed them with brought a little relief.

I lingered in the shade, oddly reluctant to ride on. Gallus nosed at the sparse grass under the trees. What would Cillian have thought of the changes Casil had wrought here? Not that they were much different from how they had changed Ésparias. Roads and bridges, aqueducts and temples. Those were Casil's visible declarations of their power and dominance, but at least equally important were other changes. These foothills and the first spread of the plain below them had been home to a scatter of villages, producing enough food for themselves and no more. Now they helped feed an empire, the dry land transformed to fields of grain.

The clop of hooves broke my reverie. Approaching the watering station from the south was a small group—and the tallest among them had fiery hair. Rielo and his charges. I'd wanted to meet a student or two. Had I secretly hoped Rielo would be escorting them? I'd take advantage of the chance meeting, in any case.

They dismounted, greeting me with the usual courtesy of the road. Horses watered, they drank themselves, then washed the dust from faces and hands. I walked over to them.

"Good morning," I said. "Who won the most at dice last night?"

Heads turned in surprise. "I did," one of the boys said. His quizzical look changed to recognition. "You were at the post inn last night."

"I was. I'm taking a message north, but I have a question for you. All of you," I added.

"Which is?" Rielo. Not threatening, but the question was asked with authority.

"I'm also looking for a young man, maybe with a woman. A family disagreement over his future." All true, so far. "Did your school have a new student arrive recently? Dark haired, about fourteen?"

The boys shook their heads almost in unison. "No," one said.

"You didn't ask at the academy?" Rielo asked. Scepticism laced his tone.

"Generous contributions to the upkeep of a school can convince its teachers to overlook certain facts." Or if the right person—or someone seen as the right person—asked. Linrathe's *Ti'acha* had hidden a prince of Varsland for almost a decade.

Rielo nodded in acknowledgement. "True enough. The boys are correct, unless the one you look for has been kept away from the other students. But likely I'd have heard whispers in the kitchens or from the guards, and I didn't."

"And you are, please?" I asked. "So my report is precise."

"Rielo. In the employ of Annius, the procurator of Beria," he said easily. A man who understood the demands of imperial business, and who had nothing to hide.

"Lena," I said, offering a hand. He took it. A firm grip, as I expected.

"Don't take offense, but—" I grinned. "I'd have taken you as a man from the northern lands, with that hair." Close to him, I could see the freckles under the hairs of his arms and across his cheeks. His eyes, with the fine lines of a man who spent long hours outdoors radiating out from the corners, were a colour somewhere between green and brown.

He chuckled, a deep, rich sound. "Not the first time I've been told that. Nessus there"—he flicked his thumb toward one of the students—"thinks I floated down the Ubë as a baby on a Varsland trader. Or at least one parent or the other did."

The boys, occupied with seeing to their horses, had stopped paying any attention to us. "There's a story there," I said.

"Not much of one. But if you want to ride with us for a while, I'll tell it to you in exchange for another, or some news. Better than listening to this lot prattle and brag."

~

On the road we dropped back, letting the boys ride a short distance ahead. "So," Rielo said, once we were settled into travel. "Who is the boy you're looking for under the guise of delivering a letter?"

"A son of one of the important families in Ésparias." I'd worked out a story as I rode, in case I was questioned. The truth was too dangerous. "The betrothal made for him wasn't to his liking, and one of his aunts agreed. She bribed a trader to take them east, but to where, we don't know."

"What's wrong with the girl? Twice his age, or something else?"

"She's a girl. That's the problem."

He laughed. "When did that ever stop a marriage among the *dignitasi*?"

I matched his expression. "I know. But he's fourteen, and not of a mind to listen to reason. And his aunt is sympathetic, for her own reasons."

"Who'd be important?" he said. "I like my life much better. As long as I do my job properly, the rest of it's my own."

"What is your job? Other than minding the procurator's son? Nessus, was it?"

"That's him. I guard him in Occida, make him practice his swordplay and archery, dole out his allowance, and keep him out of the wrong bathhouses and *tabernae*." He grinned. "The last two've been a challenge this winter."

"My sympathies," I said. "I used to be a bodyguard. But what's this story about the Ubë?"

A burst of laughter from the boys caught his attention, but it wasn't repeated. "Just a story," he said. "There's no truth in it, not that I know. But the first years after the Casilani came, there was resistance. People died, mostly not the Casilani. I was found in the ruins of a razed village, screaming in rage, or so I'm told, my face as red as my hair. The soldiers brought me to one of the estates, and they took me in. Raised me, educated me a bit, gave me work. I can't complain."

"Which village?'

"I don't know. If the soldiers said, no one remembers. Doesn't matter."

His question about my real purpose on the road had told me he was also more than he claimed. Working for the procurator, that didn't surprise me, and guarding a student in the port town—one who frequented bathhouses and *tabernae* in his free hours—meant he'd hear both gossip and news.

"And you? You don't sound Casilani."

I didn't. I was fluent enough, but I spoke Casilan with inflections that were not quite right. I'd learned the languages I needed—Casilan and Linrathan—but no one would ever mistake me for a native speaker. Unlike my children, who spoke three languages perfectly, and two more with competence.

Why I was thinking of them now wasn't hard to work out. My gut trusted this man, but could I trust my gut? He isn't Turlo, I reminded myself.

"I'm not. I'm Ésparian, but I went east early on, to join the horse archers."

His eyebrows shot up. "Really? Were you bodyguard to the empress, then?"

"Only as one of many, when she travelled from the palace. But we also escorted young *dignitasi* women, to the baths or to summer villas." Well within what I might have done, and Junia had told me enough that I could improvise effectively, I thought.

"You have all my respect," Rielo said. "From what I hear, girls can be more of a handful than these boys."

"I could tell you stories," I said with feeling, thinking of our students over the years. He laughed.

"And now you're a messenger." A question, but one I could easily deflect, if I chose.

"I served my twenty-five years. But I was restless, and I wanted to see Ésparias again, how it had changed."

"A lot, I'd wager." His head went up, his attention on the road. "Nessus! To your right, and dismount."

Cresting a slight rise north of us was a marching regiment, four abreast, preceded by mounted officers. As they approached, I could see they carried full packs and weaponry. No baggage carts followed them. They were travelling light, to meet the ship sent for them in Occida, I guessed.

Gallus stood quietly, unperturbed by either sound or sight, but I understood why Rielo had ordered the boys to dismount. Horses, unfamiliar with the noise of so many marching men, the flap of the eagle banner, or even sunlight off shields or weapons, could spook. With the regiment on one side and the ditch on the other, an out-of-control horse could injure soldiers, its rider, and itself. Better to be careful.

The officer leading them nodded to us, his eyes travelling over our group. The boys stood respectfully enough, quietly watching the soldiers march. Perhaps a third of the regiment had gone by when the officer turned his horse to ride back to us.

He did not dismount, nor try to speak over the noise of the regiment's passing. But his eyes, after a glance at the boys and a longer one at Rielo, were on me. The last of the soldiers went by. "Messenger," he said.

"Sir?"

"Where are you coming from?"

I told him. "Carrying a letter from the governor of Ésparias."

He ignored that. "You were at the docks yesterday? Were there troops boarding ships? Or did you meet another regiment on the road?"

"I have met no other soldiers," I said, "and the only ship at the docks transporting soldiers was from Ésparias."

He grimaced, clearly annoyed. "You will take two messages for me." He reached into his belt pouch for two sealed letters. "One to the procurator; one to Hathusia."

Where was Hathusia? "I work for the procurator," Rielo said. "The boy with the grey horse is his son. I'm escorting him home from the academy. I can take that message."

The officer's eyes travelled to Nessus. "He should be on his way to Casil," he said, his lips tightening briefly.

"He was meant to be," Rielo said. "Later this summer." He dropped his voice. "But now? Would you send him, if he was your son?"

"He can use a sword? Then yes. You too, redhead, were it up to me." The officer turned back to me. "Ésparias is a royal province, with its own troops, if I remember correctly. Are they being sent too?"

"Some," I said. "Major, where is Hathusia? I am not familiar with these lands. Who would I be taking a message to there?"

"Hathusia is a town some distance east, on the shores of a lake. There is a fort there, on the road between it and the Ubë. The message would be to its commander, if he is still there, which he should not be."

The expanse of high, dry plain with its sparse grasses and silver-leaved plants had begun to descend. Below us lay the lake, shining in the sun, its waters beckoning. Cillian had made us wait, watching for signs of people, before we had allowed ourselves to give into its call. Even on its shores, we'd looked for footprints and fish traps, assuring ourselves we were alone, only then plunging into the cold, cleansing waters to wash away the dust of travel . . .

"Messenger?"

"I'm sorry." I came back to the present. "The fort is east of the lake? I have seen it on maps. I didn't realize there was a town as well."

"You will have an opportunity to add to your store of knowledge," the major said, without smiling. He held out the letters. I reached up for them. I had little choice; he had the authority to direct an imperial messenger, unless I could prove the letter I carried was urgent.

"Major, could you take a message to Occida, to be sent on to Ésparias?" I'd seen and heard enough to be sure there had been no conscription. Gwenna must be informed.

"Is it written?"

"No," I admitted.

"Then no. I have no time to wait." He held out his record book and the box containing his writing implements. Crouching, I took out the vial of ink and the small brush, fished my messenger's seal from my belt pouch, and brushed its pattern with ink. Then I carefully pressed it to the page where, neatly, he had listed the two letters. The responsibility for the messages was mine now.

Book and box returned to safety, the major nodded to me and swung his horse back to the road. Then he stopped again. "You can fight now, or later," he said to Rielo. "The boys too. Don't expect to be unscathed." He clicked his tongue and tapped his horse's flanks with his heels. The animal broke into a trot.

"Is there really going to be war here?" Nessus asked, as we remounted. Both apprehension and excitement threaded his voice.

"Maybe." Rielo sounded calm. "Army men, it's how they think. Or a bargain will be made, for money or lands or both, and a treaty signed."

"These lands?"

"Maybe. Maybe further east. How should I know?"

It had been Boranoi troops who had taken these lands, their prince newly married to the Empress Eudekia. A marriage more to Casil's advantage than one to the son of a man who claimed to be Emperor of a small and forgotten land. Eudekia had chosen what had seemed to be stability and power for her empire and her son. Had she foreseen it twisting into betrayal and rebellion?

Chapter 15

~Lena~

IF RIELO NOTICED MY PREOCCUPATION as we continued north, he didn't comment. We rode mostly in silence, the boys' chatter diminishing as the day grew hotter. Close to midday, he called a halt at a small village that had grown up around a mill. Its inn was shaded by tall trees, their spreading crowns creating shade for both the yard and the buildings.

Without being told, the boys removed their horses' tack, then led them to the water trough. Rielo and I did the same, washing dust from their eyes at the same time. The sweat that soaked the horses' backs would dry while we ate; we would brush them down before resaddling. We left them tethered in the shade, chewing on hay, tails swishing against flies.

Inside the inn was dim and cool. The inn-girl brought jugs of weak beer and food—bread and goat cheese and withered apples—without asking, or offering a choice. "It's a long ride east," Rielo said, after slaking his thirst. The boys were at another table.

I almost said, 'I know', but stopped myself in time. I shrugged. "It's a long voyage by ship, too, and I'd rather ride than be crammed in with too many soldiers."

"I suppose." He broke a piece of bread in half. "You'll miss asking about your runaways at the other ports, though."

I had no good answer for that. "I'm fairly sure they're headed for Casil," I said finally. "The woman—she's asked me a lot of questions about the horse archers, and she has the skills."

"And the nature, which is why she's sympathetic to the boy?"

I nodded. We ate without speaking for a few minutes. "I'm guessing," Rielo said quietly, "as you say you were a horse archer once yourself, that you're not exerting yourself to find them."

"I'll fulfil my task." After I had crossed the plain and seen the lake again.

"I'm sure you will."

We finished the meal. The boys were still eating. Rielo called to the serving girl. "The messenger here needs a hat."

"There's a few," she replied. "Travellers forget them." She moved the heel of bread to the boys' table, picked up our plates, and disappeared into the kitchen, returning with two hats of woven straw. "Either of these?"

One fit and wasn't too scratchy. I hoped, as I paid the girl for it, that its previous owner hadn't harboured lice. She accepted the coins, enough for the hat and the meal—this wasn't an imperial inn—then slid onto the bench on Rielo's side of the table. "What news, Rielo? Not about the war. Tell me what happened in Occida this winter."

I left them to talk, going out into the yard. I'd brush Gallus down; grooming a horse had always been a calming activity for me, and not one I'd done for a long time. The stableboy found me a brush. I led Gallus away from the other horses to another shady spot, and began.

Why was I so convinced I should ride east? The road was rebuilt, and a town covered the shores of the lake. I would recognize little. But it felt—necessary. I had begun to heal there once, from an act of violence. I had trusted my instincts and the man I was with, hoping together we might overcome that violation and let me reclaim my life. I'd been right to do so.

The horse stamped and blew, a contented sound. I murmured nonsense to him as I brushed the dust from his coat. Was I wrong to think I might find another healing at the lake? On that night so long ago, I had turned to Cillian because I could see a future I wanted, a future with him. I had known I loved him, and that had propelled me past my fears. What future called to me now?

I glanced at my wrist, where the *li'ítho* bracelet should be. I had told Sorley it was not a jess. But where was home for the falcon, where there was no falconer to hold out his arm?

Sorley. I wrenched my mind away from him. The call was to ride the road east. I would trust my instincts one more time.

~

"There's a post inn at the next crossroads," Rielo told me after we'd been riding for another couple of hours. "I'm turning left there. The twins' father's estate is up the hills. He'll give me and Nessus beds for the night. Probably you too, if you wanted."

"I'll stay at the inn," I said. I had no desire to stay with hospitable strangers; the inn was different. Payment there was in coin, not in news and stories, and if I retired early to my bed, no one would feel offended. "But I've appreciated your company today."

"If you wait a bit in the morning, we can ride together again. Or if you want to move faster, give me the letter for the procurator. I'll ensure he gets it."

"I could lose my license," I said, with an apologetic smile. A license I didn't have, but I'd come to a decision while riding. A letter must go back to Ésparias, and the procurator could ensure it did. If I had to tell him who I really was, I would, but only if the governor's name didn't carry enough authority. The letter would be sent to him, with another for Gwenna enclosed.

Rielo nodded. "I just thought you might be eager to reach the road to Hathusia."

What had he noticed? I had planned to ride the road north only as far as I felt I needed, and then return to Occida and a ship to Casil. The governor's message could have been entrusted to someone else; it contained nothing of importance. The additional messages I carried should have felt like an imposition, an impediment to my plans. Instead, something else stirred inside me: the first, faint feeling of—not excitement, not quite, but anticipation.

"I like riding new roads, seeing new places," I said, "but there's no hurry."

We rode on. My hips and thighs and lower back ached now. It had been years since I'd ridden this far, and while Gallus was both well-schooled and even-paced, he was broader than my mare at Wall's End. The boys too slumped a little in their saddles. Only Rielo, on his chestnut whose coat almost matched its rider's hair, seemed unaffected.

By the time we reached the crossroads and the post inn, I was wishing I had brought Apulo, or, at the very least, that the inn had a bathhouse. I slid off Gallus's back and handed the reins to the stableboy with relief. Rielo and the boys waited while I unstrapped the saddlebags and slung them over my shoulder.

"Can we have a drink here?" one of the twins asked. Rielo glanced at the sun.

"One. Quickly. Let the horses drink, then come inside." He dismounted, handing his horse's reins to Nessus. "Keep Herti and Lena's horse apart, or someone will get kicked," he told the boy.

Together we entered the inn, its common room much the same as the last. Much the same as the new inns in Ésparias, too, built to the same plans. Casilani efficiency again.

The innkeeper was equally efficient. I signed my name and stamped his ledger while he rounded up someone to show me to my room. "Are there baths?" I asked, when he returned.

"Wood will be added to the boiler immediately," he promised.

"Then I'll go to my room until they're ready." I wanted to stretch out, rest, perhaps think. "Say goodbye to the twins for me?" I asked Rielo.

"I will. Nessus and I will be back here three hours after dawn."

I grinned, despite my fatigue. "He won't like that." Dawn came very early now, the days progressing rapidly to midsummer.

"We've a full day's ride."

"I'll be ready."

He nodded. I followed the inn-girl to the stairs up to the bedrooms, hearing the boys entering the common room behind me. At both the *Ti'ach* and Wall's End, I'd always liked the students of their age, still not quite adults but aware that their time for youthful frivolity would soon be past. War, of course, would end it immediately. As it had for me, although I'd been considered an adult when it had come. I hadn't been, not really.

I wanted the boys—boys I barely knew—to have one last carefree summer, for their practice with sword and bow to be for nothing more than prowess and competition, without serious meaning. I couldn't drink beer with them and listen to their chatter about war. Not knowing what I knew; not while I worried about my own son, and about the choices my daughter had to make. Not now I was alone.

I closed my eyes against the clenching pain. Evenings and early mornings were the worst times, except when I woke in the silent, empty night. One deep breath, then another, and another, willing the anguish to fade again, back into the void inside me. I would go to the baths, I told myself, and eat something. I might, given how tired I was, sleep soundly tonight. Perhaps.

~

The hot water stung my sunburn, but it also soaked some of the aches away, and all the dust. I ate a quiet meal in the common room, exchanged a few words with the innkeeper, and went to my room. I had letters to write.

Neither took long. I wrote the same report to both the governor and Gwenna, adding a few words of reassurance to my daughter's, telling her the inns were comfortable and I had company on the road. Then I folded both letters, leaving them unsealed. I might learn something more from the procurator.

Regardless of the weariness seeping through my body, I wasn't sleepy. I stood to close the shutters. My room looked east, over an outbuilding or two to the plain that stretched to the horizon. Close to the inn, the squares of garden plots made a green-and-brown gameboard; beside them, paddocks for the horses and the inn's goats again divided the ground. Beyond these, a grain crop rippled in the light breeze like the surface of the sea. A memory rose of an endless sea of grass, sere in early autumn, flowing like water in the wind. It had called to me then, just as the road east across the plain did now.

I'd ridden the road south in Ésparias many times since, and the memories of my time with Garth, just the two of us crossing the grasslands, had been blurred by later experiences. Buoyed by victory and hope and youthful love, we'd known our time together on that ride was only an interlude in our lives. But my walk across the plain—our walk, Cillian's and mine—had been a journey of survival, with only the faintest hope we might find a safe place to take us in. We had become necessary to each other, beyond even our mutual dependence while crossing the Durrains.

Over the years, life and work and family—not just children, but everyone we lived with—had lessened that need, at least on the surface. But not in the deepest recesses of my heart. I'd nearly lost Cillian twice: once to Eudekia, once to war. Both times—

I stepped away from the window. My thoughts were taking me somewhere I didn't want to be. I'd go outside, ensure Gallus was comfortable, maybe walk a little. Maybe then I could sleep.

Gallus was drowsing, one hip cocked. He'd been groomed, and both the hayrack and the water bucket were full. I found a gate in the stableyard leading out to the garden plots. Just as I was pushing it closed, the inn's dog, a curly-coated animal blotched in black and tan and white, slipped through. It looked up at me expectantly. "I don't know where I'm going," I said to it. It wagged its stump of a tail and trotted ahead.

The breeze carried the sweet scent of the growing plants, and a hint of damp soil. The garden plots had been recently watered. I walked down the path between the vegetable beds. Swifts arrowed and chattered overhead, hunting insects.

At the edge of the grainfield I stopped. The air was suddenly colder: the sun had dropped behind the mountains. The dog nosed along the field, scenting for rabbits, perhaps. No one else was out in the falling dusk.

I stood, facing east. The first stars began to appear. I waited, letting my thoughts drift and circle. I'd meant to ride alone, to be the anonymous messenger treated with courtesy and disinterest. If Rielo hadn't been red-haired and with the bearing of a soldier, I might have found some excuse to not join him and the boys on the road. I'd let both my apprehension and his similarity to Turlo divert me, grasping for the answer to a mystery and a lessening of an old pain. So many losses. Too many.

The longer anyone lived, the more they left behind, through choice or circumstance. Or from anger and pride and hard words, sometimes. Even after half a lifetime of love.

The breeze must have shifted slightly, or a door opened. I heard a burst of laughter from the inn. Then silence, and then, drifting towards me, the notes of a *cithar*, played with skill. A man began to sing. My hands clenched. I squeezed my eyes shut, wishing the music away. I'd been trying so hard to ignore this other grief, to not think of what had been said and not said the night before I'd left.

Tears rose. I looked up at the glittering sky, and let them fall. Oh, Sorley.

Chapter 16

~Gwenna~

THE RAIN CONTINUED. A delegation of Casilani landowners came to see me, asking to hire Ésparian troops to go to war in their stead. They would pay their salaries, they said, plus a substantial amount into Ésparias's coffers. I refused. They were Casilani citizens, I pointed out, and I could not countermand an order from their Emperor.

"But we can offer privately? Not to men of your army, but others?"

"I cannot stop you," I told them, reluctantly. "Whether that will fulfil the orders from Casil is a question for your governor."

They went away, half-satisfied, and I sent messages to Ruar and to Garth on Leste, alerting them. After some thought, I wrote a third letter, apprising the king of Varsland of the possible recruitment of men to fight in the east. The scheme, I told him, did not have my approval, but was an entirely private venture.

I went to see Sorley before I sent that letter. I wanted to include him when I could, to make him understand that I valued his opinion, even if he'd never officially been my advisor. He was struggling to find a role for himself within our family now.

He'd never apologized for what he'd said to me, but neither had he made contact with Daragh. Ruar, I thought, had made him see sense. But we skirted around the subject of my mother; he didn't mention her name, so I didn't either.

"You would be wise to warn Bryngyl," he said. "The Casilani could present the idea as if you were in agreement. I'll know if they do, in time, but the damage would be done."

"Surely he would know I wouldn't send the Casilani to recruit paid troops, were I in need of them?"

"I wasn't thinking of Bryngyl. I was thinking of what people here would say. Varsland men in the employ of the Casilani landholders as soldiers is one thing. But what happens when the war is over? Do those hires that survive get to come back to Ésparias and do different work here? I doubt that would be well received."

"Linrathan women were raped and kidnapped too in the war," I said. "We killed three men, you and I and Druise, for Jordis and her daughter's sake. But marriages take place between Varsland and Linrathe at the highest levels, men and women moving back and forth." Perhaps here too, before long. "How is that reconciled?

He sighed. "A long history, and the aggression not always from Varsland. It's a harder land, and breeds a pragmatism of a sort. And it's difficult to maintain hatred for people who share your blood, and many of us do."

As Varsland men and women did with people like my own cousin Teárdh. Not even cousins, I realized, but half-brothers and sisters, in some cases.

"Wasn't it exactly that, the connection of blood and family, that made you question Daragh's loyalties?" Sorley asked, but mildly.

"And it is what is said when my own loyalties are questioned," I conceded. "But it was also why we trusted Lynthe, wasn't it?"

He nodded. "Ruar said the same. Family does not always mean fidelity. His father, he reminded me, was not as lucky with his brother as I am with Roghan."

"Family doesn't always mean blood ties, either," I said softly. A glint of tears, before he opened his arms. I stepped into them, feeling the prick of tears in my own eyes, and the relief as one tension in my life slipped away.

I began to cross the courtyard to my own rooms, and stopped. It wasn't raining, and overhead, patches of blue showed through tattered clouds. I turned my face to the sky, feeling warmth. Impulsively, I turned back to Sorley's door.

"Let's go for a walk," I said. "It's not raining, and there's actually blue sky."

"It won't last," he said, but he was grinning. "Let me see if Druise is free."

"I'll fetch Gwyllar, and meet you at the gate." My son had been equally frustrated by the days of rain, keeping him from his pony and simply from being outside. I'd give his nursemaid—and his guards—a bit of a respite, and burn off some of his nearly inexhaustible energy.

In a few minutes we were all gathered outside the villa. I inspected the sky. Blue patches still gleamed through a layer of clouds, thin and moving quickly east. The ground was sodden; even the paths squelched underfoot. "G'uaga'?" Gwyllar asked.

"All right," I said. "But not to ride, not today. Just to say hello."

He ran ahead. "Should I catch up with him?" Druise asked.

"Let him go. He knows the way."

We walked slowly, enjoying the thin sunlight and the warmth. Skylarks sang without ceasing above us, the notes caught and scattered by the breeze. "You've never written their song into your music," I said to Sorley.

"No," he agreed. "Perhaps I should."

"For the *cithar*, yes?" Druise said. "A better tuning."

"The *ladhar* would work too," Sorley argued. I listened to their discussion, amused. The clouds were thinning even more, the sun's heat causing a faint mist to rise from the wet ground. A hare sprang from the heather beside the path, making me jump. We laughed.

"Mat'a!" Gwyllar called. He ran up to me, tugging at my hand. "Stop talking. See my pony."

"All right," I agreed, laughing at his determination. The shaggy piebald was in his stall, his head out the open half-door, sniffing the air. Sorley picked Gwyllar up so that he could stroke the pony's nose. He was smiling, watching my son. He looks better, I thought. Less ravaged.

The drains around the stable block gurgled with water, and the butts placed to catch rainfall off the roof were overflowing. The cisterns would be full this year, and the springs wouldn't run dry, as they occasionally did. I hoped today's sunshine heralded a change in the weather. It would be one less concern.

"Lambs!" Gwyllar announced, still in Sorley's arms. "See the lambs."

"I can take him," Sorley offered, "if you have work to do."

I did. But I didn't want to waste this rare good day, either. "I'll come," I said. Sorley put Gwyllar down. We walked toward the lower pastures, the path degenerating into a track. Our steps left foot-shaped puddles in the peaty soil, and I felt water seeping into my shoes. But there was birdsong all around us, and the buzz of bees foraging, and ahead of us lambs frolicked for the sheer love of life.

"Look!" Sorley pointed. Overhead, an eagle soared, the sunlight picking out the golden sheen of its head and back. Looking for afterbirth, or a weak lamb. The shepherd would have seen it too, and would be keeping an eye on it. I watched it circle, adjusting its flight with the briefest movement of a wing.

I glanced back at my son, ahead of us on the path, and a sudden dizziness made me stumble. I put out a hand. Sorley was at my side immediately, steadying me. "Gwenna?"

I stood still. The world stopped its gyration, although I still felt off balance. "I'm all right," I said. "Just looked up too long, I think." I kept my head down, eyes closed, waiting for the light-headedness to pass.

"Gwyllar!" A note in Druise's voice I'd never heard. "Bear!" I looked up. He was running, running towards my son—who was at the edge of the deep, fast-flowing stream that came down off the hills, crouching down, reaching for something.

"Gwyllar!" I screamed, and I was running too, and so was Sorley, Druise strides ahead of us. I saw my son unbalance, saw him topple into the torrent. I was screaming and Sorley was past me now but it was Druise who dove into the stream, whose strong arms propelled him with the current and grabbed Gwyllar.

Sorley was at the bank, flat on his belly, arms out. He took Gwyllar from Druise, knelt, put him down. Another stride, two, and I was there, to catch my son up, hold him close, sobbing in fear and relief. Gwyllar wailed. Sorley helped Druise out of the water.

"I didn't know you could swim," I said, which was stupid, I should be saying thank you, thank you—and then Druise's grin became a gasp. He put a hand to his chest. Groaned. Fell to his knees. Sorley shouted his name. Druise collapsed on his side, one hand still on his chest, the other groping for Sorley. Oh, dear gods . . .

"Amané." He could barely make the sounds. Sorley had his hand. I closed my eyes. No. Please, no. "Blue . . . eyes." A breath, released. "Yes?"

And then nothing. Nothing. Nothing, ever again.

Chapter 17

MY SCREAMS HAD BROUGHT THE SHEPHERD RUNNING, and the stable hands. Men bent to Druise's body. Someone took Gwyllar from me. I protested. "He's shivering, *Principe*," a voice said. "Let me dry him. Keep him warm."

I was cold too, but inside. I knelt beside Sorley. He still held Druise's hand. The other men had stepped back. I put an arm over Sorley's shoulders. There were no words to say.

People came from the fort, with a stretcher. Gently, they made Sorley release Druise's hand and stand back. He wasn't crying. He was white, and silent. His eyes tracked the men carrying Druise's body away, but he made no move to follow.

"Come," someone said to me. One of the guards assigned to Gwyllar. I wanted to shout at her. Why hadn't she been watching him? But I had dismissed them, and my own guard. Druise had been with us. We hadn't needed them. He'd keep us safe.

He would give his life for you, Sorley had told me, more than once. I moaned, and the tears began, becoming deep, racking sobs. I covered my face with my hands, gasping for breath. Why had I let Gwyllar run ahead? Why had I taken my eyes off him to look at the eagle?

How could Sorley ever forgive me?

I raised my head to look at him. He'd dropped to a crouch, staring at nothing. I said his name, a hoarse croak. Nothing. I tried again.

This time he heard me. His eyes met mine, expressionless, empty. After a long moment he moved his head side to side, just slightly. In accusation, or absolution?

~

Someone led me back to the villa. "Gwyllar?" I asked, at some point.

"In his nursery. He is safe, and no harm done," was the reply. There was a cloak around me now, and a cup of wine in my hand. Tears trickled down my cheeks. I couldn't stop them.

"Sorley?"

"With Druisius. Apulo is with him." I realized it was Talyn who sat beside me. She reached out to stroke my hair. The gesture—my father's—undid what tiny bit of control I'd mustered. The sobs began again. Talyn took the wine from me, then gathered me into her arms.

"Shhh," she crooned, as if I were Gwyllar's age. She let me cry. Only when my tears had subsided did she speak. "Drink the wine, Gwenna. There is a little poppy in it, and valerian. You must sleep."

"Why?" I said, petulant as a child.

Her arms were still around me. "Because you are the *Principe*, and you must think of what Druisius did for you in that role, and for that you need to be calmer."

"Cannot I just be me?" I pulled away from her, anger heating my words. "Druise was—was my second father. I could barely grieve for my real father, because I am the *Principe*. Now I must think of—replacements? For Druise? Whose death is my fault?"

"It is not," she said. "Gwenna, it is not. Apulo told me his heart could have burst at any time. Druisius knew that; the physician had told him."

"And he still—?" Oh, Druise, Druise. My face crumpled. Talyn held me as I wept again. Then she dried my eyes, and held the cup to my lips until I took it from her and drank, welcoming the oblivion of sleep.

~

We buried Druise in the soldier's cemetery the next day, his *cithar* laid on his chest and the coins for the ferryman on his eyes. No one knew what he'd believed, beyond his offhand 'The gods decide.' Men and women of the guards carried him to his grave, but both officers and soldiers crowded the burial site. Druise, with his insouciant grin and good nature, had been well-liked, whether he'd been dicing outside the barracks or playing music in the senior commons.

I managed to say a few words, recalling his friendship with my father and his long service to Ésparias. I could not speak of what he'd been to me: that was not for the *Principe* to voice publicly. Afterwards, I attended the gathering in his memory, briefly. Sorley did not. He remained remote, unspeaking: a man in shock.

I went to see him, later, although I doubted he wanted to see me. Or anyone, although he hadn't sent Apulo away. But Apulo was good at being unobtrusive.

"Sorley?" He acknowledged me, barely. "I won't stay," I said. "Just a question. Someone must write to Marius. Will you, or shall I?"

"You do it." His voice, like his eyes, was expressionless.

"All right. Is there anything else I can do?"

He shook his head. I bent to kiss his cheek. It was smooth, and he smelt clean. Apulo's doing, I was sure. "Let me know if there is." Useless, empty words, but what else could I say? I wished my mother were here: if anyone could reach him, it would be her.

Then I crossed the courtyard to my rooms, went to my desk, and wrote the hardest letter of my life. And when it was signed and sealed, I turned my *Principe*'s mind to two questions that could not wait. One was simple: Druise's replacement as head of the guard here at Wall's End would be his second-in-command.

But who was to be my spymaster now?

~

"I don't know." I knew Talyn had thought about the question: she'd raised it to me, the previous day. "Druisius was not forthcoming about his informants. Not even, I believe, to Cillian."

I exhaled in frustrated agreement. "Not even to him." I'd asked, once, to be told Druise felt it better that no one but he knew. "But my father said that Druise would have a plan. That someone would come forward, if needed."

"Did he?" Talyn raised a sceptical eyebrow. "Let's hope he was right. Is there anything else you know?"

"I know his brother is involved, and I suppose his nephews, in the information that comes—came—from Casil." I thought back. "And that someone high up in the governor's staff was involved." Who? Hadn't he mentioned a name? Or at least a position? My mind was far from clear. "There's Ferand, of course. But he won't know much; he's too junior."

"It's worth questioning him, though. Should I have him attend you?"

"Perhaps." Something was nagging at me; something Druisius had said that I couldn't quite remember. "Let me think a minute." We'd been talking about additions to the council. I remembered, with a pang of pain, Druise grinning, offhand as always. *They would not suggest Leste's procurator, if they knew what his son does for me.*

"Valle," I said. "He is head of the guard at the Eastern Fort. A man I could rely on, Druise said." Pieces were falling into place. "I don't think Druise told me that without reason. If he did know his life was uncertain, I think he was telling me who should succeed him in that role."

I told Talyn the context, and Druise's exact words. She nodded, slowly. "I tend to agree with you. Druisius rarely said more than he needed to, and if he did, it was important. Garth's son!" She pursed her lips. "Dern must know him."

"Was that who Dern sent to Garth to judge the level of unrest in Leste?" I wondered. "He would have had to ask Druise's permission for that, if Valle is head of the guard in the south." But that connection was there. *Sometimes Dern gives me information.* I was beginning to think half of Ésparias had, at one time or another.

But not Finn. *Finn, I do not know.* Finn, who had let Lynthe board the ship to Casil with Constyn. That was what had been nagging at me, when his name had been suggested for the council. A mistake born of assumptions and inattention in a fraught time, or a deliberate oversight?

Finn was Sorley's age, more or less. He'd served my grandfather, been part of the hierarchy of the military before the treaty with Casil, one of the relative few who'd survived the Marai invasion. My mother counted him a friend. Could he harbour resentment at my leadership of Ésparias now? Of a woman's, I amended; I doubted it would be me personally.

Or was it? I'd been brought up in Linrathe because, at the heart of it, my father had been a target of resentment too, his loyalties to Ésparias in doubt. We'd quieted that unrest, I'd thought—but had my choice of Ruar as the father of my heir brought them to life again? Gwyllar could be seen as more Linrathan than Ésparian—and Finn would remember when Linrathe was the invading enemy.

I leant back, exhaling my frustration. The logic didn't hold: I'd cast doubt on Daragh's loyalties because his mother was Marai, so why would Finn—or anyone—see Constyn as a better choice as *Princip*? His mother was Linrathan too, Ruar's sister.

But logic often didn't hold, not when human emotions were concerned. Was Lynthe's resentment of Ruar, of Gwyllar, of her own position or Constyn's logical? Not in the least. If I was suspect in part because I'd been brought up in Linrathe, the opposite argument held for Constyn: he was Ésparian-raised, at Wall's End, where he'd seen the day-to-day actions of the military—and of governance—since babyhood. A natural choice as *Princip*, some might say.

"What are you thinking?" Talyn had been sitting quietly, not disturbing my reverie.

"That," I said, the thought forming as I spoke, "I will go to the Eastern Fort, and meet Valle there. It has been too long since I was in the south." I would question Finn myself, and perhaps gain a sense of people's feelings on my journey. I should have done this weeks ago, once Casil's withdrawal was commonly known. No wonder there were concerns about my leadership.

"Except if I do, I have to leave Gwyllar," I said, doubts creeping in. "He's already confused: too many people have disappeared from his life. His grandfather, Lynthe, even Ruar. And now Druise. His nursemaid says he's clinging to her more than usual, and I see the same."

"Then take him with you."

"He's three," I protested.

"Travel by ship," Talyn said. "He'll think it's an adventure. And you can visit some of the coastal villages on the way, talk to the people, let them see your heir."

"And gain support from the villages?" I studied her. "You're suggesting the discontent stems from the army?"

"Women have only been part of it for a generation," she reminded me. "Old ways of thinking are easily awoken, and in times of change they seem safe, a return to a past that never was. Don't forget what you learned about Tain village: the discontent is not just from some of the soldiers." She cocked her head, clearly thinking. "But you know, you can claim a link to those past ways, one that perhaps you should remind people of as you travel."

"What's that?"

"Gwyllar was fathered through a liaison, not a marriage or partnership, as all our children once were. As I was, and your mother, and Lynthe and Faolyn, for that matter."

"That," I said slowly, "was my mother's doing. Her advice, I mean."

Talyn nodded. "Lena always felt that in marrying Cillian, she had set herself apart from the women of Ésparias. Almost, I would say, betrayed them: she had placed the attitudes of Linrathe over the traditions of her own people. But they could not have had the years at the *Ti'ach* without the marriage, and she wanted that, for him and for herself, after all the devastation the Marai wrought."

"I wish she were here now," I said.

"For Sorley?"

"For him, yes." I tried a smile. It didn't really work. "And to tell her I understand now, a little, why she had to leave. I would like some time and space to mourn Druise properly, and to consider the future too. But—"

"But you're not going to get it," Talyn finished for me. "Although a week or two on a ship might provide a little. Shall I send Ferand to you?"

"I'll see him," I decided, "and then Captain Eidyn."

~

I didn't really learn anything new from Ferand, except from his answer to my last question. I'd finished asking him about what he'd witnessed at the Eastern Fort, the sequence of events and what had been said. For a young lieutenant, he was composed and confident in his replies.

"Lieutenant," I'd said, "you had instructions from Major Druisius that another of your rank might not have had, did you not?"

His composure had barely slipped. "Yes, *Principe*."

"Who else within the guard command might have known that?"

"No one here, *Principe*. But the senior guard officer at the Eastern Fort did."

This was the man to entrust with the letters I had to write, I'd decided. "It is an honour, *Principe*," Ferand had said, when I gave him my instructions.

"Be ready to ride in an hour," I'd told him. "Return for the messages."

I wrote three letters: one to Finn, one to Garth, to be sent on to Leste, and one to Valle. I told them all of Druise's death, adding I would be travelling south later in the summer and would meet with them then. Valle, I asked to come to me as soon as possible.

As I wrote, a second plan began to form, and by the time I had finished the letters, it had solidified.

"Is Eidyn here?" I asked the door guard. I'd requested Druise's second-in-command's presence. "Send him in."

Eidyn was a man in his forties, square-faced, brown-haired. He'd spoken yesterday at the burial, not quite dry-eyed. I'd met him once or twice prior to that, when Druise had thought he should be part of a discussion about the guard. He'd seemed competent, and if Druise had promoted him to his current position, that had been enough for me.

"*Principe*." He stood at attention.

"Sit, Captain," I told him. "This is difficult for us both. Would you like wine?"

He declined. "Is there anything to do with the guard assignments you think I should know?" I asked. "The most recent recruits have finished their training and been assigned positions, am I right?"

"Yes, *Principe*. Several weeks ago."

I came right to the point. "Just before Druisius died, he spoke to me of unrest among some factions within Ésparias. Did he make you aware of this?"

His jaw tightened. "To an extent, *Principe*."

"Are you cognizant of how he obtained this information?"

Understanding flashed in his eyes. "Aware, yes, *Principe*. Privy to the—channels, no."

Why not? "You are Ésparian by birth?"

"Yes, *Principe*. From Torrey, in the south. May I speak freely?"

"Please."

"Major Druisius was a man in a thousand. He and I could hear the same conversation in the senior commons, and yet he would know things afterwards that I didn't. He would ask me, you see, and then tell me what he had gleaned from the talk, or at least some of it. I—" He shifted, uncomfortably. "I cannot be as useful to you as the major, *Principe*."

I appreciated his honesty. "That in itself shows me you are perhaps more perceptive than you realize," I said. "But it is also something I must consider. You will command the guard for now, while I weigh my options. I may assign you permanently. I may not."

"Yes, *Principe*." I thought I saw relief in his eyes. A man content to be a second-in-command, perhaps, not wanting the responsibility of leadership. I felt a brief pang of envy. Some of us had had no choice.

Chapter 18

OVER THE NEXT FEW DAYS, I met with Talyn several times, primarily to discuss the reduction of garrisons at the coastal forts. We couldn't keep full complements of soldiers at each: were we better shuttering half of them, or dropping most of them to half—or quarter—staffing?

I looked down at the map spread over the table. "If we kept a full garrison at these two forts"—I pointed to the most southerly, and the one at the mouth of the Taiva—"and reduced the others to six soldiers, two for each watch, would that be enough?"

"Why choose the fort at the Taiva?" Talyn's new adjutant was studying the map.

"The estuary makes for easy landing, if the tide is right. But—" How to explain? "We're not expecting Bryngyl to invade. If there is an attack, the assumption is it will come from a faction of dissatisfied and restless men, seeing us as weak and disorganized." I'd worried about this, ever since Ruar's blunt words. "To win a battle at the Taiva, against me, at the spot where my mother killed Fritjof—"

"Might be seen as redeeming their honour as Marai men," Talyn finished for me. "I concur. We"—she indicated her new adjutant—"will take a closer look at the deployments, but the idea is sound."

~

A ship had been made ready for my departure, small enough to make harbour at one or two of the coastal villages or forts. I wasn't yet ready to go, but when I did, I would be accompanied by a small guard cohort, Gwyllar's nursemaid, and, because I needed someone with whom I could share ideas, Muire and Garia. We'd be cramped on the small vessel, but the voyage wasn't that long.

"Perhaps I should place her on permanent detachment to you," Talyn had said, when I'd asked for Garia to accompany me. "If she is to be part of your council, many of her other duties will need reassigning as it is."

"You should. Muire too will need to consider his staff and their responsibilities."

"What are you planning to tell them?"

"Only that we need to reconsider trade with Varsland, and to a lesser extent, Leste, at this point. I will explain it as a way to maintain peaceful relations. I want to judge their reactions to that idea first, and to what information Daragh supplied."

Daragh's report had arrived the day before. On first reading, Muire had told me, it appeared to be a fair analysis of the reduction in trade to be expected, and its probable effects on both Linrathe's and Varsland's economies. Nor, Muire had added, did it appear to be slanted towards Varsland's concerns.

One line in the accompanying letter had given me pause. With the *Teannasach*'s approval, Daragh had written, a copy of the report had also been sent to Bryngyl. Ruar had not discussed this with me.

"It's not inappropriate," Muire had said mildly. "With the Casilani withdrawal, Abher Tabha is Linrathe's, and a significant source of income. The *Teannasach* needs to maintain cordial relations with Varsland's king, as well as with Ésparias. I don't envy him, really, a man with sons who tie him to both countries."

I'd almost told him my concerns, then. I hadn't, but I had wondered— still wondered—how much Muire had deduced. Perhaps he should know before Garia, to help explain to her the thinking behind my father's vision.

But not Ruar's other suggestion. That I had told to no one. The idea weighed on me; frightened me, were I honest. I thought about what Sorley had said, and it only increased my concerns. And yet, if I looked at it dispassionately, I could see why it might be to our advantage. To the western alliance's advantage, at least. But could I alone make such an enormous decision for Ésparias? And if I did, would more of my own people turn against me?

I wished I could talk to my father, hear his calm and reasoned analysis of the idea. Or see Druise's response, whether a chewed lip or a grin. But that reassurance was forever beyond my reach.

I could ask Talyn's opinion. But I did not yet know my own mind; I hadn't properly weighed the benefits against the possible problems; too many other things had taken precedence. Until I had done that, I would be too easily swayed.

"Where do you plan to stop on your trip south?" Talyn asked.

"Tirvan, just so Kira can see Gwyllar again. One or two of the forts, and another village. Torrey, perhaps: it has an easy harbour."

"May I suggest you visit one of the forts where the garrison will be reduced to a half-cohort? Assure them their work matters?"

A good idea, and I told Talyn that. "But only one, at least on the way down. Time also matters."

"It always does," she said. Her expression changed, softening. "How is Sorley?"

"Not good." I met her eyes. "Devastated. I'll go to see him now, but so far he's barely acknowledged me."

"The poor man," Talyn murmured. "I know this is hard for you too, but he must be completely adrift."

"He is." I stood. "Thank the gods for Apulo."

I stopped to see Gwyllar before I went to Sorley, simply to raise my spirits. I still hadn't found a tutor for him, and there was little point in appointing one now. I'd wait until after we'd returned from the Eastern Fort. Maybe I'd start to teach him *xache* on the ship.

He was playing with his farm animals, retrieved from my mother's rooms. I sat on the floor with him for a few minutes. A goat was on its side. I reached to right it. "No!" he said. "Dead." I withdrew my hand. Gwyllar patted the goat gently.

"We've had a lot of dead animals," his nursemaid said quietly. It was to be expected, I thought. I'd done my best to explain Druise's death to my son, but how much had he really understood?

Gwyllar looked up. "Where So'ley?"

"He's not well," I said.

"Oh." Gwyllar got to his feet, his favourite wooden pony in his hand. He proffered it. "I give to So'ley?"

What to do? I didn't know how Sorley would react to Gwyllar. On the other hand, didn't my son need to know Sorley hadn't disappeared too?

"All right," I said. "But he's not feeling well, Gwyllar. He won't play with you. But we can go to see him."

I carried my son across the courtyard. The door to Sorley's rooms was closed. I knocked, gently. Apulo opened it. His eyes went to Gwyllar.

"Gwyllar has something to give to Sorley," I said, clearly, and, I hoped, loudly enough for Sorley to hear.

"Come in," Sorley said from somewhere. Apulo stepped aside. The room was dim, the shutters closed. I put Gwyllar down. He gazed at Sorley, sitting listlessly in a chair. Then he held out the pony. "Here," he said.

For a moment I thought Sorley would refuse, or just not react at all. But he extended his hand. Gwyllar gave him the toy.

"Better?"

"A little. Thank you, Gwyllar." A weak smile accompanied the words. Relief and love swelled inside me. I'd been so afraid he'd blame my son.

Gwyllar hugged Sorley's leg. "D'uise dead." He looked up, tears welling, then overflowing. "D'uise dead," he said again, resting his head against Sorley's knee. Sorley took a deep breath.

"Yes."

"I'm sad."

"So am I." One hand moved to Gwyllar's head, smoothing his hair.

"Gwyllar," I said gently. "Time to go. Say goodbye." I extricated him from Sorley. One thumb went to his mouth.

"Bye-bye," he said, around his thumb.

"Thank you," I said to Sorley.

He looked at me, unsmiling, hollow-eyed. Old, suddenly. "Druise loved him."

"So much."

"Bear," Sorley said. "Little Bear. That's what Druise called him. Don't let that be lost. Please, Gwenna?"

His words brought something home. I would never be Kitten again. "I won't," I said, understanding, wishing, hurting. I kissed Gwyllar's cheek, damp with tears. "Right, Bear?"

~

I'd eaten alone in my workroom again, the windows open to the damp evening air. A small fire burned in the brazier, not for warmth but an attempt to drive away some of the moisture. I worried for my father's library, and had ordered fires to burn there constantly, and the books and scrolls to be inspected for mould.

My neck ached. When I'd finished my meal, I'd turned to my journal to record the events of the last few days. I stretched, then got up to walk to the door that opened onto the courtyard, nodding to the guard. The villa was so silent. Only a few months ago—weeks, really—there would have been voices, laughter, Sorley or Druise's music. Now almost all the rooms were shuttered and dark. A pang of self-pity arrowed through me. My family was gone, scattered or dead or mired in despair, a loss not just personal. They'd been my mainstay, guiding and advising, shaping my actions and decisions. Now I was almost completely alone, and lonely. Too much was being asked of me. I was only one person.

Voices at the gate caught my attention: a friendly exchange. Who was here? The thought of company lifted my heart; a distraction was more than welcome. Garia crossed the courtyard. Talyn must have sent her.

"Major." She was dividing her time between me and Talyn, while the new adjutant learned his duties. Well, good; we had things to discuss.

"Good evening, *Principe*." Very purposely, she unpinned her insignia of rank, grinning as she did.

"Garia?"

"Come on, Gwenna," she said. "Let's go drinking."

I'd thought we'd go to the senior commons, but instead she took me to the house Muire and his *quincala* occupied within the fort. I didn't know Bronah well—she was a few years younger than me, closer to my brother's age—but she was excellent company. Her youngest was nearly the same age as Gwyllar, so we spoke for a little while of the vagaries of three-year-olds, and then turned our minds to dicing and drinking.

It was good to just be normal again, to push work and grief to one side. Maybe, I thought, my personal life could go on, not just my public one. I had friends, although I'd neglected them over the winter, and through the demands of work.

"Gwenna?' Bronah sat back on her heels, flushed with wine and laughter. "Why don't you bring Gwyllar to play with our two sometime? Or I could come to you."

I liked the idea. Gwyllar hadn't been around other children very much. I hadn't either when I was little, not ones my own age, but I had been surrounded by the *Ti'ach*'s students. Remembering that made me think of something else. "Do your children have a tutor?"

"For part of the day," Muire replied.

"I was thinking it was time for me to find one for Gwyllar."

"Why doesn't he just join in with ours? They do lessons in the morning. His nursemaid could bring him over."

"His nursemaid and two guards," I said. "Do you really want two guards at your door?"

Bronah laughed. "We live in a fort. Do you think we'd even notice?"

"Do you have time to come and watch tomorrow's lesson?" Muire asked. "Meet the tutor before you make up your mind?"

I would make time. "You and I have some things to discuss; perhaps we could do that as well?"

He suggested a time, which suited me. Bronah tossed the dice in the air and caught them again. "Are we going to finish this game?" Her grin was challenging. "Because if we stop now, I've won."

Bronah kept on winning. Garia paid my losses; I'd brought no money, assuming we were going to the commons. We fastened our cloaks and stepped out into a dark night, a fine drizzle falling. My guards appeared.

"I hope you kept dry," I said to them.

"Yes, *Principe*," one said, although the beads on moisture on her cloak suggested otherwise. We walked through the torch-lit fort to the gates. It was very late.

"I'll pay you back tomorrow," I told Garia. "Thank you for this."

"I thought you needed it," she said. She'd known me since her days as my bodyguard, in the year I'd spent as a junior trade envoy. We'd diced together then, too, in unruly groups in the junior commons. She and Lynthe and Muire and half-a-dozen others, back when I could mostly ignore who I was. As a group we'd worked and played together, and some of us had spent nights together too. Usually that had been casual pleasure, but sometimes it had become more. As it had for Lynthe and me, or so I had thought.

Maybe it had been, once. I wanted to believe the love between us had been real. I felt little but regret now, tinged with a deep sorrow. And behind that, a deeper reluctance to consider what I would have to do when she was brought back to Ésparias.

"I did," I told Garia. "We should do it again, maybe at the villa." I paused, realizing I had no sense of the answer to what I was about to ask. "Is there someone you'd like to bring along? A partner?"

"Not here. He's at the Eastern Fort," she said.

"And neither of you have asked for reassignment?"

She shook her head, chuckling. "It's not that serious. We see each other occasionally, enjoy ourselves when we're together. Perhaps a bit like you and the *Teannasach*? Or like it was here, when Partition still was the law of the land."

Garia was older than me. "Do you remember that?"

"Not really. I was five when my mother took me to Casilla for safety. I remember cows, lots of cows. And the cellars where the butter and cheese were kept, dark and cool. That's almost all."

"You're from Ballin originally." They still made cheese there. Good cheese, sharp and crumbly.

"Originally. Didn't your mother tell you about life under the Partition agreement?"

"I know the facts. How self-sufficient the villages were, and how they were governed. The apprenticeship system for the girls, and the boys leaving at seven. But *Mathàir* left at eighteen. I'm curious, now, about how the councils worked," I said, realizing as I spoke the words they were true. "Were the villages always independent, making decisions only for themselves?"

"As far as I know."

I'd read the history written by my grandfather's twin brother, of course: both my parents had ensured that. I thought there'd been something about other governance—by guilds? My mind was too blurred by wine and the hour to remember. Tomorrow, if I got a chance.

At the villa I spoke to the guards outside Gwyllar's rooms. All was quiet, they told me. I hadn't expected otherwise. The only threat to my son's life had been my own inattention, and Druise had died as a result. The thought twisted my gut. A guilt I had to learn to live with. How?

Callan never forgave himself. Nor did Casyn. My mother's words, when she'd told me how the man for whom my brother was named had died. Both the Emperor and his younger brother, she'd told me, had realized the king of Leste's murderous intent a moment too late. Colm, Callan's twin, had not. He had taken the knife meant for the Emperor, had died to save his brother.

Druise had died to save Callan's great grandson. Were we really that important? *Are our lives worth more than Druise's?* I'd asked Sorley, half my lifetime and more ago. *For who you are, yes,* he'd answered. I wondered if he still thought the same.

Chapter 19

I WOKE ONLY SLIGHTLY MUZZY-HEADED, nothing that washing in cold water couldn't cure. My hair had been damp when I'd gone to bed, and it had dried into a mess of tangles. I cursed the comb's tug, but eventually I tamed the thick waves. I wondered, sometimes, why I kept it long; short hair was far more practical. Dressing my hair high was a Casilani custom. Did I need to continue it?

After breakfast with Gwyllar I went to my father's library. I opened the shutters to let in some light; for once, it wasn't raining, although clouds still obscured the sky. The braziers held coals, giving off a little heat, and the room felt reasonably dry. I stood in the centre of the still, silent room. The shelves held bound books, as well as rolled vellum, and his *xache* set, the position of the carved ivory pieces telling me of an unfinished game. Beside the *xache* board was a wooden coffer, the wood polished and inlaid with shell. I knew what it held.

I put Eudekia's last letter to your father with the others, my mother had told me, just before she left. *I haven't read it. You may wish to, for what she might have said about Casil and the future.*

I touched the lid of the box, then withdrew my hand. I thought I knew why my mother hadn't read it, and the same reluctance suffused me. Whatever name you gave to the connection between my father and Eudekia, it had been something separate from the bonds that had held our family together. Should I not honour my father's privacy even now?

Besides, whatever the Empress-Dowager might have said, the information was now months old. I had more important things to consider. I found the history with no difficulty; my father's books—mostly mine, now, although he had bequeathed some to Colm, too—were arranged in an orderly and logical manner. I pulled out the chair, and sat down at the desk to read.

In the third year of the reign of the Emperor Lucian . . . The first chapter concerned itself with the attempt to conquer Linrathe, and the conflicting views that had led to Partition. Guilds were mentioned here, but only in terms of the village guilds, the legal entity that had been required for each settlement at Partition. I skimmed the text until I came to the third chapter. There, among the discussion of land ownership and the percentages of the harvest owed to the army, was one line. *Prices for goods traded among the women's villages were set yearly by the governing guild of that craft.*

The governing guild of that craft. So my vague memory had been correct. How had they worked? 'Set yearly' suggested an annual meeting. Of each guild separately, or all together? And what had happened to these guilds?

A knock on the door—I'd left it ajar—made me look up. "Garia."

"Talyn sent me to you. She's working on troop assignments, and her new adjutant can help with that as well as I can. But—" The look on her face was odd, as if she'd seen or heard something she didn't quite believe. "Captain Valle is here. From the Eastern Fort. He just arrived."

"I'll see in him in my workroom," I said.

~

The man before me was of medium height, his eyes hazel, his hair dark. Like other men and women I knew from the southern coast, his skin was several shades darker than mine, but a little lighter than Druise's had been. Valle held himself with quiet confidence, seemingly not disconcerted to have been summoned by me. But then, I thought, he'd know why. Druise must have told him that he was his chosen successor in at least one role. He'd knelt when he'd first entered the room, staying down, head bent, until I told him to stand.

"*Principe.*"

"Captain." It might be major, when he left my presence. "Please sit. You know why you are here?"

"I do. A terrible loss, *Principe.*"

"Both public and personal," I agreed. "Druisius told me I could trust you. He had told none of us that he was ill, but in the context of how and when he spoke those words—" I watched Valle's face, still impassive. "Druisius rarely said anything directly, or unnecessarily. You have been important in the flow of secret information that he controlled."

"Yes, *Principe*."

"How important? Do you know the sources, and how they are paid? Whom to ask to investigate, or listen?"

"In Ésparias, yes, *Principe*. And the ships that come from the east, those that bring information—their captains know to deliver their information to me, one way or another."

"Are those ships all part of Druisius's family's merchant fleet?"

Amusement touched his eyes. "Of course. His immediate family—his nephews, now—do not come themselves. It was thought—his brother Marius thought—that too obvious a connection would lead to talk. There would be accusations of favouritism, and perhaps more. So the captains that bring messages belong to a second fleet, owned by Druisius's family in Icoris, but that ownership hidden. How, I do not know."

"And who do not do business in Casil itself?" I guessed.

"Never. No further east than Sylana on the north coast, but to Cyrenis on the south."

This was more than I had known. *So many secrets,* Sorley had said. *So much I didn't know about him.* And yet this man did. It spoke of more than trust; it spoke of preparation for an ending Druise knew was coming.

Or more than one ending? Druise's ties to his family in Casil had remained strong, letters back and forth. A thought for later, when I was done with Valle. Just now, another matter needed attention. Druise had done more than gather information for me. He'd analysed it, too, compared it with what he knew after a lifetime of observing and listening—and discussed what he'd learned with my father, and later me. And there was an enormous gulf between knowing a set of facts, and even how they related to other facts, and the wisdom and insight to understand what those relationships might or might not mean. To see every move on the gameboard.

I'd thought I could do that. I doubted it, now.

"Why?" I asked, without planning to. "Why did Druisius choose you?"

He blinked. "I was recommended."

"Recommended? By whom?"

"My father."

Garth. Procurator of Leste, but long, long before that, a spy for my grandfather, the Emperor Callan. With that thought came another realization. He was Garth's son, which meant— "You're my cousin."

"Of some degree, yes. We share a great-grandmother."

I remembered something else, too. Something I must ask, have clear between us, even if Druisius had chosen this man.

"Your mother died under my mother's command," I said bluntly. "Is that a problem?"

"No." He hesitated. "I never knew her. But it was your mother who told my father of my existence, which saved me from the only life open to an unclaimed boy, that of a servant on a retired officer's estate. I owe her much. You should have no doubt of my loyalty, *Principe*."

I had grown up knowing my father's relations, accepting as mine the ties of blood and responsibility he had shouldered half way through his life, assuming my support as *Principe* came from them. That my mother's family, living their lives in Ésparias's villages or its army as they had for generations, might also be concerned with, or invested in, my life hadn't really occurred to me. I'd liked the sense of connection having Kira act as my midwife had provided, but, to my shame, I'd never thought of a political role for them. Except for Garth, but he was—or had been—a Casilani administrator, part of their bureaucracy, not mine.

I knew what had shaped this thinking: my mother's own attitude. Oh, she'd taken me—and Colm, later—to Tirvan, made sure I knew Kira and Teárdh, but she'd never stayed. I'd spent a few weeks there, both as a girl and a junior trade official, but they'd never really been part of my life. Or my mother's, since the war. There'd always been some excuse. *Kira would be too attentive.* And my father had not countered it. I had been brought up to consider myself the heir to a tradition that, even if by a bare thread, descended from Casil.

It is not your task to blindly follow Cillian's dreams, Ruar had said. Or ignore the biases in his thinking—or my own. The idea needed examining, but not now. Valle was waiting for me to speak.

"I hope," I said, "that I will gain that loyalty for my own sake, not just my mother's."

"The Major," Valle said, "believed you deserved complete loyalty. Who am I to differ with the man who was my commander?"

"You are you own man, I hope," I said. "I need your mind, your analyses, Valle, not just an interpretation you think Druisius might have given me. Can you do that?"

"I believe so, *Principe.*"

"Good," I said, with a touch of astringency. "One more thing. You said you are capable of directing the gathering of information here in Ésparias, and from our eastern contacts. But not the north?"

"No, *Principe.*" He didn't seem apologetic. "That was the lord Sorley's responsibility. Clearly—" He hesitated.

"Go on."

"He and the Major were *consori.* They would have had much time for private discussion and analysis. I will not have the same opportunity."

"No," I agreed. "That raises another question, Captain." Two, actually. "If you are to take on Druisius's work for me, who replaces you at the Eastern Fort? Not as commander of the guard, particularly."

"My second in command, in both roles," he said. "The Major's choice, a few years ago. You might know her." He told me her name. I did know her; she was my age, and we'd had classes together for a few years. I'd seen her sometimes around the fort later, guarding a door or a gate, and occasionally she was part of the crowd I drank with.

"The Major's choice? Not yours?" This mattered. Valle had to trust her.

"Mine too. But, *Principe,* may I speak freely?"

"Always. You are free to disagree with me, Captain, and to tell me things you think I may not want to hear. I need that from you. Do you understand?"

He nodded. "Then, *Principe*, I gather from what you have said you want me here at Wall's End. I think that is a mistake. I think you need to move your headquarters and your council to the south."

He told me why, concisely, a reporting of the facts as he saw them. There was, he said, resentment of my absence from the south, and rumours of Linrathe's influence were persistent. More so, he'd said, since Gwyllar's birth. But that wasn't all. The anger at the conscription of Casilani men was spilling over into doubts about my leadership. Had I sent more Ésparian troops, it was said, the Emperor would not have ordered Casilani men east.

"Did Major Lynthe fuel this anger in any way?"

"Indirectly, through her presence, as brief as it was, as she has been your representative in the south several times." She'd be a recognizable figure to many; her visits on my behalf had been extended. "But—and I heard this only on my journey north, so Major Druisius would not have known—there is talk now that she took herself and Prince Constyn to Casil to convince the Emperor to order Ésparian troops sent."

"A rumour she began, or conjecture?"

"I'm not sure, *Principe*. I sent a message back to my second-in-command to investigate."

"You know there is talk I should abdicate in favour of Constyn, when he is of age?"

"I heard that too, *Principe*. One leads from the other, does it not?"

I liked Valle, I decided. I liked the conciseness of his reporting, his thoughtfulness, his calm demeanour. Druise had chosen him. I had one more question to ask.

"Captain, give me your thoughts on Captain Eidyn. Is he competent to lead the guard here?"

Silence. His jaw twitched. "*Principe*, Captain Eidyn's promotion to his rank came some years before mine."

"That cannot matter. I may ask you to pass judgement on a general, or on the Commander of the Fleet. Or even on the major Druisius himself. Can you do this?"

I saw the decision on his face before he spoke. "I can, *Principe*. Captain Eidyn is competent to lead the guard in its deployment and duties, when those duties are physical. He has not been part of the dissemination or gathering of information, although he is aware that some guards have that added responsibility."

I smiled, slightly. "That is Captain Eidyn's opinion of himself. I thought it was not just modesty, but I am glad to have a second opinion." I ordered my thoughts. "Captain, I intend to promote you to major, with overall command of the guard. The position includes a place on my advisory council." A flicker of surprise, at that. "Which means I need you at Wall's End, for now, but I also realize you may well need to return to the Eastern Fort to arrange matters. You have a trusted officer there. Who is here that you can equally trust?"

"General Talyn," he said, without hesitation. So Druise had told him that much. "But . . ." He stopped. "There is someone else."

"Someone known to me?"

"The general's adjutant, *Principe*. Major Garia."

Do you have a partner? I'd asked her, not long ago.

Not here. He's at the Eastern Fort.

"You're partners? I was aware of an attachment, but my impression was of something casual."

He shrugged. "Doing what I do—how close can I let anyone be, lover or friend?"

"Would you welcome the chance to change that?"

"Were it possible." A hedged assent.

"Garia has also been appointed to my advisory council." I watched closely. He hadn't known. "There will be few secrets. I won't say none."

"There are always some," he said. "Even in the closest relationships."

A surprising comment. "Major, thank you," I said. "I'll see to the official promotion today. You'll want to meet with Captain Eidyn, I imagine?"

He nodded, his shoulders straightening, the guard once again. "Who can brief me on the current intelligence from the north?"

"Not the lord Sorley, I'm afraid," I said. "I can, in the morning."

"Certainly, *Principe*."

I stood. He did too, of course. "One moment," I said. I opened the door between the workroom and the antechamber. "Major?"

Garia came in. She didn't meet Valle's eyes, beyond a brief nod.

"Major Valle is my new commander of the guard. Please introduce him at the senior commons and to the appropriate officers." I thought about what else I had to say, and decided I didn't know Valle well enough yet to tease him. "Valle, would you wait in the anteroom for a minute?"

He saluted—I'd have to tell him not to—and stepped out, closing the door. "He will need a room, too." I allowed myself a grin. "Or not, as you may decide between you."

Garia turned quite a deep shade of red. I laughed. "Just let the steward know. *Consori* are entitled to more space. When you are finished familiarizing him with Wall's End, meet me at Muire's quarters, please." I took Colm's *History* from my desk, holding it up.

"I'll be observing the tutor for a while. While I do that, could you keep reading this? Come and see what I found." I showed her the line. "I want to know if it says more about these craft guilds, or anything similar."

"I don't remember that line." She was composed again, the efficient adjutant.

"Why should you? As cadets, we studied Colm's history in the last year before we decided whether the military or administration was to be our future. We were what, fifteen? But in all my later education as a trade envoy, I don't remember it either."

"Who sets those prices now?"

"No one," I said. "Prices for anything that comes to the forts and garrisons, whether the Casilani's or ours, are set by us. But what Berge sells to off-duty soldiers, or to Delle or Tirvan or anyone, is up to them. Whatever people will pay. Surely you've been to the market at Berge?"

"I have. I just never really thought about it."

Neither had I.

~

The tutor was a slight man of perhaps twenty or twenty-one, educated at one of the Ésparian *Ti'acha*. He'd dropped to one knee when introduced, but protocol done with, his attention had been on the children. I watched him making games of the lessons, encouraging and gently correcting. The room they learned in was spacious, with two windows letting in air and light. I liked its feel, and I liked the tutor.

A nursemaid came to take the children for a break, giving me a chance to ask the man a few questions. The lessons had been conducted in Casilan. Did he teach in Ésparian as well?

"Yes, *Principe*," he answered. "In the second hour, after this break."

"What about Linrathan?" I wanted Gwyllar to speak his father's language.

"I learned it." His blue eyes crinkled, ruefully. "But I am out of practice." Really, I decided, that was of little matter; I could speak it with my son, and encourage Sorley to as well, in the future.

"Can you handle a third child, and one unused to the schoolroom? His nursemaid will attend him."

"I believe so, *Principe*. It would be an honour to teach the prince."

"I want him treated no differently from the other two," I warned. "He is far too young to be called by anything than his name, or to be encouraged to think of himself as special. Praise or discipline, he is the equal of the Major's children. It is how I was brought up, and how he will be, too."

"Of course, *Principe*, if that is your wish." He smiled, a little tentatively. "May I say, that while mine were excellent, I envy you your teachers?"

"You might not, had you been at the *Ti'ach na Cillian*," I said. "My father could convey more disappointment in a student's response by what he didn't say than most men can in a diatribe."

"Still," he said, "I would have risked that, I think."

The exchange reassured me. This was a man who honoured teachers and teaching. I would entrust Gwyllar to him for a few years, to learn his letters and numbers and a bit more. After that? I'd decide when the time came.

~

Garia joined me for the last part of my discussion with Muire. "I was aware of the trade guilds," he told us, "but they have been defunct for many years, except in Casilla. They own sections of the town, and rent living quarters and workshops to their craftswomen—and now craftsmen, too."

"But they don't set prices for the goods produced?"

"Not under Casilani governance. Before that, I'm not sure. Perhaps in Casilla's market, which traded regularly with the military and the retirement farms."

"The *History* says they did at one time," I reminded him. "I wonder when it stopped?"

"I'll have one of my staff go through the old records," Muire said. "But that will take a while. What interests you about this, Gwenna?"

"I've been wondering how independent each village was, before we became a province of the Eastern Empire, and what they expect, I suppose, now the Casilani are gone."

"I wouldn't change anything quickly, were I you." Muire looked thoughtful. "The villages have been fairly independent, as far as management of their lands and their day-to-day concerns. Other than setting the taxation rates, the Casilani didn't interfere much. Perhaps the biggest change now will be where the Casilani have abandoned their farms; villages close to them provided some of the labour for them, and that loss of employment will change the economies of those villages."

"Should we allow that land to fall fallow?" I held up a hand to stop Muire from answering. "That's a question for another time." So much to think about. Too much.

"Is it?" Muire glanced at Garia, including her in the discussion. "Before you joined us, we were talking about new taxation rates." It hadn't been all, but it was all she needed to know, for now. "We still have an army and an administration to feed. What happens to land the Casilani farmed may affect the ability of the villages to provide grain and other foodstuffs in sufficient quantities."

And there was the thinking behind Ruar's proposal. I still found it hard to accept, though.

"Well," Garia said, "why don't we ask the villages?"

"We are," Muire told her. "I'm sending people now." He and I had decided that earlier. Now we knew the Casilani withdrawal was complete—Oriacus had said his farewells, taking ship to travel east with the governor—it had been possible to calculate the food and other supplies to meet our needs. I'd done a similar task in my first and only year as a trade envoy, visiting villages to let them know what was expected at harvest, whether it had been grain or smoked fish, cheese or cured meats. A much simpler life, even when the headwomen had argued.

Perhaps, I thought, I should do it again. Speaking directly to one of the headwomen, or the village council, would give me a better feel for their concerns. Impulsively, I said, "Muire, give me the tally for Berge. I'll go to see Kyreth and her council myself."

His look of surprise changed to one of consideration. "That may be a good idea."

"I'm so glad you approve," I said tartly.

His face creased into a broad smile, followed by a chuckle. "You have them occasionally."

Grinning, I made an obscene gesture. He grabbed my hand, curving my fingers into a loose fist. Laughter bubbled up—along with a recollection of Muire's hands on other parts of me. Just a good memory, nothing more, but it added to the moment. Life was continuing, and perhaps happiness could return.

Something in Muire's eyes—not desire, just reminiscence—told me his thoughts had gone along the same path. The sense of connection, of both a shared history and a shared future, warmed me.

"The guards," Garia said, trying to control her own laughter, "will think we're drinking. Or dicing. Or both."

"You know what the guards can do," I said.

If we laughed any harder, they would come in to see what was going on, I thought. I brushed tears from my cheeks, then pinched the bridge of my nose. "Enough. We are people with important work to do."

~

Walking back to the villa, the information regarding Berge's taxation tucked into my case of papers, I thought about our moment of silliness, and the previous night of games and laughter. When had I grown so serious? There had been a time, not so long ago, that Lynthe and I had visited friends or gone to the senior commons regularly. A tacit understanding had been agreed: I was only Gwenna on those evenings, not the *Principe*. Druise, I remembered, had approved. "'Sorley and I, we do this too, yes?" he'd said. And, with a shrug, "But not your parents."

Had my father ever spent an evening in laughter and games and too much wine? I'd guess my mother had, but my father? Sorley might know, I thought. Perhaps I'd ask him, later: it would give me an excuse to see him, and maybe the question would draw him out of himself a little. He worried me, still. Regardless, I vowed, would make more time for my friends, and pursuits that lessened, even briefly, my concerns.

I was late, and so Gwyllar was napping when I went to see him. I spent a few minutes explaining to his nursemaid where she was to take him in the morning. "The Lord Sorley brought his wooden horse back this morning," she told me. "Should we take it tomorrow?"

"A good idea." Sorley had come to see Gwyllar? A hopeful sign, after all these weeks of worry.

"The poor man," the nursemaid said softly. "He looks so bereft. And I miss the music."

"So do I." Should I go to see Sorley before I went to Berge? Briefly, I decided.

Any hope I'd had that I'd see an improvement in him vanished as soon as I entered Sorley's rooms. He sat, doing nothing, his face haggard. He'd lost a lot of weight, and while he could have easily afforded to lose some, it had gone far beyond that.

"Gwenna." His voice was hoarse, as if speaking was difficult.

"I came to see how you were," I said, "and to thank you for giving Gwyllar his toy horse back."

"He asked me when Druise was coming back."

"Oh . . . I'm so sorry, Sorley." Why hadn't the nursemaid told me that? "He's only three," I said gently. Sorley just nodded. I hesitated a moment. "Would you come and eat with me tonight?"

"No. I have no appetite." He lapsed back into silence. I stood, indecisive. Apulo, hearing my voice, I supposed, came in from another room. He gestured with his head. We went out to the courtyard, walking some distance from the door.

"Gods, Apulo, he looks terrible," I said.

"I thought he was a little better this morning. I convinced him to take the toy back to Gwyllar, but I should have thought about it more. Of course the boy would ask about Druisius, seeing Sorley. They go together in his mind."

In all our minds. "Are you with him all the time?"

"I am always near. As I was for your father."

And that means you are not getting enough sleep, or even rest, I thought. "I am going to have Lairís found, and ask her to return to Wall's End," I told Apulo. "After my father died, Druise said Sorley needed his family—his other family—around him. If that was true then, it must be even a greater need now."

"Perhaps that is wise," he said. "I am doing my best, but with little effect."

"I know you are." I touched his arm in thanks. "I'll come to see him more often. If he won't come to eat with me, I'll have my suppers in his room. Maybe that will help."

Chapter 20

I RODE TO BERGE. IT WASN'T THAT FAR, but unless I went by the road I'd arrive muddy. The coastal track was fast, and it led directly to the woman's village. Beyond the traditional boundaries of the village another settlement had sprung up, serving the garrison at Wall's End with places to drink and game, have anything from a tunic to jewellery made, and, I guessed, purchase services of many kinds. The days of twice-a-year Festival were long past, and with the Casilani had come the *scraptae*, male and female. They'd been frowned upon at first by most Éspariani, but with time—and perhaps knowing the profession was regulated and considered, if not quite honourable, also not shameful, by the Casilani—the complaints had died down. The new area was not governed by Berge's council; it had been considered a Casilani responsibility, and abided by the laws set by the procurator.

Which was another issue being dealt with: how were these settlements to be managed? But not a question for today, unless Kyreth raised it.

The tide and the fishing boats of Berge were out. I could see the small craft dotted over the sea below me, and children gathering shellfish from the exposed rockpools on the shore. Even from the clifftop the red legs and beaks of foraging sea-pies stood out among the gulls and small brown birds also searching for food. I liked this ride, even though the track had been rerouted much further back from the cliff edge after the collapse that had killed Faolyn. Wisely, I thought, looking at the new falls of soil and rock caused by the months of incessant rain.

I found Kyreth in her garden, harvesting herbs. I should have sent word, I realized: she could have been attending a birth. She looked up at me.

"Good thing I'm already on my knees," she said. "Be welcome, *Principe*. What can I do for you?" She rose, a little stiffly, and brushed soil from her leggings.

"Not kneel to me, for one thing," I said. Other women had, too, as I'd ridden through the village. I had never been comfortable with it, not from the time in Casil when it had been first Dern and then my family— my father excepted, of course—who had knelt to offer me homage. "Did people kneel to my grandfather?"

"I don't know," she said. "Before my time, really. We women had little to do with the Emperor. Ask an old soldier. But that's not what you came to see me about, surely?"

"No. I came to speak to you about taxation this year, and what Berge can reasonably supply."

Her brow shot up. "I'd expected that conversation. I hadn't expected to have it with you."

I grinned. "Why not? You've known me since I was born."

"Aye," she said, returning the grin. "And what a beautiful babe you were, all that black hair. Even the physician said so. Speaking of physicians, how's your brother?"

"He was fine, the last letter we had."

"And your mother? Any news?"

I shook my head. "It's a bit too soon." Although she could have sent a letter from any of the coastal towns where her ship would have docked for food and water.

"Well, come to my workroom. I'll put these herbs in water, and then we can talk. Would your guards like a drink?"

I declined on their behalf, and went into the house with Kyreth. The first room was a large kitchen, herbs hanging from the ceiling. Beyond it was a room with a sizeable table and four chairs, and a shelf of books and ledgers. "Do you still record who fathers a child?" I asked spontaneously.

"Of course. Many partnerships are still brief. Plenty of women want a child, but not necessarily a man about all the time."

"Or the other way around?" Druise would have been—had been—a wonderful father; Sorley, too.

"Sometimes," Kyreth said. "Now, *Principe*, taxes?"

I went over the expectations with her. Berge provided fish, fresh and smoked, to Wall's End, and a certain amount of woven woollen cloth, as well as lamb and mutton and barley for beer. "We can meet most of this," she told me, after reviewing the figures. "It's been a good year for fish. Not so much for the sheep—a lot of footrot, I'm told, with all this rain, and the barley's poor, too. If you'd wanted the amounts we owed when the Casilani were here, that would have left us hungry."

"We wouldn't have," I protested. I remembered discussions with Muire about adjusting the levies in bad years.

Kyreth looked a little abashed. "A turn of phrase. Oriacus was a reasonable man. So is Muire, and Michan before him."

"Tell me," I said. "If you wanted to buy horses from Han, say, how do you negotiate the price?"

"They tell us what the army was paying," she said promptly. "But if the horse isn't good enough to be a military mount, or pull an army wagon, then we start at half the price, and haggle."

"Half the price?" I remembered bargaining for silk scarves at the market in Sylana. "That wouldn't pay for their keep."

"And we don't expect to pay that little. But the offers and counteroffers are part of the fun."

I'd always thought so, from the time I'd made my first independent negotiation as a junior trade envoy. It would, of course, be a skill that the council leaders needed too. "But the starting price is always what the army pays? If you were going to sell dried fish to Han, could one fisherwoman decide to sell at a different starting price?"

"Ah. No. Fish and wool and mutton and grain—all the things you've asked for—are Berge's common holdings. Doesn't matter who caught the fish, or grazed the sheep or planted the barley. So we sell as a village, not as an individual, do you see? But if one of our boat builders makes little boxes in her off time, and sells those to hold jewellery or whatever, those are hers to set the price on, and keep the money."

"When were Berge's common holdings decided?" Why didn't I know this?

"Generations past. Maybe at Partition, or shortly after?"

"When the village guild was formed?"

"Probably." She paused. "Would you like some tea, Gwenna? I'm thirsty."

I accompanied her to the kitchen. She raised flames from the coals expertly, added a little wood, and swung the kettle over the fire. It boiled quickly. The cup she handed me a few minutes later smelt—and tasted—of mint.

"One more question," I said, after a sip. "In Linrathe, all the landholders within an area decide together what the price for their fleeces or fish will be, so they don't compete against each other. Do you discuss prices with Delle before selling to Han or Rigg?"

"Yes. But only with Delle, now. Serra once too, I'm told, before it fell into ruin." The few women who had survived the Marai raids at Serra had scattered, some to other villages, some to Casilla. We'd built a coastal fort where the village had been.

"Did you know that once a fisherwoman's guild would have set those prices? For all the fishing villages?"

"I did not," Kyreth said. "How do you know that?"

I told her of the brief line in Colm's *History*. I should have brought it with me, I thought. Not that she'd disbelieve me.

She sighed. "We lost so much knowledge in the Marai raids. So many of our elders, the women who knew these things. When you were born, Gwenna, nearly every woman left in Berge was younger than thirty, except for one or two who had been up on the moors or who had managed to hide."

Almost every one of those women had been raped. Some had been left pregnant. The same pattern, all along the coast. "Do you still hate the Marai?" I asked.

"As a people? No. But I would kill the man who—" She stopped, grimacing. "But he is probably long dead. And with few exceptions we don't hate the daughters and sons we bore, and they are part of our land, aren't they? In the villages or in the army, and they have children of their own now too. Life goes on."

"What if some arrived, looking for land to farm? Like the families from Linrathe who came after the Wall was opened?"

"Are they asking to?"

"No. I'm just trying to think of everything that might happen."

She sipped her tea, her hands cupped around it. "I think," she said finally, "if they were families, with men too young to have been part of the raids, I wouldn't mind. But I'm speaking only for myself, Gwenna, not as the headwoman of Berge."

I thought about what Kyreth had said on my ride back to the villa. The families who came from Linrathe were mostly headed by younger sons, without land in their own country through their system of inheritance. Land was passed down in the same way in Varsland; it was those landless men Bjørn had taken east to be Alekos's personal guard—and who might choose to take coin to fight there again.

Some who had gone with Bjørn would stay in the east, finding a place in the conquering armies. Some might already have families there in what had been Casilani lands, and simply settle down under new rule. Some might look for lands along the Ubë.

But some might return to Varsland, and look south, to another country known to now have land to spare. "You are suggesting I can avoid a war through planning and compromise," I'd said to Ruar, when he'd told me his thoughts. "A very great compromise."

But to make the western alliance successful, would not Varsland expect to be an equal partner? To have the same rights as Linrathe? If so, I would need to do what Ruar had suggested. If the betrothal between Trygve and Flynsà came to fruition, I would have to make that great compromise. As part of the marriage settlement, I would have to offer land in Ésparias to settlers from Varsland.

Chapter 21

~Lena~

THE MUSIC CHANGED TEMPO, became sadder. A woman's voice, now: a song of regret, of lost love, I guessed. The stars blurred and swam. I couldn't keep the memories buried any longer.

I had dined that last night with Gwenna and Talyn, Druisius and Reif, a working meal. We'd reviewed plans and responsibilities, and, once Reif had been dismissed, the codes I would use in my letters. There'd been nothing left to talk about, but still I'd been reluctant to leave the table. But I had one last thing to do, a promise to keep.

I walked out into the courtyard with Druise, the sky above us still pearly, although the sun had set. "Is Sorley home?" I asked.

"I think so. Unless he has gone to the senior commons, yes?"

"Will you ask him to come to see me? No matter how late."

Druise chewed his lip. "Alone?"

"Yes. Unless he refuses." My fingers went to the bracelet on my left wrist. Cillian had asked this of me. "I will come to him, if I must."

Druise's eyes followed my fingers. "You have not yet given Sorley the marriage bracelet?"

Some of the tension eased. "You knew?"

"We talked about it long ago, Cillian and me. A courtesy, yes? In case I objected."

"You don't, do you?"

"You have to ask that?" There should have been a grin with those words; there wasn't. Just deep sadness, in his voice and in his eyes.

We—all of us—thought of him as solid, dependable Druise. Whoever else he was in dark alleys and secret places, in the light of day his pragmatic good nature rarely wavered. But his apparent ease in living with the intricacies and contradictions of who he was—or who I guessed he was—had been helped by the depth of friendship between him and Cillian, who had had his own intricacies and contradictions. In Cillian, they had not lain lightly. Perhaps they didn't in Druise, either.

He put his hand on my shoulder, a rare intimacy. "I will tell Sorley you must see him. Not why."

In my room I took the *li'ítho* from its box. I laid it across my wrist, beside my smaller one. Traditionally it should go to Colm, along with mine when I died, to be passed to a son or grandson. But the bracelets had not come to us that way. Brother gave them to brother sometimes, and in that guise Sorley had given them, his own wedding bracelets that he would never use, to Cillian.

I slid the braided silver strands onto my palm. Would Sorley wear the bracelet? It would cause comment, although I thought little, here in Ésparias. That he and Cillian had loved each other had not been a secret, but the nature of that love had been carefully hidden in Linrathe and Sorham, as much for Cillian's sake during his years as *Comiádh* as for Sorley. The decision to wear it would be Sorley's. My responsibility was to give him the *li'ítho,* and to say the words Cillian had not been able to.

The triple knock was quiet, as if Sorley thought—or was hoping—I might be sleeping. I called for him to come in. He did, closing the door behind him, but he stayed on his feet, taking only a couple of steps into the room. "You must see me, Druise says."

"Yes." I hesitated. If I stood, would it feel like a confrontation? "Sorley, please sit down."

He did as I asked, his jaw tight. I'd dropped the bracelet back into its box and closed the lid before he'd come in. There were other things to say first. "Do you remember that night in Casil? Two planets, you said, orbiting one sun."

His jaw twitched. I went on. "And that we needed each other, the two of us, so that neither would be burnt. The light of his sun has gone out, Sorley, but does that mean we must be so cold to each other?" I felt tears threaten; pushed them back. "Cillian wouldn't have wanted this."

"He wouldn't want you to leave, either." Said flatly, emotionless.

"I won't dispute that with you," I said.

"You say you need to leave because you cannot think here, that you need space and freedom from walls to grieve, to find a way to live." Anger rose in his voice now. "Don't you think I need the same?"

"Gundarstorp," I said, understanding. "Then go home, Sorley. If that's what you need."

"How can I?" he snapped. "How can I go to where I cannot show my grief, or talk about the man I loved?"

"That's not true," I protested. "Roghan understands."

"Roghan, yes. Partly." He swallowed. "But sooner or later he will ask the question I have no answer for." He stood, pacing the floor, not looking at me.

I didn't move. The room was in shadow. "What question?"

"Why I stayed for all these years, knowing Cillian loved you more. That I was always second." He turned on his heel, facing me. "It's true, isn't it? I even made it part of our ritual, giving you the wine first every night. I took the dregs, and welcomed them."

I stared at him, shock hollowing me. "No," I said. "Sorley, that's not true. You were first, his first love. Surely you know that."

"Know that? When for so many years he would not tell me he loved me, because those were words reserved for you? He'd made up his mind to go wherever you wanted—stay in Casil, go to Wall's End—even before Gwenna was made *Principe*. We could have stayed at the *Ti'ach* forever, but when you couldn't, neither could he. Regardless of what I could do, or wanted to do." He choked back a sob. "Wall's End wasn't so far for a good horseman, he told me. I could visit."

"So you didn't have to leave Linrathe," I said. "He didn't want to ask that of you."

"And what of those visits?" He hadn't heard me, I realized. "A few hours, and him leaving me before dawn, because he had to be with you when you woke?"

"Sorley." I said his name twice before I thought I had his attention. "Cillian made his choices from his sense of responsibility to me and our children. He was honouring the vows he made. It doesn't mean he loved me more." I chanced a suggestion. "Talk to Druise? If anyone knows—"

"Druise?" He cut me off, scorn singeing his words. "I suggested we went to Gundarstorp, you know. But I come second with him too. He won't leave Gwenna."

Dear gods. If I had known this . . . "Would he go if I stayed?"

Sorley's mouth twisted. "No. I don't matter enough."

"You do," I said fiercely. "You always did. I asked you here because I have something to give you. Something Cillian asked me to do, because he knew I understood." I took the bracelet from the box, holding it out to him. "He wore it for you as much as for me, Sorley. You gave it to him in love, and now it returns to you." There were words I had to say. Could I, without tears? I took a breath. "Cillian asked me to say this: the *li'ítho* is an offering to you, in thanksgiving, and memory, and love."

Pain crumpled Sorley's face for a moment—and then anger hardened it again. "You were to tell me that? He couldn't say it himself?"

I fought against my own anger. "It was nearly the last thing he said to me, Sorley. You had left us only a moment before, to get a drink to ease your throat. I think he knew he was dying, and did not trust himself to have the strength or perhaps the time to tell you. Where I erred was in not giving you the bracelet immediately, letting you take it from his wrist. But he had just died, and I—" I couldn't say more. I stood, helpless, my cheeks wet.

Sorley's hand was clenched around the bracelet, making a fist. "And so I was robbed of even that," he said. "I am glad you are leaving, Lena. I hope you find Lynthe. You can reassure each other your betrayals were justified."

~

The dog's wet nose touched my hand, bringing me back to the present. I ran a hand over its head. It looked up at me enquiringly. "I'm all right," I told it.

I hadn't seen Sorley again. On the ship that had taken me to the Eastern Fort, I'd relived what had passed between us many times, cursing Sorley, cursing myself, cursing even Cillian once or twice. By the time I disembarked, the flaring anger had been replaced by something cold and dark and jagged, like the waste left behind after ore had been turned to iron. Something small and hard that could be hidden in the chasm inside me.

The dog whined. It was looking back towards the inn. "Go home then," I said. Over the grain fields, a white shape floated. The owl's wings curved and it dropped, talons out. One less mouse to eat the grain. Perhaps a nest of hairless babies would die now, with no mother to feed them.

Don't be ridiculous, I told myself. I'd never been sentimental, and my children were grown. I had been gone from Colm's life, except as a voice in letters, for ten years and more, and Gwenna was a mother herself. Thinking of Sorley had brought other worries to the surface, things I'd left Ésparias to try to find some peace with.

Another whine, followed this time by a sharp bark. The dog seemed determined not to leave me, but it clearly wanted to return to the inn. I turned and began the walk back. The path was barely visible in the starlight, but the dog knew the way.

At the inn's kitchen door the dog left me, trotting off to wherever it belonged. I slipped inside. The musician was still playing. I nodded to the kitchen boy, and without glancing into the common room went up the stairs to my bed.

~

Rielo arrived when he said he would, three hours after dawn. I was alone in the common room, bringing my journal up to date. I'd neglected it for a day or two, but the habit of almost all my adult life wasn't easily broken. Seeing Rielo and Nessus come in, I finished the sentence I was writing, then stood to greet them.

"I promised Nessus a second breakfast," Rielo said with a grin. "Only way I could get him moving so early."

"I'll put this away," I said, indicating my writing case and journal, "and come back down."

By the time I'd done that, Nessus had a plate of bread and olives and cheese in front of him—or rather half a plate, the food rapidly disappearing. Rielo had a cup of something. "Were the twins happy to be home?" I asked Rielo, just to make conversation.

"Happy to not be in school," he said. "But their father's unsure of what to do, stay here or return to Casil, and he told the boys that last night. So now they're half excited and half worried, and so is Nessus." He glanced at the boy. "Not enough to spoil his appetite, though."

"Does anything, at that age?" I thought about what the officer had said yesterday. Quietly, I asked, "If they return to Casil, will the boys be taken into the army?"

"I'd think so. They're old enough, and should be joining either the administrative services or the army this year." He spoke with certainty, a man confident in what he knew—and his right to say it. What was his position in the procurator's household?

"And if they stay here?"

He flicked an eyebrow upward. "I have no idea. The Casilani have always sent their sons and daughters back east to take their places in the business of the empire. Surely it is the same in Ésparias?"

"Mostly. But not all."

Whatever Rielo might have replied was interrupted by the innkeeper. "Your horse is ready, messenger," he called across the room. I raised a hand in thanks. Nessus stood, taking a last drink.

"I'm ready too."

"Then we should ride."

Even these few hours after dawn the day was already hot. I was glad of my hat. The land began to change, the low hills and rolling ground to our left cut more often by streams. Bridges interrupted the flat surface of the road, arching over the waterways. To our right, the streams were channelled into a lattice of ditches to allow the crop to be watered.

We'd seen few people on the road: too far from the market at Occida, I thought. Men worked along the ditches, dredging or repairing slumped banks, and on the higher land men and women moved among the fruit trees and the vines. Goats and sheep cropped the fields between the road and the orchards, watched by children who shouted greetings to us.

The road began to rise, curving eastward, a deviation made necessary by a high outcropping of rock. Little grew on its steep sides except gnarled trees, rooted in crevices, and the occasional tufts of grass. I gazed up at it, uneasy. A raven soared above us, its croaks echoing.

I'd expected the mountain spur to be narrow—why, I wasn't sure—but it soon became clear this thrust of rock went on for some distance. No one farmed here, although where the plain began again scattered cattle grazed the sparse grasses. "The land must change," I said to Rielo after a while, "for the procurator to have a villa beyond this."

"It does," he said. "Another mile or so, and we'll have crossed this ridge. Beyond's a broad valley, some of the best land there is here. The procurator's villa's on the far side of that valley."

"It's beautiful," Nessus said unexpectedly. He'd been quiet. "And wonderful land for horses, with good pastures. My father says there's something in the soil or the water that makes good bones."

I'd noted the quality of his horse, and Rielo's. "Do you breed the army's horses?"

"Yes." He brightened. I'd found a passion, I thought.

"In Ésparias the best horses come from two villages in the north," I told him. We talked about horses for a while. He thought Gallus was one of theirs too, from his look, but had been judged not quite good enough for a military mount.

"But I'm not sure," he said. "I wouldn't have been very old when he was foaled."

"Your grey is a handsome animal," I said, to keep him talking. My unease was increasing as the road grew closer to the cliffs, shards of shattered boulders littering its edges. I glanced at Rielo, riding ahead of us. Did I see tension in his shoulders? One hand rested on the hilt of the sword on his hip.

Was that movement? I looked up. Scree was slipping down the rockface. A gemzē, possibly, or a rock squirrel, I told myself. A raven croaked three times. Fear snaked down my spine.

The road crested the ridge. Before I could make sense of what I saw ahead of us, Rielo swore. He reined his horse around to face us. "Off the road. Out, and back, and wait." His command was for Nessus. "Now!"

The boy hesitated for a moment, then turned the grey and heeled him to a gallop back along the road. A few strides, and the horse veered, gathered itself, and leapt the ditch. A cry came from above us, and at the wagon blocking the bridge ahead of us, answering shouts echoed against the rock.

I wrenched Gallus's head around and kicked him, hard, following Nessus off the road. I leant forward, gripping hard with knees and thighs as the horse jumped the ditch. As soon as he was steady, I knotted the reins, dropping them on his neck, then reached to free my bow. With it and an arrow in one hand, I pulled the horse up, scanning the cliffs.

There! I took a quick glance at Nessus, billowing dust showing me— and the man above us—his path. A very long shot for the bowman on the crag. A long shot for me, too, but perhaps I could draw his attention away from the boy.

I nocked the arrow, murmuring to Gallus to stand. I drew, sighted, released. Swore, because the arrow would fall short.

But I had been seen, and the arrow's flight had been close enough to take the bowman's attention from Nessus. I wasn't a long shot for him. I urged the horse forward again, back towards the road and the shelter of the rockface. He'd have to shoot downward, dangerous for a man on a cliff edge. If Gallus was fast enough.

An arrow sped past me, thudding into the ground just to my right. Gallus shied and stumbled, nearly unseating me. I grabbed his mane, righting myself just before he leapt the ditch and slid to a halt on the stones, sides heaving. I leant over his neck, taking my own deep breaths.

But only for a moment. I slid off the horse, and, keeping as close to the rockface as possible, moved forward. Near the crest of the road I dropped to a crouch, and then to a crawl, until I was behind a broken chunk of rock. Below me, where a river flowed down from the mountain, a wagon, one wheel off, blocked the bridge. Four horses stood nearby, free of harness as if being rested until the wheel could be fixed—but they were bridled, with reins for riding, not driving.

Rielo had not dismounted. His sword was out, but held loosely. He was talking—negotiating?—with two men. A third was on the cliffs. Where was the fourth?

I crawled a little further forward. The day was still, but the splash of the river meant I could hear nothing of what was being said. The bowman knew I was here. There'd been no obvious route down to the road from where he'd stood, but that was based on a brief glance. More likely he'd followed the river up to the plateau, and would come down the same way.

This close to the rockface, the ditch on the left side of the road was no more than a depression. I couldn't use it for cover. I edged into it anyhow, so that my back was against the cliff. I needed to think.

I didn't get to. Head down, unalarmed, Gallus walked into view. My view, and the view from the bridge. One of their horses whinnied, a greeting or challenge. Gallus's head went up to return the call. He did sound like a cockerel, I thought, even as I re-evaluated, rapidly. Was I better to mount, or to let the men below me think the horse was wandering loose because I had been thrown or hit?

The latter, I decided. The bowman knew he hadn't hit me, but I could have been thrown when Gallus jumped the ditch. And I was less of a target on foot.

I stayed still. Gallus snorted, and trotted towards the bridge. He'd probably recognized Herti's scent, and for horses, safety was in the familiar. Not just for horses, of course.

Familiarity had many facets, though. I was alert, apprehensive, all my senses heightened, but I wasn't afraid. Keeping one eye on the bridge, pacing every movement by several breaths, I nocked an arrow, keeping the bow at half-draw. The man to the left of Rielo shook his head and spat. Herti stepped backward—and Rielo's sword swept down.

To be parried by another, held upright in two hands. Herti swung, kicking out. A trained warhorse, part of my mind observed, even as I stood and drew the arrow back. The sound of metal on metal rang in the air. From under the bridge, the fourth man ran up the bank, sword out.

He fell to my arrow, and a shout from one of the two battling Rielo. The man's glance at his fallen companion cost him: the horse's flank hit him, hard. He stumbled to one knee. But they were too close to each other for a clear shot. I ran forward, bow at the ready, down into the valley.

Movement—or was it just the sense of someone behind me, the fear that lay never quite dormant in me?—made me turn my head. The bowman, descending the cliff almost at a run. His arrow too was nocked, his bow at half-draw. At a bend in the trail, half-shielded by one of the twisted trees, he stopped. His eyes went from the fight at the bridge to me, making in that second the same judgement I had.

I had no shelter. Running, twisting back and forth like a rabbit, would be my best chance. Perhaps I could reach another of the scattered boulders. I saw him lift his bow, step into his shooting stance. He'd expect me to run back towards the cliff, I hoped. I sprinted forward— and heard a cry of surprise.

Turning my head, I saw the bowman tumbling down the slope, reaching for something to break his fall. The loose earth must have given way. I stopped and drew the bow, watching. He grabbed for a tree, caught a low branch, dropped his bow to grasp the trunk with both hands. He lay fully exposed. Such an easy shot.

But as the arrow flew he rolled to one side, and it hit him in the buttocks. I swore, and drew again. Two arrows left after this one. He had drawn his knees up against the pain. If he reached to pull the arrow out, he might lose his grip on the tree. I waited. He rolled onto his stomach, and began to haul himself closer to the tree. At the bridge, someone yelped, a sword stroke cutting flesh.

No time to waste. Another arrow should finish the man on the hillside. I nocked and drew, sighting along the arrow. I released, and gasped as sinew flew up to hit my cheek, pain as instantaneous and intense as a wasp sting. I opened my eyes; I'd closed them reflexively when the bowstring had snapped. The arrow had arced forward a short distance and fallen.

I ignored it. My first priority was Rielo. I dropped the bow and began to run again, pulling my secca from my belt. Steel clashed against steel. Herti reared, and one man stepped back, away from his hooves, panting, his sword briefly lowered. My chance. With a prayer to the goddess I only half believed in, I threw.

Chapter 22

THE SECCA TOOK RIELO'S OPPONENT in the chest. He dropped his sword, clutching at the blade. Then fell, first to his knees, and then forward, face down onto the bloody stones of the road. I didn't see the sword stroke that finished the other man.

When I reached them, Rielo was off his horse, examining wounds on Herti's front quarters. "Not too bad," he said. "They're all slashes, not stabs." He straightened. Sweat streaked his face, and his sword arm was bleeding. "I'll wash them. But we still have a problem." He inclined his chin towards the slope.

The man had got to his feet, somehow. Legs splayed, he was nocking an arrow on the bow. It had been years since I'd practiced an uphill throw. I'd have to hope my body remembered. I wiped the blade of the secca against my leggings, tossed and caught it, and with all the strength I had left, sent the knife flying.

Almost too low. It hit his thigh, just above a knee. He dropped, screaming. Rielo was already halfway to him, sword out. I turned away. I didn't need to see his end. Instead, I took Herti's reins. As gently as I could, I unsaddled him, then led him down to the river. The man who had taken my arrow lay still, blood dyeing the pale soil beneath him. His eyes stared at nothing. I swallowed bile, and led the horse into the water.

Herti dropped his head to drink while I washed his wounds as best I could. None were deep, but the cuts were ragged in places. The sword hadn't had a honed edge. I wondered how far we had left to go today. The horse should not move faster than a walk now.

I walked a little further out into the river, its bed gritty and uneven. When the water was over my knees I stood, letting its cold flow wash the blood from my leggings. I glanced down, saw the red staining the water, felt the rush of saliva. I retched, and vomited into the water.

Trembling, I leant forward, hands on thighs, until I was sure the spasms had ended. Even after all these years, part of my mind said. I scooped up water to rinse my mouth.

"Are you all right?" Rielo asked. I nodded.

"I hate killing," I said. He'd stripped off his tunic. The cut on his right forearm still bled, but slowly. He waded into the water, took Herti's reins, and led him deeper. Then he turned the horse so the water's flow sluiced the wounds, and crouched to immerse his own injury.

"You may hate it," Rielo said, "but you're good at it. I'd never heard that the horse archers were also skilled with the throwing knife. Just who are you, Lena-more-than-a-messenger?"

"I'm just Lena the messenger," I said. "But I told you I was Ésparian. Both the secca—that's the Ésparian name for the throwing knife—and horse archery are taught to cadets in their army, and that's where I learned."

He flicked an eyebrow upward. "I think only part of that is true. But I won't press you." A shout made us turn. Nessus, his grey horse lathered, rode up.

"Are they all dead?" he asked, dismounting, eyes wide. "Are you hurt?"

"A scratch," Rielo said. "Herti has a few cuts." He led the horse up to the bank. "Tether them both, then come and help me with the wagon. It has to be moved."

"Wrap that cut!" I followed them from the water. "Any strain and it'll start bleeding again."

Rielo looked at it, a wry twist to his mouth. "I suppose. But what with?"

A few years earlier, I'd still have had cloths. But I was past the monthly bleeding now. "Where's my knife?"

"Beside my sword."

I washed it, then, pulling my tunic up, made a cut in the cloth. "Use mine," Rielo protested.

"It's already done." The cloth ripped neatly. I wrapped and tied it over the cut. "There."

~

The cart took a little time to shift. The wheel was not damaged, just freed from the axle and propped against the bed to give the illusion of a breakdown. Rocks served to support the cart while Rielo lifted the wheel back into place and secured it with the axle pin Nessus found under the piled harnesses and driving reins.

We manoeuvered the cart onto the edge of the road, off the bridge. It wasn't heavy, planked only on the bed. The sides were wattle. "What now?" I asked. Above us, ravens gathered, their croaking calls encouraging others to join them. There'd be other carrion birds too, big ones, I remembered. "We can't just leave them."

"I don't see much choice," Rielo said. "We've got a fair distance yet to go, and Herti can't move quickly."

I looked at the scattered bodies. None were young men. They would have had lovers, wives, children . . . A tremor ran through me. I hadn't just killed two men. I'd subjected the ones who loved them to the darkness and terror of grief. They would hope at first that the men had been delayed. Perhaps they weren't expected home for some days. And then the worry, and the fear, and the hollow, scouring realization—

"We could put them in the cart," Nessus said. "Cover them with rocks. It'd only take an hour."

Rielo looked at the sun, doubt on his face. "Let's do it," I said.

It took two hours, by the time we'd harnessed the horses, moved the cart to each body, carried rocks. We half-hid the cart behind a clump of bushes: the ravens would gather anyway, but a traveller might think they were at the body of a gemzē.

Rielo rode the best of the wagon horses. We kept to a walk, each leading another horse. Herti followed, needing no lead rein. As we'd worked, Nessus had been quiet, just doing what he was told, shaken, I'd thought, by violence and death. "Who were they?" he asked Rielo now.

"Men bent on robbery," his guard replied. "An old trick, the broken cart, stranded travellers. Blocking the bridge made it even better. We couldn't bypass them."

"How did they know we'd be there?"

"Maybe someone saw us on the road. But probably they weren't waiting for us, just any traveller. Someone returning from Occida's markets, maybe." Rielo's voice was casual, almost disinterested.

"There are no road patrols?" I asked.

"Not now. Recalled, like all the soldiers."

What would happen here, without Casil? There was no local governance, no local army, not in a land conquered by military might. Would they return to what they had been before, scattered villages, each with their own headman? What if some of the landholders stayed?

Was that why Ésparias had maintained a semblance—a weak echo— of what it must have been under the Eastern Empire, five hundred years and more past? Had enough of its people stayed, keeping its laws and practices in place for a while? Concepts that changed with every generation, leaving us with only the idea of an empire—our empire, tiny and contained as it was—and no memory of the great one that had once ruled.

Why had I never asked this question? Cillian would have been intrigued by it. Or maybe he had been. Our lives had been so caught up with Gwenna's since we returned to Ésparias. I'd meant to find more time just to talk to him, the way we once had, but there'd always been something else that needed attention.

The sun, high in the sky, beat down. Ahead, the road shimmered as if wet. The air carried the tang of the grey-green plants of the plain, overlaid by dust. But suddenly I was back in a room, the aroma of a peat fire in my nostrils, a man, grey-haired, holding the book I had lent him. *I had meant to*, Perras was saying. *The saddest words there are.*

A sob rose in my throat. I clamped my lips shut, forced it back down. Blinked, as if the dust was irritating my eyes. The four dead men we'd left under rocks had things they'd meant to do, too, words they'd maybe meant to say. I'd cut two of their lives short, been complicit in the other deaths. What right had I to mourn?

~

Red and gold streaked the sky above the mountains when we rode up to the villa, built on a rise of land overlooking the wide valley. We'd been seen. Men and boys came to take the horses. Rielo exchanged a few words with one, pointing down the road. Herti had fallen behind. A boy went running.

Nessus dismounted, clearly tired. We all were, and when Rielo swung down off his horse I saw a grimace of pain, quickly hidden. I didn't try to hide my own. Every muscle hurt. I claimed my saddlebags before Gallus was led away, and stood, uncertain. We were filthy. Dust and sweat stained our clothes; blood, too, on mine and Rielo's. Nessus didn't wait. Without a word to either of us, he went up the few steps and into the open door of the villa. I heard him speak to someone.

"Come," Rielo said to me. He led me along a path to the rear of the villa and another door. "Zinta!" he called.

"Rielo! You are so late." A woman, dark haired, taller than me, came out from another room. She stopped, her eyes on his arm. "You are hurt."

"A cut. It has been washed. You can tend it later, but first, this is Lena, an imperial messenger. She needs to bathe, and clean clothes. Lena, my wife, Zinta."

Why was I surprised he was married? There would be children, too, no doubt.

Zinta took in my ragged tunic, its cloth matching the bandage on Rielo's arm. "I have not seen you for six months and you bring home another woman?" The words were playful, teasing. Rielo grinned.

"Be glad I did. Lena likely saved my life today, and Nessus's." His wife gasped, then said something in—Kurzemën? I thought so, although I didn't recognize the words.

Rielo replied in the same language. Zinta's eyes were on her husband and for that, I was very, very glad. I wasn't sure I could have hidden my surprise. I'd understood most of what was said this time. Rielo had named the men, two of them; he hadn't known the others. He'd had, he said, no choice in what he'd done.

Zinta's lips thinned. "This will cause trouble."

"Yes. But see to the messenger. She has a letter for the procurator, and she and I should see him together." He gave her a wry smile. "Before Nessus exaggerates it too much."

He turned to me. "Zinta needed reassuring," he said in Casilan. "Go with her; she will show you the women's baths, and find you a tunic to replace the one you sacrificed for me."

Half an hour later I was clean. Dressed in the knee-length tunic Zinta had brought me, carrying the pouch that held the letters, I found my way back to the room we'd entered. Rielo too was washed and changed, a new bandage on his arm.

Zinta had been friendly enough, brisk in her instructions; eager, I'd thought, to get back to Rielo. "Thank you," she'd said, "for what you did today." Then, before I could say much in reply, she'd whisked me along a corridor. "Rielo says you must see the procurator tonight. So you must not keep him waiting. He is not well, and he has been worrying about his son."

"Is Nessus the only son?" I asked, to make conversation.

"No. The youngest. The older son is east somewhere, with the army." She opened the door to the baths. "All you need is here. Leave your clothes. I will have them washed." Her Casilan was slightly imperfect, and accented, suggesting she hadn't learned it in childhood.

The heat of the water eased the knots in my muscles, although I knew I would wake sore and stiff in the morning. It didn't help the tangles of my thoughts. There'd been a strong implication that Rielo was somehow involved with the men who'd ambushed us today. I thought back to what I'd first seen, Rielo talking to the two men. There hadn't seemed to be much tension. Where did his loyalties lie?

Say nothing, käresta. Listen, watch, evaluate.

"I will," I murmured. If I was mad, well, so be it. There was comfort in Cillian's voice, in his advice.

Then, because I had ridden most of the afternoon in a shadow that had nothing to do with the sun, I said, "I killed two men today."

No words. But a feeling of fingers stroking my hair, brief, ephemeral. Imagined. I sank beneath the surface of the pool, my tears mingling with its water, until I could hold my breath no longer. I surfaced, and stood. There was a message to deliver.

~

"Come," Rielo said. I walked beside him through doors and rooms, their walls painted in bright colours. He was greeted by several people; he acknowledged them, but did not stop to introduce me. Just before another door, he stopped. "Zinta tells me the procurator's illness has advanced this winter. She warned me his appearance is much changed, and his energies low. Be brief."

The man in the high-backed chair was, clearly, ill. But the eyes above the hollowed, yellowed cheeks were bright with intelligence, and his smile of welcome appeared genuine. "Rielo. Welcome home. You had a serious matter to deal with today, Nessus tells me."

"Serious enough." Rielo turned to me. "Procurator, this is Lena, an imperial messenger. She carries a letter from the commanding officer of the second detachment. She also killed two of the bandits today."

"Procurator." I bowed before approaching, the letter held out for him to take. He indicated the table to his side. I laid it down. "Sir, I am travelling from Ésparias, with a letter from their governor to a cousin. But I also have"—I hesitated, not sure of how to word this— "information that needs to go to the *Principe*, regarding a fugitive prince."

"A fugitive prince?" His eyes narrowed, then grew, briefly, even brighter. "A story there! But one I will hear tomorrow. What is it you need from me?"

I explained my errand eastward, the need for a messenger to ride south to Occida. "The least I can do, after today," the procurator— Annius, I remembered—said. His breathing was shallow, rapid; talking took effort. The swell of his belly under his robes, contrasting with his thin, yellow face and hands told their story. He was likely in great pain. At least Cillian had been spared that.

"Now," he said, addressing Rielo. "Tell me."

Rielo glanced at me. "Procurator?"

He raised three fingers. "Lena of Ésparias may stay. And sit, both of you. Nessus said the men were robbers, pretending their cart was broken down. Is that all?"

Lena of Ésparias?

Chapter 23

RIELO DREW UP TWO STOOLS. "They wanted Nessus."

"For ransom?" A croaked whisper.

"Yes."

Now I was paying attention. A kidnap attempt? Then why the bowman on the cliff? I pictured the scene again. His arrow had missed, making Gallus shy, and nearly unseating me. He hadn't known who I was. Had he used the tactics planned for Nessus? A horse running loose could be killed or wounded without risking the rider.

"Who were they?" Rielo told him the names.

"He isn't safe here, then. You cannot always be with him."

"Perhaps not. But where could you send him that is safe?"

"I must think." The dying man's voice was barely audible now. With a tilt of his chin Rielo told me it was time to leave. The procurator's head had tipped down, sleep claiming him, but our movement woke him. "A guest room for the . . ." he said. His eyes closed again.

A red eyebrow flicked up. "You'll sleep in comfort tonight. But you deserve it, after what you did today."

Or the courtesy extended because of who I was? I was nearly sure the last sound from the procurator's lips had been the first syllable of 'general'. "It is very kind," I said. "And these aging bones will appreciate a soft bed."

~

The guest room was well appointed, a small mosaic centred on the floor and the walls painted with vines. I barely noticed. The events of the day, the long, slow ride and the heaviness of my thoughts overwhelmed me. I was asleep almost as soon as I'd extinguished the lamp.

Birdsong woke me, the light filtering through the shutters telling me the sun had been up for some time. I stretched, winced at the protest in every muscle, and carefully got out of bed to find the latrine. As I returned to the bedroom, a quiet knock sounded on the door.

A serving woman entered at my call, with a tray of food and a pitcher of something. "Good morning," she said, placing the tray on a low table. "I am to tell you the procurator will see you in two hours. Until then, the gardens or the library are yours to use." She left with the untouched food from last night. I hadn't even seen it.

The bread was fresh, still warm from the ovens, and the soft goat's cheese tangy. The pitcher held cold water, flavoured with mint. We'd stopped to eat at some point in the afternoon yesterday, bread and olives and figs, but that had been many hours previously. I was ravenous.

The library? Cillian's voice said in my head. For the first time, I smiled at his imagined comment. "I think he knows who I am," I replied.

The gardens were inviting, but after I finished the food I took my journal from my bag to record what had happened yesterday. Somehow, knowing the men I'd killed had been attempting to kidnap Nessus relieved most of my racking guilt over their deaths. Robbery didn't deserve death. Kidnap was far more serious. I'd killed a kidnapper before, although it had been the least of his crimes.

I shifted to ease a cramp in my back. Thirty years since I'd shot an arrow from horseback with the intent to kill. That shot had hit its mark. Longer since I'd used the secca to end a life. *You're good at killing*, Rielo had said yesterday. I had been, once. It seemed I still was.

I looked at my hands, then down at my body. Who was I? I'd been a fisherwoman, and had expected to be one all my life. Instead, I'd been a warrior, a wife—both once incomprehensible—and the mother of both the leader of my land and a son I'd known until he was fourteen, not seven. A student and a teacher. A general. A traveller and a chronicler of the events of my time. What had happened to Lena of Tirvan?

I didn't know. Maybe that was what I was on this journey to discover. The girl I'd been, before Casyn had ridden into our village that spring afternoon. Before war, before killing. Before Cillian.

~

Zinta came to take me to the procurator. After finishing my notes, I'd found my way out to the gardens. They faced the mountains, snow still visible on the higher peaks. To the north, the shape of a distant crag caught at my memory. But we had crossed the Durrains from the eastern end of the Wall, at least two weeks' journey beyond this point. Just a similar arrangement of cliff faces and crests.

Annius greeted me with more strength to his voice. He bade me sit, dismissing Zinta with a smile. "She is your housekeeper?" I asked, wanting to ease into the questions I had to ask.

"She is. And a very good one." He gestured to a plate of small tarts. "Please, help yourself. I have little appetite, but I remember them as very good."

I took one, to be polite. It was good, tasting of something sharp behind the sweetness of honey. I poured myself a cup of water as well. The cups were deep blue glass, beautifully formed. The procurator, I saw, had one by his side.

"Lena of Ésparias," he said. "What are you doing in Beria, posing as an imperial messenger?"

"How did you know?"

"Nessus told me your name, and described you as a woman of middle age, skilled with bow and knife. That was enough to make me wonder—I have read of your exploits, of course, in your husband's excellent histories. Then you said you were seeking a fugitive prince."

"I am," I said. "And his aunt, who took him from Ésparias. Why, we are not sure, but they fled east."

"Your son, and—" He frowned. "Your sister?"

"No, Procurator. The sister of the previous *Princip*, and his son."

"Call me Annius," he said. "A rival claim to the leadership?" Illness had not dulled his mind.

"We assume so."

He nodded. "And so someone of authority must go after them. Have you found any trace?"

"No. Likely they went straight to Casil, or to Sylana at least." He sipped his water.

"Then I will ask a more precise question. What else are you doing in our lands?"

He had the right to ask. I had violated expected courtesy, if not law, by not informing the man who embodied Casil's power in this province of my presence. Had he been in Occida, I might—might—have requested an audience, explained.

I rose, taking the letter of introduction from the governor from my belt pouch. He unfolded it, fumbling a little. In silence, he read it. "I had no chance before," I said.

"Pallius asks for cooperation. You have it, of course." He held out the letter. "What were Casil's orders to him?"

"Half the troops, for now."

"Just the Casilani? Or your soldiers too, General?"

"Only the Casilani were ordered to go, but both troops and civilian men. Any Ésparian troops are volunteers. Am I right in thinking the orders here were for a complete withdrawal of soldiers, but no conscription?

"Yes." His body sagged. I saw a man at the edge of defeat, not just by illness but by circumstance. "What will happen to this land? What will happen to my sons?"

"My son is a physician, somewhere on the eastern battlefields," I said. "My daughter, I expect, will soon be the sole leader of our land. I share your concerns, Annius."

He nodded, looking away, his eyes clouded. "Empires rise, and empires fall," he said. "I did not expect to witness Casil's fall. Not that I will. My end will come before that happens." His voice strengthened. "What are your husband's thoughts on these—events?"

Perhaps in normal times the news would have reached the procurator. "Cillian died earlier this year."

"I am so sorry," Annius said. "A brilliant mind. And a difficult time for you. I lost my wife a decade past, and I miss her still." We fell silent.

Without knocking, Zinta came into the room, carrying a cup. "Your broth," she said to Annius. I rose. This was my signal to leave the ill man. He waved me down.

"Stay, please," he said. "I have something to ask of you."

I glanced at Zinta; she nodded, and left again. Annius took a few sips of the broth before putting it aside. "Where should I send Nessus? What would you do, were he your son?"

"How old is he?"

"Just seventeen."

A year younger than I had been, when I had faced Leste's invaders. A year younger than Gwenna, when she'd become *Principe*.

"What do you think?" I countered, fighting back the surge of anger I couldn't quite understand.

"His duty is to Casil," Annius said. "But would you send your son to almost certain death?"

"When I was a cohort-leader, barely eighteen, I sent a friend to her death," I said. "She was the first, but not the last. I risked my life and all I loved to save my land, in the face of near certain defeat. As you must know, Procurator, if you have read Cillian's histories."

He had closed his eyes, against the chill in my voice, I guessed. I looked around me, at the exquisite mosaic floor, at the fine frescoes on the walls. I thought of the gardens that looked up to the grandeur of the mountains, the wide pastures, the handsome horses, the kindled pride in Nessus's voice when he'd spoken of them.

"How long have you been here?" I asked, gently.

"Twenty-five years."

The procurator knew what he should do. He was also dying, and he— and his son—loved this land. It was all Nessus knew. Casil was a story, nothing more.

A story that had saved my land. But my loyalties—as complicated as they were—were not the boy's.

"He cannot stay here." I didn't make it a question. "Where else is there?"

A grimace of pain—physical pain, I realized—twisted Annius's mouth. One hand went to his side. He moaned, whispering something. I bent over him, smelling the sourness of his breath. "Fetch Zinta." He grasped my wrist. "Talk to Rielo."

"I will." He moaned again. In the corridor, I looked both ways, seeing no one. I called Zinta's name. From an opposite room, a younger woman appeared.

"Is it the master?" At my nod she ran off.

I returned to Annius. He had vomited, a thin yellow bile staining his tunic. Zinta had brought a napkin with his broth; I used it to wipe his lips and chin, then offered him a sip of water. He refused, turning his head away, his eyes closed.

"Thank you," Zinta said from behind me. "We will do what is needed now."

Quietly, I left, embarrassed for Annius; he would not have wanted me to see him like this, the proud mind fighting the diminished, failing body. Cillian had been spared this loss of dignity, a small mercy.

Where would Rielo be? With Nessus, I guessed—and where he might be wasn't difficult to work out. A gardener gave me directions to the stables, set a good distance from the villa. The boy was out in a paddock of mares and foals, but the man leaning on the gate wasn't Rielo.

"With his boy," he said. "Out behind the granary." He pointed.

I found him on a bare training field, teaching a boy of six or seven to use a bow. I watched them without speaking for a while. Rielo was patient but firm, correcting the boy's stance and hold with both words and touch. When the child went to take his arrows from the butt, I called Rielo's name.

"Your son?" I asked.

"Mikal. He's seven." The boy approached us, a little shyly. "Keep practicing," his father told him. "I'll watch, but I must speak to Lena."

"I did this," I said. "Taught archery, and other weapons, although rarely to children so young. Is he your only boy?"

"The little one's not yet three." He grinned. "A bit too young. There's a girl in between."

"Teach her too."

The eyebrow flicked. "I might, after what I saw yesterday."

"About that," I said. "You asked me a question. I didn't give you a truthful answer."

He was watching Mikal. "So who are you really?"

I told him, which made the eyebrow stay up a little longer. He did look like Turlo, sometimes. "The procurator guessed," I added. "He has—read of me."

"I've heard the tales," Rielo said. "You crossed the mountains." He looked up at them. "Zinta says there are stories among her people, of others doing the same."

"Others did," I said. "When we were found by a hunting party out from the village that took us in, one of the men was a soldier from our land, exiled, as we were." And perhaps your father crossed them too, I thought.

"But not the other way?"

"No." Why not, though? "If you had a mind to go exploring, maybe the plain would be more enticing?" I suggested.

"Maybe." He looked up at the peaks again. "I've never been beyond the high pastures."

"Rielo." He heard my change of tone. "Annius asked me to speak to you. About Nessus."

He nodded. "Mikal! Enough now. Go home, and make sure you put your bow and arrows away properly." We waited until the boy was on the path back to the villa. Swallows darted over the pastures around us, hunting insects. Below us, the river wound through its valley, reflecting trees and sky. The breeze carried the scents of clover and horses. A beautiful place, as Nessus had said. He would not want to leave.

"Can you keep him safe here?" I might as well be blunt.

"Maybe. I was not expecting him to be a target for ransom," Rielo admitted.

"You knew the men," I said. "What did Zinta mean when she said killing them would cause trouble?"

This time both eyebrows went up—but only for a moment. "You speak Kurzemën," he said. "Of course. You wintered among them."

I nodded. "Badly, and I have forgotten most of it, but it appears I still understand what I hear."

He rubbed his chin. "Shall we walk?"

We went towards the river, through fields set aside for hay, the grasses almost up to my knees. Dragonflies rested on the tallest blades, rising into flight at our approach. "Annius requested retirement late last year," Rielo told me as we walked. "When his illness first began to sap his strength. The reply from the palace was that someone would be assigned in the spring."

"But no one came," I said. "Is there no sub-procurator?"

"He took the request to Casil on the last ship of winter, with a letter from Annius recommending his promotion to the role." A small falcon, stubby-winged, dropped from a branch to take a dragonfly out of the air.

"You are well informed." The procurator trusted Rielo with more than his son. A friendship like that between Cillian and Druisius, I thought, deep and valued despite their differences in background and education.

A path, marked by hoofprints, ran beside the river. A favoured place to exercise the horses, I guessed. We followed it, the river flowing to our right. "Conquerors are not loved by those they've conquered," Rielo said. "Or not by all, I should say. Those who opposed the Casilani violently are dead, or enslaved. Others accepted the defeat, and got on with their lives. Some prospered. Some do not, and among those, and sometimes among the children who have come to adulthood under Casilani rule, there is resentment."

"In Ésparias, too," I said. "Even though we are not a conquered land."

He made a sound, acknowledging what I'd said. "Annius has governed fairly, as fairly as any representative of Casil could have. He has appealed the raising of taxes when he thought them unjust, and has been as lenient as possible in his interpretation of some laws. And he has used me—or I should say that I agreed—to be an intermediary between the Kurzemë and himself."

"A difficult role."

"Made harder by the procurator's illness and his absence this winter from Occida. Usually he is there, and the markets mean men come and go with regularity, and little suspicion, so while I supervised the boys in the taverns, not all my conversations with other patrons were casual." I suppressed a grin of recognition. Druisius would like this man.

"And then Casil recalled its soldiers," I said. "A cause of speculation in Ésparias too, speculation and uncertainty and some unbridled talk."

"It will be more than talk here. Annius is dying; Casil is leaving. My people—the Kurzemë—need a leader."

I understood his dilemma now. "But killing the men you—we—did yesterday raises questions about your loyalties. You put Nessus first."

His mouth twisted. "I have been his guard and companion for fourteen years. The men who plotted the kidnap would not guarantee his safety. They are—were—a hot-headed pair. We'd clashed before."

"They must have known you'd be with him."

"Four against two, and one of those driven off, perhaps captured. Three, or even four against one, once Nessus was restrained, was their plan." The twist of the mouth again. "I'm good, and Herti's well-trained. Even so, the odds were against me." He glanced down at me. "Except for you. A chance meeting on the road."

"Our lives turn on such things." On a road or a river. I looked east. The horizon blurred in the heat, but I thought I could see the green of the valley giving way to the ochre of the plain.

"They do," Rielo agreed. "And so a question. Would you take Nessus with you?"

I hadn't foreseen the request. Take him with me? My gut tightened, an instinctive response. Rielo waited.

"I am going to Casil," I said. "And perhaps beyond, to find my son. I could not guarantee Nessus's safety."

"Where is he safe?"

Nowhere. But I couldn't be his guardian, for all the reasons I had left Ésparias, and one more now: the journey across the plain. I wanted, perhaps needed, to do that alone.

Am I being selfish? I asked Cillian. Only silence. Then, an idea.

"What will the twins' father do?" I asked.

"Tevius hadn't decided. His wife is Kurzemë; it might be enough to keep them from reprisals, if I—if whoever emerges as the leader here is strong enough."

"They could go west," I said. "To Ésparias. With Nessus, and some of the horses if transport can be arranged. In the northeast of my country are the villages of Han and Rigg, where our horses are bred and trained. They would be welcomed."

"West." I watched Rielo's face while he assessed the idea. "You can authorize it?"

"The *Principe* is my daughter," I said, a touch drily. "I'll write the letters this afternoon."

His chin tilted. "Letters?"

"One for you, too," I said. "In case you ever need it."

Chapter 24

WE MADE FURTHER ARRANGEMENTS as we walked back to the villa: he would ensure my letters to Ésparias were marked with the procurator's seal and sent immediately. "And give me the message for the governor's cousin. I'll see to that, too."

"It's not that important," I told him. "An excuse for me to be travelling. But won't I come to his estate before I reach the eastern road?"

"No. It's two days ride north. The estate is beyond it by several days."

Two days ride? "Is there more than one road east?"

"Only one military road. There are tracks, but I wouldn't recommend them. Water can be hard to find."

I gazed towards the distant peak I'd thought familiar. Could we have drifted so far south crossing the mountains? Yes, I admitted. It had been cloudy much of the time, and valleys and passes hadn't lain in a straight line. Perhaps it explained, in part, the months it had taken to reach this side.

But in those weeks, Cillian and I had learned to trust each other, our mutual dependence slowly transforming into friendship, then deepening into something more. Without that time . . .

The days on the ancient road, drawn with the tools of an engineer before one spade began to dig, might have been the only time in my life I'd followed a straight path, I thought. Perhaps that was part of its pull.

~

I hadn't seen Annius again. "I think," Zinta told me over the evening meal, "he was husbanding his strength to see Nessus again. But now—" She gave a tiny shrug. "He has nothing left. A few days, no more."

Had I sapped some of that hoarded strength, with what I had told him, and what I had asked? Possibly. But not so much to change the inevitable end. Would Cillian have lived longer if we had stayed at the *Ti'ach*? Another unanswerable question. Our lives turn, I thought, and perhaps hasten—or delay—our deaths.

Not a thought I would voice. Instead, I praised the food, and the talk turned to their sons and daughter, and a comparison of education, here and in Casil's military schools, and at the *Ti'ach*a. When Zinta left to put the children to bed, Rielo poured us more wine, without asking.

"You speak of your husband in the past tense," he said.

"He died at the end of winter."

"Ah. I am sorry." He raised his cup slightly. I smiled, repeating the gesture. We drank. "The road—it will be much changed."

"I know."

"Should you go alone? There are no patrols, and without the military traffic the inns and the small markets will have lost most of their trade. A lone rider might be a target for robbery."

Whatever awaited me on the road east would reveal itself only in solitude. Of that I was sure. I could not take a guard.

Rielo simply nodded when I told him this. "Then will you take, with my gratitude, two things?"

"What things?"

"A horse trained to battle. And a dog."

~

The water station had little shade, not with the sun at its highest. The horse stood with one foot cocked, its tail swishing away flies; the same flies I was using my hat to repel. We had all drunk deeply. The dog—Ladon, its name was—lay in the dappled shade, head on its forelegs, but alert.

Rielo had offered three things, not two, before I'd left the previous day. The third—the sword—had seemed sensible. The horse—well, I had to ride, and I'd seen what Herti had done when Rielo had been attacked. I hadn't been so sure about the dog. A massive animal, its brindle coat set off by a white chest and paws, it wore a heavy leather collar and looked intimidating. Which was, I supposed, the point.

Ladon had certainly drawn glances at the inns, and at the marketplaces where I'd stopped to buy food. If I was on foot, he stayed at my side. When I rode, he kept pace, rarely straying more than a few lengths behind or ahead. Rielo had taught me the commands. As well as the usual ones, they'd included 'friend' and 'guard'; 'attack,' 'hold'—and 'kill'. I wondered how they'd taught the last.

Once told I was a friend to be guarded, the dog had accepted its role, and my commands. But in the five days we'd been travelling, other than a warning growl at a possible cut-purse who'd made a step or two towards me in a market, he'd been simply a companion. My imperial messenger's badge appeared to still be respected, perhaps because I made sure I paid for my lodging and food, asking for receipts. "I'll be reimbursed in Casil," I told the innkeepers, which had elicited a smirk or two.

I slapped at a fly. They were marginally less irritating when we were moving, and we'd rested long enough. Ladon was on his feet the moment I stood. I led the horse back for a last drink, then tightened the saddle's girth and mounted. Back on the road, I stopped, looking ahead. The land was beginning to slope noticeably downward. Not too many miles ahead of us lay the lake.

I glanced back at the resting place. The sun was at its highest. Perhaps I should wait another hour or two, for the animals' sake? The horse rippled its skin against the flies and snorted. I sat, indecisive. Ladon looked up at me and whined. "All right," I said to him. "We'll go on." I signalled to the horse to move. At least the dog gave me something living to speak to.

The road had changed. Except for the temple to Darcail, I had recognized almost nothing, and even that had been rebuilt, the broken pillars and inscriptions replaced. It had stood alone on the plain when we had found it. A town surrounded it now. To the west the high escarpment rose, steep sided; I'd kept looking at it as I approached. An aqueduct ran from its height to bring water to the town and the cultivated fields that lay beyond the houses, the wild force of the waterfall it had replaced channeled and tamed.

I'd spent the night at the imperial inn, a night of uneasy dreams from which I'd woken convinced someone was in the room with me. I'd reached for my secca before I realized the breathing I heard was the dog, stretched on the floor in front of the door. When I said its name I heard its tail thump the floor twice, and a soft snuffle. I'd slept the rest of the night well enough, but I'd woken feeling drained, full of doubts and indecision.

Should I have told Rielo there was a welcome in Ésparias for him and his family? Even for Tevius and the boys? I did have the authority. But who might follow? I'd told Gwenna what I'd done, before I'd sealed her letter and left it with Rielo, but had I thought out the consequences properly? I'd been too focused on the immediate, on the dying procurator's worry for his son, on what might happen to a generous, thoughtful man and his wife and children.

My mind had gone back to the temple, remembering Cillian's delight when he'd realized it honoured the hero Darcail, built by the Eastern Empire of legend. Darcail's labours, Cillian had told me, were stories to instruct, to give people hope that redemption was possible. *Is it?* I'd asked him, somewhere on this road. *Perhaps not,* he'd replied, *not for living people. Only for gods and heroes.*

I was no hero. I had only done what I had thought was needed, and people had died because of that. One had been a red-headed cadet, my fellow hostage to a truce I'd broken, a funny, brave boy intent on making his father proud. One of the losses that had driven Turlo to disappear from Ésparias. Could there ever be redemption for that?

There'd been no answer, only an echoing silence in my mind. The road that morning had still been bordered by grainfields, waves of green where I had expected ochre soil and sparse, grey-leaved plants. I'd wanted dry soils and scattered, dull plants under an unforgiving sun. I'd wanted a landscape to strip me bare, reduce life to survival, demand a choice.

Even when the cultivated fields had ended and the dry plain lay beside and before me, I'd found only more questions, more regrets. More thoughts of the woman I had been, and maybe had always been, without

Cillian's presence. Of the deaths at my hands; of the daughter I had deserted. Of the guilt I wasn't letting myself feel.

Casil had reclaimed the road from its faint traces on the land, dug out the springs to make water flow, to create shaded spots for rest and respite. But the road was only a physical thing. What I had wanted to reclaim from dust and shadow and memory could not be resurrected, not the woman, not the man. The road had changed, Cillian was dead, and I was someone riding east, restless and alone, towards a crumbling future.

An hour later I reined the horse in. Ladon dropped to his belly, panting. Ahead, the road curved back and forth down the slope before straightening again on the flat lands beside the lake, its water sparkling in the sunshine. At its eastern end, a town of some size stretched from its banks towards the fort, hidden by another dip of the land. I could see an amphitheatre, and the gardens of what I guessed were the public baths, its paths leading down to the water. Private villas and their grounds claimed the waterfront beyond the town walls.

I'd been told what to expect at the last inn, the fifth I'd stayed at since leaving the procurator's villa. The garrison was gone, the innkeeper had said; they'd marched east.

"Who do I give the letter to, then?" I'd asked.

He'd thought about that, sitting with me at my table as I ate. He wasn't exactly busy, he'd said, and did I mind? I didn't. Company took me out of the heavy fog I'd descended into again, at least for a while.

"There's a retired officer. Wasn't the commander or anything, but an engineer. He—well, his men—built the road, and most of the inns, and the towns. His villa's the first off the road, riding east. He took half the lakeshore for an estate for the Empress's husband, but when Prince Hathus came to see the town named for him, he gave it to the engineer in thanks."

I'd asked the officer's name. It didn't mean anything to me—or did it? But a vague sense of recognition was all I could dredge up. If the man had been an engineer of some note, perhaps his name had come up in one of the discussions about the construction of a bridge or road in Ésparias. I'd sat through a few of those.

I sighed, deeply. Ladon whined, as if enquiring about what was wrong. "It's all right," I told him. I would pull myself together, deliver the letter, go to the imperial inn and then the baths. Their gardens ran down to the lake; there would be somewhere I could sit, to watch the stars come out and remember. It wouldn't be what I'd hoped for, but had anything, since I left Ésparias?

Accept what fate brings you. Catilius, although that wasn't quite right. My mind shied away from the memory: a *taberna* in Casil. I forced it back. Remember the good, I told myself. Sparrows in the dust, heat, a jug of wine. Cillian raising a glass, saying the words. *Accept the things to which fate binds you, and love whom fate brings to you . . .*

He had, I thought, my breath catching as I remembered his face in the summer evening light. *We* had, all of us. We'd gone from three to four in that crowded *taberna.* I'd seen Druisius watching us, intrigued, not understanding the words spoken, but seeing in faces and bodies and laughter the binding love. He'd chosen then to leave Casil to join us. "You were like a cohort," he'd told me, much later. "When men have fought together in battle, they are more than friends, yes?"

"Did you leave companions to come with us?" I'd asked.

He'd shrugged, of course. "They were long ago. In Qipërta and Odïrya. The men are scattered, those who live. My officers—one is dead. Maybe the other is too."

"What were their names?"

"Marcellus was the first. He died in Qipërta. He taught me the *cithar.*"

"And the other?"

He'd told me. "An engineer. We built a city. In Odïrya, yes? Oppelorium."

"Is he still there?"

A shake of his head. "No. He was sent to strengthen defences in the northwest, yes? After that," the shrug again, "I do not know."

But I did, now, sitting on my horse overlooking a town he'd built, and the villa he'd been given. Druise, I thought, will be pleased. I could see his grin. I urged the horse forward, my heart unexpectedly lighter.

Chapter 25

"MY STEWARD COULD HAVE BROUGHT ME THIS." A tone of mild curiosity, not annoyance. The man before me had the cropped hair of a soldier, white now, but tinged with a faded rust, the colour of the plain's dust. On his desk, beside a scatter of other papers and a wine cup, lay the letter meant for the fort's commanding officer.

I held out my military insignia. "May we speak privately?"

His hands were square, their backs blotched with brown. He turned the insignia over in blunt fingers, examining it. When he looked up, his voice was now distinctly curious. "Who are you?"

If I was right—and I was sure I was—I had the advantage.

"Lena, General of Ésparias," I told him. No flicker of recognition. "And you, I think are the Tarquin who built Oppelorium in Odïrya, and once had an aide named Druisius."

I watched as surprise slackened Tarquin's cheeks, etched with the spider-webs of red a life outdoors could cause. A slow smile followed. "Druisius! How do you know him?" He gestured to a chair. "Sit, please, General. Now, tell me."

His interest was palpable. "Druisius is an officer—a major—in the Ésparian guard," I said. "He was also my husband's closest friend, and is a valued and beloved part of our family."

Tarquin's smile at my first words faded. "Was?"

I explained, accepted the polite condolences. "And you say Druisius was his good friend? Was he a military man, then?"

"Not really. He was a diplomat. An advisor to Ésparias's leaders, and a teacher and historian." So few words to capture a life. Little more than the words carved on a stone at Wall's End. *As if all he was are those words on his memorial*, Sorley had said, in grief and anger. No, I told myself. Don't think about that.

Tarquin blinked. "I was about to say how surprising, but perhaps I shouldn't. I valued Druisius's mind; he was observant, and intelligent, if unschooled. Analytical, too. Marcellus thought the same, although it was not why he recruited him originally."

"You knew Marcellus?" Druise hadn't told me that, but then, he hadn't told me much at all.

"He was my closest friend." Tarquin reached for his cup of wine. "Druisius was his soldier-servant. Marcellus made me promise to take care of him if he was killed. He died in Qipërta in a Boranoi raid, and I honoured my promise. To my benefit."

"And Druisius's, surely. You taught him to build? He built baths for us, a few years after he came west."

Another smile. Tarquin, I decided, was truly pleased to have word of Druise. I guessed he'd cared for him, and not just for his friend's sake.

"Forgive me," my host said. "You have ridden a distance, I think, and I haven't offered refreshment." He rang for the steward. Another cup was brought. "You will stay the night, and as long as you would like, General," Tarquin added, as he poured the wine, refilling his own cup as well. "If your business east is not pressing."

The estate ran to the lake. I could walk its shore later, undisturbed and alone. "Thank you," I said. "A night, no more, but your hospitality is appreciated."

"A room will be prepared. And the baths are yours to use, of course. Now. I knew of the Empress's decision to send troops west, of course; that reached even my ears, although long after their deployment. But Druisius was a city guard by then. He wrote me a letter. It was the last time I heard from him. He had been assigned to guard travellers from the west who claimed to have walked across this plain, and seen ruins, and he thought I would want to know the story. But why did he join the western deployment?"

I thought only two men knew the answer to that question, and one of them was dead. The simplest reply was best. It was true, if incomplete. "For adventure, I think."

"But he stayed?" Half Tarquin's wine was gone, and I had barely sipped mine. There might be another reason for his flushed appearance, I thought.

"He is part of our family, as I said." Again, I chose the easiest explanation. "He is partnered with my closest friend. Sorley, his name is. A musician. He was with us in Casil, and music brought them together. We have lived together, the four of us and our children, for thirty years." I kept a smile on my lips, hiding the wave of regret that threatened to engulf me.

Surprise, and then a grin. I liked Tarquin's face, open and honest. "I thought—" He shook his head, slowly. "I thought that after Marcellus was killed Druisius had closed himself off from caring. And music! He played only when I asked, and I rarely did. Marcellus had taught him to play, you see." Before I could reply, he frowned, a question in his eyes. "Us? You said, 'he was with us in Casil'."

"We were the travellers Druisius guarded." I told Tarquin how Cillian had seen, in the long shadows of dawn, the parallel depressions that had been the ditches on either side of the ancient Casilani road. "Without that, I doubt we would have survived the journey."

"The water sources," Tarquin said, nodding. "If they had dried up, rebuilding the road would have been almost impossible. It was hard enough, in the unrelieved sun and the heat."

I was glad of the chance to change the subject. "You built all this?" I asked. "The roads, and the town, and the fort?"

He chuckled. "Not with my own hands. I supervised the work, and designed some of it. And the fort was simply rebuilt from the ruin you saw thirty years ago."

Dust and a whistling wind, the walls colonized by wildflowers and lizards. Deserted and forgotten.

Was that what a traveller would find here, centuries in the future?

"The road has its privations, even today," Tarquin said. "I imagine you'd appreciate the baths, and to change from your travelling clothes? Do that, and join me for the evening meal. We will eat on the terrace, if that suits you. And while you refresh yourself, I will write a letter to Druisius."

~

A half-moon hung in the eastern sky, the evening star bright beside it. The food had been excellent, duck with a fruit sauce accompanied by a salad dressed with sharp olive oil and a dark vinegar. Below us, the still lake reflected clouds and light. A late heron winged its slow way to the trees at the far end.

We had spoken further of Druisius, and then of the traces of the Eastern Empire that had remained in Ésparias. "Even Casil, for all its written records, forgot its past," Tarquin said. "When as a young officer I expressed a wish to look for the ruins I thought should be present in these lands, my superiors laughed at me." Did his voice hold a trace of bitterness? If so, it was replaced by triumph. "However, I was right."

"Do you wonder how long your works will stand?" I asked. A presumption, perhaps, but it was on my mind. "All that you have built?"

"If Casil falls?" he asked. "If there is no one with the skill to repair and maintain our work? I have seen what will happen. The sands of the plain will cover the roads and fill in the ditches. Mortar will crumble and walls fall. People will take stone away to use elsewhere."

A life's work, gone. "Doesn't that bother you?"

A smile again, and again I could only call it triumphant. "Not in the least. One temple I restored was still a sacred site, after all. Perhaps the people had forgotten to whom it was raised; they had certainly forgotten who built it, beyond uncertain legends. But it still evoked awe and wonder."

He filled his cup for at least the fifth time, his hand still steady. I shook my head when he raised the jug in an unspoken question, wanting a clear mind. I glanced out at the lake. Inside the town walls, torches burned in the grounds of the baths, and lantern-light flickered in the streets. The breeze carried the scent of flowers, some night-blooming shrub.

"Would you mind if I walked in the gardens later?" I asked. More stars were out, the sky darkening to cobalt.

"As you like. May I show you something first?"

I couldn't refuse. We returned to his workroom. From a box, he brought out a drawing. A memorial arch. The name on it was his own.

I studied the plan. Engraved on the stone would be his achievements: Oppelorium was there, as well as Hathusia. "Who will raise it?"

"Some of my men retired with me. My steward, for one. They will see to it." He rolled the drawing again and tied it. "Is this hubris?"

I told him what he wanted to hear. "I think not. You were the architect of all this and more. You deserve a place in history, Tarquin."

"Perhaps. Or perhaps history will speak only of the generals who conquered these lands, or of none of us, if—when—Casil falls. Memory and the written word are as fragile as glass. But stone will outlast all."

Was that true? Cillian's memorial stone might well stand long after those who could remember him were gone. But would it outlast his written works?

"Are you returning to Ésparias?" Tarquin asked, breaking my reverie.

"I plan to."

"Then may I entrust you with records? Copies of some of what I have written in my years here. Take them back to your scholars. They may be safer there." This time the smile held an ironic edge. "I am vain enough, it appears, to wish for more than one chance to be remembered."

~

The water had felt cold at first, I remembered, cold and silky against my skin, although in the heat of summer it shouldn't have been. But it must be fed by an underground spring; no stream had flowed into it, only out. The scrubby growth that had bordered it had been cleared, and near the water's edge a small open-sided structure, floored with blocks of marble, provided a place to sit and contemplate the lake.

I carried a lantern, at the insistence of the steward. Ladon paced at my side. I'd left him at the stables earlier; why I'd let him come with me now, I wasn't sure. Perhaps to have something to pretend I was talking to, were I overheard.

I set the lantern on the marble floor, where it could do no harm. I didn't need it. My night vision had always been good, and age had not changed that. And perhaps anyone looking out from the villa would think I sat there, under shelter.

Shelter. Of all the words I could have chosen . . . Tears threatened. I wasn't going to try to stop them, not here. I walked down to the water's edge, hearing the cluck of a disturbed water bird. Something splashed: perhaps a duck, perhaps a fish leaping to catch an insect. Stars uncountable glittered overhead, spilling like milk across the dome of the sky.

I followed the shore a little further. Then I sat, my back to the faint glow of the lantern. I closed my eyes for a moment. The scent of woodsmoke, of water plants, of the mud at the lake's edge: none had changed. If I lay back, would there be falling stars?

If I waited long enough, yes. *So much sky,* I had said. *So much space,* Cillian had replied, as we watched stars fall. He had known what I needed, that night and always: space and solitude, but also shelter.

As best I could, käresta.

"You know why I am here?" I asked aloud. The dog whined. "Lie down," I told it.

I do.

"I don't want to let you go."

No reply. I could see the patient, slightly questioning look, the one he gave a student as he waited while they thought out the error in what they'd just said.

"But I must, mustn't I?" My sight blurred, slow tears trickling.

Lena. You have a life to live.

"I don't know how." My fists clenched. "I don't know what to do without you." The wail turned to a sob, anger and bewilderment and fear surging. My breath rasped in my throat, caught. I couldn't fill my lungs. I gasped and gasped again, short, shallow bursts more sob than breath, tasting the salt of my tears.

A cold nose touched the hand I'd raised to my face. A whine, and then a heavy, warm body against mine, crowding in. "Ladon," I whispered. I put my arm around him, hugging him close. He put his muzzle up to my face to lick my cheek. His breath was foul. I coughed, and then I laughed. "You stink."

I stretched out on the warm earth. The dog put his head on my stomach. I stroked his head. A star fell, then another. The moon dropped lower in the west. Silence surrounded me, filled me, and with it a deep encompassing peace. A memory—two—came, merged. Words spoken on a night before a battle, and again just before he'd fallen asleep, never to wake. *Thà mi air a bheth beànnaichte.*

I too had been blessed. After a long time, I said his name again.

Käresta?

"What do I do about Sorley?"

The sensation of touch, so light on my hair. *Do you have to ask?*

I sat up, gently dislodging the dog. The eastern sky held a hint of light, a paler darkness. From somewhere in the garden, a bird began to sing. Another day was beginning.

My grief was far from gone. One night could not free me from its anguish. I would weep again, the waves of loss threatening to engulf me. But I would no longer fight its tides; I would let it flow and ebb, rise and fall. I could steer a course through these unknown waters now.

I looked up again at the stars, then out to their reflections on the calm surface of the lake. I touched the dog's head for strength, took a breath.

"Goodbye, my love," I said.

I expected no answer. But faintly, I heard a reply, its tone almost amused. *Not yet, käresta.* And then, reflective, touched by sorrow: *Not yet.*

Part III

Tho' much is taken, much abides.
Tennyson

Ulysses

Chapter 26

~Gwenna~

A MILD NAUSEA ASSAILED ME as I swung my legs over the side of the bed, preparing to begin my day. I sat still, considering. No flashes of light at the edge of my vision; no twinges of pain at either temple. The new moon had grown to a quarter, and then to half. It was nearly full now, and I still hadn't bled. And while I wasn't always regular, I was rarely this late.

Well. My impulsive decision not to drink anash while sharing my bed with Ruar—born, I knew, in hindsight—of anger at Lynthe, and in defiance of her demands, had left me with a consequence. Another child had been in my plans, but the timing was less than ideal. I rolled my eyes at my own folly.

But neither had I been convenient for my mother. She had gone into battle carrying me, and if she could do that, then I could deal with pregnancy and politics at the same time, surely. I wondered what she'd say, wherever she was. She should have reached Casil by now. Had she found Lynthe?

Lynthe. I knew what her reaction would be to a second child. But Druise would have been so pleased. Tears pricked my eyes. I sniffed, swallowed, and stood up. A constriction in my gut, and I hurried to the latrine, my hand over my mouth. Might as well get it over with. Not that there was much in my stomach to expel. I wiped my lips, rinsed my mouth with water, and stood again, waiting to see if leaving the area was wise.

Apulo usually knocked gently when he brought my morning drink, giving me a moment if I wasn't decent. This morning, the door opened after a single, perfunctory rap. "Gwenna?"

"What's wrong?" I returned to the bedroom, alarm tingling my spine.

"Sorley," he said. My breath caught. "He did not come home last night."

"Are you sure?" Of course he was. A stupid question. I tried to think. I'd been pleased at first when Sorley had begun to go out in the evenings. But both Apulo and Lairís had reported he was drinking too much, and I'd seen the same. The memory of the *fuisce* I'd smelt on him more than once made my stomach roil, but it also gave me a probable answer.

"Check with the stewards of all the commons," I said. "Discreetly, not that I need to tell you that. If they didn't see him, try the town."

"Lairís played at the senior commons last night. He was not there," Apulo reported. "I may need help, Gwenna. If he is ill, or—" He let the words trail off.

I thought, rapidly. "Lieutenant Ferand. Druisius trusted him." He'd been invaluable in finding Lairís, too. "Wait, and I will write a note." I went to my desk, scribbling a few words. I didn't waste time sealing it.

"I forgot to make your tea," Apulo said, taking the note from me.

"Someone else can do that." He nodded, and hurried away, not his usual calm self at all. He suspected something, I thought.

I rang for a ginger infusion. I drank it when the sick headaches plagued me, so it would cause no speculation. The routine of washing and dressing did nothing to allay my worry. Even Gwyllar's hugs and chatter over breakfast—bread for me, and little else—didn't help. As soon as I could, I crossed the courtyard to Lairís's room.

It had taken some time to find her, unsurprisingly. She'd been travelling among the villages, collecting songs. But a message left at an inn, with instructions to assist her in travelling to Wall's End as quickly as possible, had brought her back.

"I don't know what I can do," she'd said, when I told her why I'd requested her return. "But I'll try."

Lairís had seemed to bring Sorley out of himself a bit. She'd enlisted his help with the songs she'd collected, comparing them to ones he knew, or discussing variations of the same tune or words. I had gone to eat with them many evenings, staying to listen to the music Lairís coaxed from her uncle. But even I could see the almost-rote way he played or explained techniques to his niece. There was no passion left.

Most evenings, Sorley excused himself early, going either to his teaching room or the bedroom and closing the door. At first I'd left then too, but more often now I stayed to talk to Lairis, enjoying her stories of travel in Ésparias. "I spent the first twenty years of my life in northern Sorham," she'd said one evening. "Casilla was almost frightening."

"You should try Casil," I'd replied. "I was only eighteen." She'd crinkled her nose in recognition, and we'd laughed at our shared experience.

Another night, she'd convinced me to play a duet with her, ignoring my arguments that it had been years since I'd touched a *ladhar*.

"Your fingers will remember," she'd said, and she'd been right. Mostly. We'd laughed a lot then too at my mistakes; a companiable mirth, shared.

Lairís looked like Sorley, more than I'd expected from what I remembered of her as a small girl. Druise had teased his partner then, saying she must be his daughter because of her musical talent, apparent even at five. But now, her hair the same pale curls as Sorley's, her eyes the same blue, and his stocky frame translated into full curves, even Druisius might have seriously wondered who her father was. If Sorley had been this appealing as a young man, I'd found myself thinking, no wonder my father fell in love with him.

The thought had startled me. But waiting for her to open the door, I knew why now. With Gwyllar, once the nausea each morning had passed, the increase in my physical desire even in the early days of pregnancy had delighted Lynthe—and me. Just what I would do about that this time—well, probably what I'd been doing since Ruar had returned to Linrathe, I supposed. Gwenna the *Principe* of Ésparias did not have casual liaisons, even if Gwenna the woman wanted to.

There was no answer to my knock. Had she spent the night somewhere else?—but no, Apulo had spoken to her this morning. She was out looking for Sorley. I turned away, torn between doing the same and the work that awaited me.

I chose the work, simply because I could see no real way I could search for him unobtrusively. At my desk, I studied Daragh's report again, trying to concentrate. But I couldn't. I kept listening for footsteps outside my room, for Sorley's voice, for something. In a very few minutes, I would have to leave for the fort. I'd agreed to meet Talyn there, as I also had things to discuss with Muire.

Sorley's absence wasn't the only thing distracting me. I put a hand on my belly. A baby. I let my mind wander, thinking of the future. Were the child a boy, I'd name him for Druise. Druisar, maybe. And if a girl . . . Perhaps for my mother.

No. Were the baby a girl, there was only one choice. Piása. Kitten, in Linrathan, and what Druise had named me to his family in Casil, disguising my true identity. Piása. I liked it. Sorley would too. He'd been there that day; I'd been posing as his daughter.

A flash of anger at Sorley, mixed with fear, made me take a breath. Fear for what he might have done; anger that he was adding to our worries. But of all of us, I told myself, searching for understanding, hadn't he lost the most? Ésparias wasn't home. I'd been to Gundarstorp, seen how much he loved its hills and coves, heard him speak of his longing for it. But he'd loved my father more, my father and Druisius, and they were gone. And without my mother, who could have supported him—maybe, I thought, knowing the terms they had parted on—where could he find any solace here at Wall's End?

I exhaled, a long sigh, and gathered my papers. I had a country to consider. I touched my belly again, low down. This one would be born into a changing world, just as I had been. I had to do my best for her, and Gwyllar, and all the people of Ésparias. As my parents had—and they, I reminded myself firmly, had not been brought up to the task, trained and educated to lead. Do your job, I told myself. Do your job.

~

Both Talyn and Garia winced when I told them Sorley was missing. I felt I had to, to explain why I wasn't thinking as clearly as I should be. "He is in so much pain," Talyn said.

"I thought Lairís being here was helping." We were silent for a moment. "Shall we look at the troop deployments? I have some ideas."

We moved to a map of Ésparias, spread out over a large table and weighted at the corners.

"These"—Talyn pointed to two spots on the map—"are bridges that should be completed. Of all the construction, those are the ones that I feel should have priority."

"We also have the mines to consider." Ésparias's metal ore had almost all gone to Casil, except what we needed ourselves. While the miners themselves were mostly civilians, settlers and Ésparian-born alike, the skills needed to build and maintain the structures and equipment of the mines belonged to soldiers. This had been Casil's way, and the practice here too when we'd been an independent country. Why, though? Why couldn't we teach these skills to civilians as well?

"Do we need to keep all the mines open?" Garia asked.

Talyn straightened, a hand on her lower back "We need metal, to replenish weaponry." Much had gone east with the troops who'd volunteered.

"I'm meeting with Muire later," I said. "It's something we'd planned to discuss."

So many things we didn't know, and even with Daragh's assessment of what Varsland needed and their vision of future trade, they'd remain that way. Everything was only a guess at possibilities. My father would have told me to consider each potential move and what its outcome could be, and I was doing my best. But no one could see the consequences of every possible choice.

Not even him. Or, I thought, surprising myself, he'd have suggested to Sorley what to do after his death, and maybe even after Druise's.

"*Principe*?" Talyn. I blinked, realizing I was frowning.

"Sorry. Just a thought, but not about this." A lock of hair fell over my eyes. When I flicked it away, my arm brushed against my breast. Its tenderness surprised me, although it shouldn't have. Just the beginning of all the irritations and inconveniences of pregnancy. "Garia," I said, "will you give the general and me a moment, please?"

"Of course."

"What is it?" Talyn asked, once the door had closed.

"I have to tell someone. I'm pregnant."

A moment of surprise, and then she grinned. "Ruar? So—" She calculated. "Late winter?"

"All being well. Not a word, though, please, until the third month."

"Of course not. But you know the villa servants will notice." No blood cloths to be washed. The ginger tea in the mornings. I would have to ask for discretion.

"Gossip is not the same as an official announcement. My concern is that I, and by extension Ésparias, will be seen as weaker because of it. If we can keep it a secret for as long as possible, the weather will be unfavourable for an attack by sea."

"Until late autumn?" Talyn sounded sceptical.

"I didn't show with Gwyllar until nearly the sixth month."

"Gwyllar was your first. You may find it different this time. Will you tell Ruar?"

"Not yet." The old wisdom. Kira had told me, when I'd been pregnant with Gwyllar, that in the days of Partition no message had been sent from the woman to the father until after the first three months had passed, when it was reasonable to assume the baby would be carried to birth. I'd waited with Gwyllar, and I'd wait this time. Ruar understood.

Partition. Something about the concept wanted attention, but it was just beyond the reach of thought. A few villages still maintained the practice . . . but that wasn't it . . .

A sharp rap at the door. "Come!" Talyn called. I turned to see Apulo, his face creased by concern. Fear blossomed again.

"Sorley," he said. "We found him. He's in the infirmary now. You had better come, *Principe*."

~

"A bad beating," the physician said, her voice low. "From the bruises, I would say likely he was punched, and when he fell, was then kicked repeatedly. And by more than one man."

Sorley lay on the bed, not conscious. He'd been dosed with poppy, and the cuts and bruises washed and salved. "Will he be all right?"

The physician rocked a hand back and forth. "It is too early to tell. He has not passed water, and if it is very bloody, or there is other bleeding inside we cannot see, the prognosis is poor. If not, then it is good. Time will tell."

He must live, I thought. Please. "And his hand?" I glanced down at the bed. Sorley's right hand, lying outside the light blanket covering him, was bandaged, and underneath the bandage each finger was splinted.

"Deliberately smashed. By a booted foot; the marks of the hobnails were visible on the skin."

Beside me, Lairís made a horrified sound. If Sorley could not play . . . He could not lose his music on top of all else, or what was left for him?

"Will it heal?"

The physician gave me a level look. "If he lives, yes. He was lucky." Lucky? "The man who did this did not twist his foot, or smash it down repeatedly. The breaks are clean."

Apulo touched my arm. "Come. Let him rest. Lairís will stay with him."

He took me to a small room, empty except for shelves of medicines and a small desk and stool. "Sit, Gwenna." I did as he told me, but I had questions.

"Where did you find him?"

"In a yard behind a *taberna*, in part of the town Druisius sometimes frequented."

"Is there any chance this was done as a warning to me?"

"I don't think so. I think this attack had a different motive."

"Why?"

He hesitated. "Were you aware of Druisius' tastes? A liking for—" I held up a hand to stop him.

"Yes. The soldiers talk. Lynthe told me. This was a place he would have gone?"

"I believe so. And I think Sorley went there to find those—friends. Perhaps just to talk to them about Druisius. Perhaps . . ." He spread his hands, not finishing the thought, allowing me to draw my own conclusions.

Sorley, whose face showed every feeling, who cried so easily, and whose emotions soared and wept in his music, too. But he'd been like stone since Druise's death, as blank as the marble head of the Emperor that graced the governor's villa. I should have realized, should have done something more than just bringing Lairís to Wall's End.

Apulo reached over to a shelf, then handed me a square of cloth. I realized I was crying. "If he lives," Apulo said, "I will fix the hand. It can be done, in time and with work."

I blew my nose. "Thank you, Apulo."

"Do not blame yourself," he said gently. "I have tried to be a friend. To listen, if he wished to talk, or just to sit with him. But he did not respond. Lairís did better."

Perhaps, I thought, perhaps he did not trust himself with you. *Sorley and I, we have ways to deal with the anger.* Druise, so many years before, when Lianë had died. I hadn't understood then. I barely did now. But I knew a little of Apulo's history, of what had been done to him as a bath slave by men who had supposedly paid only for a massage. Sorley had known too.

Or perhaps he'd just been locked in his prison of grief and guilt. I truly hoped that was the reason. But what had sent him to the dark alleys of the town?

It didn't matter. What mattered was that he recovered. "Will you stay with him?" I asked Apulo.

"Of course. Between Lairís and me, one of us will be with him always. We have decided that already."

I wiped my cheeks. My eyes would be red, but I didn't care. Muire was an old friend. I stood, and wished I hadn't: a wave of dizziness made me sit again immediately.

"Gwenna?"

"It's all right." I stood up again, more slowly. "It's nothing, Apulo. Just—" He should hear it from me. "This is only for your ears. But the dizziness is natural. Gwyllar will have a brother or sister in the spring."

For a moment his brown eyes creased with pleasure. "How wonderful. A new life is what we need."

~

Muire, apprised of the reasons for my late arrival and my distraught appearance, was horrified. "A robbery, I assume?"

"I would think so." That would be what I would say. "If—when—he recovers enough to talk, we'll know more."

"The poor man."

"Yes." I paused. "Muire, we need to decide which mines to keep open. It affects our ability to assign soldiers to the coastal forts."

"And perhaps more guards in the town?" he said. "What happened to the lord Sorley might be a foretaste of greater lawlessness, with the patrols reduced, don't you think?"

He had a point. "That too," I said. "But Talyn says we need to replenish the weapons supply, as the troops who went east took much of the reserve, so we need metals for that, as well as what we spoke of before. Do you have the map?"

~

I went back to the infirmary later in the day. "He has passed some blood," Apulo told me, "but not an excessive amount. There is fever, but no more than the physician expects."

"Can I see him?"

Sorley was asleep, his face leached of colour except for the livid bruise on his jaw. A sheen of sweat gleamed on his brow. His hair was matted, and damp at the temples. Lairís sat by his bed. Her *ladhar* rested beside her, but she wasn't playing.

"If he wakes, tell him I was here?" I asked them both.

"I will," Apulo said. "And if there is a serious change, I will have you alerted. But you must take care of yourself, *Principe*. Let me take care of Sorley."

"Apulo." I tried to smile. "What would we do without you?"

"I prefer to think of it the other way," he said. "Where would I be, without your family?"

"Are you staying now?" Lairís asked Apulo. "If so, I will leave for a little time."

"Take your time," Apulo said. "I will sleep here tonight, and every night needed. But an hour or two to bathe and rest this evening would be welcomed, if you could return then."

Together we walked back to the villa, my bodyguards a few steps behind. Two guards, now. Lairís glanced back at them a time or two: although not a *scáeli* yet, she was used to travelling alone. "I feel as if I have failed him," she said quietly, half-way between the fort and the villa. She had her hood up against the inevitable rain. I barely heard her.

"So do I," I said, and then realized how that could be understood. "Not that you have failed him, but that I have," I added hastily. "You have done far more than I."

"He won't talk about Druisius at all."

"I noticed." I had got Sorley to talk a little about my father as a young man, reminiscing about their shared time at the *Ti'ach na Perras*, and one or two stories from Casil. But as soon as the story veered towards a time Druise would have been present, he would say no more.

"Come and have wine with me," I suggested. I didn't really feel like being alone. I'd seen Gwyllar earlier in his schoolroom, heard him say his alphabet and show me colours, and more of a three-year-old's company wasn't what I wanted.

Lairís glanced down at herself. "I'm not exactly clean." Dried mud splotched her legs, and, in places, her tunic. "I went straight to the infirmary when I heard Sorley had been found, and I've been there all day."

"So?" I said lightly. "We could take the wine to the baths."

"I like that idea." She smiled. "I was pleased to discover in my travels that all the villages have bathhouses, but I especially liked the ones where the water bubbles up from the ground already hot."

"Such as Tirvan."

"Yes, such as Tirvan. Their headwoman is your aunt, am I right?"

"My mother's younger sister, Kira." We passed through the villa gates and into its sheltered porch. "Did you find songs there?"

"A few. Mostly variations on ones I'd learned already." She gestured towards the wing where she slept. "I'll get clean clothes and meet you at the baths."

"And I'll have wine sent."

A woman would bring it, and pastries, the steward said, and did I want the wine warmed? I told him yes, and to add honey and spices. A few minutes later, I joined Lairís at the baths.

Built to be used only by myself and Lynthe, the rooms the baths occupied—and the pools themselves—weren't large. Beyond the small anteroom where we'd wash first, and where a marble table for massage stood, the hot pool sat in the middle of a floor patterned by tiles in varying shades of a reddish-brown. The walls were painted warm colours, without design. One alcove held a statue of the huntress.

Lairís's curves, I noted, were even more pleasing unclothed. Behave, I told myself, and sat a distance away, half-facing her. She'd pinned her pale curls up to keep them dry, and in the heat of the baths her skin was turning as pink as the dog roses of summer.

We accepted cups of wine. I told the server to leave the tray on the tiles of the floor where we could reach it, and dismissed her. She'd stay in the anteroom, close enough to hear if I called, not so close she could hear our conversation.

"Sorley won't talk about your mother, either," Lairís said abruptly. "Why is that? I thought they were close."

"They were." I sighed. "Sorley thought my mother should stay here to advise me; he said it was what my father would have expected. My mother disagreed, and so did Druise. He—Druise—said something then: 'Thirty years together, and now you fight over who knew him best?' That's mixed up in it somehow, I think."

I realized I was making an assumption, and one that was likely erroneous. "Lairís? Did you know my father and Sorley were not just friends?"

"Druisius told me. When I arrived, and saw how distraught Sorley was. So that I understood." I sensed no shock or disapproval. "But he will speak of Cillian, not just to you, but also to me when you are not there."

"He was prepared for my father's death," I said. "As much as he could be. He was almost always at his side, and perhaps they had said all they needed to each other. Druise died without warning." My fault . . .

"With things unsaid?" Lairís suggested. She gave me a faint smile. "A common theme in some of Linrathe's sadder songs."

"Or with words spoken that are now regretted? I think that's what happened between Sorley and my mother." I remembered something. "She did make a suggestion after my father died. She thought Sorley should go home to Gundarstorp to grieve, so he had his blood family around him."

"So did my father," Lairís said. "He tried to convince Sorley of that at your father's burial, with Lena arguing for it, but Sorley would not hear of it."

"Why not?"

She gave me a rueful look. "Druisius. He wouldn't go."

"And Druise wouldn't go because he wouldn't leave me, or maybe Gwyllar," I said, understanding slowly dawning. "Gods, Lairís, I'm surprised he doesn't hate me."

"He doesn't. Don't worry about that." She slid a little further into the water, resting her arms on the edge of the pool and letting her body float. I did my best to keep my eyes on her face. "But going home—I think he should, Gwenna. When he's well enough."

"But how do we convince him?"

"We can't," she said. "But the *Teannasach* can order him home."

~

Late that evening, I sat at my desk to write to my aunt Kira. I'd appreciated her presence at Gwyllar's birth, even knowing the physicians of the fort and the midwives of Berge were perfectly competent. I'd just liked having my mother's sister with me, the all-too-rare reminder I had ties to Ésparias that weren't from my father.

I didn't have too many worries about carrying this baby past the first months, but I was under a greater strain than I had been with Gwyllar, and asking Kira's advice made me feel like I was doing my best for him or her. Her, I thought, although I knew I couldn't really know. But my mother had been convinced I was a girl, right from her first realization she was pregnant, and she'd been correct. Piása. It felt right.

I wanted, too, to give Kira plenty of time to prepare to be away from Tirvan for a few weeks. As the head of its council, she had decisions to make on a regular basis, and that responsibility would need to be handed over to someone else—one of the other council leaders. Just as I would have to designate someone to be, effectively, my regent, for the hours of labour and recovery. It had been my father, during Gwyllar's birth.

Should I have given the role to Lynthe? Would it have changed anything? Or would it have simply increased her desire for what she saw as power? I would ask her, when my mother brought her back.

I finished the letter and sealed it. It would go southward as soon as a messenger was travelling that way. It wasn't urgent. I didn't move from my desk, though. Nights, my rooms felt empty, echoing, and the bed cold. Even though it really wasn't.

I didn't miss the fights with Lynthe. I missed company: jokes and laughter and just hearing her breathing if I woke in the night. I missed lovemaking, too. I'd overlooked the occasional barbs, and her hot temper, but they'd grown worse in the last few years. Since Gwyllar, or, were I entirely honest, since I began the liaison with Ruar to conceive my heir.

Jealousy, unfounded. Ruar was a friend, much as Muire was, and a man whose experience in leadership I valued. Did jealousies and competition exist among the village council leaders, or among women who wished to be elected to the positions? Probably. People were the same everywhere. But the system used in the villages had worked for generations. I'd seen it in action the summer I'd spent at Tirvan: the council advising, the women—and men now too—voting, at least on the issues outside of Casilani governance. My governance, now.

My governance. I sat back. In all the planning of how to create the western alliance after Casil's withdrawal, we'd never really talked about how I should govern. Casil had brought an organized, efficient system of administration to Ésparias, and we'd developed a parallel one to ensure we had a voice in how our country was governed: our prerogative as a royal province.

But no more than thirty years past, Ésparias had had an elected emperor whose influence on the women's villages was minimal, except to set taxes and food levies. Nor had the women had any say in how the military was ordered and governed. My grandfather had wanted to alter that, had planned for an assembly of the headwomen of the villages to discuss and debate a new way of life. It had never happened. Three wars in quick succession—Leste, Linrathe and finally Varsland—had forced change. And then Eudekia had imposed a hereditary leadership.

I got up to pace. How much had my father's respect for Casilani thought and order colour his thinking about Ésparias's model of governance? He'd been part of Linrathe's since he was eighteen, as a *toscaire* serving as a conduit of the voices of the people to its hereditary leader, gathering their thoughts on the *Teannasach*'s plans and ideas. We had no equivalent role, not formally. In my brief time as a junior trade envoy, I'd taken notice of taxes or food levies to the villages, spoken with the headwomen, informed my superiors of their reactions and suggestions. But I'd been telling the villages what would happen, as the men and women who did that job now were. In Linrathe, the *toscairen* asked for reactions and suggestions *before* Ruar decided on a course of action.

North of the Wall, the voices who felt I should not be *Principe*, or should abdicate in favour of Constyn, would be heard; not judged, not condemned, but listened to. Not without argument, for it was the *toscaire*'s role to present all sides of an issue, both to the people and to the *Teannasach*. But men and women could say what they liked to a *toscaire*, short of direct threats, without fear of reprisal. Ruar had no secret network of informers, because he didn't need one.

I returned to my desk to begin another letter. I had two reasons now to ask Ruar to come to Wall's End.

Chapter 27

RUAR ARRIVED QUICKLY; SO QUICKLY, I thought he must have left the same day the messenger arrived at Dun Ceànnar. I was at the infirmary when he strode in, his hair plastered to his forehead by the rain, his clothes sodden.

Sorley and I had been talking, but he'd drifted back into sleep a little while earlier. He would live, the physician had declared several days before, but he was in considerable pain. Poppy helped, but he couldn't stay awake for very long. Which, the doctor had said, was all to the good. Sleep helped healing.

Ruar stopped just inside the door, looking down at Sorley. His eyes flicked to me, a question in them.

"He's improving." Physically, at least. I kept my voice low. "Another day or two and he can be moved to the villa."

Relief swept over Ruar's face. "I was so worried," he said.

"So was I," I said. "I still am. We must talk, Ruar. I need your help. He should go home to Gundarstorp, but he refuses to leave Wall's End."

"I have some thoughts on that. Your letter said his niece is here now too?"

"Yes. Lairís. She's just gone for some rest." I looked at the still figure in the bed. "Sorley will sleep now for some hours. Go and bathe and change—your usual rooms are ready—and come to the villa for the evening meal. Apulo will be with Sorley, and you and I and Lairís can talk."

Another glance at Sorley, and a nod. "I will." His face softened. He held out a hand. I rose to take it. Avoiding his wet cloak, I kissed his cheek, feeling the comfort of his hand on my shoulder.

"How are you, *leannan*? I am so sorry about Druisius."

"I miss him." Terribly. "But otherwise, I'm well." And carrying our child, I thought. But that was not for now, or even for this visit. Ruar's hand lingered, fingers playing with a loose strand of hair. Where would he expect to sleep tonight?

A delicate conversation to be had later. It wouldn't be with me. Because I, newly pregnant, beset by grief and with worries personal and political, uncertain of the future, was falling in love with Lairís.

Not that I had said or done anything to suggest my feelings. She was an adult, and had travelled to teach and gather songs for two years, both in Linrathe and Ésparias, but I had no idea of her own inclinations. And even if she shared her bed with women, what would she think if I admitted my attraction? She knew I had been partnered with Lynthe and had asked once where she was. Lairís's concern for me when I said she'd gone east with the troops had seemed genuine.

Would she think I was only looking for a casual encounter? From what Sorley had told me over the years, that wasn't unusual where either *scáeli'en* or *toscairen* were concerned. Even my father in his younger days, as unbelievable to me as that was. And perhaps if that was all I wanted . . .

But it wasn't. I was nearly sure of that.

"Come early," I said now to Ruar, "so Gwyllar is still awake."

~

"Pat'a!" Gwyllar ran over to hug his father's legs. Ruar picked him up.

"Hello, little Bear."

I'd hoped Gwyllar would recognize Ruar. It hadn't been that long since he'd seen him, and he'd asked about him once or twice. I'd emphasized to our son that his father would return; when he asked about Druise, which broke my heart every time, I'd tried to be equally clear that he was gone forever. But what did a three-year-old understand?

I left them together, going to ensure the dining room was warm—an excuse to compose myself. I was ridiculously nervous about being with both Lairís and Ruar. Had there been a fourth person to invite, I probably would have. But we were meeting to discuss Sorley, and that meant just us three.

Apulo. Why hadn't I invited Apulo? He had known Sorley for longer than I'd been alive. I could do that now, and delay the meal until he arrived. Now Sorley was out of danger, he could be left alone. I called for the steward and told him what I wanted. "Placate the cook," I added. I hoped whatever he'd planned wouldn't be ruined by a delay. I'd go to praise him—or apologize—myself later.

"I was told you were here." Lairís came in, pulling a scarf from her hair. She'd changed from when I'd seen her earlier into a tunic of a soft blue, matching her eyes. Finely worked embroidery in shades of gold edged it at neck and hem and sleeves. Honouring her *Teannasach*. She looked lovely.

"Ruar is with Gwyllar." I hesitated. "That's a lovely tunic."

"Isn't it?" She looked down at herself. "Maj did the embroidery. She dyed the wool, too."

"I had no idea she was so talented."

"She tried to teach me when I was little. But all I wanted was the little *ladhar* Sorley made for me." She laughed. "Of course, I had no idea what an honour that instrument was. The head of the *scáeli'en* council, crafting a quarter-sized *ladhar* for a child? He was just my uncle."

"Maj sings, doesn't she?" I remembered a wet day at Gundarstorp, all of us in the hall, the women singing as they worked. I'd played Sorley's *ladhar*; he'd been doing accounts with his brother.

"Yes. As my mother does, and she plays the *ladhar*, too. My first lessons were from her. Music matters at Gundarstorp."

"All the more reason for Sorley to go home," Ruar said from the door. "Hello, Lairís."

"*Teannasach*." She did not kneel. Ruar led his people, but he wasn't given undue veneration. Only at the oath-giving, done once at his acclamation to the role, and then for new landholders at the yearly council. Lairís would kneel to him only to give that oath as a *scáeli*, when she had passed her exams.

"I've asked Apulo to join us," I told them, gesturing that we should sit.

"Then until he does, let me say this to the two of you." Ruar accepted the cup of wine I handed him. I'd dismissed the servants; this was a private conversation. "Am I right in thinking you wish me to compel Sorley to return to Gundarstorp?"

"You are," Lairís said. "He cannot refuse you, can he?"

"He could have, once," Ruar said. "But I freed him from his *toscaire's* oath long ago, although I may remind him of its words. Because it may mean more, in the end."

"Why?" I didn't know what the *toscaire's* oath said, not in detail. Only the part my father had broken.

"For two reasons. If he baulks at going home, I could remind him of the years I ignored his violation of it. I am glad no situation arose where he had to choose between his loyalty to Linrathe and"—he smiled, to show the words held no reproach—"the foreign prince he loved. He always managed to find a way to honour both fidelities."

"My father was barely a foreign prince," I protested.

"Barely," Ruar agreed. "Still, it could have been argued, had there been a faction in Linrathe who wished to. But that is not what I would remind Sorley of, but the last part of the oath. He swore his loyalty to the land beneath his feet. Words, but words matter, especially to *scáeli'en*, and for Sorley, there is a great and abiding truth in them, beyond simply the oath."

"He told me that once," I said. "That he heard Gundarstorp calling to him, always. There was a word he used, but I don't remember it."

"*Cianalas*," Ruar said. "The land pulls you to it, crying for your return. I felt it, the time I spent in Casil. Linrathe wanted me home." He took a long drink. "Do you know our stories of the seljies, the seal-folk, Gwenna?"

"Isa used to tell me about them, when I was small," I said. "People who were sometimes seals, or seals who could become people. I always thought they were sad stories."

"Seljies belong to the sea, and the wild shore," Lairís said, and I heard the cadences of the *scáeli* in her voice. "But sometimes they fall in love with a man, and so they shed their skin of soft fur and take on the guise of a human. But they hide that skin, carefully, secretly, because one day they might want to return to the wild, their true home.

"And all the while with their love, they hear the waves and the seabirds crying, and their longing is great. For some, too great, and so they return to the sea, leaving behind a grieving man. But for some the love is greater, and so they abide, and count the cost worth the days with their mortal man. But when the man dies, as all mortals must, the seljie goes back to the shore where their skin of fur is hidden, and dons it, and slips again into the waves."

"Sorley is like the seal-folk," Ruar said. "He too was torn between who he loved and his truest self, which belongs to the wild shore. But you can hear his longing for Gundarstorp in his music. It holds the rhythm of the waves, the cry of the curlew, the splash of a stream. Lairís, if you will play tomorrow, I will speak of Gundarstorp, of Sorham, and perhaps I won't need to send him home. Perhaps our seljie will choose to seek his hidden skin himself."

For all we knew of each other's bodies and their responses to lips and hands, I had never heard Ruar speak this way, from his own heart. The closest was his expressed delight in Gwyllar, the first time he'd seen his new son. I could have loved you, I thought, had I seen this in you before.

"What would you have me play?" Lairís asked.

"*An dithës braithréan.* Has not Roghan always wanted him to come home?"

"Won't he know what you are doing?" I asked, shaking off the mood. "I've heard him speak of how a *scáeli* can manipulate emotion through music, helping to convince people of a cause."

"Perhaps. Probably," Ruar admitted. "But maybe it will be all he needs to do what his heart is already telling him."

I thought of what Sorley and I had talked of earlier today, of secrets kept and words unspoken. There would never be answers. But if he was to make peace with that, I didn't think it could be here. "I hope so," I said.

Apulo joined us a few minutes later. He was comfortable with Ruar, knowing him as both a student of the *Ti'ach* and Linrathe's *Teannasach*, and now as Gwyllar's father. And that of the baby I carried, I thought suddenly. Would he let that slip, assuming Ruar knew?

Not in Lairís's presence, I reassured myself. There were few people in this world as discreet as Apulo. "How is he?" I asked.

"Perhaps a bit more comfortable. I have assured him his hand will heal, and that with time and the appropriate exercises he will play well again." Apulo accepted the wine I offered, and took a seat.

"Shall we eat now?" I asked. "Once the food is brought, we can continue our discussion."

The food took a little time to arrive, so clearly the cook had waited to prepare it. The fish, baked with herbs and wrapped in leaves to keep it moist, was delicious. The steward brought a different wine to accompany it, paler and only slightly sweetened. I ate lightly and watered my wine well; I'd never suffered from evening nausea, but this wasn't a time to find out that I did with this baby.

The fish was followed by lamb, redolent of rosemary and garlic. The cook had remembered this was Ruar's favourite dish. Not that I'd said who was to be at this dinner, but the servants had their own conduits of information. When that course was cleared and the fruit and pastries brought, I told the servants to withdraw.

"Tomorrow, the physician says," Apulo said, responding to my question about when Sorley could return to recover in his own rooms.

"And to travel?" Ruar asked.

"To ride? A month, at least."

"What if it was by ship?"

"A week, if he continues to improve. And if I went with him." Apulo ate a small pastry, neatly. "How long a voyage would it be, *Teannasach*?"

"A week, I should think. Perhaps more, if the weather is poor. You would go with him? I thought Lairís would."

I started to protest, then stopped myself, rapidly. But Ruar cocked his head. "You disagree, Gwenna?"

"He will need nursing," I said, the first reasonable objection I could think of.

"More than nursing," Apulo said. "If his hand is to recover, he will need specific exercises. They will hurt at first, and later it would be easy to overdo them, and cause new damage. I—" He wiped crumbs from his fingers. "I believe Cillian would have asked me to do this for Sorley. May I have your permission to accompany him, Gwenna?"

"You don't need it," I said. "You are free to do what you want. But you haven't even asked to where."

There were times when the looks Apulo gave me reminded me that he'd changed my diapers. This was one of them. "Gundarstorp," he said. "Why else would the *Teannasach* be asking these questions?"

"Well," Lairís said, "this is assuming we can convince him. But if we do, Apulo, take your warmest clothes. It is cold there, and dark in the winter. You will need to be prepared for that, and for long days of stories and songs and games." She grinned. "And you will have both stories and songs no one has heard a hundred times before, so you will be very welcome." She pushed back her chair. "I'll go to see Sorley, and then give some thought to music, if *An dithës braithréan* is not sufficient. And thank you, Apulo. I was not quite ready to leave Wall's End, although I would have had I needed to, of course."

We bade her good night. Apulo too excused himself a few minutes later, leaving me and Ruar alone. A blackbird sang in the dusk. Ruar reached for the wine jug. I shook my head at the offer. He poured himself half a cup, added water. "Have you heard from your mother?"

"No. The last messages to the governor spoke of turmoil and uncertainty, so letters might not reach us—or the ones I sent reach Casil. It's another worry."

"To add to all the others you carry, *leannan*."

The softness in his voice disturbed me. There would be a certain comfort in his presence in my bed, for the warmth and strength of him as much as the pleasure. But Lairís had caught my eye when she'd said she was not ready to leave Wall's End.

"Ruar." I licked lips suddenly dry. "You are welcome at the villa at any time to see Gwyllar, and to dine. But I will sleep alone."

Just a tiny tightening around his eyes. "May I ask why?"

I could not speak of what I hoped, what I had read into a glance and maybe the smallest of smiles. Perhaps it was only my own wishful thinking. I would risk another reason, although wisdom said I shouldn't. "Worries are not all I carry," I said. "If all is well, I—we—will have another child next year."

Delight took all traces of confusion away. "Well." He smiled, broadly. "I hope you are equally pleased."

I laughed. "I am. I would not have told you so soon, but, as you are here . . ." I spread my hands. "I hope I have not tempted the fates."

He sobered. "You will let me know, if—?"

"Of course. But as things go as they should, he or she will be born in the late winter. Near my own birthday, I should think."

"Perhaps," he said, smiling again, "it will be a daughter this time. I have three sons."

"If it is, I want to call her Piása."

"For Druisius." I'd known he'd understand. He'd heard Druise call me Kitten often enough. "I like that."

I touched his hand. "You are a good friend, Ruar, and a good father." It was what I had asked him to be, when I'd first suggested we might have a child together.

"I do my best." He rose and bent to kiss my forehead. "Good night, Gwenna."

Chapter 28

THE STRETCHER-BEARERS WERE EXPERIENCED, but even so, by the time Sorley was in his own bed at the village the next day, he was in considerable pain. The physician prescribed more poppy, and told us to leave Sorley to sleep. Lairís stayed with him to quietly play. "Tunes that will make him yearn for home," she said.

"Sorley was not the only reason I asked you here," I told Ruar. "I have no tasks this morning that cannot wait. Perhaps we could talk?"

A thin sunshine penetrated the light layer of clouds today; we could sit in the courtyard, I decided. The fountain's splash would muffle our words, and we were close if Apulo or Lairís thought we were needed. I sent a servant for cushions—the seats were damp—and gave instructions we weren't to be disturbed.

"Are you comfortable?"

"I am. Ruar, don't fuss." He hadn't been in Ésparias for my first pregnancy; I'd informed him by letter, and again when Gwyllar was born.

He gave me an abashed smile. "I'll try. What are we talking about?"

"*Toscairen.* Do you know their history?"

"In what way?"

"To have emissaries who bring your ideas to the people, and the people's ideas to you, without judgement, is unusual. Surely you see that, when compared to how Casil functioned, or even Ésparias."

"It is not entirely without judgement," Ruar said, "but the judgement is the *toscaire*'s. They are meant to be neutral, to gather information and report it. But they can refuse to deliver a message, or counsel the sender—whether that is me or a shepherd met on their travels—that the ideas they have been asked to present are not best for Linrathe."

"Does that happen?"

"The refusal, no. The counsel, with some frequency, both to me and to landholders or perhaps even that theoretical shepherd. When I proposed to marry Helvi, the *toscairen* took that idea to the *torps*, for discussion at the yearly council, and then told me the reactions. It meant I was prepared for the objections that were presented, and could counter them."

"What if you hadn't been able to? Or if the majority of landholders had objected?"

"It was unlikely, because she brought Sorham back to us. But had that not been part of the marriage settlement, and there had been great opposition—" He made a hissing sound through his teeth. "I am not sure. I lead Linrathe through the will of the people, through their choice to swear fealty to me, and I have been lucky, because that fealty has been given by all who make that choice." His voice became harder. "But that has not always been so. At fourteen, with Sorley beside me, I fought my own people because of what Lorcann, who called himself *Teannasach*, did by siding with Fritjof. I have no wish to do that again, ever, and so I would listen carefully, and choose carefully, if something I proposed created many objections."

All I'd had to do at fourteen was accept who I was. And who my father was, and had been; not his titles, but the man behind them. Flawed, human, capable of mistakes, even betrayal. Like Lynthe. Or like the man with me, were her accusations correct.

I could not believe that. Or think about it, just now. A new idea had gripped me. "Ruar, do you think the idea of an advisor who spoke for the people, presented their concerns, might have come from the Eastern Empire hundreds of years ago? The way the men of the army electing the Emperor, rather than having a hereditary line, might have reflected the days when Casil too was led by chosen representatives?"

"I have wondered that, and debated it with Cillian more than once," Ruar said. "The election of an Emperor here seems clearer. The role of *toscaire*? I'm not sure. What is your interest in this, Gwenna?"

I needed to tread carefully. Ruar should not know what I was thinking before my own advisory council. "I'm trying to decide how to govern," I said. "How to know what the people of Ésparias want, or dislike, or would change. The army is one thing: other than minor adjustments in the sizes of cohorts and the titles of officers, it really has gone on much as it did before Casil came. But I do not head the army the way the last Emperor did. And I have no history—no recent history—to guide how I might balance the independence of the villages and the farms against my leadership." I'd said too much, and from Ruar's expression I guessed he thought the same.

"This is a discussion for your advisory council," he said, "not for me. I cannot be seen to interfere in Ésparian politics."

"I needed to understand Linrathe's system better. I would have asked Sorley, but it wasn't possible. And," I said, suddenly exasperated, "it was your suggestion I consider settlers from Varsland. If that isn't interfering, I don't know what is."

"For Ésparias, it is a suggestion only," he said quietly. "But do we not also have to consider the western alliance?"

Of course we did. And it was getting harder and harder for me to separate my two roles. "How do you do this?" I demanded. "How are you *Teannasach*," I spread my arms, "and more?"

He didn't laugh, thankfully. Or give me a pitying look. "It is more difficult now," he admitted. "Without what Lena called Cillian's directing mind. When I was undecided, when I saw a conflict between the two responsibilities, it was his advice I sought."

"There is only us now." The hard and painful truth. "Except I think that cannot continue for much longer. I am expanding my advisory council, Ruar, and the new members must be told." I had made up my mind, it seemed. "I can't do this without their support."

He nodded, surprising me. "I see that. I have had others beyond my family for almost all the years we have planned this: Sorley, of course, but his brother too, one or two more. It has been easier for me, because of our long ties with Varsland. Tell me, Gwenna, is there anyone among the Marai-fathered you could bring into your council?"

My instinctive, gut reaction was 'No!'—but why not? My cousin Teárdh was Marai-fathered, and I'd never thought less of him because of it. But he was a fisherman and a boatbuilder, not someone suitable for my council. But perhaps in Casilla, or even among the officers of the army? "Maybe," I said, "but perhaps more easily acceptable would be a headwoman or a council leader who bore a child to the Marai." Like Kira?

Even with the cushion, the stone bench was beginning to feel cold. "Let's walk," I said. The clouds had thinned even further, and the day was almost warm. "Gwyllar and his nursemaid should be on the way back from the fort. We could go to meet them."

Surprisingly, the tutor was with Gwyllar and his nursemaid, and so was Lairís. Or rather, the tutor walked beside Lairís, talking animatedly to her, a few steps behind Gwyllar's guards.

"Matra!" Gwyllar, all of a sudden, could say the word properly. He ran up to us, but it was to Ruar that he held up his arms. His father swung him onto his shoulders.

"Ruar, this is Gwyllar's tutor." I made the introductions. The two men fell into step, discussing Gwyllar's progress in his lessons. I joined Lairís.

"Apulo needed more salve, and I wanted a walk," she told me, although I hadn't asked. "I met the others at the door to Muire's house." She dropped her voice. "And suddenly the tutor decided he needed to stretch his legs on this sunny day."

"He seemed rather interested in talking to you." I kept my voice light.

"Asking about the *Ti'ach* where I was educated, and comparing it to his," she said. "With one or two questions about teaching music to very young students. I think he was hoping I would volunteer to give a lesson or two."

"Did you?"

"No. I think his interest is not in how I teach." She rolled her eyes a little, smiling. "And I have no intention of encouraging any other attention he may wish to give me." We walked a step or two. "Surely you know that, Gwenna?"

I could feel the pulse of my heart. "Should I?"

"I had hoped," she said, very softly. "But—Ruar? Am I wrong?"

"He is Gwyllar's father," I said, equally quietly, "and I am—fond—of him. But we live separate lives."

Lairís moved a little closer, so that her free hand brushed mine. "As a *scáeli* must live her own, too. But I am not one yet, and if Sorley returns to Gundarstorp, maybe I could take responsibility for some of his teaching duties here for a while."

"Perhaps we could discuss this later? Over supper?" Excitement rippled through me. I found it hard not to smile too broadly.

"I would like that," Lairís said. "Very much."

~

Neither of us ate much, the promise of the evening too much in both our minds, I supposed. But Lairís had questions, fair ones. "Would you like me to stay at Wall's End for a while?" was the first.

"Yes. But there is something you should know, before you decide."

She studied me. "May I ask my second question? It may be related."

"Go ahead."

"Lynthe?"

I shook my head. "That's over. She will face judgement, on a charge of treason. But even without that—" I told her about Lynthe's threat against Gwyllar. "Whatever she claims as her reasons for taking Constyn east, I could never trust her again."

"I'm sorry."

"I wonder sometimes if I ever knew her." For a moment, I remembered Sorley saying the same to me the day before about Druisius, his words anguished.

"What do you need to tell me?" Lairís asked.

"I'm pregnant. The baby will be born early next year. It's Ruar's, of course."

Her smile was definitely genuine. "How wonderful! I love babies and little children. I'd like to get to know Gwyllar better."

The warmth spreading inside me wasn't from the wine. "I'd like that too." There was an obvious question. "Would you have your own, some day?"

"It's unlikely." She stopped, considering. "Maybe I shouldn't say that. It would be impossible at home, because women who are *scáeli'en* cannot marry in Linrathe. But it would be possible if I lived primarily in Ésparias, wouldn't it?"

"Definitely," I assured her. I grinned, joy bubbling. "Perhaps the tutor's hopes are not so far-fetched?"

She laughed, throwing her head back. "Only if he's prepared to wait for several years. Although—" She pretended to consider. "He is rather sweet, like a half-grown puppy."

"Are you planning to make me wait several years too?" Desire was pushing restraint away.

"No," she said. She took a deep drink of wine, and slid her chair back. "Not at all. Not even several minutes. Unless—" She raised an eyebrow. "You think it wise?"

"Wisdom," I said, rising to hold out a hand, "has its place. But not tonight."

~

She was curved and soft, and a mix of confident and cautious. "Do you like this?" she asked, "and this?" Questions both endearing and exciting. Our lips and hands and tongues explored and teased, giving and taking, until we both lay panting, damp with sweat, satisfied and languorous. Lairís turned to fit her back against me, her breathing slowing. Sleep was beckoning.

"Stay with me," I murmured. The guards would know, but I didn't care.

"For tonight," Lairís said, the words barely audible, slurred with sleep.

For more than tonight, I hoped, but for now, it was enough.

Chapter 29

I WENT TO SEE SORLEY THE NEXT MORNING, after breakfasting with Lairís and Gwyllar. Lairís seemed truly interested in my son, telling him a story that had him so enthralled he had to be reminded to eat.

"I'd like to see Sorley alone," I told her, "before we join forces to convince him to go home."

"An hour?"

"Or a bit less."

"I'll go and find the *Teannasach*, then, and go over our plan again with him." We were standing in the corridor outside Gwyllar's nursery. His guards were only a few paces away. I decided I didn't care, and pulled Lairís close for a kiss. She felt so good in my arms. Or maybe I felt peaceful in hers. Either way, I crossed the courtyard smiling.

"He's awake," Apulo said to me, "and he's eaten a bit. But—" He shook his head. "There's no light in his eyes. No hope, I would say."

I saw what Apulo meant. Sorley lay in his bed, his injured hand outside the blanket. The shutters were open to a light breeze, and the room smelt of lavender. Sorley's face was slack, his eyes dull, but there was a little colour in his cheeks that was not the flush of fever. I pulled a stool close.

"How are you?"

"Gwenna." His voice was listless. He frowned. "Is Ruar here? I thought I heard his voice."

"He is. Not right here at this moment, but he'll come to see you later."

"Why?"

"Why is he here?" *No hope*, Apulo had said. "We have some things to talk about."

Sorley nodded, a brief movement. "I wish Lena were here," he said abruptly. "I miss her. But—" He swallowed. "I said terrible things to her,

Gwenna. Things I didn't mean. So I've lost her too. Lost them all." Tears pooled in his eyes.

"She'll come home. And she'll understand," I soothed. He wasn't listening.

"Not that I ever knew Druise. Not really. He had so many secrets." The tears spilled over, running down the sides of his face. He ignored them. "And what he said to me—what did that mean, Gwenna? Blue eyes?"

I had wondered the same, and I thought I knew. Or at least I had an answer, one that, if Sorley believed it, might help ease his pain. "How many songs," I asked gently, "start with the colour of a beloved's eyes?" Even the one Sorley had written for my father.

A breathed 'oh'. Then, "Do you think so?"

"I do." I hesitated, not sure if I should tell him what had come to my mind. "When we were in Casil, I challenged Druise. He wanted to stay with me, if I had married Alekos, to guard me. I said he couldn't leave you, that he loved you." I was being selective with the truth, but it was what Sorley needed.

"But he wouldn't say so," Sorley said, flatly.

"He said 'maybe'. And we know what that meant, from Druise."

Sorley's eyes closed, but his lips curved upward into a smile before his face crumpled. I touched his arm, very lightly. "Not just Druise," I said over his sobs, "and not just my father. I love you. My mother loves you. And so does your brother, and all his family."

"He told me to come home," Sorley said, his voice barely over a whisper. "And to bring Druise. That he'd find a place for us."

I hadn't known that. It told me, even more than Roghan's appearance at my father's burial, how much he loved his brother.

"I have something to tell you," I said. "An idea. One that involved Druise, in a way. Will you listen, and give me your honest opinion? No one but you can really advise me on this."

He nodded. I told him about Valle, and the way messages from Casil had been sent. And then what it had led me to consider. "Could it work? Would Marius do this?"

"Almost certainly," he said. "What did Druise say? Lives must go on, and ways to make a living, too. There is sense in this idea, both for us and for Marius's business."

"I liked him," I said, "that one time we met. A good man."

Sorley had closed his eyes again. I heard movement at the door, and looked up to see Lairís, *ladhar* in hand. She raised her brows in question. I nodded. Taking a seat, she began to play, a song I recognized but couldn't name. She didn't sing, just let the music fill the room. Sorley lay still. I thought he'd fallen asleep again.

When Ruar arrived I held one finger to my lips. But Sorley must have heard his footfall, because he opened his eyes, then tried to push himself up a bit. Pain contorted his face.

"Don't even think of it," Ruar said. "I am told you will live to play again." He bent to kiss Sorley, the traditional greeting of Linrathan men.

"*Teannasach.* You did not come because of me, I hope." Sorley's voice was stronger: he was making an effort.

"No," I said, to forestall Ruar. "He came because I asked him to. We had things to discuss. I told you."

"And tomorrow I will go home." Ruar picked up a stool and placed it on the opposite side of Sorley's bed. "For while I have both good friends and a son here, I have no liking for forts. Although they are better, I suppose, than cities."

Sorley smiled. "You hated Casil."

"With both heart and mind. I want streams running down hillsides amongst the heather and bracken, and seabirds overhead in the clean air, not fountains and pavement and kites over a stinking river." Lairís still played quietly. I heard the tune change to one I did know: *An dithës braithréan.*

Sorley's face changed, emotions I couldn't identify flickering over it. Surprise, relief, fear? They didn't make sense. Then, something that looked like acceptance.

"I may," he said quietly, "be losing my faculties, but I was playing music to influence men's choices when you were just fourteen, Ruar. I know what you are doing, you and my niece."

"Will you not be persuaded?"

"And if I am not, will you order me to Gundarstorp?"

"Have I ever commanded you to do anything, *mo charaidh gràhadh*?"

"Only once," Sorley said.

"The choice is yours," Ruar answered gently. "Think about it. You cannot travel yet, so no decision need be made today."

"I can't do anything else but lie here and think, can I?" He sounded tired again, his brief spurt of energy gone. "And perhaps go mad, if I am not already. What do you say, *Principe*? I am here in Ésparias by your request, after all."

"Oh, Sorley." Tears threatened. "Of course you are free to go home." I didn't want him to leave. In some way he was keeping both my father and Druise alive for me. With my mother gone, and if Apulo went with him, all my family would have vanished.

I could not be selfish. I had friends, and a son, and another child in the spring. And perhaps more. Lairís had stopped playing. The room was quiet. What had Sorley meant, about going mad?

A bell rang, and rang again, its sound distant but clear, the rapid, repeated peal of warning from the fort's watchtower. "What?" Lairís asked. I held up a hand for silence, listening to the message in its toll, in the timing between each strike of the hammer. The danger, it told me, approached from the sea.

Chapter 30

"SHIPS!" I TURNED TO RUAR. "I must go to the harbour." The Marai? Surely this could not be an invasion? Our intelligence should be better than that. Perhaps the hired soldiers—but they would have sent word ahead, wouldn't they, so there would be someone here to meet them?

"As I had better too. Lairís, you stay here with Sorley." Ruar didn't wait for an answer; he had given a command, and he expected it to be obeyed. He swung open the door, urging me forward. Our guards—and Garia—were waiting.

"Horses," I snapped. Someone would bring them, and I wasn't wasting time on foot. I strode out of the courtyard and through the main doorway of the villa, Ruar beside me. The horses were being led up, the need anticipated. I mounted, and turned the mare's head toward the fort.

I did not enter its walls, but rode straight for the harbour. Ruar's horse kept pace, our guards surrounding us. My mind raced ahead: if, against all odds, this was an attack, could we defend ourselves? I hoped so: I trusted Dern and Talyn to have kept our defence readied, but I wasn't sure. *And you should be*, I berated myself. *You are the Principe.*

I reined in my horse near the top of the cliff. Clearly visible, but still distant, three ships moved towards the harbour. Marai ships, almost certainly.

Below me, the chain that closed off the harbour to entering ships was being fastened in place. Archers stood in formation along both arms of the long jetties the Casilani had built to enclose Wall's End's natural harbour. Barrels were being rolled and carried out to the archers: the fuel for the incendiary arrows—another Casilani introduction. Cadets would stuff the cages below the arrow points, light them, and hand them to each archer. I'd seen it practiced. I'd never thought to see the flaming arrows used.

Hoofbeats made me glance behind me. Valle, followed by Dern and Talyn. They drew their horses up on either side of Ruar and me. "Your thoughts?" I asked immediately.

"Three ships do not make up an invasion force," Dern said. "Not against Wall's End."

"Possibly a diversion?" Valle stared out to sea, one hand shading his eyes. "Maybe not. *Principe*, look closely at the first ship."

I followed his gaze, narrowing my eyes. Was that white at the prow of the first ship, something wrapped around its carved stem? "Ruar?"

He too shaded his eyes, watching for some moments. "A *draki*," he said finally.

"What does that mean?" Talyn asked sharply.

"They come in peace," Ruar said, "and as emissaries of the king. Only his ships bear the dragonhead on the prow."

"With a white cloth wrapped around it," I said, for those whose eyes were less sharp. "There will be evergreen branches as well, but they are too far out yet to see that. They are asking to confer."

"I am getting old," Dern said, half to himself. "I should have been able to see that."

A thought struck me. "It isn't Bryngyl himself, surely?"

"No," Ruar said. "He would not bring only three ships. An envoy of some rank, I expect. Shall we go down to meet them?"

I took my eyes off the ships. "We? It is Wall's End they approach, Ruar, not Abher Tabha." I let him consider that. "Dern, have the chain taken down, and the archers—"

"Can act as an honour guard," he said, "if you allow it, *Principe*. A show of strength masked as respect. It cannot hurt."

Nor could the Casilani engineering that had transformed Wall's End's harbour fail to impress. Or so I hoped. These were the first Marai ships to sail to Ésparias's shores in thirty years, but their traders had travelled the river route to Casil itself. Stories would have been told. "Do it," I said. "Garia, we need a banquet prepared, and beds for perhaps half a dozen." Fewer was likely, but better to overestimate.

"A guard can take that message," Garia said. "You need your grey-and-white, *Principe*." I glanced down at myself. My tunic was clean; that was the best that could be said.

"And my pendant," I said. "Thank you, Garia."

"*Principe*." Ruar waited until she was gone, and even then kept his voice low. "My apologies. I overstepped."

"*Teannasach*." I gestured him away from the others. We walked the horses a few paces. "Ruar. I too apologize, but I cannot be seen to be in your shadow. Not by Varsland, and not by my new commander of the guard."

"Nor should you be." He paused. "But my presence might be of use, don't you think, if they are here to negotiate a furthering of the western alliance?"

Which I most fervently hoped was the reason three Marai ships approached the harbour. "Yes, certainly. But I should greet the envoy alone."

Dern had descended the steps to the harbour. I saw the chain being released, and commands being given to the archers. I glanced out at the ships again. I would have time to change.

~

By the time the *draki* had docked, the two smaller boats sliding into berths behind it, I was down at the harbour level, waiting. The white cloth around the dragonhead's carved neck was indeed garlanded with evergreen, and standing on board were two men and a boy. As the first ship had slipped between the harbour arms into the still pool of the inner water, flaming arrows had been shot out into the sea away from the ships. A welcome to honour, and impress, and warn.

Talyn, also dressed in the grey-and-white of Ésparian royalty, her general's insignia pinned to her shoulder, stood a few paces back from me, soldiers on either side. Their leathers and armour gleamed. I nodded to Dern. In passable Marái'sta, he gave our visitors permission to disembark.

I walked forward to greet them. The boy was Constyn's age, and I had a good sense of who he was. One of the men was older, Sorley's age, and one—

I smiled in recognition. "Earl Vidar, welcome to Wall's End." I had last seen him fifteen years past, on the road leading to the *Ti'ach*. He'd been on his way to talk to my father. By his invitation, I learned later, to discuss schools in Varsland, and almost certainly much more. He was also a cousin of Ruar's dead wife, and therefore of his two sons.

"*Principe*. I am honoured you remember me. May I present Trygve, Prince of Varsland?" Vidar's youthful arrogance had tempered into confidence.

"*Principe*." The boy was as fair as his uncle Bjørn, with the suggestion of the same handsome looks in the bones of his face. In excellent Casilani, he said, "I bring greetings from my father the king, and our condolences too for the death of the prince Cillian."

"My thanks," I replied. "We are honoured by your visit, Prince Trygve. Be welcome." He was assured for—what? Thirteen?— but so had Colm been, when forced to be the prince. And he would have had the importance of this undertaking made very clear. I would need to remember not to treat him as a child.

Trygve turned to the older man. "This is Trostann, *sjaldr* to the king." *Sjaldrën* were Varsland's equivalents of *scáeli'en*: musicians, keepers of history and genealogies, but also lawgivers, and greatly revered. His presence, even more so than Trygve's, told me this was a visit of some importance.

"Another honour," I said. The breeze off the water was cool. "Food and drink await you at the fort, and rooms for your stay with us."

"One moment," Trygve said. "My father has sent a gift for you, *Principe*."

That in itself was not unusual, but to be presented with it here and now was. Had the boy forgotten his instructions? But both Vidar and Trygve had turned to where a man stepped out from a shelter on the deck, carrying a huge falcon, hooded and jessed in fine green leather. Its breast was as white as fallen snow, its back and wings flecked with black.

Behind me, Ruar drew a surprised breath. "A *geirfalki,*" he murmured, "and a white one at that. Gwenna, this is a present nearly beyond price. Bryngyl is courting peace."

"And perhaps also a different sort of courting," I whispered. I had heard of these falcons; the prince of birds, they were called, rare and difficult to obtain. I gathered my wits. "Prince Trygve, I barely know what to say. A magnificent gift, for which I thank you—and your father the king—most sincerely."

"She hunts well," the prince said. "She will take hares and geese easily."

What was I going to do with her? There were no mews for hawks at Wall's End. And who would know how to care for her? "Will you tell me her name?"

"Fräska." Little queen. Appropriate, I thought.

"Gwenna." Ruar again, his voice very low. "One of my guards can take her. He has handled falcons before."

"To the stables?" I suggested. Ruar relayed this to his man.

"Will you entrust Fräska to this soldier?" I asked Trygve. "He will take her to where she will be housed, and see she is settled and fed."

"Her handler will go with her," Vidar said. "He is prepared to stay in Ésparias, if you lack a fawkner among your servants."

A convenient spy, I thought. But perhaps a necessity. I could not let this marvellous bird die for lack of the knowledge to care for her.

"A kind offer," I said, as Ruar's guardsman gestured to the man with the falcon. They could not climb the stairs to the fort before us, of course, but stood to one side.

"Shall we?" As protocol demanded, I fell into step with Trygve: *Principe* and prince, followed by Talyn escorting Trostann. Vidar I left to Ruar; they were, after all, family. Valle followed at the rear.

If our guests were to stay for more than a day or two, I thought as we waited for them in the dining room of the commander's house, would Trostann agree to give Lairís an hour of his time? She would love the chance to speak with a senior *sjaldr*, I was sure.

I had better tell Sorley that Trostann was here, too, although he was still too ill to play any sort of formal role. But this could wait; I should be planning my approach to them, and my answers to their possible questions.

Ruar had stayed with Vidar, but Talyn sat on a stool, waiting. "Gwenna," she said now, "we have managed, just, to imply that our visitors were not unexpected. But that falcon is a present beyond imagining. What will you give in return?"

This mattered. "What can I?" I asked. "What should I?"

"What was Ésparias's gift to Alekos on becoming Emperor?"

"The finest of metalwork," I said. "Filigreed buckles and brooches, enamelled and set with jewels."

She clicked her tongue. "Not something you have just lying around."

"No." But I had a thought, a connection made. "Send someone for Lairís, will you?"

~

When Lairís arrived, the Varsland emissaries had joined us, and we were enjoying wine and small savouries while we awaited the more substantial food. I excused myself to speak to her.

"What is it, Gwenna?"

I explained. She looked both surprised and interested. "Trostann? He is famous, the way Sorley is."

"Yes, well, he may be. He is. But the king of Varsland has given me a white falcon, and I must give him something close to it in value. So—" I took a breath. "I would do this myself, but I cannot leave my guests. Will you ask Sorley if I may have the best of whatever Casilani glass he is willing to give up? Something sent from the Empress herself, if possible."

I knew what I really wanted, the blue and green glass swirled with gold that he and Druise had purchased in Sylana. But I would not ask to take something with the memories it must hold. And Bryngyl might be impressed by the provenance, were it glass sent by Eudekia.

"How many pieces?"

"Five, I think." It seemed neither sparing nor overly generous.

"You want them brought here?"

"Yes. Ask Apulo to arrange that." I wanted to hug her, but I just touched her hand. "Thank you."

"May I tell Sorley Trostann is here? I'm sure they must have met before, and he would want to see him if he can."

If it would lighten Sorley's melancholy, yes. I told Lairís so.

"We can hope," she said, and left to do her task. The 'we' made me smile.

Chapter 31

THE MEAL WAS NEARLY OVER, only the sweet pastries and fruit left. The cook had produced a fine meal, salad dressed with oil and vinegar, fish as fresh as it could be, warm flatbread, olives from the stores, and cheeses. Trostann had watered Trygve's wine down to a pale pink, and allowed him only one glass. I too had watered and limited my wine, but in my case, it was to keep a clear head. The conversation after the meal would need all my wits.

"A fine room," Vidar said to me, as the servants handed round the plates of pastries.

"It is," I agreed. "The *Princip* before me, Faolyn, had the rooms remade in the Casilani style. The floor is particularly fine."

Faolyn had had a weakness for mosaics, but Talyn had admitted to me privately she was happy he'd had the underfloor and wall heating added. "My old bones are glad of it more each winter," she'd said.

"Faolyn," Trostann said. "His widow and daughter are at Dun Ceànnar, I hear."

"Siusàn is my sister," Ruar said mildly.

"And the boy?"

"Prince Constyn travelled south some weeks ago," I replied. "A pity, because I am sure he would like to have met you, Prince Trygve. You could have become friends." I was testing, looking for a reaction from the boy.

He obliged, sending Trostann an uncertain glance before saying, "I hope he may." Vidar's expression, I noted, was slightly amused, or perhaps indulgent. Trygve was here for a reason beyond an education in diplomacy, I was sure.

The serving girl, holding the plate of sweets, whispered in my ear. I smiled my thanks. "If I may," I said, raising my voice a little, "our gifts to your father, Prince Trygve, are ready for presentation. The docks were not an appropriate place earlier."

At my nod, the doors were opened, and one by one five trays were borne in. Each held one piece of Casilani glass, each different, each exquisite. One, I saw with a jolt of surprise, was a cup of almost-white glass with an outer shell of entwined green vines, an intricate, delicate piece of the highest workmanship, and extremely valuable.

"Each piece," I said, "was chosen by the Empress Eudekia herself and sent to my father. You will find no greater expression of the art of glassmaking than these."

"A kingly gift indeed," Trostann said. I heard awe in his voice, but whether it was real or not I couldn't tell.

"In my father's name, I accept them with thanks," the prince said. "They are beautiful. But how do we get them home safely?"

His composure had slipped; the question was asked anxiously. "Packed tightly in wool and straw, and each within its own box," I told him. "That is how they came from Casil."

"Oh, good." He smiled his relief.

"*Principe*, much of what we have to discuss will be tedious for Prince Trygve," Vidar said, almost lazily. "He is, I believe, close in age to your cadets. Perhaps he could watch them in their training?"

"Certainly," I replied. Tedious, or not for his ears? "My assistant can take him."

Talyn rose. "I'll find Major Garia. Prince Trygve, will you come with me?"

The boy stood up. With a bow to me, he accompanied Talyn from the room. The door closed quietly. Very purposely, I poured a little more wine, added water, took a sip. Giving myself time to think, as my father had taught me long ago.

"I have had no chance to offer my condolences for the loss of your daughter, Earl Vidar," I said. My sentiments were real—I had seen my parents' grief when Lianë died—but my statement also would tell the envoys I knew why they were here. Vidar acknowledged my words with a murmured, "thank you."

"Now, does this tedious discussion need my senior trade envoy present?" I asked. "Or are Princess Flynsà's uncle and grandmother more appropriate?"

Both men were too experienced to show surprise. "The latter, *Principe*," Trostann answered.

"Prince Trygve knows nothing of this?"

"He will marry as he is told," Trostann said. "To strengthen the alliances here in the west." He had not chosen those words accidentally; of that I was sure.

"As my daughter would have, and my cousin Helvi did, and"—Vidar nodded to Ruar—"the *Teannasach* of Linrathe did. Just as his sister married into Ésparias. But there are no ties of marriage or blood between Ésparias and Varsland. Yet." He gave me a wry, practiced smile. "Although I did make the proposal, some fifteen years past."

I knew the reply he had been given by my father. None of his children would make political marriages. Even the Emperor of Casil had not swayed his determination that I was free to make my own choices, for love. The King of Varsland had not been pleased, at the time.

But, I remembered with a jolt, my father had not appeared to extend that choice to Faolyn's children, or even to his own grandchildren. "'That alliance must wait for another generation," he'd said, when we'd been discussing the marriages that strengthened the ties among our lands. Was it easier to see a boy or girl as a piece in political strategy, when they weren't your own? Ruar hadn't seemed to have a problem arranging a marriage for his oldest son—or suggesting that his niece would be a suitable match for Trygve.

I had made a political partnership when I'd chosen Ruar to father my heir. But that decision had been mine, and Ruar had been free to refuse. Flynsà was twelve, and Ésparian, and all my blood and flesh and instinct said I could not betroth her to Varsland's heir. That was not my choice to make.

Talyn returned. "Prince Trygve has been taken to watch weapons training," she told us. She pushed a strand of silver hair off her face. "And since you did not want him present, this discussion involves him. And, at a guess, my granddaughter."

Vidar and Trostann exchanged glances. "I told you," Vidar said to the *sjaldr,* "not to underestimate this family."

Trostann spread his hands, acknowledging Talyn's assumption as correct. "A marriage would be of benefit to both our lands, surely? Linrathe and Ésparias have those ties, several of them, over more than one generation. King Bryngyl's daughter will marry the *Teannasach's* son in a year or two; a man who himself carries the blood of both Varsland and Linrathe. If her brother, the heir to Varsland, marries this Ésparian princess, it braids our lands even more tightly together. Which is what your father wanted, *Principe.*"

As long as Ésparias is a province of my Empire, I—we—will tolerate no marriage with Varsland. I do not trust them. Eudekia, after I had refused to marry Alekos. But Ésparias was no longer a province of her empire. I was nearly sure of that. Nearly. Could I use my uncertainty to buy time?

No. I dismissed the idea. I would look weak, a figurehead, not my country's leader.

I do not trust them. Nor did I, quite, although it was not their king I didn't trust, but some of their people; Bjørn's men who had served a foreign Emperor for pay, and perhaps those who had accepted Casilani coin now. But neither did Varsland trust us, I realized. The eighty men on the other two ships were not just an honour guard.

"You do not expect an answer now." I made it a statement, not a question. "My advisors and I will discuss your proposal. What amusements can we offer you? There are horses if you would like exercise, or my father's library, or the baths."

"I would like to meet with Sorley of Gundarstorp," Trostann said, "if he is here. It has been many years since we have spoken, or exchanged songs."

"Lord Sorley is here, but—" How to say this? "He is not well."

"Is it serious?" Trostann sounded truly concerned. "A summer fever?"

"No." I wanted no rumours of illness in our fort. "He was attacked and beaten badly not long ago."

"What?" Shock raised Trostann's voice. "Has this land no respect for a *sjaldr,* a *scáeli?'*

In both Linrathe and Varsland, to bring harm to a *scáeli* was a crime punishable by death. No such law or tradition existed in Ésparias—but I had little doubt bodies would be found, apparent victims of robbers. Sorley had been Druisius's *consor*. The guard would not be inclined to be lenient.

"The circumstances were such it is unlikely they knew who he was," I said.

"I, for one, would like to ride," Vidar announced. "And perhaps the prince might too. Exercise after days on the ship would be welcome."

"I'll have my adjutant brought," Talyn said. "He can escort Earl Vidar and the prince. Horses will be found for your guards too, of course," she added, addressing Vidar.

"And I," Ruar said, standing, "will be happy to walk with Trostann. I cannot imagine Sorley will not make the effort to see him for at least a few minutes." He was making it clear to the Varslanders that, Flynsà's uncle or not, his opinion was not being sought by me. At least, not now.

"Thank you, *Teannasach*. Trostann, Earl Vidar, we will see you for the evening meal."

"I look forward to it," Vidar said. "A question, *Principe*?"

"Yes?" I prepared myself; had he left something important to the very last, as if an afterthought?

"Who is represented by that figure on the wall?" He indicated the fresco on the far side of the room.

"Come," I said. We approached the painting. "It is goddess of the hunt."

"Beautifully rendered." He dropped his voice. "The king thanks you for your letter sent some weeks past. He has rejected the proposed purchases; it is not at this time in the best interest of either our country or yours."

I inclined my head, doing my best not to let the relief show. "Thank you, Earl Vidar. Will his direction be sufficient to prevent all sales?"

A shrug, a wry smile. "Most. Not all, *Principe*. There may be another way."

"Which is?"

He told me.

~

"Well." Talyn sank back onto her stool. "Were you expecting this proposal?"

"It had crossed my mind," I admitted. "But how can we? An arranged marriage goes against all our traditions and beliefs. Marriage itself is still regarded a strange custom by many of our people."

"And yet we need Varsland in the alliance," Talyn said.

"You're not suggesting we agree?"

"No. But if Siusàn were here, she would tell you there is more than one way to promote a marriage, without directly arranging it. Or were you too young to be aware of how she and Faolyn were brought together?"

"At the *Ti'ach*, one of the summers Faolyn was home from Casil."

"That he was heir to Ésparias, and she was the *Teannasach's* sister gave them something in common. As egalitarian as the *Ti'acha* are, it was difficult for both of them not to be aware they were not quite the same as the other students."

"As it was for me as a cadet." Which was why, I could see now, I had gravitated toward Lynthe, who shared my dislike of the titles Eudekia had imposed upon us. A commonality—but also a way for me to excuse her frequent irritability. I wrenched my mind away from those thoughts. "You think we should repeat this with Flynsà and Trygve?"

"If Bryngyl would consider sending his heir to Linrathe for a year, or a portion of it, yes. It would be a reasonable extension of his education, given his sister is marrying the *Teannasach's* heir."

"Presumptive heir," I reminded her. "Or should we suggest that Flynsà return to an Ésparian *Ti'ach,* and Trygve join her here?"

"No," Talyn said. "Flynsà would be too comfortable here. We want them both to feel a little out of place."

"How is this any better than telling her to marry him?" I didn't like it. "We're manipulating her."

"I don't like it either," she snapped. "I'm sorry, Gwenna," she said immediately. "it's just—the Casilani changed all our lives. My son is dead, and my daughter—" She shook her head. "We have no idea if Constyn is safe, or complicit in Lynthe's treason, and now we're suggesting my granddaughter be married to Varsland's heir. It's too much."

I thought her near tears. "Oh, Talyn," I said. "I should have realized. But—"

"I am her only close relation here," she said. "By our customs Ruar has no say in her future. But her mother has taken the girl to Linrathe, so perhaps he should."

"Flynsà is an Ésparian princess, not a Linrathan one. And I will have no compunction in telling Ruar that, should he think to interfere."

She half smiled. "As you did earlier."

"He knows he has no say in Gwyllar's future, so I doubt he will think he does in Flynsà's," I reassured her.

Talyn took a breath, composing herself. "In the cause of peace, I will accept an introduction between Trygve and Flynsà. If she has no interest in men, or dislikes him, we will know in time to decline a betrothal. And it buys us a year, perhaps more."

"What will Siusàn say?"

"Her marriage was happy, as was Ruar's and Helvi's. I doubt she'll be opposed." I couldn't argue; Talyn knew her son's widow better than I did.

"We would need to warn Kúsi." The *Comiádh* would have to be aware of why Trygve was there, if Bryngyl agreed to send his son. But his was not the only agreement needed. Ruar would also have to assent.

What of the obvious counteroffer: that Flynsà be sent to a Varsland *Ti'ach*? There were several now, the first established not long after Vidar's visit to my father the summer I was fourteen. How would we respond to that suggestion?

Talyn and I discussed that possibility—and what we might do if Varsland opposed any delay in a betrothal—while we waited for Ruar to return. My full council would have to be apprised, but for now, this was an issue for us alone.

He wasn't long. "Sorley was pleased to see Trostann. Happier than I have seen in some time." He poured himself wine and sat down. "I suggested on the ride over to the villa that an invitation to visit Varsland when Sorley was well enough might be well received."

Another incentive to go home to Gundarstorp, where the crossing of the narrow sea to Varsland was comparatively easy. "Did you explain to him that Sorley is grieving?"

"I did." He gave me a reassuring smile. "The *sjaldrën*, in common with the *scáeli'en*, are open-minded and accepting. It is a pity, in some ways, that my Ullach had no interest in music. But from very young it was bridges and roads he wanted to build, not *ladhars*." The oblique admission of his younger son's nature—for what else could I take from his words?—surprised me. I didn't react; perhaps he thought I'd known. But it explained in part why Ullach had come south to learn from Casilani engineers.

"What will he do, now the Casilani are gone?" I asked, momentarily diverted from my concerns for Sorley.

Ruar simply shook his head, his lips pursed. "What have you decided about Flynsà?" he asked.

"Nothing. But we have a plan." I told him what Talyn and I had discussed.

"That's the *Ti'ach* where Bjørn was sent as Sorley's son," he said, when I was done.

"Is it?" I thought back. Had I known that? "Did they ever know who he really was?"

"I don't think so, at least not officially. But it might make it more attractive to Bryngyl."

"Bjørn told me once that he and his brother rarely agreed. I had the sense that his education had given him a broader sense of the world, one Bryngyl did not share."

Ruar rubbed his lips. "That was when you met Bjørn in Sylana?" At my nod, he said, "That was true then. But the years of trade with Casi, and the exposure to thought and writings that have spilled out from the *Ti'acha* have broadened his mind. His earls—Vidar for one—like the wealth the trade has brought, and the status of having Casilani goods in their homes. The gift of Casilani glass, especially the green and white piece, was brilliant, by the way."

Lairis's doing, or Sorley's? The latter, more likely. He would understand what the colours meant. I would have to thank him.

"So you think Bryngyl might agree to send Trygve to the *Ti'ach na Kúsi*?" Talyn leant forward. "Because if anyone is to present this idea to Siusàn, it should be me."

"I think," Ruar said, "that he might, if the proposal is handled well, and perhaps I need to be part of that. What if," he glanced at me, "you tell the envoys that an arranged marriage is still not Ésparias's way, but that you have no objection to the two young people meeting. If that leads to a mutual interest and attraction, then there can be further discussions. And while they mull that over, I suggest the *Ti'ach*, with all the appropriate arguments for why it is in Trygve's best interests."

"The alliance in action," I said. "And if they wish to be part of it, as Trostann's words told us, they will agree."

"Not just Trostann's words," Ruar answered. "The gerfalcon was a message, Gwenna. A royal bird, a powerful, efficient killer—but she is white."

And the leather jesses and hood had been green. Surprised by the gift, focused on protocol, I hadn't fully comprehended the subtle diplomacy on full display. *Do not underestimate this family,* Vidar had said to Trostann. Perhaps I had underestimated them.

Chapter 32

I HAD FRÄSKA BROUGHT TO the dining room of the villa. A perch had been hastily constructed for her by one of the men who worked on the estate. It looked rough, a portion of a branch mounted on a pole, but Ruar's guard, the one he had sent with the falcon and her handler, assured me it was sufficient.

I brought Gwyllar to see her before our guests arrived. Holding him in my arms a few steps away from the bird, I warned him to make no loud noise or movement, At my nod her handler removed her hood. She swivelled her head, her dark eyes, ringed with yellow, taking in the room. She seemed unperturbed by her travels. The handler stroked her with a feather, murmuring to her nearly under his breath.

My usually chattering son said nothing, watching Fräska with fierce concentration. "Mine," he said finally.

"Ours," I told him. "Yours and mine. But you need to grow up a bit more before you can handle her." Quite a bit more, but he could learn that slowly. When had Ruar first flown a falcon? I would have to ask.

I gave a protesting Gwyllar back to his nursemaid. The falcon was hooded again, and I went to change. This evening I would wear a gown, rather than my usual tunic and leggings. My maid did my hair, braiding it and pinning it high. For jewellery, I chose only two shoulder brooches, and silver earrings made by Berge's metalworker. Simplicity suited me, Rosale—who was now the Empress-Consort of Casil—had told me once.

The memory made me pause. Whatever changes were happening here in Ésparias, they were nothing compared to what she was facing. Was she in the city, or had she withdrawn with her children to a safe place beyond its walls? I hoped so: I had liked Rosale, and had been pleased when Alekos—whether from my advice or not—had chosen to marry her. We'd exchanged a few letters over the years.

I put Rosale from my mind and returned to the dining room. Apulo was there with Sorley, and the two men who had supported him on the short walk from his room to this one. "The men will bring you back," Apulo was telling Sorley. "There is a chair they can carry, if you need it."

"I won't," Sorley said shortly. "I walked half the length of Sorham with worse injuries. I need only a stick to support myself with."

That, I thought—but had the sense not to say—*was nearly thirty years past.* But his words did give me an idea. I slipped out and went to my parents' rooms. They had that cold feel that unoccupied space seemed to hold, and a light layer of dust lay on every surface. I'd have a stern word for the steward tomorrow.

I found my father's walking stick in a corner of the room: not the black one with the silver eagle that Eudekia had sent, but the one he'd used every day, the wood polished by his hands, the bronze tip worn. I took it back to Sorley.

"I can't take it," he said.

"Don't be ridiculous," I said. "Should it just stand in a corner?' He shook his head, tears glinting.

"Sorley," I said, in my *Principe's* voice, tempered with affection. "My father would have given this walking stick to you without hesitation, the way he gave you jewels for your *ladhar* and glass for your shelves. He delighted in making you presents. Don't refuse it."

Whatever rejoinder he might have made was interrupted by the arrival of our guests, accompanied by both Ruar and Talyn. After the introductions—although only Trygve did not know Sorley—the young prince excused himself to go to the falcon, taking the feather from her handler to stroke her. He was clearly fond of the bird. Had she been meant for him, once?

We played out the expectations of protocol: casual conversation over the dinner, compliments to the frescoes and the floor mosaic, praise for the meal. When we were on the last course of figs and walnuts and a honeyed wine, Apulo and Lairís entered the room. While Lairís adjusted the tuning of her *ladhar* one last time, Apulo spoke quietly to Sorley, who shook his head. Refusing more drugs, I guessed.

"Normally," Sorley said to the table, "I would play for you now. But as I cannot" —he held up his bandaged hand for all to see— "my niece Lairís will, with your indulgence. She is not yet a *scáeli*, but that is only a matter of time."

Chairs were turned so we could both hear and see Lairís. She drew her fingers over the strings of the instrument—Sorley's *ladhar*, inlaid with the carved carnelians—then began to play *The Two Sisters*. Sorley had told me once the song was known in Varsland as well as Linrathe.

Her voice was lovely. Her years of training from Eithnë had shaped her natural ability into something greater. And when Apulo stepped forward to add his own exquisite voice to hers, the music was beyond anything I had ever heard. Even Sorley seemed awestruck. When, I wondered, had they practiced this?

"Not a *scáeli*?" Trostann said into the silence that followed their song.

"No, *Sjaldr* Trostann," Lairís replied. "I have songs to gather yet, to meet the Council's requirements."

"Come to me in Varsland," he said. "I will teach you songs. And you." His attention switched to Apulo. "What is your role here? Do you teach music?"

"I taught voice at the *Ti'ach na Cillian* for many years," he replied, "and now to a few students here." Said calmly, without deference or pride.

"I remember you," Vidar said. "But were you not also Cillian's aide?"

"I was." He offered no further explanation.

"You are Casilani, are you not?" Trostann asked. At Apulo's quiet confirmation, the *sjaldr* smiled. "We must speak further while I am here. I was saddened to learn of Druisius's death." He inclined his head to Sorley. "Not just for the personal loss, which is great, but also because I had hoped to discuss Casilani music with him. I had not realized there was a second Casilani musician of great skill in the *Principe's* household."

"You could also visit Gundarstorp, Trostann, if the *Teannasach* agrees," Sorley said. "In a few weeks, when the physicians allow, I am going home, and Apulo will be coming with me."

He had decided. I said a silent prayer of thanks to whatever gods were listening, and caught Lairís's eye. She smiled. A sudden doubt assailed me: would she go too now? How could she refuse Trostann's invitation?

Concentrate, I told myself. "And what will a singer of your capabilities do at a remote *torp*?" Trostann asked Apulo.

"I do not go as a musician," Apulo said, "but to ensure the lord Sorley's hand heals properly."

"That will not be all," Sorley said. "The *Ti'ach na Barì* is less than a half-day's ride away. There will be opportunities for Apulo to teach."

"And you too, once your hand has regained its strength." Trostann nodded his approval.

"It is where I was educated," Lairís said. "Close to home, and I imagine the lady Eithnë kept Sorley informed of my progress through the council."

What were they doing? I glanced at Ruar. He too was listening, his eyes slightly narrowed.

"And an easy trip across the *Smölvann*, if Apulo wishes to visit Varsland," Vidar said. "I have used Gundarstorp's harbour myself, from time to time."

I saw the gameboard now. Who had told Sorley of our proposal? Ruar? I had not, and I doubted Talyn had. But why should I assume anyone had? Sorley had been part of my father's intrigues for longer than I had been alive. He was more than capable of developing this plan on his own—if Trostann had told him of the betrothal they sought. I thought the *sjaldr* might have, hoping to create an ally: Varsland's ties to Sorham were very old.

"Prince Trygve," Vidar said, "the evening grows late, and our talk will be of trade now. Would you like to leave us?"

"I am tired," the boy admitted.

"Apulo, would you go with the prince and his guards? To ensure he finds his rooms, and has all he needs?"

"Of course," Apulo said.

"I'll come with you, to keep you company on the walk back." Lairís's diplomatic instincts were very good. I would have had to ask her to leave, as if she were only there to entertain us—and I hadn't wanted to do that. Although—

"Will you wait a moment?" I said to her quietly. "We may need you."

The formalities of Prince Trygve's departure took a few minutes. I dismissed the fawkner, too. When the door was closed again, I faced the table. "Trade is, I suppose, what we are discussing now," I said. "But tell me, *Sjaldr* Trostann, do I have need of a scribe, a role the lord Sorley would usually take on? Or is tonight an exploration of possibilities, without formal record?"

"The latter," Trostann said. He smiled. "The lady Lairís does not need to practice that part of a *scáeli's* duties tonight."

I thanked him. Lairís smiled at me, gave Trostann a small bow of respect, and left us. I stayed on my feet.

"For the lord Sorley's sake, and to ensure we all understand what we are discussing, I will reiterate what I believe I heard from the Earl Vidar and *Sjaldr* Trostann earlier today. Bryngyl, King of Varsland, wishes a betrothal between his son Trygve and Flynsà, daughter to the late *Princip* Faolyn. Is that accurate?"

"It is, *Principe*," Trostann said.

"Then before this night is any older, I must tell you we will not agree to that betrothal now." I paused for a heartbeat, two, assessing their reaction. But both envoys were too experienced to show me anything. "Or ever, without the consent of Flynsà herself. Women of Ésparias choose their own partners, even those of the *Princip*'s line."

I pulled my chair out and sat. Trostann, I noted, was almost smiling. The game had begun. "Have you a counterproposal, *Principe*?"

I had, during the space given by Trygve's formal leave-taking, reassessed our plans. But even if I had judged Sorley's idea correctly, they would serve. "I do," I said.

They listened. Lips were pursed, questions asked about the *Ti'ach na Kúsi*. Ruar spoke of his own sons' education there, under both the old *Comiádh*, Asgaill, and his successor. "Kúsi is a Marai name," Vidar murmured.

"He is from the Raske Hoys," Ruar told them. The islands in the sea between Sorham and Varsland were neither quite Sorham nor Varsland, although their governance now fell to Linrathe. "But there is another argument for having Prince Trygve attend a Linrathan school in a year or so. His sister Kjersti will marry my son Daragh when she is of age. Should we not give Daragh and Trygve the opportunity to know each other outside the formalities of their positions?"

"Your son is much older than the prince," Vidar said.

"Of little account to the heirs to leadership," Ruar said. "And it has been my practice, and my sons', to spend time at *Ti'acha* whenever we can, to continue to learn from the *Comiádha*, and sometimes to speak to the students as well."

"Perhaps," I intervened, "Princess Kjersti could also have a year or two at a *Ti'acha* in Linrathe? She and Flynsà are not far apart in age. A friendship between the girls could strengthen the" —I chose my words carefully— "attraction of her brother?"

"My cousin Helvi came to a Linrathan school before she married the *Teannasach*," Vidar said. "She was glad she did, she told me once."

The Varslanders seemed willing to compromise. But, excepting the possible betrothal, there was little here to strengthen the alliance between Ésparias and Varsland, and much to improve the already-strong relationships with Linrathe.

"I would hope," I said, "that if the betrothal happens, Prince Trygve might spend some time in Ésparias as well."

"And the princess Flynsà in Varsland," Trostann said, "but the betrothal is our first concern." He glanced at Vidar, who nodded. "I can neither agree nor disagree to this plan. The decision will be the king's, but I will say that I will not oppose what you have suggested. Whether King Bryngyl will approve, I cannot say."

"What might cause him to not approve?" I asked.

Trostann laid his hands on the tabletop, palms down. "I do not intend these words to cause offense," he began. "But a prince of Varsland, and perhaps a princess too, at a school in Linrathe well could be for their education. It could also be a play for power on the part of Linrathe, a country with close ties to Ésparias."

Silence. I did not break it, because the accusation was against Linrathe, not Ésparias. Ruar studied Trostann, his face impassive.

Rebuttals flickered through my mind, but one—not a rebuttal but a solution of sorts—kept coming to the forefront. A possibility, but one I could not rely on.

"*Teannasach*, if I may?" Sorley. Ruar nodded. "Trostann, you are thinking like a diplomat must. But you should have no doubt of the safety of the king's children. I will remind you that Linrathe gave shelter to Prince Bjørn when he needed it, at my request. Still, if the *Teannasach* agrees, I offer this. Do not send the children to the *Ti'ach na Kúsi,* deep within Linrathe. Send them to the *Ti'ach na Barì,* a short ride from Gundarstorp, and passage to or from Varsland. I will stand surety for their safety, and offer Gundarstorp as a home for whomever the King chooses—perhaps you, Vidar?—to watch over them."

My heart pulsed in my throat. It was a magnificent offer, one that should allay any fears Bryngyl might have. More than that, it gave Sorley a role in the alliance's future, and a purpose. It also told me that he planned to return to his childhood home to stay, not just for a few months of healing. How that made me feel wasn't something I could deal with right now.

Chapter 33

"YOUR BROTHER WILL AGREE?" Vidar asked, before Ruar could speak.

Sorley nodded. "Of that I am sure. It was Roghan who brought Bjørn to Sorham. As I imagine Trostann knows."

"I did," the *sjaldr* said. "And the king will not have forgotten. He may be amenable to this plan, if it is acceptable to you, *Teannasach*. And to you, *Principe*."

"I spent a few days at the *Ti'ach na Barì* when I was little older than Flynsà will be, when it is appropriate for her and the prince to meet." The memory brought a smile. "I would have no objection at all."

"Nor I," Ruar said. "Not to the school, and not to Lord Sorley's offer."

"Then we will await the king's decision." Trostann's tone told me he considered the subject dealt with. "Vidar—"

"A moment." Talyn interrupted the *sjaldr*. "Sorley has offered to ensure the prince's safety, and to house whoever is sent from Varsland with him. But should not my granddaughter have the same protection?"

"I am surety for them both," Sorley said, "although the *Teannasach's* niece surely needs no protection in Linrathe?"

"The *Teannasach's* niece is also a princess of Ésparias," Talyn said, "and it is in that role we are discussing her future. She is not Linrathe's responsibility."

Nor had I been. Druisius and my mother had been my protectors, until I went to cadet school and was assigned a bodyguard at Wall's End. "General Talyn is correct," I said. "Someone will be sent." Who? Once, I might have thought Lynthe. Was that possible now, if she could defend her actions to me? It would remove her from Ésparias, but with some vestige of honour.

I dismissed my own fancy. There would be someone of sufficient rank among the officers. And the unusual presence of adults, even if some miles distant, who were known to be looking out for Trygve and Flynsà would be one more thing that might bring them together.

Trostann and Vidar excused themselves some minutes later. Trade discussions were Vidar's responsibility, Trostann made clear. He was not needed, but would keep an eye on the prince, and perhaps find some time to talk and play with Sorley. "And your niece and Apulo, too," he added.

"We would be honoured," Sorley said. I could see the fatigue and pain on his face, but he spoke not just courteously, but with an undercurrent of real interest.

"Prince Trygve is welcome to join the cadets in their exercises," I offered. There were enough Varsland soldiers to supervise him; if Trostann could keep Sorley from falling back into melancholy, I'd rather the *sjaldr* spent his time with him. "But I need a day, Earl Vidar, to meet with my council. Your arrival was—unexpected."

"We kept far out to sea," Vidar said, "so as to not impede the trading ships." I knew a diplomatic lie when I heard one, but I let it go. They had chosen their route to take us by surprise.

They bade us good night. Neither Talyn nor Ruar made any move to accompany them.

"That was brilliant, Sorley," I said, when I was sure we could not be overheard.

He reached inside his belt pouch, finding a small package which he emptied into his wine. He swirled the cup and drank it down. "You understood what I was suggesting, before the formal negotiations began?"

"Yes."

"And I," Ruar said. "Although saying I had no objection is not true." His tone belied his words. "I had hoped that after a sufficient time, you might be induced to take the position Cillian talked me out of offering you a very long time ago."

Sorley frowned. "Amlodd cannot be ready to retire?"

"Not yet. But the joint-ill plagues him, and the time is not many years off when he will not be able to play. Something to consider."

Amlodd was *scáeli* to Dun Ceànnar and the *Teannasach*. An honoured position, requiring a *scáeli* of great skill with both diplomacy and music. Sorley would be exactly right for it. And my father had talked Ruar out of offering it once before?

A question there, for either Sorley or Ruar. But not tonight. Tiredness permeated me, making my neck and arms ache. I would have to be up early, too, to meet with Muire again before the formal talks began. I had one more thing to say before I retired—but it was not for Ruar's ears, as trusted an ally as he was. Or, truly, for Sorley's.

"Sorley," I said gently, "go to bed. I can see you are in pain, and exhausted. Ruar, would you go with him?"

"There's no need," Sorley protested. "Apulo will be waiting for me outside."

"Better with two of us," Ruar said cheerfully. "You're thinner than you were, Sorley, but you're not light." I guessed he'd seen through my ploy, and was playing his part. Ruar helped Sorley stand. When he handed him my father's walking stick, Sorley took it without hesitation, his hand caressing its smooth top. He nodded. "I'm ready."

"Good night," I said, echoed by Talyn. I dropped back into my chair. "Well?"

"Well played," she said.

"And you." I reached for my wine. My throat was dry. "An idea, but just for you until we know more."

"What is it?"

"If my mother brings Constyn home, and he was in no way complicit with Lynthe's plans, we send him to Varsland for a year or two, to a *Ti'ach* there. Then Bryngyl would feel it a more equal situation, wouldn't he? Exchanging princes, in a way."

"Except Trygve is the heir," Talyn said thoughtfully. "But yes, it makes sense. And if he falls in love with some high-ranking Marai girl, so much the better, I suppose."

~

I stepped out into the courtyard. The night was cool, a few stars showing through a haze of clouds. The fountain burbled. A light still shone from Sorley's rooms, but otherwise the villa was in near darkness.

"Gwenna." I jumped at Lairís's voice. "Sorry," she offered when I said her name. "I didn't mean to scare you."

"Why are you out here?"

"I was waiting for you."

"You could have—" I stopped. She couldn't wait in my rooms; I had not given the household instructions to allow her. And maybe I shouldn't, not yet. Not if she were leaving with Sorley.

"Come." In my rooms I put my arms around her, not kissing, just enjoying being held. "I'm very tired," I said into her hair. "But I'd like you to stay. You were stunning tonight, you and Apulo."

"His voice is so pure. Eithnë will be thrilled to have him teach a few lessons."

"As you will be with lessons from Trostann?" I might as well know. We could still be together for the weeks before she went north. It was just a matter of adjusting my expectations.

"How long do you think he'll be here?" She slipped out of my arms, going to sit on the edge of the bed. I sat to take the pins out of my hair.

"Ten days? Maybe a bit less, or more."

"I can learn a lot in ten days." She got up again to stand behind me, beginning to loosen my braids. I dropped my hands, glad to have even this small thing done for me.

"He invited you to Varsland," I said.

"I'm not going. Not now, anyhow. Maybe in a year or two." She reached over to pick up my comb, and began to run it through my hair. "Do you want a single braid for bed?"

"Yes, but you don't have to do this. I have a maid."

"I know. But I like to. And the maid would just get in the way." She plaited my hair, her fingers neat and efficient. "I talked to the falcon's handler tonight. A fawkner, we'd call him in Linrathe. He took that bird from her nest when she was just fledged. He wants to stay with her, but he has a wife and daughter in Varsland."

"Would he stay long enough to teach someone here how to care for her?" Standing, I undid the belt of my gown, and removed the silver brooches on each shoulder, carefully stepping out of it. I draped it over a stool. My maid could deal with it in the morning.

"Probably. Or could he bring his family here?"

The undertunic of my gown was too long to sleep in. I pulled it over my head, well aware that Lairís was watching. A thought that made me less tired, suddenly.

"Maybe," I said. "But could we talk about it tomorrow?"

~

I woke a couple of hours later, thirsty from the wine I'd drunk and needing to relieve my bladder. I wouldn't sleep through the night again until after this baby was born. Quietly I slipped from the bed, dealt with both bodily requirements, and returned. Lairís stirred, but didn't wake.

She was staying. One bright thing among all my worries and responsibilities. My father, I thought unexpectedly, would have liked her. Then I chuckled to myself, because how could he not? She was so like Sorley. Not just in looks and talent, but in her care for people. Talking to the fawkner, learning his concerns—Sorley would have done that too.

Could the fawkner bring his family? Yes, if Bryngyl allowed—but I would not let that be known yet. Because the king may have forbidden his men to fight for Casil as hired soldiers, but that was all. *Not in the best interest of either of our countries.* I thought about what Vidar had suggested to me privately. Part of it was reasonably easy. Part of it was not.

The betrothal between Trygve and Flynsà, if it happened, wouldn't be made for some time, giving me space to consider and to consult. *Yours is the directing mind now,* my mother had said. Directing, yes. Deciding? Perhaps not, or not alone.

I listened to Lairís's quiet breathing. There had been free movement between Linrathe and Ésparias since the Casilani peace. Not that many people had come south: younger sons with no land to inherit; a few women who wanted to be soldiers. People joining lovers, or coming with their partner of the same sex to where they could live openly together. A few came to learn from a specific teacher, like Ruar's younger son. Some Ésparian men and women had gone north for love or learning, too.

Linrathe had been our enemy once, but few on either side of the border had objected to the gates of the Wall standing open. But for all our history of war, their men—or ours—had never been as cruel and vicious as the Marai. I could not invite settlers from Varsland unless the women of Ésparias agreed they were welcome.

Certainty settled over me. I knew what I had to do.

Chapter 34

THE DAY AFTER THE VARSLAND SHIPS arrived the weather turned warmer, the sun occasionally showing through the clouds: a perfect day for Vidar to take Trygve riding. They could use the exercise, he said. I suggested the road that ran beside the Wall. They had some of their men with them, and I sent Eidyn and guards he handpicked, so it was a large party that rode out that morning. I should, really, have been among them, but my council would be expecting to be told why the envoys were here. And what else I had to say to them could wait no longer.

My first order of business was to introduce Valle. When that was done, I began. "You all want to know why Varsland has sent envoys," I said, "and why the king's son is with them. Earl Vidar and the *sjaldr* Trostann are here for certain negotiations, in peace and good faith." I saw sceptical expressions, but no one interrupted me. "That is one reason the prince is with them. But primarily he is here because King Bryngyl is proposing a betrothal between his son and Flynsà, Talyn's granddaughter." I watched my advisors closely. Dern didn't look surprised, but Garia and Reif did. Valle's face remained impassive.

"The proposal was refused." I told them why, and what the counterproposal had been, and that we expected it to be accepted. "I cannot say this was unexpected. Fifteen years ago, the king of Varsland asked to be betrothed to me. My parents refused." I caught Dern's eye. "But, as some of you have likely deduced, the *Teannasach* of Linrathe's marriage to a woman of Varsland, and my cousin Faolyn's marriage to the *Teannasach*'s sister were not coincidental." I paused.

"What I have to tell you now requires secrecy. So much so, I will ask for your promise, your oath, before I go on. You may not agree with what I say, but it must not be discussed with anyone beyond this room, not even among yourselves unless you are completely sure of privacy. Talyn alone of us knows what I am going to say. Do I have your oaths?"

One by one they gave it, with varying degrees of interest or puzzlement on their faces. When the last—Garia's—was given, I composed myself to speak.

"For the past thirty years, almost since the Casilani arrived, some of us—my parents and later myself, Talyn, the lord Sorley and Druisius, and others scattered across Linrathe and Ésparias and, yes, Varsland— have been working towards an alliance of our countries, for the time when Casil left us. That day has come."

"What," Garia said sharply, "will this alliance entail?" I heard doubt, and perhaps an undercurrent of fear, or at least caution. Reif too was frowning.

"That is to be negotiated," I said. "Trade, certainly. Closer blood ties among our leaders."

"Free movement? The Marai coming here to settle on our land?"

Purposely, I didn't answer, but took my seat. I leant forward, hands interlocked on the tabletop. "Should there be?"

"No!" I'd never seen Garia so agitated, and I'd known her a long time. "How can you even consider it, *Principe*? After—" She didn't finish her statement, just shook her head.

"What if," I said, "we allowed no-one who was an adult then to come? No one over thirty, perhaps? Do we hold what their fathers did against our own citizens like my cousin Teárdh, who was conceived in the violence of that invasion?"

"If we did," Dern said, his voice mild, "if we had shunned them, or lessened their rights as citizens, I'd be without half my sailors, at a guess."

"And me," Reif said. "I am Marai-fathered."

"But you were brought up in Ésparias," Garia argued, "not Varsland. You're one of us."

"Varsland is ruled by a king whose father was murdered by the same man who led the invasion against us," I reminded her. "He has no pride in what Fritjof did, or any desire to emulate him." I straightened, no longer the sympathetic listener. "Garia, I hear your concerns. I share some of them. Let me tell you what I see.

"Casil is gone, and I doubt they will return. Before they came—not just the soldiers, but those who came to work, to farm the land or set up businesses—Ésparias was a land of scattered villages, two roads, army camps and a few forts, isolated, alone except for our historic enemies north of the Wall and the sporadic trade with Leste. Now we know—know again—that we are part of a wider world; we have welcomed that knowledge, benefited from it in trade and education and skills learned."

Garia was listening, her expression still doubtful, but not closed. Beside her Reif leant a hand on a fist, intent on what I was saying.

"We do not know what the future brings. Will Casil's conquerors send their armies west? Or will they learn from the records kept, and see that no profit was made from our little country, and we are not worth invading?" I nodded to Muire to continue.

"Varsland trades east, as you all know," he said. "Not just from the trading port at Abher Tabha, but by a river route which bypasses both Linrathe and Ésparias—and I have little doubt they will continue to do so, no matter who sits on the Emperor's throne. It is my understanding that the rivers flow through a land suited to grain, and grain is the bulk of what Varsland buys from Ésparias. To transport grain along the river route is difficult, but it is not impossible, if they cannot trade with us for it."

"You are afraid of an alliance eastward, one that could have implications for Ésparias and Linrathe." Valle spoke for the first time, not a question, but a summary.

"I am," I said. "Such an alliance could isolate us, return us to being a small and vulnerable nation. Because—" I had to say this, had to take the long view. "Linrathe's connections with Varsland have a long and complex history. Whatever our ties of blood and friendship now, that could change." In a heartbeat, or the ceasing of one.

"Since the Casilani farms were developed," I went on, "Ésparias has grown enough grain not just for our own needs and Casil's demands, but to trade north as well. But last year's harvest was poor, and worse in Varsland—and even the previous one there was not good. Nor is this year's looking promising. Bluntly, Varsland needs grain." Half of Vidar's message to me, and the third time I'd heard of the need. I let that sink in, with all it suggested. "Muire?"

"There is an alternative," he said. "The lands on the southern shore of the Nivéan Sea, Cyrenis and Icoris, grow grain; they too supply Casil. We have not needed southern grain; we may, this year, but it is sure, as the *Principe* has said, that Varsland will, and possibly Linrathe. What is being proposed is to buy grain from Icoris for our own needs, and to trade north."

"What do we have that Icoris will want?" Reif was frowning in concentration. "Or are you considering an outright purchase?"

"Metals," I said. "Whether refined to bars or further to coin. It makes up the bulk of our trade with them, currently."

"What do we buy from them now?" Garia asked.

"Figs and dates, and some oil, and cloth," Muire answered.

"What leads you to believe they will sell us grain?" I was glad to hear probing questions from Reif. I glanced at Talyn and then Valle, seeing the amusement on my new advisor's face.

"One family controls most of the trade from Icoris," I said, "although that has been, and is to be, kept quiet. The man who will decide whether to sell us grain is Marius. Druisius's brother."

"You are certain he will do this?"

"I believe," I said, "the possibility has already been discussed and planned for." My father had played *xache* with forethought and precision, the moves following a pattern. Druise had diced, a game of chance—except when the dice were weighted.

"Is Ruar aware of this plan?" It was the first question Talyn had asked.

"No. But it was he who told me that Varsland's harvests have been worse than ours, and you have heard the concerns about how the reduction in trade at Abher Tabha will affect the country. I doubt Linrathe will find much to object to."

Or Varsland, for that matter. The fine details I would leave to Muire and his staff. I had one more thing to say. "A final consideration. We will always want to grow as much grain as we can; relying on purchased supplies is foolish. Harvests fail in Icoris and Cyrenis, too. We must think about keeping the land farmed by the Casilani here in production. I doubt very much many of the men who sailed east will return." I stopped speaking. Waiting.

"So we need more people," Garia said flatly. "That's what you're saying, *Principe*?"

"I think we need more people," I said, "and Varsland may have younger sons and daughters looking for land. As part of the alliance as my father envisioned it, offering land in Ésparias creates strong bonds. But I also think this is not my choice to make."

This time, Dern was the first to speak. "You are the *Principe*, Gwenna. Who else should make this decision?"

"I am *Principe*, yes. A leader, not an Empress." My next words would commit me to my plan. My breathing was suddenly shallow, rapid. "I want to know what the people of Ésparias think about asking Varsland to send settlers to farm the land we likely cannot. Only with the agreement of the villages will I make this offer. To this end, I will call an Assembly of village headwomen. To ask their feelings, to participate in the debate, and to be bound by their vote."

Chapter 35

I CALLED FOR REFRESHMENTS, and as we ate the food provided, I gave my council more of an idea of what my father had put into motion when I was just a baby. The work Sorley had done, and Ruar; the Varsland earls bringing the young prince Bjørn to be fostered in Linrathe to protect the royal line; the role the *Ti'ach*a had played in spreading ideas, in the guise of teaching the works of Catilius and other philosophers of Casil and Heræcria.

"Wasn't this sedition?" Reif asked, at one point.

"Yes," I said. "Had there been anyone else on the throne of Casil, we would not have survived. But Eudekia chose to see it as only forethought, the planning all good leaders do."

"So she knew?" Muire sounded incredulous.

"Yes. And Alekos, later, although we never spoke of it openly." I looked around the table. "As you cannot, you understand? Not until the Assembly next year."

"Did you know," Talyn asked, her wine glass half empty in front of her, "that it was Tirvan's headwoman, generations past, who forced the Emperor Lucian to call the first Assembly?"

It chimed faintly in my memory. "Yes, but I'd almost forgotten."

"She might have been your many-times great-grandmother. The role of headwoman tends to stay within a family. Your aunt Kira may know, actually."

"From the midwives' records." I considered this. "It might be worth finding out."

"Callan wanted a new Assembly, too," Dern said, his voice deep. "Your mother could tell you more about that: she was involved in spreading the idea." He paused. "Finn, too, might remember what Callan said at that last midwinter meeting. He was at the Winter Camp that year." He rubbed the back of his neck. "When will you call this Assembly?"

"Late spring or early summer," I said. "After planting is done, and lambing and calving are over. But with the intent relayed to the villages and towns this autumn, to give them a winter of discussion and debate."

"There will be opposition," he warned.

"I know."

"It's more complex than that," Talyn said. "There will be people who choose not to accept their council's decisions. What happens to them? Where do they go?"

"And what say, if any, do the Casilani who stayed have?" Reif asked.

"We have a winter to decide these questions," I said. "I am by no means presenting you with a completed plan."

"So much change," Garia said, so quietly I knew she was talking to herself.

"As there was for Dern and me, and all our generation, three decades past," Talyn responded. "Violence and destruction and death, and then to be governed by a distant empire, with new laws. You have no idea, Garia, none at all." She closed her eyes, briefly. "Forgive me. You can know only what you have experienced. But I was a mother, happily breeding and training horses in Han. Gwenna's mother was a fisherwoman. We had never fought, never dreamed we would need to. Women didn't. That we are now generals in this army—" She shook her head. "I could never have seen it, and I doubt Lena could have either. Our world is changing again, yes. But it is change that we are directing, choosing, controlling, and have largely planned for. Be grateful for that."

There was quite a bit more discussion, until Muire caught my eye. "Gwenna," he said quietly, "if the trade talks are to start tomorrow, we need to do some planning." I excused myself, leaving Talyn—and Dern, who'd had a fair idea of what had been happening, even if he hadn't been fully part of it—to finish answering Garia and Reif's questions.

I needed the fresh air, too. We walked over to the fort and Muire's office, and spent an hour reviewing the expected issues. Nothing would be decided tomorrow, only the first proposals made. Maybe.

"If they mention direct trade with Leste," I told my trade envoy, "until Garth has had an opportunity to tell me what he thinks—and that includes whether their harbours are suitable—we can make no decision at all. So that's for later."

He made some notes, then stretched, bending his head from side to side. "I'm expecting a long week."

"If I'm needed, let me know."

"I will. Do you want to go to the senior commons to eat?"

I hesitated. I hadn't spent much time with Muire recently. But I wanted to see Sorley, after his public revelation last night that he was going home. I had something to say to him, and a question, too.

"How about a drink this evening? You might have more questions then."

We agreed on that. I walked back to the villa, revelling in the warmth of the day. Maybe later I'd take Gwyllar to the stables to see the falcon.

Would Lairís be with Sorley? As much as I wanted to see her, I hoped not, because if she was, I couldn't ask Sorley what I needed to. When we'd woken this morning, I'd wanted to tell her—well, everything. And I couldn't. Which disturbed me, partly because I didn't want to have secrets from her, and partly because it reminded me of being with Lynthe, before my father had told her some of the plans.

Over the years Lynthe had eventually become party to most of the thinking, although some of the people involved were never revealed to her. I hadn't liked that, but now I was glad. *Mathàir*, I thought, as I walked through the summer sunshine, *I hope you've found her.* Before she could do real harm, to me, to Ésparias, to the western alliance.

~

Sorley was sitting in a chair outside his room. There were cushions under and around him, padding the wood, and his feet were resting on a small stool. I realized with a pang that it was my father's chair, and his stool. Apulo must have brought them from wherever they had been stored—and Sorley hadn't refused to use them.

"It was too nice a day to be in bed," Sorley said, at my greeting.

I settled onto a bench close by. "Have you eaten?"

"Apulo just went to fetch me something." I'd ask him to do the same for me, I decided. We sat listening to the fountain, and the chirp of sparrows—which ceased suddenly as one of the villa's cats ran from the shelter of a shrub. Half-grown, its leap at one of the birds got it nothing but air between its paws, and laughter from Sorley and me.

"You're better," I said.

"Given how much laughing hurt, not entirely."

"You know what I mean."

"Yes. A little. But Ruar was right, Gwenna. I must go home. There are"—he hesitated—"many reasons." He reached his good hand out to me. I folded my fingers around it. "I will write your mother a letter, before I go. You will give it to her?"

"Of course."

Apulo appeared in the courtyard, carrying a tray. Seeing me, he smiled. "Would you like something too, or are you joining Lairís and Trostann in the dining room?"

"Something here, Apulo, if you would."

He laid the tray on Sorley's knees. "I won't be long."

"Eat," I said to Sorley. The fish and beans wouldn't benefit from getting cold. "I suppose I won't worry about you, with Apulo to take care of you."

"Apulo on the journey, and Betis and Maj to fuss over me when I'm there," he said. "I'll send Apulo home when my hand has healed."

"Maybe he won't want to come back." I took a bean from Sorley's plate. "Sorley? What does Lairís know, about the work to create the western alliance?"

He swallowed his bite of fish. "She must know some of it. Her father sent messages to Barì with her, I know, and she's far too bright not to realize they were about more than the price of fleeces. And I don't know what she might have heard in her travels. Why?"

"I was wondering how much I could tell her."

"Tell her?" His expression changed, first to puzzlement, and then to a questioning delight. "Are you the reason she's not coming home with me?"

My cheeks warmed, although I didn't know why. "I'm afraid I am."

His grin was one of real pleasure. "Really? And it's serious?"

"I think so, yes."

"She's—" He stopped, chuckling. "I was about to say she's a lot younger than you. By ten years, which was exactly what there was between Cillian and me."

"She looks like you," I said.

"And you are so much like your father." He'd cry in a minute, I thought, but not entirely from sadness. "Oh, Gwenna, I didn't expect this."

"Neither did I." I knew I was smiling too broadly, but I couldn't stop.

"She'll have to travel," he warned. "And take the *scáeli's* exams."

"As you did," I said. "But there is work for her in Ésparias, just as there was for you." I hesitated. "And always will be, you know." He was the only parent I had now, until—unless—my mother returned.

"I know." He was quiet for a moment. "If Bryngyl accepts our proposal, I'll do what I said, and keep an eye on the prince and on Flynsà. And maybe when Amlodd is ready to retire, I'll become Dun Ceànnar's *scáeli*, and maybe I won't. I can't see that far ahead."

"I'll come and see you some day. Gwyllar should see his father's land. And so should this one." I touched my stomach. "It's a girl, I think. If I'm right, I'll name her Piása."

That did make him cry. I took the tray, placing it on the ground, and knelt to hug him. "Druisar if it's a boy," I murmured, which brought tears to my eyes too.

"Gwenna!" Apulo's voice, and disapproving. I looked up, then followed his gaze to the half-grown cat, eating the fish that had been left on Sorley's plate. I laughed.

"Sorley can have mine," I said. "I'll go to the dining room. I apologize for the extra work, Apulo."

~

For the next week I divided my time between the trade talks—usually just brief visits there, to make my oversight clear to Vidar—and my plans for a spring Assembly. I brought Kyreth into those talks as well, not just because she was the closest headwoman, but also because she had been midwife to girls and women who'd born children to the Marai. She could be one voice for them, until the Assembly.

Along with the questions raised by my advisors, there were many more: some philosophical, but some simply of management. The Assembly site should be central, and capable of housing and feeding a large number of people. A good water supply was important. I assigned this task to Garia and Reif; the organization of sending letters to every village I would give to Muire—or rather his staff—after the trade talks were done.

In between, I visited Sorley every day, found time for my son, and kept my evenings for Lairís. She was excited, full of what she was learning from Trostann, and I thanked Sorley silently for my musical education, because it meant I understood most of what she told me. She'd play for me, in our rooms, and I couldn't help thinking of the way Sorley and Druise had played for my parents. That Lairís did the same for me felt like a connection; a continuation.

I told her a little of what we were doing, enough for her to understand the significance. "My father has gone back and forth to Varsland for years," she said. "I knew it wasn't just for his own business, but I thought it was just for Ruar. Although now I understand why Sorley came to Gundarstorp so often."

"One reason," I said. We were curled together after lovemaking, the room lit only by the moon. "Lairís, I saw how he was torn, all these years, between his love for my father and Druise, and his love for Gundarstorp and all of you. I don't want you to feel the same conflict."

She turned a little so she could see my face. "And your mother. He loved—loves—her too. What happened between them?"

"I don't know, not all of it. But there were hard words spoken between them before she left." I thought about it. "She and I fought, too, after my father's death. I wanted him buried here; she wanted him to lie at the *Ti'ach*. She was right, but I was hurting too much then to see it. I think it was something like that, each believing they'd known best what my father wanted."

"I hear her name sometimes, when he's talking to Apulo," Lairís said. "I don't listen."

"Isn't listening and remembering part of a *scáeli's* skills?" I teased, wanting to lighten the mood.

"I'm not a *scáeli* yet."

"But you will be," I said, serious again. "You will be. And if I have to continue to lead Ésparias from Wall's End, so you can go back and forth to Linrathe as you need or want, then I will." Although I should go south for a time this autumn, before riding grew too uncomfortable. But maybe Lairís could come with me.

Not if my mother brought Lynthe back. The thought jolted me out of my increasing drowsiness. I recognized its truth. I could not deal with Lynthe, as either *Principe* or as her once-partner, with Lairís accompanying me. It would be unfair to both women.

Even if I could pardon Lynthe, if her motives had been misguidedly good, she could not return to Wall's End, or even to her position in the army. Maybe, I thought, there was something she could do on Leste, under Garth's watchful eye. It was an idea.

~

Muire had asked for my presence to discuss landing fees at Casilla's harbour. Vidar was arguing for the fees to be waived if the ships docked only to exchange goods for further movement.

"The harbour must be maintained," I pointed out, "and a harbourmaster and others paid." I refused his suggestion, but I would tell Muire later to offer a reduced fee if the ships involved transferred their goods without the use of harbour cranes and carts. If they found they needed them after all, there would be a price for their use.

I'd just stepped out of the meeting room, wishing all problems were as easy to solve as questions of trade, when a cadet came running. "*Principe,*" he said, "there is a messenger asking for you. He is with General Talyn."

I thanked the boy, and turned towards Talyn's office. My stomach was growling—the nausea had lasted a little longer this morning, and I'd eaten only a little bread—but hunger would have to wait. A messenger from where? I wondered, trying to mentally prepare myself. I really didn't want something more to deal with. Were I lucky, this would be something I could hand over to someone else.

"*Principe.*" The messenger stood. A military messenger. "I have a letter for you, from General Finn."

I glanced at Talyn, whose eyebrow quirked just slightly. What news had Finn sent separately from his regular reports? I took the letter, breaking its seal and reading rapidly. Then I read it again, more slowly, trying to understand its repercussions.

"Wait outside, please," I said to the messenger. "I will want to talk to you shortly."

"What is it?" Talyn asked.

"A ship arrived from the east," I said. "Not from Casil, but from Beria, beyond the Durrains. Bearing a family, and the son of that country's procurator, and horses."

"Horses?" Talyn frowned.

"Breeding stock. They are looking for refuge in Ésparias. And they have a letter offering it, signed by my mother."

"Dear gods," Talyn said. "What is Lena doing in Beria?"

"Pursuing Lynthe, I suppose." I read the last part of the letter again. "Finn says nothing of that. This family—the man is Casilani, his wife from the local people—were landholders, wealthy. The procurator's son is with them because his father has just died, and he and the family's sons are close friends."

"What are they fleeing? Surely the eastern threat has not reached Beria?"

"No." Or the implications for us would be unthinkable. "Local unrest. With the procurator dead—there was no governor—and the troops withdrawn, there is fighting among the people whose land it was, several factions vying for leadership. And most not friendly to the Casilani landholders who remain."

"Where are they now?" Talyn asked.

"At the governor's villa. Apparently his steward stayed to take care of the estate, and Finn convinced him to take them in." I put the letter down. "I will have to go south immediately. I must talk to them, get a sense of how many more people we might expect."

"Maybe not just from Beria," Talyn said quietly. "Sylana, too."

"Or even Casil?" We stared at each other. "This may change our approach to Varsland."

"And your plans for the Assembly?"

"Perhaps. Perhaps the questions asked will be different." I hadn't prepared for this; hadn't even seen the possibility. What had my mother been thinking?

Part IV

Omnia vincit amor: et nos cedamus amori
Vergil

Ecl. 10.69

Chapter 36

~Lena~

"SINCE WHEN," THE GUARD at the gate asked, "do imperial messengers have dogs?" Ladon had dropped to the ground at my command. The guard, I noted, was keeping his distance.

"Since there are no soldiers patrolling the Empire's roads." I might be dressed as a messenger, but my tone was the one I used with insubordinate cadets. I was tired and troubled, in no mood to tolerate delays. "I carry an official letters from Ésparias to the palace. The dog has helped ensure I deliver them."

"Ésparias?" the other guard said. They were both grey-haired; veterans called from retirement, I guessed. "How'd you end up on the northern road?"

"I had business in Hathusia," I said. Beyond the guards, a line of people and a few donkey carts waited to be let through. They'd join those I'd passed on the road over the last few days: men, women, families both poor and rich fleeing Casil before the enemy reached it. I'd spoken to some. The Emperor was dead, a man said, and the war lost. Another disagreed, but feared it would soon be true. Nothing official had been said, they admitted, when I probed more deeply.

"That garrison's already arrived," the first guard said. "Are there more to come from Ésparias?"

"I left several weeks ago," I said. "Some were shipping out then. They should have docked by now."

An impatient shout came from a man driving an ornate carriage. "Fucking *dignitasi*," the guard murmured. "Keep your hair on!" he shouted back. To me, he said, "Yes, they came. I hope there's more on their way. You'd better go in." He stepped to one side, holding up his hand to keep the ragged line from surging forward. "Imperial messenger!" he called. "Let her through!"

People stepped aside, but as much from fear of the horse and dog—or my grim expression—than from respect for my role. At the first square I reached, I stopped. Another guard was patrolling here, but this one was a woman.

I called to her. Then I dismounted, and led the horse over to where she stood. She was square and muscled, her dark hair streaked with grey. Close to my age, I guessed.

"Messenger?" Her voice was friendly enough.

"Where do I stable the horse?"

"You don't know?"

"I've always arrived by ship before." I was barely being polite. On the ride from Hathusia, alone except for the dog, the peace I'd found at the lake had stayed with me. The darkness and cold inside had lessened. I'd felt as I did in the first days after midwinter: despite the harshness still to come, the world had turned. I'd been content with that. I couldn't conjure Cillian's voice, not quite, but I had a sense of him, distantly, like the memory of music after the song has ended. I was content with that, too.

But in the last day or two, I'd found myself increasingly short-tempered, easily irritated. It wasn't hard to work out why. The families I met on the road, travelling west, worried me: rumours swirled and swarmed like starlings at dusk, darkening my thoughts. What would I find in Casil?

The guard gave me directions to the stables. "You can leave the dog there too," she added. "Nice animal."

I had one more question. "Where could I find your captain? Junia."

"What's your business with her?"

"She's an old friend." And possibly my way into Eudekia's presence. I had no idea whether the Empress would choose to see me, or what Lynthe—assuming she had arrived and asked for an audience—might have told her.

A flicker of interest in her eyes. "Is she? Don't hope for much. She'll be at the palace, with the Empress-Dowager, and she's rather occupied just now."

"I thought she might be," I said. "But maybe she'll have a few minutes to see me."

"Maybe." She looked me up and down. A smile lifted the corners of her mouth. "Are you an old enough friend to know the baths we use?"

I kept my answer short. "I am."

"If you're looking for company after days on the road, I'll be there this evening. Most evenings, after my shift. Or the *taberna*. See you there?" She grinned. "Life's short. Live while we can, eh?"

I wasn't going to feign interest. "Thanks for the information," I said. I mounted again, slowly riding through the streets. The clop of hooves made people at the fountains and market stalls turn. Many stepped back, sometimes with hands to mouths. Ladon's hackles were up, sensing the tension.

At one *taberna* three men stepped forward, blocking the street. Ladon growled. "Down," I told him. He dropped, but the deep rumble from his throat continued. I held up both hands. "Imperial messenger," I said. Slowly I swung my leg over my horse's withers and slid down, my eyes on the men.

The man in the middle stepped forward to look at the badge pinned to my tunic. He grunted. "From where?"

"I began in Ésparias. Hathusia was my last stop. I'm taking the horse to the stables." I had my secca. The dog would attack, either at my signal or on his own. But there were more men at the *taberna*, watching.

"Petrius!" the man called, without taking his eyes off me. "Come here."

From the shadows of the *taberna* an old man shuffled out. Gaunt, white-haired, his bowed legs told of long hours in a saddle. "Ask her something only a messenger would know."

"You came from Hathusia?" he asked. "How did you cross the river?"

"On the longest bridge I've ever seen," I told him. It had spanned the Ubë on a series of arches, high enough above the river to allow ships through. More of Tarquin's work, I'd been told.

"The inn, two days after. What's different about it?"

"There's a cave behind it, running back into the hillside. A long way back." The innkeeper had told me stories of ancient bones, and drawings on the rock of its sides and ceiling. Some said there were spirits, ghosts. He'd walled off most of it, and kept his barrels and amphorae in the part he hadn't.

The old man pursed his lips when I added this, nodding. "She's been where she says she has. Can't say more."

The lead man relaxed. "Apologies, messenger. A rider, with a sword— we're nervous."

"Understood," I said. I tried a tired grin. "I'll lead the horse."

"Probably best." He hesitated. "A drink, to say we're sorry?"

I was thirsty. And perhaps I could learn a few things. "One," I said, "and thank you."

The beer was thin and bitter, but it wet my dry throat. I listened, trying to discern the probable truth from the rumours and speculation. A ship had arrived the day before from the east, a small, fast vessel, Casil's eagle on its prow. Several men had disembarked and gone straight to the palace. The soldiers who had manned its oars were kept on board, and the ship anchored out in the harbour. No announcement had been made.

"It can't be good," the man who had offered the drink said. "Even a small victory, there'd be something said."

Silently, I agreed. "Where's the Empress?" I asked.

"At the palace," Petrius said. "Where else would she be? She's never left Casil in times of trouble, and she wouldn't start now."

"That's the old one," someone replied.

"She's still the Empress, in my eyes," Petrius stated. "The young one's doing her duty, but she's nothing on Eudekia."

"I meant the Emperor's wife," I said.

"She's there too." The speaker was confident. "The young empress and the two children. So my wife's sister says, and she works in the palace kitchens."

"If the barbarians come," a voice said, "those children are dead."

~

Three hours later, washed and changed, I stood outside the messengers' inn where I'd stabled my horse. Near the city walls, northeast of the palace, from its height on the hill I could see the southern reach of the walls, glimpses of the river—and, on its own hill, its walls white with lime, the palace itself.

The air hung heavily over the city, smelling of cooking fires and the river. Kites and crows circled lazily, or perched on rooftops alongside rows of pigeons. I began to walk downhill, passing large houses, shuttered and quiet. Against the heat of the day, or empty? When I'd ridden through the low mountains northwest of Casil, the road running easily over a gentle pass, summer villas and their expansive estates had lain on either side. The *dignitasi* were already arriving, the innkeeper had told me that night, even though the hottest months weren't yet here. At least, she'd added, the wives and children, if only some of the men.

I missed Ladon padding beside me, but I couldn't have brought him. I'd left him to guard my room at the inn, not that I had much to guard besides a few clothes, my journals and Tarquin's papers, and my bow and sword. Everything of real value was in my belt pouch.

Sweat dampened my armpits and face by the time I reached the palace. I knew where to go: Druise had told me before I left. The entrance was guarded, of course, but my badge and the seals on the letters should be enough.

"Show me the knife," the guard said, after studying the proffered letters. Imperial messengers were exempt from the prohibition of weapons inside Casil's walls, but there were still regulations around the length of the blade. I handed it to her. She nodded, and handed it back.

"The waiting room's down the corridor on the left. Tell the clerk there who the messages are for."

This level of the palace was cool, the thick stone of the walls keeping out the heat. I found the waiting room and presented myself to the man at his desk. The room was empty except for him.

"Junia?" he said. "The Commander?"

"Yes."

He frowned. "I doubt she'll see you."

"She knows me. Give her my name."

"Who is your message from?"

"Gwenna, *Principe* of Ésparias."

"Ah." He put his pen down. "Is this to do with the pair who arrived two weeks ago?"

I shrugged, hoping in the low light my face had given nothing away. "How would I know?"

"There might have been talk," he said. A man who traded in information, I thought. What palace official didn't? But, I reminded myself, so did I—and this man's question meant I was now better informed.

"I will send a boy," he said. "Take a seat."

The benches weren't comfortable, but I appreciated sitting; my feet weren't hardened to long walks on flagstone and cobble. The room was dim, the clerk's desk situated where light from a high, small window reached it. His pen scratched on paper. The sweat on my skin dried. I thought about what Lynthe might have said, what might have been believed, and what I would say to counter it. Gwenna's letter made it clear Lynthe's—and Constyn's—act was one of rebellion, a false claim. But even so, she'd wanted leniency for them both. "I don't believe Constyn conspired in this," she'd told me.

"And Lynthe?" I'd asked.

I'd watched the emotions cross her face: anger, hurt, loss. The memory, perhaps, of love.

"This was treason," I'd reminded her, gently.

"I know," she'd said. "But even treason can be forgiven, can't it? Callan did, and so did Eudekia." She'd straightened her shoulders then, a decision made. "Bring them home. Lynthe will face trial here."

~

The boy returned. "The messenger will be received," he told the clerk. I followed the boy through corridors and up steps, the halls growing wider and the walls and floors more elaborate. Apprehension began to tighten my gut. We stepped out into a level I recognised. Two guards—

both women—stood at doors half way down the corridor. My throat dried, suddenly. I wasn't being brought to Junia.

I'd stood before the Empress twice, once to sign a treaty, once in support of the daughter she wanted as her son's bride. Never as anyone close to an equal, even though the second time I was wife and mother to the royalty of Ésparias. Excluding me from rank had been a deliberate choice on her part.

She was beautiful, and learned, and intelligent, as capable of intricate, incisive thinking as Cillian. Who had admired and respected her—and if that had been all, my heart would not be pounding now, nor would there be the darker thread that was insinuating itself into the misgivings I felt. But I did not believe, had never believed, for all I had tried not to, that there hadn't been more.

Anger, or jealousy, or resentment—whatever it was, it had to be kept in check. I realized I had stopped. The boy—he couldn't be more than eight or nine—looked up at me. "Messenger?"

"Just catching my breath," I told him. "Keep going."

The door guards took my secca. They'd tried, the last time, but officially I'd been guarding the senior prince of Ésparias, and Eudekia herself had let me keep it. A magnanimous gesture, or a subtle message that Cillian was in no danger from her that day? The latter, I'd decided in the end.

Then one turned to open the door, and I stepped forward, in my creased clothes and dusty feet, into the presence of the Empress-Dowager of Casil.

Chapter 37

I WAS PREPARED TO KNEEL. But the man standing beside the Empress turned a gesture of protocol into something I couldn't help. All strength drained from my legs, and I dropped with no grace at all. Nor was I looking at Eudekia, but at the figure, dark-haired and tall, advancing towards me. Confusion—and a touch of fear—fogged my mind.

My throat closed. I couldn't say Cillian's name. I fought for clarity, for sense, and just as he spoke, the fog cleared. I saw the hazel eyes, the sunburnt skin. My son crouched beside me. "*Mathàir.*" He opened his arms.

I sagged, letting him hold me. "Colm." Hot tears rose. I blinked them back. "You're safe."

"I am," he said. "Many aren't."

I didn't care. He did; I could tell from his grim voice, but until this moment I hadn't known just how afraid I'd been, how much I'd wanted to know he was alive. I put a hand on the face of the man who'd taken the place of the boy I'd left in Casil twelve years before. "You look like your father."

"I must agree." With a jolt, I remembered where I was. I straightened my back and looked past Colm.

"Empress. Forgive me."

"Stand." Colm rose, graceful, lithe. My heart clenched. He slipped a hand beneath my elbow, helping me to my feet. I was still unsteady, although it was relief that drained me now. He kept his hand in place.

Eudekia's hair had faded to a dull ochre. Her bearing was as regal as ever, but the skin beneath her eyes looked bruised. "Lena. Before anything else, may I offer my deepest sympathy?" For a second she hesitated. "As I have told your son, Cillian was an extraordinary man. He will be greatly missed. And mourned," she added, softly.

"Thank you," I murmured, holding back the raw, resentful reply I wanted to make. What right had she to mourn him?

"One among so many," my son said.

"But not to be diminished because of that," Eudekia replied. Gently, but still a chastisement. "General, time is short, and there is much to arrange. I must ask: why are you here?" With a movement of her hand, she indicated we should sit.

Taking my place at the table gave me a brief moment to gather my thoughts. My personal reasons were of no interest to her. She had made that clear.

"A major in Ésparias's army, the sister of the late *Princip* Faolyn, took ship for Casil using falsified documents," I said, handing her Gwenna's letter. "With her is Faolyn's son Constyn. I am here to take them back to Ésparias. The major must answer for her actions."

"That won't be possible," the Empress said. I forced myself to stay calm, as Cillian would have.

"You would protect her?" The political implications of this—could I sort them out quickly enough?

"No. It is not possible because the major in question—Lynthe, is it not?—is not in Casil. She asked for protection for the boy, and then joined the recalled troops. They have gone east to the war."

What did this mean? "Protection from whom?" I asked.

"She indicated that Ésparias was in danger from Varsland again, and that Faolyn's son had been sent east so that someone of the royal line was protected. An argument that made no sense; what safety can there be here? But you have arrived in time to take the boy back to Ésparias."

"Are there still ships travelling west?"

"There are always traders. I am sure passage can be arranged." To my ears, her answer sounded evasive. But why? Probably, I told myself, she just didn't care—and why should she? Lynthe had left her nephew at the palace and gone off to fight. What would the palace have done with him, if I hadn't arrived? Was that why Colm was here?

How I was to return to Ésparias would never have been the palace's concern. "May I see Constyn?" I asked.

"When our business is concluded," Eudekia said. "A question, General. Did my last letter to Cillian not reach Ésparias, or are you ignoring what I asked in it?"

Her last letter; the one I hadn't read. "It arrived after he died," I said. "I didn't open it. He didn't share your letters, Empress, only portions he chose. A private correspondence. I—I thought I was respecting that."

Her head dropped slightly. One hand touched her brow, her eyes unfocused. "I see. It doesn't matter," she said. "Because my son had the same thought as I, and sent your son to see it was done."

"May I decline that task now, Empress?" Colm asked. "As my mother can take my place?"

"Wait, please." I looked from my son to Eudekia. "What was it you asked of Cillian, Empress?"

"Thirty years past," she said, "he asked for sanctuary for a princess of Varsland, fleeing war and retribution. I asked him for the same, for the Empress-Consort and my grandchildren, Selekos and Philita."

My breath stopped. The potential consequences of what Eudekia was asking were enormous. If a pursuing enemy reached our little land— I reached for Cillian, for his advice. Nothing. But a question was forming.

"The Emperor also asked me to take his wife and their children to Ésparias." Colm spoke quietly. "He thought if I brought them, not as a physician but as what else I am, my sister could not say no."

What else I am. Colm had never wanted to be a prince. Medicine had been his passion since boyhood, and in the medics' tents at the edge of a battlefield, it was his skill that mattered, not his birth. But when had events ever allowed us to be who we wished? Cillian had wanted only to be *Comiádh*, and I . . . I had forgotten what I had once dreamed of. "Empress," I said, turning to her, "why did you ask this of Cillian, when it was a request properly made to the *Principe*?"

Eudekia didn't answer. I recognized her expression: I'd seen it on Cillian's face often enough. She was waiting for me to see the thinking behind her move. "You have never written to her," I said, working it out. I thought of the clerk in the office many floors below, asking questions, trading in information. "A letter would have aroused suspicion, fed rumours."

"Indeed," the Empress said.

"You could have made the request through your governor."

"I could have, yes. But that would have been inefficient. Clumsy. More messages and travel and meetings would have been needed, the trappings of diplomacy. Much easier to ask a father to speak to his daughter."

Something twisted in me, something dark. I spoke before good sense stopped me, wanting to hurt. Knowing I lied. "I have no authority to grant this. It is not a military matter."

"Sorley did it for Bjørn," Colm protested. "Without consulting Ruar."

"Linrathe is not Ésparias," I told him. "The *Teannasach* leads his people, but his authority is not absolute. He is bound to listen to his landholders and his *toscairen*, and Sorley was both. But tell me. Did Alekos order you to do this?" If so, then there was no question. He was Ésparias's emperor. My cruel words—words I already regretted—would not influence the outcome.

"No. It was a request to a friend." He glanced at the Empress, a question in his eyes. Her face tightened. She nodded. "*Mathàir*, this cannot be repeated beyond this room. Alekos is dead. The rightful emperor of Casil and its provinces is a six-year-old boy."

History repeats, Cillian had told his students. But always with small variations, and one here was key. Rosale, as I remembered her, was kind, and intelligent enough to be more than simply Alekos's bedmate and mother to his children. But she lacked the steel within to do what Eudekia had, to hold a city and an empire for her son. Nor had Eudekia faced an enemy like the one that now threatened Casil.

I could not let my resentment—my irrational resentment—of the Empress threaten the lives of children. "Empress," I said, "May I speak to my son privately?"

"I will have refreshment sent," she said, rising with the unopened letter in her hand. "You have half an hour." She closed the door to the room beyond.

Silence, for a heartbeat, and another. Colm's shoulders dropped. He ran a hand through his hair. "Lives will be lost because Alekos sent me back to Casil," he said.

"To save his wife and children." I kept my voice gentle. "He has put their lives in your hands now."

"But you are going back to Ésparias, with Constyn. You can take Rosale and the children too." The skin around his eyes tightened, revealing tiny lines, more than a man of twenty-five should have. "To say you don't have the authority—I don't understand, *Mathàir*."

"I haven't. To give sanctuary to the Empress and the heir is not a general's decision. That is all I am, Colm." I was prevaricating, trying to convince myself my refusal was justified.

He grimaced. "But Ésparias is a province of Casil's empire. Surely the Empress-Consort needs no permission from anyone."

He was a physician, not a diplomat. "We were a province," I said. "By asking permission of the *Principe*, and through your father, not the governor, we are also being given a message. Casil is turning its back on us, just as your father always thought they would one day."

"Look back over the past, at the empires that rose and fell, and predict the future," Colm quoted. "I remember." He looked up, his eyes hollow. "Your letter, the one telling me he had died—I had been in the surgery tents for days, saving some lives, losing more. Ten days ago, maybe. The Emperor, and Bjørn—they came to sit with me, to honour his memory, when they should have been making plans." He swallowed, hard. "Before dawn, before the battle started, Alekos came back. To ask me to save his wife and children. I argued. But he ordered me back to Casil, and so I am here."

"Ordered you back to Casil, but not to Ésparias?"

He nodded. "He said he had never ordered Gwenna to do anything. He even laughed, and said he was afraid to. But that he felt sure she would grant the request, as he had once granted hers."

The Empress had not given us enough time together now for me to explain all that had happened twelve years before. On the ship home, I thought.

"His order was to an army physician," I said. "His request was to his friend."

"I should be there."

"Alekos thought differently. Both as your emperor and your friend. He entrusted you with his wife and children. A different way of saving lives."

"I understand," he said. "I must act as the prince. Something I have not done in a dozen years. So advise me, *Mathàir*, as you have advised my sister the *Principe* for all that time. Can I, Prince Colm, order you to take the Empress-Consort of Casil and her children to Ésparias in his stead, and present the request to the *Principe*?"

This close to him, I saw the pallor beneath the sun-browned skin, the taut jaw and the flick of a tiny muscle beneath an eye. "No," I said gently.

"You can't. No more than Constyn can." His friends are dead, I reminded myself. So were too many others, soldiers he'd known, fought to save. Their blood on his hands, their screams and prayers in his ears.

Cillian, confronted with the news of the Marai invasion and the deaths they had caused, had wanted to go home, into that fray, to avenge and atone. To go to war, even though he lacked the skills to fight. What his son wanted was little different.

"Colm," I said. "I understand. I lost friends, good ones, both when Leste invaded and when the Marai were the enemy. Some died because of my orders. But I think there is little a physician can do now, and you are no soldier."

"I can use a sword," he said. "You taught me. Sword and bow and secca, remember?"

"You were a competent twelve-year-old. When was the last time you practiced?"

He looked away, tension apparent. Holding back an angry retort, I guessed. "Have you seen Constyn?" I asked.

"Yes," he said, his tone short. Then, "Yes, I have. He was glad to see me, when I told him who I was." Colm half smiled. "I am a hero in his eyes, because his mother ensured he knew that I had given him his dog."

An opening here for an argument for his return to Ésparias, but not one I would make. "The prince's dog," I said. "That's how Peritas was known around Wall's End. He has his own memorial stone. Did Constyn tell you that?"

"No. Really?" The thought brought a smile, for a moment. "He was a good dog."

Another good dog was guarding my belongings at the inn. I would have to return to him today. There was something I had to do first, though. I took the small leather bag from my belt pouch. "Your father wanted you to have this." I handed the bag to our son.

The ring dropped into Colm's palm. He stared at it. Then he closed his fingers around it and raised his fist to his mouth, the knuckles white. "Why? What is its meaning?"

"He didn't say. It was his father's."

"His father the Emperor. I am a physician."

"Your father was a teacher," I reminded him. "Before anything else, and always, even after Eudekia made him a prince. You can be more than one thing, Colm."

He didn't reply. He slipped the ring onto the middle finger of his left hand. "It fits," he said quietly. "Gwenna's was too big. She had to wear it on a chain, beside her pendant."

"Until we returned to Ésparias, and had it made smaller." I remembered something. "Do you still have your pendant?"

"Somewhere. Why?"

"Because your father made sure you had that, the sigil of the royalty of Ésparias, in case you ever needed to prove who you are. His intent in giving you the ring was something different." Something, perhaps, that even Cillian found difficult to put into words. Not just honouring the memory of the father he had known so briefly, and whose absence—and then presence—in his life had shaped so much of who he'd been, but asking, perhaps hoping, that Colm might remember him, too, with love and respect. "He loved you deeply, you know," I added.

Sudden tears glittered in his son's eyes. "I know." He smiled, then sobered. "How are you coping, *Mathàir*?"

"I am—adjusting. It isn't easy."

He nodded. "And Sorley?"

A question I hadn't expected. "Not well," I admitted.

"At least in Ésparias he can openly mourn." Before I could say anything, he said, "Gwenna told me. To save me from worrying like she had, she said, once I realized *Athàir* and Sorley were more than friends."

"Would you have?"

"Realized, or worried? Neither, probably."

That made me laugh. I would let him remember his life in Ésparias, the people he'd loved there. Perhaps that, coupled with the responsibility Alekos had entrusted him with, would be enough for him to choose freely to come home. I had one more move I could make, one that robbed him of choice. I didn't want to make it; I wouldn't, not yet. Not unless I had to.

Chapter 38

COLM AND I HAD NO CHANCE to talk further. Eudekia entered the room, and with her a woman I recognized. "Junia!" I said, with real pleasure.

"Lena." Her smile was one of genuine welcome. "It's good to see you again, even under the circumstances." The smile became a grin; in her own way, Junia was as irrepressible as Druise. "The messenger's uniform suits you."

"It's served its purpose," I said. "You look well." She did, wiry and muscled, her hair, streaked with grey, cropped short.

"I am." She glanced at Colm. "I'm sorry, but I need to take your mother away."

He nodded. "Commander. Perhaps I'll go and play *xache* with Constyn. It will keep us occupied."

"Come," Junia said to me. Eudekia had disappeared into her private rooms. I followed Junia along the corridor to another room, this one with a long table. I recognized it: I'd signed the treaty here. I recognized what lay on the table, too: a map, weighted at the corners, game pieces representing armies arranged on its surface.

Armies and ships, I saw as I drew closer. All far too close to Casil. "The military advisors are debating," Junia said, a tip of her chin indicating another room. "But I see no escape. The enemy outnumbers us, and without the Emperor—" She shook her head.

"I see." I studied the map, but I saw nothing to contradict Junia's analysis. "Who is regent for Selekos?"

"Eudekia. But that is a closely held secret. No official announcement of Alekos's death has been made."

"You are sure, though?"

"Yes. A reliable report. His personal guardsmen protected him for much of the battle, but they fell to greater numbers, and shortly after, the Emperor was killed."

"Bjørn too," I murmured, with a pang of regret, remembering the sword the handsome prince of Varsland had entrusted to Cillian. The blade had been Bjørn's private gift to Alekos, along with an offer of a band of Marai men to act as the young emperor's personal guard. An offer Alekos had accepted, not long after.

"Yes. And many of his men. Not all."

Something in her tone made me ask. "Not all?"

"Some may have changed sides, when they saw how the tide of battle turned. Always a problem, when soldiers are not fighting for their country or their families."

Among those traitors would be those who would know that Alekos's young physician was also a prince. Colm would be a target: for retribution, possibly, but more likely to be held for ransom. "How long?" I asked Junia.

"Days."

"Will the Empress leave?"

"No." Junia's voice was level. "She is adamant. Rosale and the children must try to find safety beyond Casil, but Eudekia will stay in the city."

Selekos, if he survived, would be an emperor without an empire. Eudekia wanted him sent to Ésparias. A spider of alarm crawled up my spine. I regretted not reading her last letter to Cillian. There were implications I needed time to think about, and questions I needed to ask. And time was short.

"Can I see the Empress again?" I wanted answers now.

"Not immediately. She is with her advisors for some hours." Advising on what? What plans did you make, when your city was about to fall? Junia must have seen my frustration, because she said, "I haven't eaten. Have you?"

"Not since this morning."

"Then let's get some food, and I'll have a room prepared for you."

"My things are at the post inn by the north wall," I told her.

"I can send someone for them."

"No," I said, "You can't. I'll have to go myself." I'd have sore feet, and—

"Why?" Junia asked, frowning.

"There's a dog," I said.

~

The walk back to the inn—mostly uphill, it seemed—had me sweating. To my surprise, Junia had come with me. "There's a good *taberna* near that inn," she'd said. "I might as well eat there one last time. His beer's good, too."

One last time. I didn't ask. If Eudekia would not leave the city, neither would Junia. The enemy would not let the Empress-Dowager of Casil live, nor her bodyguards. Could I be as calm as Junia, knowing what she faced?

At the inn I paid for the room—the innkeeper would never collect my fee from the palace now—and walked up the stairs to my room. "Ladon," I said, before I opened the door. He was on his feet, tail gently waving. It stopped when he saw Junia.

"Friend," I told him, and the tail tip resumed its movement. She offered him her hand to smell. He sniffed, tentative, and then swiped at it with his tongue. Junia pulled her fingers back before he made contact, smoothing his head instead.

"He's fierce looking," she said.

"Trained to kill, apparently." Ladon whined, barely audibly. "I should take him out."

"I'll stay here with your bags," she offered. I took the dog out into the yard of the inn. He sniffed around, found a post to his liking, and lifted his leg. I waited. The animal had good bladder control. Finished, he went to the horse trough, put his paws on the edge, and lapped up water. Then he returned to my side.

Ladon trotted up the stairs in front of me, and into my room. Junia was sitting on the bed. She stood when I entered. "Lena. I haven't said how sorry I am. About Cillian."

"Thank you," I said, because it was all I could say.

She put out a hand to touch my hair. "You're almost as grey as I am, *amané.*" Her hand slid down to my shoulder. I heard my own wordless sound, and then her arms were around me, not asking anything, just holding me, as no one had for so long. I didn't weep. We stood like that for what felt like a long time, until she drew back a little and bent her head, just a little, to kiss me.

"I can ask for a room for you at the palace," she said softly. "Or you can share mine."

To be held; to feel another's skin against mine, to remember, perhaps, that there was still pleasure and comfort to be found in the world. "We'll share," I murmured.

"The dog," she said, "stays outside."

~

We were older, but neither of us had forgotten what gave the other pleasure, even if the small flask of olive oil Junia kept by her bed was needed. We'd gone to the baths first. Then I'd sat in her room while she did her last check with her soldiers and the Empress. I'd sipped unwatered wine, slowly, waiting. Wanting. Not just the comfort of another's skin and scent and touch, but the solace of familiarity.

One small lamp burned, afterwards. We lay with fingers entwined, facing each other. "Roll over," Junia whispered. I did as she asked. She curved her body against mine, her arm around my waist. "Thank you," she said.

"Shouldn't I be thanking you?"

"Not this time. I didn't want to spend my last nights of this life alone. The huntress heard my prayers, I think."

"Maybe." Junia's belief in the deity of the horse archers was deep and complete, her initiation into the temple rituals far past that of a novice. I had blamed the huntress for my youngest daughter's death: a life for a life, I'd thought. The gods had given Cillian back; the goddess had guided the arrow I had loosed from too far away to kill Fritjof, in vengeance and triumph. Both must be paid for, I had thought, and Lianë had been the cost.

Junia had taught me otherwise. Lovemaking was part of her worship, but only between women. 'No man,' Junia had told me then, 'may see the huntress unclothed. We all carry her within us, and if we are sworn to her, we are sworn to shun men. But you are not; you never have been. She would exact no price from you.'

She'd seen the doubt in my eyes and grinned, wickedly, playfully. 'But another woman may see the huntress's acolyte unclothed without being sworn to her, if the acolyte so chooses. And I choose, Lena. Do you?'

I had. Without guilt, without a sense of betrayal, because this was not for simple pleasure, but to begin to heal a hurt that Cillian could not, because he shared it; because in loving we had made Lianë, who had died, and that memory hovered between us, casting a shadow.

In time we'd found our way back to a communion not clouded by loss, but neither of us, I thought, had done it alone. I wondered now, lying against a woman who hadn't expected anything from me in our days together, what had passed between Cillian and Sorley in that time. Something had changed between them, but in the upheaval of our first year in Ésparias, and our slow return to a new equilibrium, had that shifted again?

Why did I stay, knowing he loved you more?

I'd never thought Cillian had loved me more; quantifying his feelings for us wasn't something I'd even considered. What I did know was that he had loved Sorley first. I'd put that puzzle together slowly, remembering the bits and pieces Cillian had told me in the first months of our exile.

This wasn't the time to think about it. But when I was alone again, I would.

Junia kissed my shoulder, her lips light. Not an invitation, just to make the contact, I thought. She'd needed to make love as much as I had, if for different reasons. Perhaps her goddess had brought us together for a night or two.

"Sleep," I murmured, drifting.

Her arm around my waist tightened, her body tensing. "There's something I have to tell you."

"Now?"

"Yes. I should have told you earlier, but you might have set the dog on me." Lightly said, but there was doubt in her voice.

"What is it?"

"The officer you're chasing, Lynthe? She's dead."

"Dead?" I lay still. Relief, anger at the waste of a life, sorrow for Gwenna—all roiled in my mind. *Oh, Lynthe. You foolish, foolish woman.* "When? How do you know?"

A long pause. "Junia?"

"I ordered it."

I moved away and sat up, facing her. The lamp cast a faint light, and no warmth. "Why? And how?" But before she answered, I knew. "Druisius." Protecting his Kitten.

"Druisius. He sent a message. I can show you, but it's coded, won't make sense." She propped herself on one elbow. "He said she was a traitor, and dangerous."

"She was." Regardless of what she'd told the Empress, I didn't believe she could have thought Constyn safer here. Her intent, I was sure, had been to use him as a bribe, a prince of Ésparias to lead their invasion of our land. Slowly, I worked it out.

"She went to battle so she could contact the enemy, make the offer of herself and Constyn. Before the chaos when they reach Casil and the palace."

"That was my assumption. And I trust Druisius's judgement."

He would have done it himself, had it been possible, I thought. Better this way.

"It looks like she died in battle?"

"Yes. The arrow that took her is one of theirs." Collected from the field. No one wasted arrows, regardless of who had made or loosed them.

A profound sadness filled me. Another grief, for Gwenna, for all of us, and the sense of a burden shouldered. I would never tell Gwenna the truth. Let her believe her misguided, angry lover had died fighting for Ésparias. Druise's role in Lynthe's death would remain my secret, mine and his.

Unless—"What happened to the messenger Druisius sent with the letter?"

"He went east, to fight."

He too was likely dead. I reached for Junia's hand. "I won't set Ladon on you," I said. "But it was a terrible thing for Druisius to ask."

"I've known Druisius a long, long time," she replied. "He wouldn't have asked without good cause." She smiled. "He protects your family like I protect Eudekia. He'd give his life for your daughter. Or for any of you, I think."

I thought the same. Junia sighed, and lay down again, holding out her arms. "Come," she said. "We really should try to sleep."

I slid into her embrace. She pulled the blanket over us and blew out the lamp. Lying in the dark, I felt her breathing change as sleep claimed her. A long time passed before it took me too.

Chapter 39

JUNIA WOKE ME AT DAWN, not purposely. "I'm on duty." She touched my cheek. "Tonight again, the gods willing?"

I made a noise of assent, not properly awake. I heard the creak of the door opening. "Out?" she asked Ladon. He'd spent the night curled on the floor of the corridor. "No? Well, go see Lena." Claws tapped. Warmth breath tickled my cheek.

"All right" I said. "I'll get up."

I washed and dressed, the dog watching. Last night Junia had led me through hidden passages, the ways servants moved between floors. "I don't need my guards giving me knowing looks," she'd whispered, "and neither do you." I'd go back the same way, I decided.

I came out onto a lower floor. One flight of stairs took us outside. The door guard let me pass without question; Juna would have ensured that on her rounds the previous day.

I knew what I had to do next, but it was too early. I walked towards the forum, quiet except for a few priests and *scraptae*. Ladon padded alongside, alert.

"Messenger?" a priest called.

"Yes?"

"Is there any news?"

I shook my head. "I came from the west. I know no more than you."

He went on his way. The day was already warm, the air heavy. I could find the market, I thought. Druise had led us along this path, turned—where? Here, I decided, the shape of a building tugging at my memory. Noises and smells drifted my way. Hunger stirred.

"Messenger?" Another query. I was beginning to regret my green tunic. I repeated my answer. But more people approached. Ladon growled, deep in his throat. I put a hand on his collar. "Peace," I told him.

"Messenger?" More voices now.

"I have no news," I called. A hand reached for my arm—and Ladon's quiet rumble changed to a snarl. His hackles went up. He began to bark, each deep sound beginning with a growl. The man backed away, blanching, hands held high.

"Peace," I told the dog again. His barks subsided, but his tail stayed low, and his eyes never left the man who'd tried to touch me.

"I told you," I said, pitching my voice to carry, "I have no news. Now let me pass to buy some bread, or I will not stop the dog next time."

The bread was fresh, and warm, and the woman selling it didn't want to take my coin. "A small compensation," she said, "for the disrespect."

"It wasn't you who was disrespectful," I said, putting the coins into her hand. But I did let her give me a scorched loaf for the dog. One less for a beggar child, but Ladon had earned it. I sat on a low wall, tearing chunks off each loaf, tossing the dog his between bites of my own. Thinking about what Junia had told me last night, and what I must tell Constyn today.

We returned, unmolested, to the palace. Perhaps word had spread about a woman messenger and her vicious dog; if so, I was glad of it. I asked a question of the door guard, and was directed, as I'd expected, to the upper floors, to a room overlooking the central courtyard. A guard stood there, too. Seeing me, she stepped forward.

"General?"

"I would like to see the prince Constyn."

"I was told to expect you." She eyed the dog. "He's bigger than I imagined."

Inwardly, I chuckled, imagining Junia's description to her soldiers: "A slight woman, about my age, with a large dog." Ladon was proving useful in ways I hadn't imagined. The guard opened the door.

Constyn was reading, the remnants of his breakfast on a low table beside him. He looked up. The book dropped to the floor. He stood, relief flooding his features.

I could take one of two approaches. I only trusted myself with one. "Cadet, report," I ordered.

"General." He straightened. Saluted. "Where should I begin?"

"You were sent to the Eastern Fort as an aide to Muire. An order from the General Talyn. Am I correct?"

"You are, General."

"Garia was the senior officer in that party. How did you come to be under Lynthe's command?"

He blinked a few times, collecting his thoughts. "Lynthe is my aunt," he said, "and the *Principe*'s *quincala*. As you know." He looked embarrassed, I thought, explaining this to me. But he had been taught to give a full report, which included details he could expect the officer taking the report to know. Assumptions led to misinterpretations.

"Go on."

"She—Lynthe—suggested we walk after dinner one night. I think—" He hesitated, suddenly unsure. "I think she told Muire she wanted to know how I was feeling. After . . ."

"After Cillian's death?" I asked gently. Constyn had been Cillian's last student. "A good mind," he'd told me. "He will make a diplomat, should he choose that path."

"Yes." So Lynthe had used her nephew's emotions to make him trust her, taking advantage of his vulnerability, pretending to be his friend and confidant. Had she used those same tactics twelve years earlier, when it was Gwenna who was confused and unsure?

"And then?" I damped down my anger. Lynthe was dead. A grief for those who had loved her, but they were free of her machinations.

"She asked if I understood what was happening with the Casilani troops. I told her I did. Then she said that Ésparias was in danger from Varsland again, and Gwe—the *Principe* wanted me out of the country, so there was someone royal to lead Ésparias if she—the *Principe*—and her son were killed."

The son Lynthe had threatened. "You believed the major?"

He wanted to squirm; I could see it, but he managed not to. "At the time, General."

"But not later."

"No, General. Her explanation was flawed."

"But she outranked you, both in your military role and your private one," I said.

"Yes, General."

"Thank you, Cadet." I smiled. "Constyn. You can relax now." He'd had no conscious part in Lynthe's betrayal, I was sure.

His shoulders dropped. "What's the dog's name?"

"Ladon." To the dog, I said, "Friend." His tail wagged, and if a dog can be said to smile, he smiled, looking up at Constyn. The boy dropped to his knees.

"Come here?" he said. Ladon looked at me.

"Go," I told him. A memory surfaced: twelve years earlier, in this same room. Gwenna, asking Colm what he wanted for the dog he'd left behind at Wall's End.

"Let Constyn keep him," he'd said. "He'll need a friend, now his father's dead."

Colm had known then he was staying in Casil. I knew we were not, and what I would do with Ladon I had no idea. But I could lend him to Constyn for a while. He might need a friend again.

The dog was licking Constyn's face. "Ladon," I said. "Guard."

Constyn frowned. "Guard? There are guards on the door."

"I know. But now he'll stay with you when I leave. He's trained to protect someone, if that command is given. And I don't need him following me all around the palace."

Delight showed itself in a broad smile, and a hug for the dog. "Constyn," I said, "we need to talk about a few things before I leave."

"All right." Reluctantly he got to his feet. "Down," he told the dog, which dropped immediately, to my pleasure.

"What do you want to know, General?" he asked.

"You said Lynthe's explanation was flawed. Can you explain?"

"Two things, or rather one thing, twice." I liked the precision. "I am not the only person of royal blood outside of Ésparias. My cousin—" He paused. "Your son, Colm, was already here. And he is the *Principe's* brother. Lynthe is here now too. I am the third and youngest. It made little sense that the *Principe* would have ordered me from Ésparias as a—" He searched for words. "As a contingency."

Had he chosen that word at random? Or had Cillian spoken to him about contingencies, about when planning for a different future was prudent preparation, not treason?

What would you have said to him now, Comiádh? I asked. But only to focus my mind. I sat on one of the stools, gesturing to Constyn to do the same. "But what if both Colm and Lynthe were dead?"

His forehead furrowed. "Then, yes. But they aren't."

"Until a few days ago, Colm was a battlefield doctor, working in great danger. And Lynthe, after she ensured you were safe here, went to war."

He caught my tone, the unsaid words. The realization showed in his eyes. "She's dead," he said flatly.

"Yes. I learned late last night."

He blinked several times, his bottom lip quivering. The cadet in front of his general, I realized, not wanting to show emotion. "I'll leave you for a few minutes," I said. "With Ladon." He nodded, not speaking. I'd give him half an hour. The dog knew what to do.

Chapter 40

CONSTYN WAS CALM WHEN I returned. His eyes were red, but he had control of himself. "What happens now?" he asked.

"We're going home, as soon as I can arrange it."

"How?"

"By ship, I hope." I thought I knew who would take us, or at least find us passage. But while I'd sat in the courtyard, giving Constyn time to weep for Lynthe, I'd had another idea. One I was slightly ashamed of, but I'd remembered something Sorley had told me once, about how he'd helped convince a room full of sceptical landholders to accept Ruar, no older then than Constyn was now, as their *Teannasach*.

"It's their hearts you want to convince, when their heads are reluctant," he'd said. "Music and songs are good for that."

I had neither, but I did have a boy Colm had once felt sympathy for, and a dog. The dog, I thought, might tip the balance.

~

In the corridor a guard approached. "The Empress requests your presence, General."

I couldn't take Constyn with me. "Do you know where my son is? The physician," I added, at her blank look.

"He's gone out, General. He had his physician's bag with him."

I swore, silently. Had someone called for him? Or had he simply gone to find a doctor he could assist?

The latter, I decided. Who would know he was here? "Then—" I turned to Constyn. "What would you like to do?"

"I'd like to see the city. I've heard so many stories from other cadets whose fathers or grandfathers came from here. And from the *Comiádh*."

Cillian had continued to use his Linrathan title with his younger students, with Ruar's blessing. His senior students, on their way to becoming officers or officials, had called him Major, at least to his face. When they spoke of him among themselves, he was 'the Prince', said with affection and respect.

"What is the news?" I asked the guard.

"Nothing, General. He'll be safe enough in the public squares, with guards and the dog,"

"Can you arrange it? I can find my way to the Empress."

"She's in her private rooms."

I hadn't expected that. The guard gave me directions. I found them easily enough, and was allowed in immediately. Eudekia was standing, looking out at the city from an open window. She turned at my entrance. I began to kneel.

"Don't," she said. I straightened. She was wearing a simple gown of a green not so different from my uniform, but of a richer fabric. Her hair was braided and pinned, a style she could have done herself. Only her bearing spoke of her position and her power. "May we speak as mothers? Or more correctly, grandmothers?" She smiled a little. "Perhaps matriarchs is the right word?"

"For you, perhaps," I said. Hearts and heads. She was appealing to my heart, looking for common ground. But she was also a woman whose son was dead, and perhaps there was more than manipulation behind her words.

"I think for you too. Your daughter is *Principe* of your land; her son will succeed her. You began a royal line. Matriarch is appropriate."

"Perhaps," I said. "But I am only a soldier."

"When I said that to Cillian," she said, "he told me how wrong I was. And I was. Will you accept my apology for that long-ago slight, Lena?"

I inclined my head. "Empress." What point was there in that grudge now?

She laughed, although I could see it was forced. "Empress. I was only a scholar's daughter, you know. I should have married a junior tax official and followed him to Halachia or Odïrya or another province, like my friend Ennaia. But love had other plans. As it did for you, did it not?"

"It did."

"Had Philitos lived, I think he would have matured into a man as notable as your Cillian. Our fate was to love great men, and bear the cost of that."

Your Cillian. A tacit admission? I thought so. The Empress-Dowager of Casil did not speak casually. Where was this dance of words taking us? "You became great yourself," I said.

"As did you, if in a different way." I raised an eyebrow. "The slayer of Fritjof; a scholar of history; now a general?" she said. "These are not small things."

"I would dispute the scholar," I said drily.

"Your husband did not, and his judgement surely supersedes yours in that? Or are you saying love blinded him?"

"Love," I said, suddenly enjoying this game, "surprised him. But it never blinded him, Empress. Cillian always knew exactly what he was doing."

Something flickered in her eyes, a memory. "Yes," she said. "I know. Even when it was dangerous."

"Even then."

We looked at each other. Eudekia spoke first. "I concede the draw. Shall we leave this gameboard, and enjoy some morning tea as two grandmothers may? Although—" She tilted her head. "Did you know your grandmother, Lena?"

"Not really. I was very small when she died."

"Let me tell you about mine."

~

I was spluttering with laughter after Eudekia finished telling me about how her grandmother had confirmed Philitos's father's capability for another, diplomatic, marriage. "My father was horrified," the Empress said. "And she had said it so matter-of-factly, as if she'd been testing whether he could keep up with her on a brisk walk, not meet his marital responsibilities." She took a breath, let it out slowly. "I loved her. She made it possible for me to marry Philitos, and she left me her island villa.

I used—" Her voice caught. She swallowed, and continued. "I used to take Alekos there in the heat of the summer, away from the city, if Casil's affairs allowed. It is where I would have sent Rosale and the children, were the threat not from the east."

Now I knew why I was here. And perhaps I could turn Eudekia's tactics to my own advantage. Because there was a simple solution to the question of Rosale's request for sanctuary, and under other circumstances, the Empress would have seen it.

"You want me to take her west," I said.

"As you know. Why have you refused?"

"For the reasons I gave. I haven't the authority." I met her eyes. "But my son does."

Comprehension flashed across her face. "And you want to use that to make him return to Ésparias, when he wishes to stay here."

"I want him to choose to return, and your request for sanctuary for the Emperor's family is an argument I will use," I said bluntly. "Colm is a good man, I believe, but he is torn between two loyalties, and one is more real to him than the other."

She considered my words. "I could strengthen that argument," she said. "I am regent for Selekos, although that has not been officially proclaimed, of course. While I still have the power, I must appoint a successor. A regency council, I think. Rosale, and the *Principe* of Ésparias, and her brother. Would that not solve both our concerns?"

And create many more. I sat back, thinking. What did it change? If the Boranoi alliance learned where Rosale and the children were and came after them, did it matter if they had simply been given sanctuary, or that Gwenna and Colm were regents for the boy?

It did. Because it gave my children the right to govern Casil and its empire until Selekos was of age, and that made us an enemy of the Boranoi too. If they were determined to conquer all the lands once held by Casil, we would face war against an enemy we could not defeat.

I closed my eyes, trying to see the gameboard, all the possible moves. *Cillian,* I said silently. *I don't know what to do.*

A night not long before an imminent war. A bed, disordered by lovemaking, the room dark except for one flickering lamp. A conversation, and a decision. I do not think we have the right to refuse the succession for our children.

Thank you, I said, to whomever—god or shade—had sent the memory.

"This is not my decision," I said to the woman trying to shape a future, not for herself, but for her child's children. And perhaps for the city and the empire she had given her life to. "I propose this: appoint Rosale the regent, and suggest that Gwenna and Colm be her advisors. There are dangers to Ésparias if the *Principe* or her brother are co-regents, as I am sure you must see."

"You wish to give them time to weigh those dangers, and the implications for your country," she said.

"Yes."

"I doubt the enemy that is nearly at our gates will find much distinction between an advisor and a co-regent," she warned.

"The Boranoi envoy with whom Cillian negotiated the treaty you needed was subtle and skilled," I countered. "Have they lost that sophistication in thirty years?"

"The Boranoi? I believe not. Although their king is not subtle, or not to his people. But the kingdom with whom they are allied? We had little chance to find out." She stood, a motion of her hand telling me not to rise, and went to the window. "I have given all the days of my adult life to this city and its empire. In a short time, those days will end. There is no time for argument and negotiation. I will do as you ask."

Loss, I thought, cannot always be avoided. Every sun sets. Cities fall, men die, regardless of how much they are loved. "Must all days end for you?" I asked. "Why should you not come west too?"

"I held an empire for my son for almost two decades," she answered. "I lost the husband I loved; I expelled two babies from my womb to ensure Alekos had no rivals. I had my second husband poisoned when he conspired to give the throne to his descendants." She turned from the window. "Do I shock you?"

I hadn't ever expected to feel compassion for her. "I have blood on my hands I cannot forget either."

She nodded. "I have never left Casil in times of strife, and I will not now. No one will say I fled."

Such pride. But she was the last ruler of an empire that had stood for nearly a thousand years. I searched for words. "You are very brave."

"Not so very," she said, her words quiet. "Junia has her instructions, when the palace is taken." She left the window to sit again, across from me. "You are also brave, inviting me to be an exile in your country, when only a minute or two ago you were worried about giving the Empress-Consort sanctuary."

"In Ésparias, Rosale cannot be known to be the Empress-Consort," I said, "nor can the children be known by anything by their names, and perhaps not even those."

"A small issue," Eudekia said. "But you speak as if you have decided she is to go. What if your son refuses to be her protector?"

"When you gave refuge to Irmgard of Varsland, it was neither Cillian nor the General Turlo who asked," I said. "Perhaps because she could not speak to you herself, your memory is unclear. Irmgard was a princess, perhaps briefly a queen. It was her ship that brought us here, and the request for sanctuary was hers. Cillian was only her translator."

"Of course," she said. "But Rosale cannot do that, without revealing who she is. Which could put her and the children in danger, again, as well as your country."

I should have known Eudekia had thought of it; why did I think I could see a solution she could not? "But," she continued, "a general of your land escorted Irmgard to the palace to make that plea. Cannot another general of Ésparias do the same? You can find some pretence to bring her to your daughter, I imagine."

There was one very plausible reason she would be introduced to Gwenna. "I can," I said.

Eudekia laid her hand over mine for a moment. "Thank you. And now plans must be made. We have little time. Passage for—six people?—must be arranged."

"Seven, I think, if there is someone to help Rosale with the children. Although the girl is how old?"

"Philita is eight. They will not need help. And a nursemaid might draw attention. But so will a woman travelling alone with children. Questions will be asked."

"Not if she is travelling with her husband and his mother, and his younger brother. A family fleeing Casil together."

"Oh, very good. Very good indeed, Lena." She gave me a smile I could only call conspiratorial. "Do you think Colm will agree to this? Have you stopped to think that his reluctance to leave Casil may also be for personal ties?"

Chapter 41

I HADN'T. WHICH WAS FOOLISH, but somehow, I hadn't fully accepted Colm wasn't a boy now. Surely, at his age, there would be someone. Man or woman? I had no idea. A man would be easier; for the duration of a voyage, the pretence of Rosale being Colm's wife could be maintained. Another woman—especially if she was truly his wife--might not be willing to go along with the ruse.

But no. Had Colm married, he would have told us. Surely?

I thought back over the years of letters. In the beginning they'd reflected the excitement of what he was learning, his first small surgeries, travelling to Gnaius's summer villa. Descriptions of birds and animals new to him; the delight of swimming in a warm ocean. Then more serious discussions, of the limitations of medicine, of his responsibilities to those he treated; when to offer hope, when not to. And then, less often, and sometimes clearly in haste, the letters written at the edge of battlefields, the lives he had saved, the ones he had not.

Only two names had been mentioned with any regularity: Alekos and Bjørn. No, a third: an assistant, but I had no recollection of a name. Perhaps, though, the relationship of mutual accommodation and affection that existed between many officers and their aides? Turlo and my father; Casyn and Birel. Tarquin and Druisius. Even Gwenna and Lynthe had begun that way, although Lynthe had been her bodyguard, not an officer's assistant, and there were those in Ésparias who believed Cillian and I had too. Probably Eudekia had thought that, once.

"Not one I know of," I said now to the Empress. "Is there someone you are aware of?"

She shook her head. "No. But it should be considered. You may need passage for seven after all."

"I must talk to Colm," I said. "But he left the palace early, with his physician's satchel. I have no idea where he might be."

"I do. This day each week, the physicians of Casil gather at the Hepasian temple to discuss whatever it is physicians discuss. Difficult cases, new treatments? He will have joined them."

"And he will not appreciate his mother running after him."

"I rather think not," Eudekia said. We laughed, mothers together, but the sorrow in her eyes was untouched by mirth. I liked her, I realized. Far too late.

"Eudekia," I said. "I lost a daughter. There is life afterwards. You won't reconsider?"

"No," she said. "No. But thank you, Lena. You have been generous, always."

I could give her one last thing. Was I strong enough? "Cillian," I said, "was a man who did not love lightly, and for him love was inextricably bound to responsibility. His vows were to me, and to Sorley, and to his children. But—" I took a breath, willing the words. "In another life, they would have been to you."

For a moment I thought she would break down. Her hands visibly trembled, and tears swam in her eyes. She closed them, raising one hand to cover her mouth. "Thank you," she whispered. "Thank you."

She rose again, walking to the window. Regaining her composure, I knew. I didn't speak; I wasn't sure I could. After a few minutes she turned. "His letters," she said. "I kept them. I think you should take them."

I did not want to read what he had written to her. I started to refuse. She held up a hand. "Not for you, but for your daughter. We discussed, many times, the problems and perils of governance, and solutions to disputes. If he thought to keep mine, then together they might be an— an advanced education? One that might be shared with Selekos, at the appropriate age."

I couldn't say no. "He did keep yours," I said. "I'll take his letters, for Gwenna and for Selekos."

"I will have the box sent to you."

A knock at the door interrupted us. A guard handed the Empress a note. She scanned it, eyes narrowing. "The same went to the others?" she asked. "I will meet them in ten minutes at the most." She turned to me. "Ships approach from the west. This will be the last of my troops from Ésparias, and perhaps some of yours as well. I must meet with the war council to decide how they are best deployed. Would you join us, General?"

I began to agree, and then a thought struck. "Are you convinced of the generals' loyalty, even in the face of death?"

She looked surprised. "As sure I as I can be. What are you thinking?"

"That as few people as possible should know a general from Ésparias was here, and then gone, at the same time the Empress-Consort and the heirs left the city."

A slow nod. "You are right. My intent is to use the troops to defend the city now, at the harbour and on the walls. Would you do anything differently?"

"Where are the vulnerabilities? For the advancing enemy, not for the city, first."

"The bridges, for the troops on foot. A command was sent to our retreating armies to destroy all bridges and ferries, and to block roads wherever possible. The harbour will be chained, and ballistae and fire arrows are waiting. The river will be blocked near the mouth, preventing boats from easily accessing it, and creating a flooded area difficult to pass through." She listed these calmly, sure of the preparations.

"On the walls?"

"Archers and slingers, and outside, ballistae and all the engines of war."

"What of the small boats, the river transport and traders' skiffs?"

"What are you thinking?"

"Order them hauled up and hidden. Or sunk. And ban all cooking fires once your intelligence tells you the enemy is close. Long ago," I explained, "at home, we hid our fishing boats, and lay in wait, hidden and silent, to fool our invaders into thinking our village was deserted."

"I doubt we can make Casil seem deserted," the Empress said. "But depleted, perhaps. My thanks, General. Perhaps you might go to see Rosale now, to apprise her of our plans?"

"Certainly," I said. "Where do I find her?"

"Not here in the palace. She and the children are hidden for their safety, at the house of Marius the merchant."

"Marius? Druisius's brother?"

"Yes. Like Druisius, Marius remembers my father, and then I, were once his family's patrons. A loyalty older, and perhaps stronger, than the obligation all Casilani owe their Empress. I trust him implicitly, both with information and with my family." She glanced at the door. "I must go. Can you find the house?"

~

I stopped to check on Constyn, but he was still out in the city somewhere. The door guard gave me directions. The streets changed from wide, lined with houses of the wealthy, to narrower, with shops at ground level and living accommodation above. I kept to a good pace, and didn't look at the shopkeepers calling to me. My stride and green tunic should have told them not to bother, but small merchants live in hope. At least I wasn't accosted as I had been at the market.

The street came out onto a small square. One side had a display of amphorae under awnings striped in blue and white: Marius's business, his and his sons' now. I knew from Druise that they traded in oil and grain and olives, their routes taking in all the Nivéan seacoasts. But not beyond: they did not trade directly with Ésparias. I had my suspicions why, strengthened by something Eudekia had said today.

The three shopfronts under the awnings looked well cared for, prosperous. They had once been separate businesses; each had a door leading to the inside. Which one would take me to Marius?

As I stood, irresolute, I noticed something. Unlike the small merchants' shops I had just passed—and, I saw, looking around—the other storefronts in the square, Marius's were shuttered, and so were the windows above them. Had they gone somewhere? Fled?

Not with Rosale and the children, common sense told me.

A woman came out from the nearest shop, one with green awnings. "Can I help, messenger?"

"I was looking for Marius."

She pointed with her chin. "Unless it is important, come back tomorrow. There was bad news today, and they are a house in mourning."

That explained the shutters. A ship lost, I thought. Or were his grandsons old enough to be soldiers? "It is important," I said, wishing it were not and I could leave them to their sorrow.

"The last door, and up the stairs. But do not linger."

I climbed the stairs slowly, and tapped lightly on the door. Footsteps, and then it was opened by a tall woman, her hair half-covered by a scarf, golden bracelets on her wrist. She was drawn, her face taut, her lips chapped and bitten. The Empress-Consort of Casil, newly widowed, soon to be an exile. "Rosale," I said softly. "I am Lena of Ésparias. Gwenna's mother."

Recognition lit her face, but then it fell again. She frowned. "How are you here? Marius will want to see you, of course. You were his friend. Did you come all this way to tell him more?"

Apprehension—no, fear—lodged like an arrow in my chest. *You were his friend*. "Tell them more about what?" I said sharply. "Who is dead, Rosale?"

Her hand covered her mouth. "You don't know. Oh, Lena, I am so very sorry. Druisius. It is Druisius who has died."

Chapter 42

A WAVE OF PAIN SWAMPED ME. I was a small boat in a storm, fighting to stay upright. "No," I heard myself say, and then, "Oh, Sorley." I'd put a hand on the doorframe, but still thought I might fall.

Distantly I heard Rosale calling for Marius, and then a man was there, taller than Druise, but so like him. Rosale explained who I was. I stood in a fog, a blank of disbelief, while people moved and spoke around me. A strong arm went around my shoulders.

"Come," Marius said. He led me to a chair, made me sit. Someone handed me a cup. "Drink."

I sipped. Wine, unwatered, strong. I drank some more. The fog receded a little. "What happened?" I asked.

"There is a letter. It came this morning." Marius fetched it. The seal—and the writing—was Gwenna's.

I skimmed the words, then read them more slowly. A sudden death, she had written; his heart, the physician thought. The rains had been heavy and continuous this spring; Gwyllar had fallen into a stream in spate. Druisius had run to save him. Gwyllar was safe, but Druisius had collapsed and died immediately after. He had died a hero, she wrote, and deeply loved. When Sorley was capable, he would no doubt write, she'd added, and then four more lines.

'Druisius was a second father to me. He taught, admonished, and advised me, girl and woman. I could not do the work fate has given me without his influence. He will be properly honoured here in Ésparias.'

She'd signed it Gwenna, *Principe* of Ésparias.

"Kind words," Marius said, "from the *Principe*."

"She meant every one," I said. "Druise—Druisius—was her guide in so many things." I glanced at the letter again, for the date. Six weeks past.

"He brought her here once," a woman's voice said. "The princess. He called her Piása." Kitten.

"His name for her since she was a newborn," I said, smiling just a little. "You are Vita, I think?"

"Yes." She smiled, gently. "It is good of you to remember. These two"—she introduced two women— "are my sons' wives."

"My sons are at the warehouses," Marius said. "Business cannot stop, not now. We will honour my brother properly tonight."

"You don't need to explain," I said. "I understand." Business, for the *Principe* and her advisors, hadn't stopped for long when Cillian had died. Nor would it have at Druise's death, at least not for Gwenna. But for Sorley? *Sorley will write when he is capable.* Fear for him twisted inside, almost filling the hollow space that had begun, until now, to shrink a little.

I took another mouthful of wine. The shock was receding, and with it the fog. I pushed the fear down, searched for words. "Druisius spoke of you often, both of you," I said. "And his nephews. He was proud of you, of the business you had built."

"We were in frequent contact," Marius said. "He was happy in Ésparias, with your family."

"His family," I said. "He was part of it." I brushed tears from my eyes. I would grieve properly later. There would be time. "Forgive me, Marius, Vita. But this is not what brought me to your door. I must speak with your guest."

"Are you here to take me west?" Spoken calmly, as I would expect from the Empress-Consort. "I and the children?"

"Yes. If passage can be arranged."

"That is in hand," Marius said. "It is what my oldest son is organizing at the harbour. But he expects the ship to go across the Nivéan Sea, to our family in Icoris. Are you suggesting Ésparias instead?"

"It is what the Empress asked for," I said, confused. "The Empress-Dowager, I mean."

"Icoris was a contingency," Rosale explained. "If no one came from Ésparias, and we thought no one had. I—we—did not think it safe for us to remain in Casil any longer. Marius thought his cousins there would give us refuge."

"But not without risk," Marius said. "They would be noticed. There are many people now in Icoris from Casil and Sylana and even further, but still a paler-skinned woman, with two children the ages they are—" He shrugged, and for a moment I saw Druise. My heart constricted. I took a breath, exhaled.

"Can the plans be changed? Ésparias, and there will be six of us, or perhaps seven."

"I will send a message now." He turned to one of his daughters-in-law. "Where is your youngest?"

"In the storeroom downstairs. I will fetch him."

While she went for the boy, Marius moved to a table under a window to write. I remembered something. "Marius," I said. He looked up. "There may be a dog, too. A large dog."

Gwyllar should have had a dog, some insidious voice heard only by me said. *A dog would have kept him safe, and Druise wouldn't have died.*

Then, a whisper in my mind: *His left arm pained him, and he tired easily.*

"A dog," Marius said. "On a crowded ship? Is it necessary it comes?"

I thought of two children being taken to a future they couldn't imagine, and Ladon's instinctive understanding of when comfort was needed. "I believe it is. It is a very well-trained dog."

The shrug again. "There is seawater to sluice the deck." He folded and sealed the note. The seal surprised me for a moment, until I realized the true identity of their guests would not be known to the younger members of the family. A wise precaution.

The boy—he looked about ten or eleven—came for the note. "You may stay at the harbour if your father allows," his mother told him, "but be useful."

"And now," Marius said to Rosale, "I must ask forbearance, *Domina*. There is something I must discuss with Lena that is private business."

"I will go to the children," she said. He glanced at his daughters-in-law.

"There are preparations to be made for dinner. Come, sister." They left us. Vita remained.

"I am sorry to have disrupted this day," I said.

"For this, it is good you are here," Marius said. "Letters would have sufficed, but it is better in person. It concerns Druisius's will."

"Did he have one?" A will meant he had thought of the future, and that was unlike Druise.

"I insisted. I have it. It is properly done." He paused, arranging his thoughts. "A portion of the business's profits has always gone to Druisius. He took very little of the money, and the business has done well. My brother died a rich man, Lena."

Rich? Druise? Marius, watching me, smiled slightly. "You are surprised?"

"To say the least." Had Cillian known? Had Sorley? I thought of the shelves of beautiful, expensive glass in their room, and Druise saying to Daragh, in the spring: *I will tell you what I would pay in Casil, which is less* . . .

"Lena?"

"I'm sorry. Please go on."

"There are bequests to his nephews, and a description of items, some for your daughter, some for Sorley." The glass, I thought. "Half the rest goes, in the names of my sister and her daughter, to a temple here in Casil to support their work." He paused. "I may not distribute that, until it is clearer what happens in Casil. The rest—and it is substantial, Lena—is to establish a school in Ésparias dedicated to the teaching of medicine, with your son to lead it."

Too much had happened too quickly. I couldn't make sense of it. Druise was dead. The fact echoed in my mind like the tolling of a bell. He had left money—a lot of money—for a school for physicians. It will be somewhere for Apulo, I thought.

And for Colm. Marius was still speaking. I forced myself to listen. "It will take a little time to get the money to you, Lena. I had it moved, over the past months, to Icoris. It is safe there with my family."

"That's fine," I said. The money wasn't real, or important, except that it was what Druise had given Ésparias. How would Sorley feel? He didn't need money. Roghan too had ensured that, sharing Gundarstorp's profits with him, the years there were any.

My mind was wandering. I breathed in, and out, concentrating on what Marius had just said. "You had the money moved? You saw what was coming?"

"I saw what might happen, yes. Our warehouses are not full, either: full enough that we could help feed a city under siege, or a returning army. And full enough that a victorious enemy can plunder them, but not so full that the loss will destroy our business."

"And when the streets are washed clean of blood, and someone new sits on Casil's throne, you will begin to trade here again."

"My sons will," he said. "It is our living."

"Not you?" *Marius remembers my father, and then I, were once his family's patrons.* I looked at the man before me, his skin greyed with grief, perhaps not just for his brother. I thought I knew what Druisius would have done now, had not adventure and something more taken him west so many years ago. "Marius," I asked, "are you staying? To protect Eudekia?"

"No," he said, regret threading his voice. "I spoke with her, a few days past. When she asked me to shelter the young Empress and the children. I know her plans." He fell silent, his eyes seeing something not in this room. Then he raised his chin. "I—we—are going across the sea, to my father's land. My homeland; I was born there. But I will leave business to my sons now, and their cousins, and do my best to enjoy the years I have left."

"Something is happening." Vita spoke sharply. She stood at a window, the shutters open now. I could hear voices and movement. I went to stand beside her. People were passing through the square in both directions, rapidly. Families, women, men.

But not equally. Families and men and women moved towards the river, carrying bundles and bags. Who walked or ran the other way were almost all men; men and older boys.

Marius had joined us. "Rumours fly through this city like the winds before a storm," he said. "But do you see? Some are fleeing. Some are going to the palace, or the gates, to stand against the enemy."

"Do not!" So there had been discussion. Marius touched his wife's shoulder.

"I will not. Eudekia made me promise, and so did you. I will honour those promises." He watched the scene below for a few minutes. "It is time, I think. Lena, can you be back here in two hours, or fewer? We must get the young Empress and her children to the ship, and that may have its difficulties."

"I can." Could I? If Colm was back at the palace. Constyn must be; his guard would have returned immediately if they sensed trouble. But surely the physicians would not have sat calmly discussing remedies and techniques while the city erupted?

"Then go."

~

The river of bodies, once I edged and sidestepped into the right stream, carried me close to the palace. I kept a hand on my secca. One or two men told me to go back; more frowned, seeing me, but I ignored them.

Then, with some distance yet to travel, the flow of forward movement slowed and stopped. Men stood fifty deep or more, spread between the palace and the Arénas, a wall of humanity come to stand—and fall—for their Empress and their city. Men in rich tunics and threadbare, men who smelled of lavender and those who reeked of sweat. Admirable, brave, foolhardy—any or all, but I had to get through and into the palace.

"Messenger!" I shouted, pushing between two men. "Imperial messenger. Let me through!" They stepped apart. I continued shouting, forcing passage. Someone trod on my foot, hard; I winced, and shoved.

"What the fuck?" He turned, hand raised.

"Messenger," I snapped. The man beside him grabbed his arm.

"Get out of her way, idiot." He raised his voice. "Imperial messenger! Clear a path!" Whoever he was, he'd used his voice to reach crowds before, both in volume and the note of authority. People moved out of my way.

He stayed behind me, shouting his commands, until I was free of the mass of men. "Thank you," I said, over my shoulder, before I ran for the entrance.

The guard knew who I was. "You are to go to the Empress." I nodded, catching my breath.

"Is the physician Colm back? Or the young prince?"

"Neither, that I know of," she answered. "But there are many doors."

~

I had seen Eudekia only a few hours earlier, but in those hours she had become gaunt, her eyes huge above cheekbones that pushed sharply through the stark, pale skin of her face. Was she ill? Was that knowledge behind her decision not to leave Casil? I had no right to ask, and what did it matter now?

She'd been watching the crowds below. "Are the arrangements made?" she asked.

"Yes. We leave today. Two hours, Marius said, at most."

"I have the box," Junia said from the other side of the room. "It's with your bags and weapons. Is there anything else you need?"

Time, I thought. Time to try to make sense—a little sense—of everything that had happened. But I didn't have it.

"Is Colm ready? And Constyn?"

"They have not returned." Eudekia said.

"What?" Fear, like the bite of a blade in my gut. "Where are they?"

"Perhaps looking for a way through the crowd," Junia said.

My heart spoke before my head. "I won't leave without them. Marius can take Rosale to his country, or she can go to Ésparias alone."

"This is not your war, Lena," Eudekia said. "An army will descend on Casil soon; they are advancing on us now. An army that will cleave history as lightning cleaves an ancient oak. Men will write of the time before Casil fell, and the time after. Go home to shape the time after. That is your work, the work you have planned for the past three decades." Unbelievably, her lips curved in the slightest of smiles. "It was never sedition. I told Cillian that, and your daughter."

"I won't leave without them," I repeated.

"He is a physician. They are unlikely to harm him," Junia said.

I had lost Cillian. Druise was dead. I couldn't think about what Sorley might have done. Too many people I loved had died. I would not leave Colm behind, or Constyn.

Not just for myself, but for Cillian, who had predicted this day, and worked to shape a future to follow. For Druisius, who had given his life to save Gwyllar. For Gwenna, who wanted her brother at her side, and for a country who needed them, the man Colm was and the man Constyn would become.

"This matriarch," I told the Empress, for the third and deciding time, "is going nowhere without her son."

~

I paced, fear making me nauseous and at the same time closing my throat, constricting my breathing. Sweat pricked the back of my neck and my chest. Outside, the crowd grew larger. Eudekia watched them, silent.

"Look," Junia murmured. "The statues."

The crowd was parting for a procession of sorts, men bearing marble images on their shoulders.

"They are brought from the temples only at times of great importance," Eudekia said, without turning.

"Casil is honouring you." Junia came to stand beside her. "Should your people see you, Empress?"

"Of course," she said. "Come."

She turned, walking rapidly. We followed, out of the room and along a corridor. "Bring torches, and what is needed to light them," she said to us. Torches? It was full daylight. But she was the Empress.

At a door that led out the roof of the lower floor, Eudekia walked out into the sunshine. She stepped to the low wall and raised her arms. Shouts from below, and then cheers.

"Light the torches," she said to Junia.

Eudekia held the torches high, then lowered and crossed them in front of her, so the flames appeared like burning wings folded low, holding her in their embrace. She left them there for a dozen heartbeats, more, then raised them again. What was she doing?

Below men had knelt. Others shouted, and one cry was taken up, spreading through the crowd like fire: *Casil! Casil!* And interspersed, *Casillia! Casillia!*

I had called myself a matriarch a few minutes earlier, but it was a false claim. Eudekia was one. Mother and grandmother, yes, but mother to her city and her people, too, the spirit of Casil made flesh: Casillia. If Casil must die, so would she, but like the phoenix, Casil—and its spirit— would rise again.

We cannot shape the circumstances to fit our lives, only our lives to fit the circumstances. What defines us, as men and women, is how we respond to those circumstances. Casyn's words. I had been eighteen. Tears rose in my eyes: tears for the inevitable ending; tears for all the deaths there had been and those yet to come, for the loss of a magnificent, shining city, and most of all for this courageous woman who had responded with strength and grace and determination to the circumstances that fate had chosen for her.

She stepped away, handing the torches to Junia, who held their burning ends below the wall, hidden from the crowd. "If any survive," Eudekia said, "they will tell stories, and with each telling the story will change, until even the teller believes he saw a woman become a bird consumed by flame."

"As you meant it to be," I said, oddly reluctant to speak to her, as if she had become something too exalted to be addressed.

"As I meant it to be. And now come. I cannot be seen again."

Chapter 43

IN HER ROOMS EUDEKIA poured wine, watering it well. She gestured for us to serve ourselves. I took only water; my throat was dry. "Marius will not wait much longer," she said.

Junia, her face set, stepped out into the corridor again, calling to the guard at the far end. "The physician and the prince? Have they been seen?"

Had she answered in the affirmative? Junia's footsteps receded, returned. "They're here," she said. "Gathering belongings."

"Then you must go," Eudekia said. Even as relief coursed through me, a different fear made itself known.

"How?" I said. "How will we get through the crowd, without being thought cowards and stopped, or worse?"

"The way we came into the palace," Colm said. He dropped his bags onto the floor. "Constyn will be ready shortly. Do you remember, *Mathàir*, that when we were here for Alekos's investiture, I spent time with Gnaius in the lower levels of the Arénas, where the fighters and the animals are treated?"

"The tunnel!" Junia said. "Did you come through the tunnel?"

"We did," Colm confirmed. "Full of cobwebs and dust, but it was passable."

Junia almost laughed. "If it had worked as it was meant to, it would have been full of much worse. It was supposed to be a sewer, joining one from the palace, but the engineers got the angle wrong, or some such, and it didn't drain, just backed up. The story is it was kept because some emperor liked to have lions and bears from the pens in the Arénas brought into the palace and paraded at dinner parties."

"There are other stories," Eudekia said, drily. "Perhaps not just animals made their way to the private quarters of royalty. You have a good memory, Colm."

"I was fourteen, and interested in the animals as well as medicine, Empress."

"Empress?" I said. "Eudekia? You would not be seen."

"Someone would," she said. "Someone would see a red-haired woman, at the docks, or on a ship passing westward . . . I cannot."

Hair could be cut, a head covered. But she had made her choice. I knelt. "You will not be forgotten," I said.

Beside me, Colm knelt too. "Empress. My thanks for your care of my cousin."

"And mine for the care you will give my son's wife, and his children. I charge you with their safety, Prince."

I heard him swallow. "I accept that charge."

He was coming home. By choice, or nearly so. Not from my insistence, or his sister's command. Or to fulfil Druise's wish. I would tell him about that later.

I rose, into Junia's tight embrace. "May the goddess be with you," she whispered.

"And with you. I hope—" What could I say? "I hope she grants you strength," I said, feeling tears threaten again.

"So do I." Junia touched my cheek. "Now go."

I'd expected a tunnel like the ones from my childhood, earthen and wood, narrow and with only just enough room to stand. This was a Casilani tunnel, though: a wide, tall archway of brick, the floor slightly concave. Dusty, as Colm had said, with the sediment of ages, but perfectly passable. Not even dark: the occasional grate brought a dim light from above.

At the Arénas end an iron gate barred our way. But Colm and Constyn had come this way. How?

Colm removed something from his satchel, then knelt before the lock. He inserted what looked like a needle. His fingers, I noted, were like Cillian's: long, supple, sensitive. The lock sprang open.

"He did that on the way in, too," Constyn said, a note of pride in his voice.

"Where," I asked my son, "did you learn to pick locks?"

"Gnaius taught me," he said. "Sometimes physicians need to remove chains that have been locked to the legs of prisoners or slaves. It's precise work, done mostly by feel. Good practice for a surgeon, too, although," he added, with a wry smile, "that needle will need replacing."

"Useful," I said. I put the box I'd tucked under one arm down. Carrying it, and my sword and my saddlebags was awkward. I'd given the bow and quiver to Constyn: he could use them, if the need arose.

"Is there any room in your bags?" I asked Colm. The dog stood at Constyn's side, panting, waiting for us to move again.

"Maybe a little. Why?"

"The box is difficult to carry, and if the streets or the boats are crowded, I'm afraid I'll drop it."

I knelt to open the box. Inside the folded letters were neatly piled. There were so many. "Maybe Marius will have a bag I can use," I said.

"Until then," Colm said, "leave only what you absolutely need in your saddlebags, and put them there. You'll have to borrow tunics, if you can. Your messenger's green will cause questions."

He was right. I'd have to beg clothes from Vita, or the sons' wives. I sorted the contents of my bags quickly, keeping only Tarquin's papers and my journal, a few underclothes and my comb. The letters fit, although the bags bulged. I folded my discarded tunics and leggings into the box and pushed it against the wall. It was a beautiful box, carved and painted, probably valuable. Someone would find it, someday.

"*Mathàir*? Where is your marriage bracelet?"

"I left it at home," I said. "I couldn't wear it, not as a messenger." Taking it off had been hard. But Cillian would have understood, I had told myself. If I'd had other motives, I hadn't recognized them then.

He nodded. "I could never wear one, not as a surgeon."

An oblique message? Perhaps not. Perhaps only an observed truth. This wasn't the time or place to ask.

~

We came out of the Arénas through another unlocked gate to a set of steps that led up to the street. A busy street, but less crowded than the surrounds of the palace, and most people were headed away from the heart of the city, laden, like us, with bundles and bags. Fleeing, to the river or the gates. No one impeded us: no cutpurse or bag thief would come near Ladon.

Marius was waiting, his face smoothing into relief at the sight of us. Rosale sat, her children on either side of her, a very few bags at her feet. So little for an empress used to the luxuries of the palace. I made quick introductions, ignoring titles.

Constyn crouched in front of the children. "Do you want to meet my dog?" he asked. Ladon had been left outside. "He's coming with us."

My dog. I'd thought to give Ladon to Colm, but it appeared the decision had been made for me. I doubted my son would mind. The children, at their mother's nod, scrambled to their feet to accompany Constyn down the stairs.

"Tactful," she said. It had been. The more I was in Constyn's presence, the more I understood Cillian's praise of the boy.

"Empress," Colm said. "I will not address you as that again, but at the Empress-Dowager's request, as Prince Colm of Ésparias, I offer you my protection and support."

Rosale sighed, deeply. In relief, or resignation? "Prince Colm," she said. "I accept, and am honoured."

"Now," he said. "To practical matters. My mother"— he glanced at me—"has suggested we pose as a family: husband and wife, our children, my mother and my younger brother." I had told him this in the tunnel, quickly. He hadn't agreed or disagreed, just nodded, then. "If you are agreeable, we would continue this deception in Ésparias; it will not be noted if I take my wife and children to meet my sister the *Principe*."

"An admirable solution," Rosale said, but her voice was flat.

"You are grieving," Colm said. His face, his bearing, imparted sympathy: this was the physician at work. "Perhaps we will say there are elderly parents you have left, or a beloved brother?"

Tears shone in Rosale's eyes; she blinked them away. "Eudekia is beloved to me," she murmured. I must tell her soon what I had witnessed, I thought.

"Then we will tell a close truth: a mother who refused to leave," Colm said. "Are we ready?" His confidence, his command of what was needed: Gnaius had shaped this man. Watching him, pride warming me, I almost forgot what I needed.

"Not quite," I said hastily. I explained my requirements to Vita.

"Come," she said, and led me to their bedroom. From a chest she took several tunics. "Will these do?"

They were all shades of blue, not a colour I favoured, but what did that matter? Vita was close enough to me in size I had no worries about the fit. "Thank you."

"I would have left them behind, so"—her mouth twisted—"you might as well take them, rather than the barbarians."

"Are you coming with us now?"

"No. Marius says we must not be seen to leave. It could cause problems at the warehouses. We will go in the dark. Tonight, very late, with our sons' wives, and the younger children."

"Not your sons?"

"Tadius must stay here. He will not argue with the invaders, but make the grain and oil available. And offer to bring more. There will be soldiers to feed."

And trade would go on. As it must. It was a necessary part of life, and life went on, demanding we go with it.

Or burn in the fires of our grief. I pushed the thought away.

"They are waiting," Vita said. "Go safely, Lena."

"And you," I said. "Later, if you can, come to Ésparias. There will be memorial stone for Druisius you might want to see."

She nodded. "I will tell Marius."

Constyn and the children had returned, and with them a man of middle years. "My oldest son, Valens," Marius explained. "He will take you to the harbour, to the ship that will take you west."

Valens had his mother's eyes, his father's smile, and Druisius's big, competent hands. "Should I carry bags or the boy?" he asked.

"My bags," Colm replied, "if you will. A father should carry his son." This, too, I thought, was the physician's mind: once a decision had been made, it was acted upon without hesitation or doubt. Rosale, pale with apprehension, took her daughter's hand.

"Thank you," she said to Vita and Marius. We descended the stairs, into the afternoon and an uncertain future.

The crowds increased as we neared the river, men and women calling to the boatmen, offering coins, goods, and even their bodies in exchange for passage. "There are not ships for them at the harbour," Valens said, his voice low. "There will be trouble. Be prepared."

Trouble began long before the harbour, before we had reached the landing stage belonging to Marius's family. Too many people seeking to leave Casil, too few barges and skiffs. People slipped in the mud of the riverbank, or were pushed down by others frantic to leave. Mothers handed children to family members—or perhaps strangers—who had made it onto a boat. Bodies pressed around us. Valens strode forward, his deep voice demanding to be let through.

Philita started to whimper. Rosale picked her up. The bag on her shoulder slipped; unbalanced, she stumbled, righting herself almost immediately, but Philita began to cry, sobs of fear and confusion. "I want my father!" she wailed.

Colm stopped. His eyes met Rosale's. "Wait a minute. Then give her to me." He put Selekos down. Constyn immediately took his hand. Philita sobbed, asking for her father. People pushed around us, and Ladon growled, then began to bark. We were being noticed.

Colm had taken his bag from Valens. From it he took a small vial. He dipped a finger into it, and then, firmly, taking her by surprise, grasped Philita's jaw and ran his fingers over her gums. She gasped. He did it twice more. Her sobs began to subside, and her head wobbled.

Colm corked the vial, returned it to his bag, and took Philita from Rosale. "The undiluted juice of poppy," he told her, quietly. "I dislike using it on one so young, but—"

"But it was necessary," Rosale said. "Thank you. I'll take Selekos now."

Ladon's barks had become grumbles, but the dog had been heard—and seen—by the people around us. They gave us a wider berth. "Fucking *dignitasi*," someone shouted as we approached the landing stage. Two large men, armed with clubs, guarded it. Moored at its end, and also guarded, a river barge awaited us.

We made our way on board. Philita was asleep; Colm handed her to Rosale as soon as her mother was seated on the sacks of grain that took the place of benches. Selekos's eyes widened as the barge rocked a bit, but he didn't cry. "Quickly," Valens urged, his eyes on the riverbank. Constyn ordered the dog down, the two men who had guarded the barge came aboard. One pushed the boat from the dock, and we began to move downstream.

The men rowed at a steady, measured pace, but the river was crowded with vessels. If the Empress had given the order to ground the boats, it had been ignored. Most were packed with people; too many, I thought. Ours wasn't. Several men, noticing, ran from the bank and began to swim towards us.

Valens swore. "Can you use that sword?" he asked me. He'd picked up the boathook.

"When I must," I said. I stood, legs apart for balance, unsheathing it. The dog got up, immediately.

"Ladon," Constyn said, "down."

Ladon ignored him. "He's trained to battle," I said, "and he was told to guard me. Let him be."

The men had nearly reached us, but they had stopped swimming, treading water. Seeing the weapons and the dog, reassessing. Watching us, and not the boat approaching them.

I shouted a warning, but it was too late. The oar hit a man in the water, hard, knocking him below the surface—but also unbalancing the over-loaded boat. It skewed, and tipped slightly. People slipped and slid to one side; some fell into the river. Others grabbed its sides, hanging on—and the skiff tipped further and overturned.

Rosale moaned, a sound of horror. My stomach churned. "Keep going," Valens commanded his oarsmen. Colm began to protest, then fell silent, his lips tight. He clenched his left fist, his eyes on his father's ring. I could almost read his thoughts: he had to be the prince now, not the physician.

When the lighthouse that marked the entrance to the harbour came into view, Valens directed us into another landing stage, this one also guarded. "We can go no further," he said. "The water is too fast, where it spills over the dam." We disembarked. "Come," Valens said. His men took our bags, allowing us to move faster. Colm carried Philita; Rosale, Selekos. Valens strode ahead, over ground broken by the dam's construction. And stopped, holding up a hand for us to do the same.

The quays swarmed with people; the same scene as at the river, but here there was no chance of further escape. The boats lay at anchor in the harbour basin, far out from the jetties. There was no sign yet of the ships approaching from the west.

One of the anchored boats was ours. But how to reach it?

"Go back," Valens said. "To the landing stage. Wait. I will swim to our boat, and we will bring it up around the harbour arm to the river mouth, under the dam. But the water is turbulent there now, and others will see what I am doing. Be ready to move, and be ready to fight."

"Can you swim that far?" Colm asked. Valens grinned.

"Of course I can. I'm a harbour rat."

I both wanted to watch, and not. What we'd witnessed earlier on the river; Valens's grin, so much like Druise's; the storm I'd sailed through to rescue Gwenna as a baby: all swirled in my mind, confusing me. I turned away, fighting for clarity.

One of his oarsmen called to us in a harsh whisper. "Come," Colm said, taking charge. I was relieved to let him. Other people were coming towards us now, from other landing stages above the dam.

"Why are you turning back?" someone called.

"We are waiting for friends," Rosale said, before I could think of a response.

"I wouldn't," the man replied.

At the landing stage we waited. Philita had awoken, but she was still groggy, clinging to Rosale. "I don't want to drug her again," Colm said quietly. Rosale had given Selekos some food; he'd sat on the ground to eat the bread, and then rolled onto his side and gone to sleep. I hoped he'd stay that way until we were on the boat.

Sleep felt like a good idea to me, too. The fog that had clouded my mind had returned, just when I couldn't let it. My legs and arms and the world all seemed too heavy. Could I even lift my sword, or throw my secca?

I closed my eyes. Could I sleep for a moment? Colm would stay awake.

"*Mathàir!*" I struggled up, my head clearing. The trader—little larger than Irmgard's ship had been—was rounding the long breakwater that protected the harbour. Men and women had followed the boat along the stone wall—but some had realized its heading, and were running towards us.

Two oarsmen, two guards, with clubs. My sword. Perhaps Constyn's bow. And the dog. I glanced at the boat; the oarsmen were working hard.

"Rosale, behind us," I said. "With the children. Colm, you too."

"No," he said. "Give me your sword, *Mathàir*. You have your secca."

"Should a physician kill?" I said. I pulled my secca from my belt and gave it to him. "Only if you must."

The men approaching would have knives, but nothing else. "Constyn," I said. "Give me the bow. You take the sword."

He stripped off the quiver, handing it and the bow to me. I took another look at the boat. Not close enough. I nocked an arrow, drew, released. It arced into the ground before the running men, as I had intended. "Stop!" I called.

One or two did. The others didn't. The next arrow took the lead man in the shoulder. He fell with a cry of pain and surprise. Beside me, I heard Constyn's ragged breathing, but his sword was held at the ready.

Two more arrows; two more men down. Most had stopped now. One man hadn't. I nocked and aimed. A flash of movement stopped my draw. Ladon launched himself at the man's throat.

"Hold!" I screamed the command. The dog's head turned a fraction, to sink his teeth into a shoulder. His momentum toppled the man, driving the breath out of him. He lay still, perhaps stunned. Ladon did not let him go.

"*Mathàir!*" I turned. The boat was at the landing stage. Beyond it, another group of people stood, gaping, one of the guards facing them, his club held menacingly.

"Go," I said to Constyn. He ran for the boat.

"Release!" I called. The dog did as commanded. "Come!"

He turned in one fluid movement and loped towards me. The man lay still. I doubted he was dead, although he might die of blood loss or infection. But I hadn't wanted to risk the children seeing a man's throat ripped out by the dog they thought was their friend.

I grabbed Ladon's collar as he trotted up to me, taking him down to the water. Then I washed the blood off his muzzle. He didn't object. He lapped up some water, then followed me onto the landing stage to leap onto the boat.

We pushed from the dock. Valens uncorked a small bottle to pour wine onto the water. "For a safe journey and calm waters," he told me. Recorking the flask, he grinned. "I can't say you need any other protection. There will be stories told about this!"

That worried me. How long would it take for someone to add up what had been seen today? The personal guard of the Empresses of Casil were the horse archers. Women highly skilled with the bow. Had I just revealed who the mother and two children travelling west were?

Chapter 44

~Gwenna~

THE HORSES WERE MAGNIFICENT; even I could see that. Five mares, all in foal, Nessus told me, and a bay stallion whose neck arched proudly. I wondered what Talyn would think of them.

I leant on the fence at what had been the governor's estate, listening to the young man beside me tell me about the horses, grazing in the sunshine. They'd brought a groom, too, but he'd been seasick for much of the short voyage, so the care of the animals had fallen to Nessus. He hadn't minded, he assured me.

"Can I learn here to use a bow from horseback, like Lena? General Lena," he amended. "Forgive me, *Principe*."

"It's of no matter," I told him, "in private. And yes, you can. I imagine you can use a bow already, and ride very well?" He nodded, eagerly.

"Even if you choose to breed and train horses here," I said, "it's a skill you'll need. Our horse archers' mounts come to them ready for battle."

"Will there be fighting here too? Among the people, I mean, like in Beria?"

"Not among the people here," I said. I hoped I was right. In our six-day journey from Wall's End to the Eastern Fort, I'd heard little of real concern. The idea that I should abdicate in four years to give Constyn the title hadn't found fertile soil in which to take root among most of the villages and farms. The traditional villages, in the shadow of the Durrains, were a different matter. And so might be factions within the army. But with both Lynthe and Constyn gone for so long now, it was possible the brief support Lynthe had raised had died away. What would happen when my mother returned—if my mother returned—with them waited to be seen.

I was still debating if Lynthe was more of a threat to me—or rather to Ésparias—alive or dead. Whatever conclusion I reached would likely be purely intellectual; I didn't really think I could bring myself to order her execution.

Voices called to Nessus; the twins, calling from the stables. "Go," I said to him. "It's time I rejoined their father anyhow." We'd taken a break from Tevius's analysis of the possible outcomes of the infighting in Beria, and the potential threat to Ésparias. His wife was not well, and he had wanted to consult the doctor who'd been called. I'd been happy to accept Nessus's offer to show me the horses.

At the governor's villa, Tevius had a relieved look on his face. "The doctor thinks only shock and exhaustion," he told me. "The speed of the upheaval, and leaving our villa with so few possessions. We had been there for over twenty years."

"If the unrest is controlled, might you return?" I asked, gesturing him to sit again. He was, I estimated, Ruar's age, perhaps a bit older. The twins were his only living children, he'd told me.

"Perhaps. If it is Rielo who emerges as the leader, and if he tells us it is safe. But I cannot see it. The people have seen what their land can be, now we have showed them how. Why should they not be the ones to farm it?"

With only a few exceptions, Tevius had told me, those who had come from Casil to develop the lands in the shelter of the Durrains had relied upon local labour; in fact, they had been directed to do so by Casil's fiscarius. "It was meant to show them the benefit of being a province, of adopting our ways. My wife is Kurzemë; that too was encouraged, marriages with the daughters of men who held rank among their villages."

"How many more Casilani might come to Ésparias?"

"I cannot say. How many more might your mother have invited?"

"I cannot tell you that, either," I said. "She sent no letter to me."

"Or it was lost," he suggested. "If it bore the procurator's seal, or even her own, those would have been worth stealing, to pry off and use again. Anything to speed a departure. The harbour was chaotic. Finding a ship to bring us here took more of my money than I had expected."

"Please don't worry about that," I said. "Tell me how many Casilani estates there were, if you can. And perhaps merchants and artisans, in Occida?"

"I will make a list," Tevius said. "There are the teachers at the Academy, too, and some physicians."

They would not—surely?—all come. I'd directed Valle to find out what he could from the few traders who were still arriving from the east, so far bringing only goods, not more people. I had one more question for Tevius, at least for now. "Have you any family among the Casilani who came to Ésparias? Even distant family?"

"No," he said, regretfully. "It will be the same for most. We were younger sons of men with few connections, without uncles or cousins to help us on our way, even if we were minor *dignitasi*. It is why we took the land offered. But Nessus might."

Would he know? But he would know his parents' ancestry, and questions could be asked among our own Casilani. Family ties were strong, and even distant cousins considered a responsibility. Perhaps, if someone did claim kinship to Nessus, they would feel an obligation to the family who had brought him here. Time would tell. Until then, they could stay at the governor's estate, under the watchful eye of the steward.

Who, I had learned, had claimed a few more years of life than he actually had, to stay. Because of Finn, who had been his lover for many years. Which explained, at least, why he'd been willing to provide us with information: his loyalty to Finn had been stronger than to his employer. Had the governor known this, and let it happen, glad of the clandestine flow of information? I thought it likely.

"Thank you," I said to Tevius. "I've taken enough of your time. Send the list when it's done; that doesn't need to be today, or tomorrow."

"My time?" he said, rising as I did. "I have been honoured by yours, *Principe*."

I rode back to the Eastern Fort with Valle, thinking. I hadn't needed to go to the villa—I could have ordered Tevius to come to me—but I'd had a reason beyond meeting the Berian and his family. On the ride south, largely along the new road that ran diagonally across Ésparias from north to south, I'd passed through many Casilani farms. What I'd heard, beyond the worry for husbands and brothers and sons, had been concern for harvest. Almost every farm had men still, those over sixty—or claiming to be—and under fourteen, but not enough. Not enough, even in this wet, unproductive year.

The governor's steward had concurred. Garia and I had met with him first. The farm manager had gone east with the governor, but there was an older man, this one genuinely over sixty—closer to eighty, the steward said—who could at least advise. And here in the more populated south, close to Casilla, it had always been easy to hire workers, men and women, at harvest season. They would, he thought, manage.

It would be prudent, I thought, passing through the long lines of grapes on either side of the road back to the fort, to offer Tevius the use of the villa until the spring. He too had grown grapes and apples on the eastern slopes of the Durrains, and from what he'd said to me, he hadn't left the running of the place entirely to his manager. The boys were old enough to be useful, either on the farm or among the senior cadets at the Eastern Fort.

Valle rode beside me, not speaking. He was, I'd discovered, very good at being quiet, a trait I liked. I'd had to instruct my other bodyguards, over the years, to not talk when we travelled. It was thinking time for me, and, as Druisius had pointed out when I was still a girl, a bodyguard whose mind was engaged in conversation wasn't fully paying attention. Two other guards followed behind.

A flock of starlings rose from among the vines, chattering as they swirled above the grapes. The first varieties were nearly ready to be picked; the birds and the children hired to chase them away would be in constant motion all day. At least it wasn't in sloppy mud: here in the south there were now more dry days than wet. Not the days of full sun there should be, but the rain had mostly stopped.

We crested a rise, and there before me lay the Eastern Fort, and beyond it the sea and the first of the islands that divided the Edanan Sea from the Nivéan. A small trader was making its way past the last of the islands. We had spoken of those islands yesterday, Finn and I, in the context of the possibility of invasion from Casil's conquerors. "They should be our first line of defence," he'd said. "We need fortifications, garrisons, supplies of weapons. Fire arrows and possibly even ballistae. The watchtower is useful, but it isn't enough."

"Do it," I'd said, seeing the sense.

"I'll need more troops, and ones with experience in building would be helpful."

I'd signed the orders. Bridges could wait; ferries or floating bridges had served, and could keep serving. They were not conducive to moving troops or supplies rapidly, but Finn was right: this had to take precedence. I liked the man: he was both thoughtful and decisive, and Valle told me his troops respected him, finding him fair and firm. But, I thought, he was tired, or perhaps somewhat despondent. Like my mother and Talyn, he'd defended Ésparias against more than one invasion. After thirty years of peace, he would have been hoping to quietly retire, and now he was overseeing the construction of defences against yet another aggressor.

Or the possibility of one. He'd suggested something that none of my advisors had: the alliance between the Boranoi and the Kidari invaders was new. How solid was it? The young king of the Boranoi wanted Casil, had wanted it for years. The Kidari king—if that was his title—wanted it too, assumedly. There was, he'd said, a real possibility their alliance could crumble rapidly, once the city had fallen.

"Did you say that to my mother?" I'd asked.

"Yes. We spoke a bit about historic alliances, what your father had taught her of the agreements among the eastern lands, before Casil rose to power."

I could trust him, I'd decided. He'd had no reason to doubt Lynthe, who'd been both my *quincala* and my designated representative, when she'd explained the diplomatic mission she'd told him she was being sent on. She'd even shown him a letter purported to be from me, although she'd hadn't needed to.

"Maybe I should have questioned her more," he'd said. "Taking the prince. But the letter of introduction mentioned them both, and your name was on it. An excellent forgery," he'd added, ruefully.

"Did my mother," I'd asked, "mention newer alliances, here in the west?"

"Yes. Not in detail. Just the possibility that peace among us would continue, because of the marriages and trade agreements." He'd hesitated for a moment. "Nothing more than I had deduced for myself, *Principe.*"

I'd nodded, smiling. "Shall I say only that it has been actively pursued, almost since the Casilani came? My father particularly liked one saying of Catilius's: *Look back over the past, at the empires that rose and fell, and predict the future.*"

"A wise man," Finn had replied.

"*Principe.*" Valle broke my reverie. "There is another family arriving. Look at the harbour, and the trader that has just docked."

I reined my horse to a stop. The trader, a medium-sized ship, had tied up. People were disembarking: a tall man; a woman, two children, with a very large dog. Another man, slighter. Then another woman. My breath caught. Was it? She turned to speak to someone on the deck, gesturing, and I was sure.

"That's my mother," I said, and urged my horse forward.

Chapter 45

~Lena~

"PATRA," SELEKOS ASKED, "are we nearly at our new home?"

"Nearly," Colm said. In the six weeks of our voyage, he and Constyn had made a game of having the children call Colm 'father'. It had begun with Constyn saying Colm was so old they had to call him 'Father Colm'. They'd giggled about that, and done it, and slowly, simply, it had become just 'Father'.

Colm lifted the boy up. "Look for flags and a fort, Elekos-Selekos." Another game, but more and more the boy was just Elekos. Philita had become Lita. "Once we're past this island."

Valens had refused, last night, to pass through the unknown waters between the islands as dusk approached. One more night, he'd said, would make little difference. Now we stood on the deck, waiting.

"There!" Selekos pointed. High on the headland, but below the watchtower the Casilani had built, stood the Eastern Fort. Above it, blowing landward with the breeze, one flag flew alone: the white horse of Ésparias on its green field.

"The flag," Colm murmured. He would never have seen Ésparias's flag flying proud, without the eagle of the Eastern Empire above it.

"It's got a horse on it!" Selekos said. "I like horses."

"And you may have one, or at least a pony, soon," Colm told him. "You too, Lita."

Valens guided the trader in. Once the marsh and tidal mud of an estuary had lain below the fort; now a dredged harbour with low breakwaters and stone jetties replaced it. We'd been seen, of course. Two soldiers awaited us, standing with weapons out, but at ease.

It was Constyn who leapt from the deck to the jetty, rope in hand and Ladon at his heels, and it was Constyn whom the soldiers recognized.

"Good gods, Prince, you've grown," one said, forgetting himself. He scanned the rest of us. I didn't know him, and he didn't recognize me, in my blue tunic and hair grown longer than it had been in years.

"You'd better salute," Constyn said drily—when had he become so adult? "Or the General Lena might have something to say to your commander."

Two sets of eyes widened, and two hands went up in salute. I returned the gesture. "Is General Finn at the fort?"

"Yes, General. Would you like an escort?"

"I can find my way. But someone can bring the bags." I stepped up onto the jetty and turned to help Philita up. Colm handed Selekos to Constyn, and gave Rosale a hand—and then we were all walking up the jetty, and our arrival home to Ésparias hadn't been momentous at all. Except for how my heart had clenched, seeing the flag.

"Are we to live here?" Philita asked her mother.

"I don't know," she murmured. "Ask Patra."

"For a while," Colm answered. "Then we'll see."

"Who's that?" Selekos asked, pointing. I looked up to see—and realized it was Gwenna, running down the steps as if she were Constyn's age, a man following at a more sedate pace. I strode forward to meet her, my arms outstretched.

Gwenna threw herself into my embrace, almost unbalancing me. I hugged her, hard. From behind me, I heard a grumble, followed by a questioning whine. "Friend," Constyn told his dog.

My daughter stepped back. "You cut your hair," I said.

"It was getting in the way." Her eyes scanned the others, widening briefly at Rosale and the children; questioning for a second at Colm before softening as she realized who he was. A smile tugged at her lips, escaped into a grin. "Colm. You were shorter than me, when we left you in Casil."

He grinned back. "And you were thinner. Gwenna, may I introduce my family? The children are Elekos and Lita, and this—" He took Rosale's hand. "Is Sallah."

Not a flicker of surprise from Gwenna, I noted. "Sallah, you are most welcome. And so are you, Elekos, Lita." She crouched, smiling at the children. "I have a son, younger than you. His name is Gwyllar, but we call him Bear."

Druise's name for him. I fought back the pang of grief, and the question that was eating at my gut.

"Does everyone here have a different name?" Lita asked.

"Not everyone," Gwenna told her. "Just very special people. Now, shall we go to the fort and find you food and drink and baths and proper beds?" Not a word more than the listening guards would have expected to hear, just a woman welcoming her family home with the decorum appropriate to the *Principe*.

"And welcome home, Constyn," Gwenna said, turning to the boy. "Although I see you have brought a monster with you." A warning, in her jocular tone.

"His name is Ladon." Constyn's hand dropped to the dog's head. "Lena gave him to me. He is a loyal protector, *Principe*." A subtle message.

"Good," she said softly, then, "He is housetrained?"

"Yes."

"Then he can enter the fort, and not be confined to the kennels. Now go ahead. I want a word with my mother, but we'll be right behind you."

Her eyes had gone back to the ship, where the man who had accompanied her—her bodyguard, I guessed—had gone to speak to Valens and the crew. Watching, I realized, to see if a prisoner was being led out. So it was up to me to do this. "Gwenna." I put all the warning I could into my tone.

She closed her eyes. "She's dead, isn't she?"

"In battle. In Casil's defence. Honourably." Not the truth, but no one alive but me knew that, and no one ever would.

I saw her shoulders heave, the choked sob, and I took her into my arms. Twenty-nine and a mother, but she was still my daughter, and she was grieving. Had been grieving, already, and I'd just added to that pain. "I'm so sorry," I murmured. "Shhh."

She sniffed, and shook her head. "I'm all right. It's just—one more death. After *Athàir*, and—" She stopped, her eyes suddenly doubtful.

"Druise. I know. His brother told me." *Athàir* and Druise. Not Sorley. Hope unfurled, a tiny loosening of one tension. But I couldn't ask, not yet. There was more to say, more pain to cause.

"I'm afraid it's not just Lynthe," I said. She stiffened, stepping back from my embrace. Her shoulders went back.

"Alekos? That is why Rosale is here?"

"Alekos," I confirmed. "And Bjørn. And, Gwenna—" My own resolve wavered. I was close to weeping. "Eudekia." Junia, too, but Gwenna hadn't really known her.

"Then Casil is fallen?" Only the rapid flicker of thought in my daughter's eyes now. "The boy is the emperor in exile."

"In theory, yes, with his mother as regent." I glanced up the steps. "We should join the others."

She nodded. "One moment. Major!" The man speaking to the captain of the trader turned, raised a hand, began to walk towards us.

Major? Then he was more than a bodyguard. He reached us. Something about his eyes was familiar.

"General, may I introduce Valle, Commander of the Guard?"

He saluted. "General."

I returned the salute. "Major. We have met before, although you won't remember. In Karst. You were three? Four? I was with your father, and stood witness to his acknowledgment of you."

"I knew that," he said. "My father told me, and more. I am more grateful to you than I can say, General."

A kindness done, a righting of a wrong three decades past; I'd given it little thought since then.

"Major," my daughter said, "the man waiting for us is my brother, with his wife and family. They will need guards. As will Prince Constyn, although from the look of it, the dog might suffice."

I smiled. "It would. Ladon is a trained dog of war, and was my only guard for much of my journey."

Suddenly, I had to know. I would not be able to concentrate on what needed to be done now unless I did. "If I may? Major, will you escort my son and his family to the *Principe's* quarters? We still have private speech to conclude."

He glanced at Gwenna for permission. "And arrange for the baths for their private use," she said. He nodded. I watched him climb the steps to introduce himself to Colm. Gwenna waited. I took a breath. "Sorley?"

"He's gone home," she said. "To Gundarstorp. Apulo went with him." She told me, briefly, what had happened. I barely took it in, relief and sorrow warring inside me.

"He'll play again?" It was what mattered most. He could not lose his music.

"Yes. Apulo was confident."

"I was so worried," I said. "After I learned Druise was dead. About what Sorley might choose to do."

"We all were." Pain clouded her face.

I touched her hand. "Tell me later. But now, *Principe*, there is much that needs your attention."

Chapter 46

~Gwenna~

SALT ENCRUSTED MY MOTHER'S HAIR and whitened the skin of her arms. Her tunic was stained with the grime of travel. She looked drawn, as if the voyage home had been fraught and dangerous.

"No," she said, when I asked. "Once we were free of Casil's harbour, it was not difficult. I am just tired, Gwenna, and wondering if I have brought you—brought Ésparias—more trouble."

If she had, it was just one more. "You have brought me my brother," I said, "and you are home again. Anything else can wait until you've had a chance to bathe and rest."

"Let Rosale use the baths first," she said. "She will need time alone, to gather herself. We can talk, and then I'll wash and change."

Where to go? If Colm and Rosale and the children were in my rooms, I could not take my mother there yet. We needed privacy. The room I'd taken as an office, I decided: I shared it with Garia, but she might not be back from the governor's estate. I'd left her with the steward, making lists of the Casilani estates, and who among the men had stayed behind. Information we needed, both for immediate consideration of the harvest, and for future planning.

Garia wasn't back. I requested wine, and while my mother went to take care of bodily needs I arranged cushions on a chair. I thought them necessary. She was thinner even than when she'd left, and not all the white in her hair was from salt.

My mother smiled her thanks for the cushions, and took the cup of wine gratefully. She drank, deeply. "I don't know where to start."

"Lynthe," I said. "Once, and not again, except for what I must say at some point to Talyn, and then officially. What did you learn?"

"She took Constyn to the palace, requesting he be kept safe. She told him, and Eudekia, that he had been sent east, so that if Varsland invaded there was someone royal in a safe place. And then she went to fight the Boranoi."

"And Eudekia believed her?" I said. I could not imagine that incisive intelligence accepting Lynthe's story.

"No. Nor did Constyn, after he'd had time to consider. You have no need to doubt his loyalty, Gwenna. Eudekia gave Constyn shelter for her own reasons, an incentive for someone to bring Rosale and her children east. She was expecting someone to come for them: it was what she asked of your father, in the letter I did not read. To give them sanctuary. She thought that was why I was there."

"I didn't read it either," I said. "But then why is Colm here? Did you tell him I ordered it?"

"No." She explained Alekos's request. "I told Eudekia I hadn't the authority to grant sanctuary, but that Colm did. A lie, and she knew it, but she also understood why I had made it. I—we—used Colm's sense of responsibility to sway him into accepting the Emperor's entreaty. You need to be aware of that, in whatever you ask of him. In that respect, he is very much like your father."

"Does he look like him? When you first knew *Athàir*?" I'd never known my father except as a man whose hair had been streaked with grey, his face scored by pain.

"Yes. Except his eyes are lighter. But so do you, with your hair short." She smiled then, her gaze travelling over me. Stopping. Narrowing, at the fullness of my breasts against my tunic. The smile grew.

"You're pregnant."

"Yes. She'll be born in the spring, near to my own birthday. She's Ruar's, of course. He's pleased."

"She?"

"I feel certain, the way you said you did with me. Piása, she'll be, if I'm right."

I watched pain temper the pleasure on her face. "A beautiful tribute," she said.

"I felt dizzy, walking," I said, feeling the need to tell, to confess. "Probably the first sign of this one." I touched my belly. "Everyone took their eyes off Gwyllar to help me." Tears rose. "I should have brought Gwyllar's nursemaid, or a guard. I didn't think we needed one, with Druise there. And he's dead, because of that, and Sorley—" I couldn't go on. Tears choked my throat.

My mother did not rise to hold me, but she did touch my hand. "He knew, didn't he?" she asked gently, "The signs were there, when I look back."

I swallowed, nodded. "Apulo said he did. The physicians had told him."

"Let me tell you what else Druisius did for you. Dry your eyes," she suggested, as if I were Philita's age. I did, on the sleeve of my tunic. I'd change later. "Now listen."

I could barely believe her words. "Druise was wealthy?"

"He was. The business is more than successful."

"I know," I said. "They control almost all the grain trade from Icoris. But—a medical school?"

"A way to entice Colm back to Ésparias, I think. But I didn't tell him until he'd already made the decision to come home."

"He'll work it out, won't he?"

"Maybe. He may have already. I told him early on the voyage. After that—" Her mouth twisted. "I was not paying attention. All I could see was grey. Sound, words, were muffled, scattered. So many losses. Your father. Druise. But also Eudekia. Her courage, Gwenna, her choice to stay, to be—what did you say at the council table before I left?—a reminder of their history?"

"Those were *Athàir*'s words," I said. "When we were in Casil. He said that I and Faolyn and even he were symbols; that we reminded Ésparias we were more than a province of Casil, with a history of our own. It was, he said, a source of Ésparias's strength."

"Eudekia made sure her people saw her as a symbol, and perhaps too a source of strength. What she did will live in legend, as she intended." My mother told me of the torches, the crowds below watching, a message that would transform into a memory of a phoenix, rising to live again from the flames. "I hated her, almost, for too long," she said. "Stupidly. I told Sorley once that I could never hate him, because how could I hate what Cillian loved? So how could I have hated Eudekia? She was a greater woman than I, for all she tried to tell me it was not so."

"It sounds," I said, choosing my words carefully, my mother's admission reverberating in my mind, "as if you became friends before the end."

"We did, I think," she said. "I offered her sanctuary, too. She refused."

"A phoenix," I said, "cannot fly away." But it left an egg—or a hatchling—and that hatchling was currently being bathed in a room not very far away. Ésparias was being asked to nurture him, disguised as a lesser bird—and this was not a decision for a council, or an Assembly. Whatever my intentions, in this I had to act on my own.

Chapter 47

~Lena~

AN HOUR LATER WE GATHERED in Gwenna's sitting room, in the set of rooms kept for her at the fort. Bathed and in clean clothes—borrowed, for the most part—we sank gratefully onto the comfortable chairs and couches. Plates of food had been placed on a low table, with jugs of wine and water and the juice of apples.

"Look," Rosale—Sallah—said to her daughter, handing her a cup of juice. "Even the cup welcomes us." She pointed to its rim. "What does that say?"

"Be glad that you are here," the girl read, translating the Heræcrian with ease. "Are you glad, Matra?"

"Very glad." She touched her daughter's back. "We are safe here, Lita." The girl didn't smile, but she raised the blue glass to her lips and drank. Neatly, in small sips, although I thought she must be thirsty.

"Perhaps," her mother said, "someone could take the children to another room?"

"I will," Constyn said. "I'd like to, unless I am needed here? They trust me."

He filled a small plate with food, including several of the small pastries. Selekos went with Constyn without demur, one hand on Ladon's back. Philita followed, but only after several glances at her mother and Rosale's firm encouragement. The room fell silent.

"She is old enough to understand this is not an adventure," Rosale murmured. She composed herself, turning to Colm. "Is it good to be home?"

"It's good to be somewhere with baths. I itched." Colm smiled, to gentle his words. "But Ésparias isn't home. I've spent no more than a few weeks in this country that calls me its prince, and that as a boy Constyn's age."

"But where is the country of our heart?" Rosale said softly. "The one we were born into, or the one where our loved ones are? And when those we love are scattered, or dead, where do we call home?"

Where is home for the falcon, when there is no falconer to hold out his arm? In my mind I saw the sea, the sun setting, fishing boats returning home.

"I need you here, Colm," Gwenna said. "There is much to do, much to plan for. But first, Empress, I assume it is sanctuary you seek?"

"Not for Rosale," Colm said. "Surely my wife would not need it?"

His wife? "We will marry, as soon as possible," Rosale added. "Who can do that, here?"

"But when did you decide this?" I asked.

"On the ship," Colm replied. "The children have just learned to call me father, a necessary deceit in our travels. They have been uprooted from all they know. I—we—would not deprive them of a father a second time."

"Well," Gwenna said, grinning. "I stand corrected. I told Ruar you would not make a political marriage. Do you plan to formally adopt the children?"

Her brother hesitated, glancing at Rosale. "I don't know. There are many considerations."

"Before the Taiva," I said, the sound of the sea in my mind receding, a tide ebbing, "before Eudekia changed the game board, before your father even knew I was carrying you, Gwenna, he and I made a decision one night. We knew any children we had would be Callan's heirs. Your father removed himself from the succession, for many reasons. But we did not think it was our right to take that choice from you, either of you. You must ask yourself the same, Colm, Rosale. No matter what the future looks like now, Selekos is Alekos's heir."

I could see from their faces that this already weighed heavily on both Rosale and Colm. "The letters I brought at Eudekia's request—Gwenna, they are Cillian's to her; she kept them all. She thought that coupled with the ones she sent to him, they would be an education in leadership, one she thought might be instructive. For you, she said, and for Selekos, at a later time."

I thought of the other papers I had brought: Tarquin's could be added to the library at Wall's End. His letter to Druisius I'd given to Valens, for his father. Knowledge and ideas to be passed down, memories to be kept.

"She did not," Rosale said, "say that to me."

"Perhaps because she thought your instincts as a mother, in the danger of Casil in its last days, you would have refused the idea?" Gwenna, speaking softly. "I know I might, were it Gwyllar whose life was threatened by events."

As it might be—as all our lives might be—if Rosale and the children were pursued. If. An unknown, but one that needed to be planned for.

"Before you decide," I said, "there is more to consider. Rosale, you are Selekos's regent now. Eudekia thought a council might help you share that responsibility. She suggested Gwenna and Colm."

I let them work out the extent of the implications. This was for the *Principe* and her brother the prince to decide, not me. I carried no rank beyond General, no position beyond mother and advisor.

"Just me," Colm said. "Not Gwenna."

"No!" Rosale spoke forcefully. "I cannot ask that of you. There is too much danger in it."

"If we are married, the assumption will be made in any case."

"Then we won't marry."

"We must. For your safety, and Lita's. And for Alekos's son and heir."

"Do you think," Gwenna said, "that if the Boranoi, or whatever they call themselves after this, send men after Rosale and the children, it will matter who is officially regent, and who isn't? We will all be in danger for harbouring them."

"Danger." Colm made a small sound, not quite a laugh. "There is always danger. Physicians know this. I could have cut myself during surgery, and died of the festered wound. Or caught a disease from an ill man; there were rumours of illness among the eastern troops, something contagious and fatal. We take precautions. We act with care and forethought, but we act. I swore an oath as a physician to never harm, to never act wrongly. To leave Rosale alone in this responsibility would be to act wrongly."

"Then I should join you in this regency, with Rosale's agreement," Gwenna said.

"No. Your responsibility is Ésparias."

Gwenna stared at the brother she had not seen for nearly twelve years, who had become a man neither of us knew. Her eyes went to his hand, to the ring on his finger, and then to the one on her own hand.

"I will leave the decision of regency to the two of you," she said after a moment. "I will witness any papers you draw up, and place my seal on them. As for the marriage—Rosale, you asked who can do that. I can. And I suggest I do, privately, so that your real name can be recorded. And then a second ceremony, if you feel it necessary, under the name Rosale will use here."

"Marry us, yes," Rosale said. "The ceremony is—necessary—to me. But do not record my real name. That might offer Colm some protection one day. Just speak it, so we and the gods hear."

"We need two witnesses, do we not? Constyn is not of age," Colm said. He had not refuted Rosale's suggestion. "*Mathàir*, but who else?"

"Valens," I said. "He knows who Rosale is, and the children. We trusted him to bring us here. We can extend that trust to this."

~

A guard was sent for Valens, and another to find Constyn and the children. "Selekos will not understand," Rosale said, "but Philita will. I would like them to be here." Colm turned to her then, speaking quietly. Gwenna beckoned me to a corner.

"This is in my power," she whispered. "But, *Mathàir*, I've never done it. What words do I use?"

"I doubt it matters," I whispered back. The vows Cillian and I had exchanged had been Linrathan, and in any case, not appropriate. *The love you share.* Nor would there be an exchange of *li'ítho*, their interwoven silver strands representing the newly entwined lives.

"Simply their names, and titles if you wish, and ask them each if they enter into this marriage honourably. That should be sufficient."

"It seems so brief, for such an important step."

"A step they have already chosen. This is only a confirmation."

"Gwenna?" Colm approached us. "After whatever is said to marry us, can you state that the children are under my protection, as a prince of Ésparias."

"With their real names?"

"Spoken, yes. But recorded as Elekos and Lita, son and daughter of the widowed Sallah of Casil."

"I will. But—" I left them talking, crossing the room to Rosale.

"Are you sure of this?" I asked, softly.

"Yes. This is the best protection I can give my children." She smiled, her eyes softening. "I know you were much in the world of your thoughts on the voyage here. But Colm and I spoke at length, every day. He is a good man, your son. He will not ask more of me than I can give, and both Selekos and Philita love him already."

Accepting what she must do, given circumstances over which she had no control. Casyn, I thought, would be proud of this woman. *What defines us ...*

I had carried those words with me since I was eighteen. They had shaped how I had seen the world, where I had thought my responsibilities lay. I had another response to choose soon, one that would change, in the eyes of some who loved me, their idea of who I was. And for all my travelling, and the time spent in the dark places of my mind, I still didn't know that myself.

No? Cillian's voice, faintly.

You're dead, I thought back.

But he isn't, käresta.

~

The ceremony took only a few minutes. The vows made, Rosale beckoned the children to her. Philita had watched from my side, attentive, solemn. Valens had held Selekos, mostly, I thought, to keep him still and quiet.

Rosale murmured to the children. They stood in front of Colm. He placed a hand on each child, one on Selekos's head, the other on Philita's shoulder. "I, Colm, prince of Ésparias, pledge my protection to these children, Philita and Selekos, born to the Emperor Alekos of Casil and Rosale of Halachia. Their father was my friend, and his children will be brought up to honour his memory and his legacy."

He looked down at the children. "I will love you as my own," he said. "In Ésparias, you will be known as Elekos and Lita. A new home and new names, but without diminishing or forgetting your history. In this your mother and I are agreed. Are you, Lita?"

"Yes, Patra." Her eyes were huge. How much did she understand?

"And you, Elekos?" The boy was far too young to comprehend, but this was pageantry. His mother whispered to him.

"Yes, Patra!" he said, grinning.

Colm bent, to kiss each child on their hair; his father's gesture. Responsibility and love, inseparable.

I hope you are proud of him. Of them both, I thought fiercely, into silence.

Chapter 48

~Gwenna~

NIGHT; THE LATE WATCH ON DUTY. Through the window of my room, stars glittered. From the chair where he reclined, his long legs stretched before him, my brother regarded me, cradling his cup of wine. Everyone else had gone to bed.

"I doubt," he said, "it is safe for Ro—for Sallah and the children to remain in the south, if I understand where the Casilani largely settled. Even if it is mostly women, and older men, some will have travelled back and forth to Casil, been present at the games or other entertainments. They may recognize her."

Rosale was striking, both her height and her high cheekbones making her memorable. Colm's concern was valid. "I'd hoped," I said, "you'd stay with me. I—" Speak the truth, I told myself. "I need you, Colm. *Mathàir* is the only family I have left."

"We've been apart for nearly half my life. I am a physician, Gwenna, not brought up to the intrigues and dances of diplomacy."

"You were for the first fourteen years," I said, with some asperity. "And Gnaius was a court physician, and you, you were a close friend of both the Emperor of Casil and a prince of Varsland. Do not tell me you are just a doctor, Colm."

He grinned, tiredly. "Perhaps not. But I *am* a doctor, and I have, it appears, a medical school to be responsible for."

"In the fullness of time. I have an idea about that, as it happens." An extension of something proposed by Valle, as we rode south. The road had taken us through what had been the Casilani's principal fort and its accompanying settlement, once the site of my grandfather's winter camp at the southern edge of the grasslands. The Casilani, Valle told me, had flattened the shallow valley ringed with hills level before building their fort. It had been extensive, larger than Wall's End or the White Fort, even if built to the same ancient model. Now it stood empty.

"You could do worse than take this over, make it your own," Valle had suggested. "It might be wise for you to be away from either coast. Easier to protect you, here."

I'd thought about that, on and off. It was Valle's job to keep me safe, and if invasion came—almost certainly from the east—I would not be riding at the head of our army, or even directing the defences. That would be up to my generals. My greying, aging generals—or their younger, untried successors.

But no. What was an alliance for, after all? I was almost confident of Varsland, now they had made their approach. If a threat came from the east, Ésparias should not need to stand alone against it.

"Gwenna? Are you going to tell me your idea?" Colm's question brought me back to the immediate.

"Do you remember talk of the Winter Camp?" He frowned, made a rocking gesture with the hand not holding his wine. I explained. "It's all built, with Casilani skill, in the last thirty years. There will be an infirmary, and barracks, as well as the commander's house, and others. We could make it into the school Druise wanted for you, as well as my seat."

He considered this, his eyes dark in the lamplight. "I would need to see it," he said. "But if it is as you say—Gwenna, there are men and women in Casil, other physicians, who, if they live, I could invite to come? My own experience—" He shook his head. "I am twenty-five. I am a good physician, and a more competent surgeon than I was before the war. But there are better teachers than I, with more knowledge."

"I imagine Valens could find a way to make that invitation known, and perhaps provide passage." It would be asking a lot of a family balancing its loyalties and livelihood. But Valens knew who he had brought to Ésparias, and their faithfulness to the family who had once been their patrons still ran deep. That wouldn't stop them trading with Casil's conquerors, but I didn't think it would stop their dealings—of many kinds—with us, either.

"The school—could it be more than a medical school?" I asked. "Because if I do move there, I have my son to consider, and there would be Lita and Elekos, too." And the child I carried, and perhaps Lairís's children, in time.

"A *Ti'ach*? Why not? But maybe the senior students, the ones who come to learn medicine, would be from all over. Perhaps not just Ésparias, in time, but Linrathe and Varsland and even Icoris and Cyrenis." He didn't look tired any longer, but animated, excited by the idea. He had a purpose here now, to be more than the prince he'd never wanted to be.

He'd have to be that too, but he'd learn that role—and developing a school for physicians that brought both teachers and students from across the world was a different sort of diplomacy—but it was still diplomacy. Had Druisius understood that? Probably. I wondered if my father had known of his bequest, if they had planned it between them. I'd never know.

Silence fell, a companionable one. I drank a little wine, thinking about what I was feeling. It surprised me, a little. "I've missed you," I said.

He looked up, flashing a quick smile. "I'm astonished. I have a clear memory of you chastising me with some force."

I returned the smile. "You deserved it."

"I suppose I did." He fell quiet again, but only for a moment. "Sometimes, in the heat of Casil's summers, I'd remember the *Ti'ach*, the coolness of its valley, the sound of the stream, the feel of the air. And the peace of it, the ordered days, the talk and the music."

"The love," I said. He nodded.

"We could do the same. The commander's residence is large, and could be extended. You and Sallah and the children, I and—" I would say it, make it real. It had been Lairís's thought first, after all. "And Lairís, and Gwyllar and whoever this is I carry now. To begin with."

"You're pregnant?"

"Yes. You can help her into the world next year, if you like."

"Perhaps. Physicians are advised not to attend their own family. Who is Lairís?"

"My partner. Sorley's niece."

He frowned. "Wasn't Lynthe your partner?"

"She was." I didn't really want to talk about her, but he should know. "She betrayed Ésparias, Colm, and she threatened Gwyllar's life. I'll tell you the whole story another time, but—" I swallowed. The room was dark beyond the circle of lamplight. I could say this here, now, and never again. "When *Mathàir* told me she was dead, part of me was relieved. Because I didn't have to try her for treason, and order her execution. I don't think I could have done that. Not to someone I once loved."

"I have," he said, after a minute, "tried to save the lives of men I knew and liked, who were my friends. Sometimes I succeeded. Sometimes I didn't, and sometimes what I attempted hastened their deaths. It is the only way I have ever killed, and each death has weighed on me, although I have learned from them, too.

"Physicians deliver death, whether in a surgery that does not succeed, or in diagnoses. Neither is easy. But to order the end of someone's life—" He shook his head. "I could not. Cannot, by my oath as a physician. You must know this, Gwenna. I will hold to that oath above all else."

"I understand," I said. "But do not judge me if I must."

"I saw our mother kill," he said, "to protect us as we left Casil. Without those deaths, we would not be here. They were only men trying to escape Casil too, but they would have killed us to do so. She did what was necessary. So will you."

I hadn't known this. "*Mathàir* hates killing," I said. "Was she ill, afterwards?"

"Yes." He paused. "Not physically. But on the ship, once we were safe, she fell into a melancholy that lasted some weeks. I treated it with what drugs I had, but there is little that can be done for these dark periods of the mind. They happen to soldiers, after battle and after the loss of their comrades. She seems better now, but don't ask too much of her." He yawned then, and sighed. "I should go to bed."

"So should I."

He placed the wine cup on a table, and pushed himself up. Looked down at me, and was abruptly still. "Should I have waited for you to stand?"

I laughed. "Gods, no. You're my brother, and we're alone. Protocol is for public rooms and council meetings, not for family."

He grinned, crookedly. "Good. Because I am too tired to deal with being chastised by my older sister yet again. Not on my first day back."

I stood, offering my arms. We hugged. "Good night, Colm."

"Good night, Gwenna."

I heard him speak to his guard before the door closed. Something else he'd have to grow used to, their ever-present shadowing. I walked to the window to close the shutters. The night was quiet. I could hear, faintly, the jingle of ships' rigging down at the harbour. The breeze was strong. I leant on the windowsill, breathing in the cool air, suddenly certain that I could, now, face whatever was to come.

Chapter 49

~Lena~

TYSTIE WAS READY. My supplies and almost all the belongings I'd chosen to take were stowed, wrapped in waxed cloth. Across the harbour, Valens's trader was also being loaded. It would take my son and Muire back to the Eastern Fort. Two weeks earlier, it had brought us—Colm and Sallah and the children, and me—to Wall's End.

Gwenna had stayed in the south, with Garia and Constyn. For many reasons, she'd told us. Some practical: if more people came seeking refuge, she wanted to be able to question them herself, and she needed to consult with Finn over the defences being planned for the islands, and Garth over trade. But also because she needed to be seen, the *Principe* among her people. "I neglected that," she'd admitted, privately, "in these past few years. Colm and I, and even Constyn, should be perceived as working together for the good of Ésparias. I hope that will smother the seeds of unrest Lynthe planted."

"Casil had a ruling council of three once, didn't it?" I'd asked, remembering Cillian leading the students in a discussion around the table at the *Ti'ach.*

Gwenna had given me a wry smile. "It didn't end well. But Constyn is too young to involve completely, and I cannot see my brother suddenly deciding to depose me."

"Do you still intend to call an Assembly next year?" She'd told me her plan, and the reasons behind it.

"I do. I want their approval of settlers from Varsland, should that be raised as part of a marriage settlement between Prince Trygve and Flynsà. To do otherwise would be—unfeeling. Callous."

"It would make you enemies." A simple truth.

"Yes." She'd given me a level look. "As would the presence of the Empress-Consort of Casil and her son, were it known. They are a danger to us, an invitation to invasion. But that is not for discussion and debate at an Assembly. I realize that I cannot consult the people on all issues. Some information, some choices, are not even for my advisors."

I climbed the steps back up to the fort. It would be several hours before the tide turned. I would take *Tystie* out on its flow. There was a good breeze, and I'd have some hours of light before the late summer sun set. Time to say my goodbyes.

Talyn first. She looked up from her desk when I knocked. "You're ready?"

"I have one or two things still to do. But, yes."

"I can't dissuade you?" I smiled, shaking my head. She'd been a mentor and a friend these last three decades, and she'd made her own sacrifices for Ésparias. I'd been the one to tell her Lynthe was dead. We'd shared an evening of talk and tears and memories, and the choices we'd both made. Although Talyn had continued to express concern about mine.

"You're leaving things far better organized for Garia than I did for Reif," I said. "But I suppose he'd been carrying much of my work for months, even before I left." Wall's End would have two new generals this autumn. Talyn too was retiring, to return to Han, to her sister and the grasslands and the horses. I'd already resigned, after presenting my adjutant with his general's insignia.

"And now you're leaving again." She half-smiled. "You're braver than I am, Lena. All I'm doing is going home."

"I hope I am too." Sometimes home was a person. She nodded.

"If it doesn't work out, Lena, you know you can come to Han."

"I know. And thank you, Talyn." Perhaps I would, if Sorley turned me away. There would be shared memories with Talyn, too; some.

Children's laughter filled the courtyard of the villa. They had no lessons today; Muire, after the last ten days of negotiations with Valens, had wished to spend time with his own children before travelling south to finalize the agreements with Gwenna. Elekos and Lita had been given a few days to settle into their new home, but their mother had wanted them to have a normal life as soon as possible. So the tutor suddenly had two new students—and a senior cadet with a gift for languages as an assistant, to teach Ésparian to the children our world would know as Colm's.

But today they were free to play, and I listened for a moment. Even Lita was laughing. I'd given Colm and Sallah the wing of the villa that had been mine and Cillian's; there were rooms enough for them all, and Cillian's library there for their use. And a bed wide enough for a mother who needed, in a strange place, to comfort two uprooted children.

Over the laughter, I heard Colm's voice, gently reprimanding Elekos. Or maybe Gwyllar; someone was being told to not climb on the fountain. I crossed to where he sat with Sallah.

"It's not time to go?" my son asked.

"No. You have several hours. They're happy," I said, indicating the children.

"Very," Sallah said. "Although Lita still has bad dreams. And she is anxious about her Patra going away."

"Again," I said softly.

"Again. Although, before—Alekos never promised to come home. Only told her to be brave."

"I've told her where I'm going. Back to the Eastern Fort, and her aunt. And that I will be home before winter," Colm said, "and there will be letters."

Sallah smiled. Her hand, I noted, covered my son's. "You are a good father, Colm."

"I had," he said, "the best of examples."

His words undid me. I covered my face with my hands, not wanting the children to see me weep. Colm's arm went around my shoulders. "I miss him too," he said. "Do not be ashamed to grieve."

"It is true," Sallah murmured. "I loved my husband. I also weep still. They were magnificent men, our princes."

What had Eudekia said to her, of Cillian? What had Colm? Memories and stories. I wiped my eyes and cheeks. "Read the letters," I said to my son. "I couldn't. But you should, you and Gwenna." I turned to Sallah.

"And you. You had a decade of being who you were, in a world more complex than ours. Use that to help Gwenna and Colm lead Ésparias."

"I had Eudekia to guide me." A rebuke? Maybe. She had been an Empress.

"Avia!" Gwyllar launched himself at me. I caught him.

"Hello, Bear."

"We're playing catch-me!" He touched the *li'ítho* on my left wrist. "Pretty," he said, before running off again to join Lita and Elekos.

"Isn't he confused by his two names?" Sallah asked.

"Three, in a way," Colm said.

"Three?" I frowned at my son.

"Lairís calls him Bear, but in Linrathan."

"Druise used to call you Cub," I remembered. "Sometimes in Casilan, and sometimes not."

Colm laughed. "That's right. I'd forgotten. Probably because it was the same name, regardless of language."

"What is Bear in Linrathan?" Sallah inquired. "And were you really called Cub? I think I like that."

"Artos," Colm said. "And please, no. Not Cub. What respect would a physician called Cub have?"

They were easy together, I thought. Something about my son—his ready smile, perhaps—reminded me of Dern when I'd first known him, at about the same age. The recollection brought a reminder.

"There is something I need to give you," I told Colm. "For Gwenna. She's expecting it. I'll be back in a minute."

I crossed the courtyard, avoiding the running children. I was sleeping in what had been Sorley and Druise's rooms, for reasons I couldn't quite give words to. I'd stood in their silence, the first day back. Exquisite glass still on the shelves, but with gaps where pieces had been removed. One or two instruments left on the walls. In another room, a bed nearly as wide as the one I had shared with Cillian.

And a teaching room in use. I'd waited until the music had ended and the student had gone. Then I'd walked to the door. "Hello, Lairís,"

"Lena! When did you get back?" *She is so much like Sorley*, Gwenna had told me, colouring a little. I'd seen a resemblance when she'd first arrived, but preoccupied then with my concern for Cillian, I hadn't given her much attention. But, in that room, the *ladhar* in her hand and her pale hair curling around her head, I'd seen what Gwenna meant.

"Just now, here," I had told her. "To Ésparias, many days ago. I've been at the Eastern Fort, with Gwenna. I left her well, and missing you." The message I'd been asked to convey, although there was a letter too. "But I've brought her brother and his wife and children with me, and perhaps you should come to meet them?"

A meeting that had gone well, and I thought now that Lairís and Sallah were well on their way to being friends. Would Gwenna choose to tell her partner who Sallah really was, someday? I believed so; I also believed that, after Lynthe, she would be slow to do so. I hoped Lairís would understand that, and more.

I opened the door to my rooms, thinking of one of my last conversations with Gwenna, after she'd told me about Lairís, and her concerns about what she could and couldn't tell her about the western alliance, the years of planning that had gone into it.

"Explain why you can't tell her everything," I said. "What matters is honesty. Carrying secrets hurts both of you." I'd told Gwenna then what Sorley had said to me, that last night. "Your father was wrong," I'd said bluntly. "Sorley needed to know he was loved, and had been for all those years they were apart. Cillian's apparent rejection of him hurt him terribly. Even after he knew why, and saw the pain it had caused your father, Sorley still saw himself as lesser, because Cillian had been able to love me openly."

"Lynthe could never have accepted me loving someone else." She'd looked away then, and back, meeting my eyes. "Did *Athàir* love Eudekia?"

"In a way. But not to any detriment to us." I'd watched where my daughter's hand went, unconsciously. "Ruar?"

The question had startled her. "Maybe," she'd admitted. "I don't know. It's something more, now, than when I conceived Gwyllar."

"Does Lairís know?"

"I haven't said, directly. We've talked about us both having children, so there's no expectation of exclusivity. But . . . I don't know myself how I feel."

"Talk to her," I'd said. "Be honest in this too. Eudekia was a world away, but it was her intelligence I was jealous of, her intellectual connection with your father. I was never, for a moment, worried about Sorley, although"—I'd smiled, remembering—"Cillian took some convincing of that. But it was not only your father who loved him. Which is why, Gwenna, I am resigning as your advisor, retiring. I am going to Gundarstorp."

"But—" I'd watched the conflicting emotions cross her face. "I wanted you to help me plan the new Assembly. You knew what Callan was going to do."

"With a very different intent. You don't need me, Gwenna. These are your tasks to do, yours and Colm's and your new council's, not mine."

Her eyes had gone distant, thinking. I'd waited. "Colm said you were not well on the ship. A dark period of the mind, he called it. Is that part of it?"

"Yes. I am still mourning your father, but now—" I had gestured, not finding words. "What Eudekia did—it shocked me. She will live in story and song, Gwenna. I will not, and nor should I. Perhaps you will, or your father, or one of your children. But I was only a village girl once, and I would like to end my days as one. With a few years of peace before that end."

"You will only not live in song if Sorley's *danta* is forgotten," my daughter had said, tears gleaming in the lamplight. "There is a letter from him to you, in your room at the villa. Maybe you shouldn't decide until you've read it?" Then, hesitantly, "Can you truly forgive him, *Mathàir*? After what he said to you?"

"I can. It was just grief speaking, Gwenna." In all its layers and complexities and contradictions. "Just grief." But had Sorley realized that too?

When my daughter spoke again her voice was firm. "You are right. These are my tasks to do. Perhaps I relied too long on *Athàir*, on all of you, but the foundation you built for me is why I can look to the future with some confidence. For that, for so much more—thank you, *Mathàir*."

"Oh, Gwenna," was all I could say, before my own tears had spilled over. It had taken a long embrace and several minutes before either of us could speak again.

"I have a task for you to consider," Gwenna had said, as briskly as she could manage. "Now Flynsà is a possible bride for Varsland's prince, she should be—not guarded, but watched over, as Sorley has offered to do for Trygve. Something a retired general who was once a village girl could do, perhaps?"

"I could," I'd answered, because it was reasonable and my daughter wasn't arguing; she was letting me go with dignity and grace and love. Like the *Principe* she was, or like an Empress.

I went to the bedroom, where the small chest that held the last of my belongings was waiting to be loaded onto *Tystie*. Not until the ship home to Wall's End had I realized how I could tell her what Casyn had asked of me, how I could share the ideas and conflicts and secrets of that time. A small sacrifice, perhaps, but one I would gladly make.

I knelt to open the chest, feeling my knees creak. I removed a few items, glancing again at one before setting it aside. Near the bottom, wrapped in layers of oiled cloth, were several leather-bound books. I undid the strings and took one out. The man for whom my son was named had given it to me at the Winter Camp. The first of my journals, a record of that year when my life had changed forever. A record of what Casyn had asked of me, and then the Emperor himself, and what I had done in response.

I would send it to Gwenna. The others I would keep, for now. In my mind I felt the briefest brush of approval. I smiled, and ran a finger over the journal's worn cover. Then I opened it and read the first words I'd written so very long ago.

I was seventeen the spring Casyn came to Tirvan.

Chapter 50

I SWUNG *TYSTIE* ENOUGH to let me watch the ship leaving the harbour, bearing Colm and Muire back to the Eastern Fort. Lairís and Sallah hadn't brought the children to see us sail, and for that I'd been glad. The day had turned grey and breezy, and I needed to concentrate on handling my little boat.

For some distance north I knew the coast and the waters; I'd sailed this way on my occasional mornings or afternoons away from my desk or the council table. But not too much further out, and I was into unknown seas. I'd sailed this coast only once before, in a stolen boat, and I'd been unconscious for the last half-day.

But you brought us home, I thought to Cillian. *You became home, for Sorley and me, and maybe even Druise.*

No answer. I hadn't expected one. In the water, dovekies floated and dived. I'd named my first boat for the little black-and-white birds. I passed a fishing boat, a bit further out, the two men aboard raising a hand to me. I returned the wave. The breeze was strong, and I was making good time.

As dusk fell I found a small, sheltered cove and anchored *Tystie*. The sky was clouded, but it didn't feel like rain. I'd sleep aboard. I built a driftwood fire for warmth, and to boil water for tea, and ate some of the food I'd brought. A passing thought both surprised me and made me smile: I wished I had Ladon with me. But he was Constyn's dog now. And how the sheepdogs of Gundarstorp would have reacted to him, I didn't want to know.

How would I be received? Not by the sheepdogs, but by Sorley? I glanced over at the boat. In the chest stowed and strapped in place lay his letter to me. I hadn't read it. I'd told myself that he was safe, alive, and that was what mattered, but in truth I hadn't had the courage to read what he'd written. In my last days at Wall's End, I'd had enough strength of mind to do what I had to. But not enough to cope with another rejection from Sorley.

I'd half expected the *li'ítho* to be enclosed, but the folded and sealed letter was one thin sheet. That had reassured me a bit. But he'd said nothing more to Lairís about me, before he'd left.

Should I read his letter? Not yet. I would, before I reached Gundarstorp, I told myself, so that I knew what resistance I would be facing. But what I had to say to him I was determined to do face to face, and not in cold ink on paper. I'd leave again, if he wanted me to.

And he well might. I looked up at the starless sky. Far to the east, the sky over a lake was likely clear, shining with stars. The memories I carried of that place belonged only to me, before chance or fate had brought us to Sorley and Turlo and the desperate request of an Emperor. But a decade before that, Sorley had fallen in love, and his memories of that night belonged to Gundarstorp. Almost his only memories unchanged by my presence. *One night alone*, he'd written in his song for Cillian.

I'd go to the *Ti'ach na Barì,* and from there I would ride to the edge of Gundarstorp. There would be a shepherd or his boy I could ask to fetch Sorley. Then I could say what I needed to, without intruding on memories that belonged to the hall and night and music. If needed, Barì would give me a home for the winter, or longer; it was my right, really, as someone who had been the Lady of a *Ti'ach*.

It wasn't what I wanted, deep in my heart. But it might be what Sorley did. I would have to honour that, although it would be another grief to carry for the rest of my life. Cold was seeping through me; the fire had burned down. I got up to place more wood on it, and fetch my blankets from the boat. I'd sleep by the fire, not on *Tystie*, or I'd wake too stiff and sore in the morning to sail.

~

The weather held, except for spatterings of rain. The wet and cold of the early part of the year had finally given way to summer, I'd been told, but it had remained too often damp and cloudy. Now, as autumn approached, the weather had become drier, but no less grey.

I navigated the rocks and small islands without difficulty, although in places rowing with the sail down. Seals slipped into the water if I came too close, their sleek heads and huge dark eyes looking up at me. Between the islands, I glimpsed a trading vessel much further out. Whose? It was sailing north, too far away for me to identify it. But I was stopping at Abher Tabha for food and water. I'd find out then.

~

I didn't have to ask. As soon as I brought *Tystie* into the trading basin, I saw the ship moored at the jetty—and the leopard's head on its prow. *Leste.* Gwenna's talks with Garth must have been productive. Who had they sent to negotiate the terms of trade? Garth would not have come himself, and I had no idea who his trade envoy was. And, I realized, it was not my worry.

I tied *Tystie* up among some other small boats, but I didn't disembark. I sat, considering. I'd need to report to the harbourmaster's office, so my boat was identified, but beyond that there were no requirements for me to register my presence. I didn't want there to be any chance of a message sent, purposely or casually, to Gundarstorp; nor did I want to meet Daragh, who could be about his duties at the harbour.

When the sky had darkened to night, I walked along the jetty to the harbourmaster's office. The clerk barely looked up. "The boat is *Tystie*," I told him in answer to his questions, "in berth five. I'm Galena, of Berge in Ésparias. One night, to resupply." My long-dead father would forgive me—or perhaps, from what I'd known of Galen, approve—I thought.

I paid the fee, asked my own questions about where to not be cheated on food and water, wondering as I did if I would be more conspicuous if I didn't ask about the catboat than if I did. The former, I decided. "The ship out there, with the cat's head—where's that from?"

"Leste," he said. "An island south of Ésparias."

"I've heard of it," I said. "I've never seen their ships." Except the one we'd burned at Tirvan's harbour, the summer I turned eighteen.

"A nine-day's wonder," he replied, glancing out at the harbour, "but I'm told they'll be a common sight soon. The Casilani ships used to come here, to pick up the cargoes from Varsland. Now they're gone, Leste will be taking over. Or so I understand." He did look at me, then. "Why are you here?"

I grinned. "There's a man. I met him in the spring. He invited me north, and now the fishing's almost done, I thought why not?"

"May the course of love run truly," he said, returning the grin. "The inn halfway up the hill is decent, if you don't want to sleep aboard."

I went back to *Tystie* to fetch a bag for food and a jug for water, thinking about catboats, and Garth, memories from that long-ago summer. I'd been glad Garth hadn't arrived for his meetings with Gwenna before I left the Eastern Fort; I hadn't wanted to see him. Nor had I been comfortable in Dern's presence in the spring. I knew why; in the irrationality of grief, that these two men I had cared for—loved, in Garth's case—were alive when Cillian was not made me angry. Perhaps another thing I should tell Sorley, if he would listen.

The inn, I decided later, was preferable to a chilly night on board *Tystie*. There was little chance of Daragh frequenting a sailor's inn, and I would leave as early in the morning as the light allowed. Fine rain, almost a mist, was falling. I walked up the hill in the gloom. The inn's windows shone with lamplight, and inside the common room was warm, and crowded, and noisy.

I made my way to the serving area, asked for a room. The innkeeper pursed her lips. "Expensive," she said. "There's no other women."

"I can pay." How many times had I done this now? In time the recollections blurred, became a blend of conversations and sights, scents and tastes. Where was it I'd had rabbit stew, or lamb? Where had there been lavender in flower?

Would I remember a woman with torches, or a phoenix rising?

~

The clouds were heavier in the morning, and the wind sharper, from the south. I added a layer of clothes, trimmed *Tystie*'s sail, and headed out of the harbour. Out beyond its shelter, my little boat ran north rapidly, the wind behind her, the sea miles slipping away. I was making excellent time, even through the islands and rocks of the Maw, but I didn't like the look of the sky.

Still, I didn't take refuge at one of the *torps* or fishing settlements I passed. I wanted to reach the *Ti'ach*, and there was exhilaration mixed with the thread of fear running through me. I was sailing in a trance, my adjustments of sail and tiller done beyond thought. Until lightning split the sky, followed by a crack of thunder—and in my head, Cillian's voice. *Lena!*

Tystie heeled over. I scrambled to right her, to drop the sail. Another flash, another roll of thunder. The waves were suddenly huge, storm-driven, boiling. I struggled with the sail, sodden, whipping away from me in the fierce wind. I couldn't tie it down. I wasn't strong enough.

The sail billowed, pulling ropes taut. I reached to haul it in, my feet slipping on the drenched deck. My boat was still upright, still afloat—but being driven into the shore. Lightning illuminated the rocks ahead, just before *Tystie* struck them.

Chapter 51

THE SEA ENGULFED ME. I kicked, trying to surface, to get my head above the waves long enough to breathe. I broke through, gasping—to be driven under before I could fill my lungs, taking in water, coughing, trying not to inhale more. I strained upwards—or what I thought was upwards. My chest burned. Panic rose. I flailed, trying to find a rock, or a piece of my boat, anything. Lights flickered across my vision. My arms and legs were growing heavy, the cold sapping strength.

The terror faded, the peace of resignation beginning to replace it. An easy death, it was said, if I just gave in. *Cillian,* I thought. *Be there? Please?* I stopped fighting the waves. Darkness was encroaching, dimming the flickering light. I'd never know what Sorley had written, I thought, distantly.

Hands grasped my arms, pulling me up, dragging me through the waves. I started to cough, from the force of movement, of trying again to breathe. "Walk!" a man's voice said. "It is shallow now. A few more steps. Yes, good. We are on the beach."

I collapsed onto my hands and knees, coughing, vomiting sea water. A fist thumped my back. I gasped, gobbling air, vomiting again. My throat felt torn, corroded, and I was shaking, my heart pounding. I let myself drop to the shingle. My rescuer turned me onto my side. "Safer," he said.

When my heart and breathing had slowed, I sat up, with difficulty. I seemed to have no strength left at all. In the dark and the driving rain, I could see only a shape beside me: a man crouching, then standing to offer me a hand.

"Thank you," I rasped. "You saved my life."

"Óski sent me," he said. "He tells me when there is a person in danger, sometimes."

"Óski?"

"The god. I saw him, as a boy. He blessed me, and this is his gift."

A simple man, I thought. But Cillian had heard a god's voice, too.

"Come," he said now, helping me to my feet. "Out of the storm."

"My boat—"

"In the morning. What there is left to find."

He led me, patient with my slowness, up a path. I had to pause to catch my breath more than once. "Where are we?" I asked, my hands on my knees.

"The *Ti'ach na Barì*," he replied. "I take care of the animals. Not the sheep, except sometimes." We climbed a little higher. "Look," he said. "See the lights. There is the *Ti'ach*."

~

Eithnë, with the calm practicality Sorley had told me about more than once, wasted no time on questions. *Fuisce* with honey in it, a hot bath, soup. Blankets around me at the fire, while my hair dried and I drank the soup. The rain rattled against windows. More *fuisce*, and this time I tasted valerian as well as honey. A bed, warmed with a hot stone, and finally, sleep. But before it, at the edge of dreams, a thought hovered, drifted, disappeared.

I woke into full morning light. I had missed breakfast, I guessed, but there would be porridge or bread in the kitchen.

I dressed in the clothes I found on a chair, and made my way to the warm, stone-flagged room. Tea and buttered bread were provided, the housekeeper not fussing except to click her tongue when I coughed. I sat at the table to eat, considering. I ached, but it was only strained muscles and bruises. My lungs still burned, but I was coughing less than when I had first got out of bed.

"Lena?" Barì came into the kitchen. "Is that tea fresh?" he asked the housekeeper. At her confirmation, he poured a cup and sat down. "How are you feeling?"

"Sore," I said. "Inside and out."

"Drink a lot," Eithnë said, joining us. Barì poured her a cup of tea. "It will help with getting rid of the salt in the water you swallowed. Otherwise, willow-bark and rest." She drank, thirstily. "Voice lessons," she explained. "Which I took only because Apulo did not come from Gundarstorp yesterday, I assume because of the storm. Do you want a message sent there?"

"No," I said, a bit too forcefully. She looked at me quizzically. "Sorry," I offered, "but please, no. I am not entirely sure Sorley wants to see me."

She and Barì exchanged glances. "I won't ask. But I will say I doubt that."

I decided not to ask her why; inevitably, I'd have to explain my feelings, and I didn't want to do that. "Will the man who rescued me say anything that might get back to them?"

"Blindi? No. He doesn't speak to many people. He's good with the livestock, though."

"He said his god told him I needed help." I guessed he'd seen my boat from a hillside, without fully registering it, until the storm began and part of his simple mind remembered, sending him to the cove.

Barì nodded. "He has visions. His mother brought him here, not long after the *Ti'ach* was built. The others in their village—they are trappers, not tied to any *torp*—were afraid of him. He was blessed by a *gubbë* when he was small—that's one of the wandering holy men of the north—but he's convinced it was a god in disguise, as the legends say."

"He's saved a few other people," Eithnë added. "Not always from drowning, but you're not the first. He's brought your chest, by the way. It's all that's salvageable. The boat is in pieces, I'm afraid."

A boy of about eleven pushed the kitchen door open. He carried a tray with empty plates and cups. "Thank you," Eithnë said to him. She stood. "Lesson time. If you can tolerate hearing music played by students, you're welcome to use my sitting room. It's warm, and more comfortable than the kitchen."

"When you next are free," I said to Eithnë, "I have news of Lairís." I got up to follow her. "And you're forgetting we were seventeen years at our *Ti'ach*. I've probably heard every wrong note that can be played."

She laughed. "Or sung, no doubt. And you did some very good work with the words of the *danta*, and whose voices they represented."

"A long time ago." We crossed the hall to her teaching rooms. Beyond them were her private quarters, sitting room and bedroom. A peat fire glowed in the fireplace, my box sitting close to it. Raw wood showed in several places where it had scraped against the rocks, but the latch was still closed.

"I had it brought here. I thought you would want privacy while you saw what damage had been done," Eithnë said. "And now I must go." She closed the door. I knelt, wincing, and opened the chest.

Most of its contents could be salvaged; even my journals, their wrapping protecting them from being thoroughly soaked. But the three letters I had carried – two from Lairís, to her family and to Eithnë, and the one Sorley had left for me—fell to pieces in my hands, the faint blurring of ink on the scraps all that was left of the words that had been written. I would face Sorley unprepared.

~

I spent most of the day in Eithnë's rooms, drinking tea, dozing, thinking. The faint music, of varying quality, was familiar and somehow reassuring. The midday meal had been brought to me, so that I hadn't needed to eat with the students. More soup, sheep's cheese, a good barley bread.

Late in the afternoon Barì came to see me. "You look much better," he observed, sinking into a chair in a way that told me it was his usual place.

"I feel better. I've stopped coughing, and my throat isn't raw now."

"The sky's clearing. Tomorrow should be fine, at least in the morning. I can offer you a horse, if you think you can ride. Someone will bring it back, or—"

"Or I can, if there is no welcome for me at Gundarstorp," I finished for him.

"Yes. And if that is the case, you know there is a place for you here. To write, to study, to teach if you wish."

"I might accept that." It wasn't for me to tell him of the students he likely would be asked to take in the next year or two, or the role I would then need to play. Gwenna and Ruar would make that request, if Bryngyl agreed to their plan.

"We would be honoured if you did." He smiled, an open, honest expression. "But I think it unlikely. Now, will you take your meal at the long table tonight? There are two of my senior students who would love the chance to talk to you, if you feel up to it."

They would ask about Casil's withdrawal, about what it meant for Ésparias and for Linrathe, and possibly even about the relationship with Varsland. Questions without real answers, but I could shape my responses as my own questions, hear their thoughts, guide them a little. I'd watched Cillian teach that way for years, and I'd taught senior cadets in the same way. Like the faint music throughout the day, it would be familiar, a return, briefly, to a life I'd known and loved.

"I'd be glad to, *Comiádh*," I said.

~

The morning dawned as clear as Barì had promised, only a few wisps of clouds over the sea. He had given the students the evening to themselves, and the three of us had talked, or Eithnë had played and Barì and I had listened, until late.

"Lairís and Gwenna?" Eithnë had said, clearly pleased. "Does Sorley know?" She'd smiled, delighted, when I said he did. "That's like a continuation of love into the next generation. There's a song in that, you know."

"Which of course you will have to write." Barì's tease had been accompanied by a smile, the love between them not hidden in these private rooms. I could come back here, make a home, I thought. Rest, heal, find peace.

But something inchoate, unformed, had disagreed. Something from a dream? I couldn't quite reach it: it was as blurred and fragmented as the sea-soaked letters. When I had gone to bed a little later, the feeling was still there, unidentifiable, like a shape glimpsed through fog, or the notes of music heard from too far away.

I had doused the lamp. The room had been utterly dark. I'd whispered Cillian's name.

Nothing, except, at the edge of hearing, the pulse of the waves.

~

Now, as I mounted the chestnut mare I'd been given, the same pulse was in my throat. The animal was half hill-pony, its legs feathered, suited to the rough tracks of this land. What belongings I'd salvaged were packed into two canvas bags, tied on either side of the cantle.

"Do you want someone with you?" Barì asked. Eithnë stood beside him, come to wish me well.

I shook my head. "I'm better alone."

"I understand." In the sunlight, the flecks of grey in his hair stood out. He cupped his hands to give me a leg up.

"Thank you again, *Comiádh*, Lady," I said, the formality for the stableboy. Then I raised my hand in farewell, and turned the mare's head north.

I kept the chestnut to a walk, both for the slipperiness of the wet path and from a reluctance to face what awaited me. Regardless of what both Barì and Eithnë had indicated, I had no idea what my welcome would be.

Skylarks trilled above me, and the occasional grouse scuttled across the path. Sheep grazed on the hillsides below the crags. Up in those rocky peaks, *fuádain* would nest, but it was early in the day for them to be flying.

At its crest of a ridge, a stand of rowan grew along the path. The breeze caught the leaves as we passed, showering us with water. I pulled the mare up. Below us, the land lay in sunlight, the white foam of waves breaking on the rocks and shingle of the cove. I stood in the stirrups to brush water from the chestnut's face. Then I swept my own hair free of droplets, and looked down.

Fishing boats dotted the sea, men hauling nets. Around the boats, gulls cried and circled. The hall—more a long farmhouse—nestled into the side of a hill, sheltered from the worst of the weather, and scattered around it were outbuildings and cottages. As I watched, a woman came out to peg laundry out in the breeze. She didn't look my way.

Beyond the stubble of harvested grainfields, a drystone wall divided the cropland from the sheep moor. Part of the wall had collapsed, no doubt from sheep pushing against it. A man was rebuilding it, lifting stone into place, his pale hair tied back off his face, tunic sleeves rolled up. And wearing gloves, to protect his hands against the roughness of the stone.

The thought—no, the words—I hadn't been able to remember came back, as clear as the skylark's song. *You are almost home, käresta.*

All fear left me. I took a deep breath.

A dog barked, a sharp yap of warning. Sorley looked up, scanning the hills. We had ridden together so often. He would recognize my figure on a horse.

He stiffened, seeing me. Then he stood still, making no gesture of welcome, but not turning away either. I rode towards him. A few paces away, I stopped. This close, I saw the glint of unshed tears, and heard his ragged breath. We stared at each other, unspeaking.

Sorley moved first, to strip off the leather gloves and hold out his arms. I slid off my horse and into his embrace. I heard the gulls crying, and the faint lapping of the waves on the shingle. Smelt the scent of baking bread rising from the hall below, and heard the distant sounds of rigging and shouts from the fishing boats and the closer, unceasing baa-ing of the sheep. Sorley's arms were tight around me.

"You came," he said. "He said you would."

He said you would. "He talks to you too?" I murmured against Sorley's chest.

Sorley tensed, just slightly. "What? I meant—" He stopped. "Yes. I hear Cillian." His voice changed. "I thought I was going mad, Lena. That I was mad, as I was after I was beaten and left for dead before. I heard Druise then: did I ever tell you? But that was only once or twice. Cillian—" He broke off, stepped back to meet my eyes. "I'm not alone in this? Are we both mad?"

"Perhaps," I said, "Or perhaps we are just greatly loved." A god had spoken to Cillian once. What might he, with all his subtle, quiet persuasiveness, have negotiated when he had faced that god for a third and final time? "You showed us once that love could conquer death. Maybe it has again."

"If that is true," Sorley said slowly, "then I think—I think he will fade. Leave us, finally."

"Now we're together? Yes." I felt the truth in Sorley's words. Whatever bargain Cillian may have made with the god of death, it could not have been for more than a passing reprieve. All things faded, were temporary, after all. Even a long peace, or a long life. Except, if we were blessed, love.

"And that will be bearable," he said. "Now." He paused, blinking. "Lena—what I said, it was unforgivable, and not true, ever. Lies I cannot forgive myself for. I hope I made that clear, in my letter."

"But it was true, or at least how you felt was. You're a *scáeli*. You don't lie." I'd tell him about the letter in a bit, and the man whose god had sent him to rescue me. "Sorley, I could have said similar things to Eudekia. I was so angry that she mourned him. I wanted to tell her she had no right. But she did. She loved him, and he her, and I finally admitted it. To myself, and to her. There is room for many, Druise said to me once."

Sorley's face tightened at Druise's name. "Let's sit," he said, indicating a ring of boulders a few paces into the field. My horse grazed among them.

The stone, flecked with orange lichen, was mostly dry, and cool. "Do you think," he asked, after we'd settled, "Cillian talks to her, too?"

"Talked," I said softly. "She's dead." I laughed, surprising myself. "They're probably playing *xache*."

After a moment, he smiled. "With Druise guarding them both?" There were tears on his lashes.

The brief moment of mirth left me. "Sorley, I am so sorry I wasn't there."

"Better you weren't." He too had sobered. "I was so angry. So lost, Lena. You can imagine."

I nodded. "So you came back to Gundarstorp."

"There was nowhere else. And Cillian told me to."

Overhead, ravens croaked. I looked up at the two circling above us. Thought and memory, birds of the god, in the beliefs of the north. Sorley looked up too. "They call us home, it is said," he murmured. He brushed the tears from his eyes. The fingers of his right hand were slightly crooked. On his wrist, a silver bracelet caught the light. I reached out to touch it.

"You wear it."

"Yes. I will not pretend, or hide who I am. Or who I loved." His own fingers went to the bracelet, a habitual gesture, I thought. "Not any longer." He glanced at my own wrist. "But *li'itho* bracelets are not meant to be separated. By right and tradition, you should be wearing them both."

"To honour the love, even in death," I said. "By tradition, perhaps. But not by right. That is as much yours as mine. And—" I grinned. "They won't be separated now, will they?"

"Oh, Lena." Fresh tears glittered in his eyes. I blinked hard against my own. Sorley pulled me into another hard embrace. He smelt of woodsmoke and sweat, and beneath that, of himself, familiar, loved. "Will you stay? Or are you here to take me back? As it must be one or the other."

I looked around, at the sky and sea and hills. The breeze was cold on my skin, carrying with it the salt of the ocean. Sunlight silvered the water, brightening the fishing boats out in the bay. *You are almost home.* Certainty settled inside me. Here there was space: space for memories and grief, yes, but for laughter and song too, and a friend who would share them all—and who would share, too, the work still to do.

Not almost, my love. Thank you.

"I'll stay," I said. "If you'll have me, that is."

Sorley stood. He reached for the chestnut's reins before holding out a hand to me. "In that case," he said, "you'd better come and meet the family."

Epilogue

~Colm~

"Come." I call Lita and Eli to me, crouching so they can see the small bundle I hold. I push back the cloth their sister is wrapped in. She opens her blue eyes, blinks.

Lita touches her cheek. "What's her name?"

"Rosian." Honouring her lineage, a combination of her mother's real name, and my father's.

"Rosín," Lairís says, giving my daughter's name the pronunciation of northern Sorham. She is holding my sister's daughter, barely two. "This is your cousin, Piása. She'll be a friend for you when she's a little older."

Piása's thumb is in her mouth. She looks doubtful. I stand, so Piása can see Rosian more closely. "You were this tiny once," I tell her. She frowns, disbelieving me.

"You were," Eli says. Elekos, but Gwyllar shortened it to Eli. "I remember."

"So were you," his older sister says.

"Even I was once," I say, to forestall the argument. "We all were."

A knock on the door before it is opened by the physician who attended Rosian's birth. "Your wife is ready for you," she tells me, "and the babe will be hungry."

"Gwyllar hasn't seen her," Eli protests.

"Gwyllar," Lairís says, "wanted to finish his *xache* game. It's his own fault he isn't here. He'll see her later, with his mother."

Gwenna was in one or another interminable meeting. I probably was told which one, but when Sallah's pains began in the night, all other thoughts vanished. I understand now why physicians are counselled against attending their own family, except in direst need. Had there been problems I doubt I would have been capable of the detachment needed in those circumstances.

Sallah looked tired, but she had been washed and her hair tidied, and her smile of welcome was for both me and the child. I sat on the edge of the bed and handed Rosian to her, watching as my wife bared a breast, its blue veins prominent beneath the white skin, and guided the baby to its nipple. Rosian snuffled and groped with her mouth, then, finding what she instinctively wanted, began to suckle. I had seen this countless times before. It always brought a smile to my lips, but never before tears to my eyes.

~

Sallah and the baby are sleeping; so are the children. A half-moon hangs outside the window, open to the breezes of the summer night. Gwenna and I are alone. This is our habit, this time together to discuss the business of the day. We have ignored Gwenna's meetings tonight; there was nothing, she says, that cannot wait. I am glad of this. I doubt I could focus.

"Rosian is lovely," my sister says, handing me the cup of wine she has poured for me, "even if Gwyllar wasn't terribly impressed. She'll have Sallah's hair, I think. Our father's beard had red in it, if you remember."

I did, vaguely, a memory from the voyage to Casil. "I wish he could have seen her. Does Gwyllar remember him?"

My sister shakes her head. "He was too young when *Athàir* died. So he is only a story to all our children. Lita and Eli remember their father, don't they?

"Lita does, and she tells Eli about him," I say. "I don't know if he can separate what he really remembers from those tales. But, Gwenna, how could Alekos have left them to go to war?" I cannot imagine that: there is a hot, fierce protectiveness in me now. I hadn't expected this: I loved Lita and Eli, and I had thought I would love this baby in the same way. I was protective of them, but not like this.

"Because he had to," Gwenna says simply. She is sitting with her feet tucked up, as if she were Lita's age, not a woman of thirty-two. "He was father of his city and his empire, not just his children. But he made sure they were safe."

Will you take my wife and children to safety in the west? Alekos had asked. Then: *Tell my wife I have loved her. Tell the children the same.* The memory holds pain, but also gratitude. I had not wanted to leave Alekos; my place was at the battlefield, saving lives, I had thought. I had said that to my Emperor.

You will be saving three important lives, he had responded. Three lives I loved now, as I had loved, in a different way, the man who had entrusted them to me. Had Alekos hoped for that? Perhaps not. I had said after my baby sister had died when I was fourteen, I would never marry, or father a child. The pain I had felt at her death had been more than I could bear. Better not to love. When Gnaius had offered the chance to stay in Casil as his student, I'd wanted it not just because it was a chance to study with the greatest physician of our time, but because it would remove me from the complexities of my family; from the confusion of love and grief.

Gnaius had taught me the balance between compassion and detachment in treating patients, and when I had agreed to bring Sallah and Eli and Lita—the Empress Rosale and her children—to Ésparias, compassion for Selekos and Philita had led me to offer marriage to Rosale, for protection and stability, nothing more. I had little interest in physical desire; indeed, were it not for Gnaius's advice that release was needed for the health of both the body and the mind—I would have ignored it completely.

But if I had, Rosian would not be in the world, and I would not be a father.

"Aren't you glad now Sallah encouraged you to her bed?" Gwenna asks, her voice teasing.

I sip my wine, feeling my face heat. "Do you read minds at the negotiation table too?" I ask, deflecting a little. But this is my sister, and we have few secrets.

She grins at me. "Sometimes. Although it is really reading faces and bodies, and knowing what has gone before. Sallah is my friend, and friends express their frustrations with their partners, sometimes."

You may be happy with a celibate life, Sallah had told me, *but I am not. I loved Alekos, but it is time for me to live fully. I will not take a lover unless you give me no choice.* She had paused, smiled, a little sadly. *And I would like us to have a child together. At least one.*

She had, it appeared, said much of this to Gwenna, too. What had Sallah reported after I'd agreed? Only one lamp was lit, hanging above us. It cast little light, for which I was grateful.

Gwenna laughs. "You look so discomfited. Don't worry. I will allow confidences only to a point. There are things I do not want to know about my brother." She sobers, and her voice becomes serious, the tones of the *Principe*. "But you have a daughter now who belongs entirely to Ésparias. It will change how you think about our future, both our family's and our country's. I know Gwyllar and Piása did, for me."

I frown. "Eli and Lita belong to Ésparias now too."

"But only in part. You—we—cannot ignore who they are; that Eli is really the Emperor Selekos, and that some day—in ten years, or twenty—he may choose to act in that name." A name almost never spoken, and only when we are sure of privacy; a secret known only to five people. No, six. Lita must remember, even if her brother doesn't.

Gwenna tilts her head. "Have you noticed that Constyn is nearly as protective of Lita as Druise was of me? She adores him."

"I thought she adored the dog," I protest.

"Ladon? She does. But also his owner. Do not be surprised if that friendship becomes something more, in time. Eli's true identity will be a bond between them."

I can't take this in. Tiredness is coursing through me, and I have a daughter I want to see again before I sleep. "Do I need to worry about this now?"

Gwenna smiles again. "No. Finish your wine, go see your wife and daughter, and go to bed. But you will need to concern yourself with it at some point, with all its complexities and implications, my brother prince."

Her quiet reminder. One that prompts another thought: my tiny daughter, who, I hope, is either asleep or suckling, is a princess. Her life will be inextricably caught up with the fate of our land. I understand, suddenly, what my sister is telling me. And why Alekos left his children to fight for his empire, for their future.

I am twenty-eight. I am head of a school that I am working to make a beacon of learning in the west, where men and women from the known world may come to teach and learn; not just medicine, as my benefactor planned, but music and engineering and philosophy and history too. I advise my sister the *Principe*, her closest confidante for concerns of politics and diplomacy. These are tasks I can do, with some competence.

To be a father to a helpless, newly born child is another matter entirely.

"Don't forget," my sister is saying, "to write to Gundarstorp. *Mathàir* and Sorley will be awaiting the news. But the morning will be soon enough."

I expect I will write tonight; I doubt I will sleep. There is so much to consider. I stand, leaving my wine unfinished. Run a hand through my hair. I feel unbalanced, as if the mosaic beneath my feet is shifting. Hear Gwenna laugh.

"Colm," she says, her voice amused. "Stop worrying. Sallah's already had two children. So have I, and there are Lairís and Constyn too to help bring her up. Rosian will be surrounded by people who love her. You're not doing this alone. She'll be a child of the *Ti'ach na Colm*, just as we were children of the *Ti'ach na Cillian*. What more could you ask for her?"

"Nothing," I say, tears pricking. Gwenna is right. I tell her so.

"Of course I am," she says. "I'm your big sister, remember?"

The Vocabulary of Empire's Passing

The languages spoken in my books are my inventions, but they are based on existing or historic languages, and some words are identical to ones in those languages. while pronunciations and grammar may not follow existing linguistic conventions. Roughly, Casilan is based on Latin; Linrathan primarily from Gaelic, both Scottish and Irish, and Marái'sta from Scandinavian languages. The dialect of Sorham is an analogue of Norse Gaelic.

Word	Meaning	Language
amané	lover	Casilan
Athàir	father	Linrathan
Avia	grandmother	Casilan
cithar	stringed instrument	Casilan
comiádh, comiádha	professor(s)	Linrathan
consor, consori	partner(s)	Esparian
danta	saga	Linrathan
dignitasi	patrician	Casilan
domina	lady	Casilan
draki	dragon-headed ship	Marái'sta
eirlysa	snowdrop	Linrathan
fiscarius	financial comptroller	Casilan
fuádain	peregrine falcon	Linrathan
fuisce	whisky	Linrathan
geirfalki	gyrfalcon	Marái'sta
gràhadh	beloved	Linrathan
gubbë	holy man	Linrathan
käresta/kärestan	beloved (f)/(m)	Linrathan
ladhar	stringed instrument	Linrathan
leannan	dearest	Linrathan
li'ítho	marriage bracelets	Sorham

Word	Meaning	Language
Mathàir	mother	Linrathan
Matra	mother	Casilan
mo charaidh gràhadh	my beloved friend	Linrathan
mo charaidh	my friend	Linrathan
mo	my	Linrathan
na (as in Ti'ach na Barì)	of	Linrathan
Patra	father	Casilan
Princip(e)	leader, prince,princess	Casilan
quincala/um	formal partnership (f)/(m)	Casilan
Smölvann	narrow sea	Marái'sta
scáeli/scáeli'en	bard(s), skald(s)	Linrathan
scraptae	sex workers	Casilan
sjaldr/sjaldrën	bard(s), skald(s)	Marái'sta
taberna(e)	tavern(s), eating place	Casilan
Teannasach	chieftain; leader of Linrathe	Linrathan
Ti'ach/Ti'acha	school(s)	Linrathan
torp	farmstead & cottages	Linrathan
toscaire/toscairen	envoy(s)	Linrathan
xache	board game	All

The Characters of Empire's Passing

Characters in italics are deceased at the beginning of the story.

Character	Role
Alekos	Emperor of the East
Annius	Procurator of Beria
Amlodd	*scáeli* to the *Teannasach* of Linrathe
Apulo	Cillian's body servant
Asgaill	*Comiádh of the Ti'ach na Asgaill*
Barì	*Comiádh* of the *Ti'ach na Barì*
Betis	Roghan's wife
Bjørn	Prince of Varsland, Commander of the Emperor's Guard
Blindi	worker at the *Ti'ach na Barì*
Bronah	Muire's wife
Bryngyl	King of Varsland, Bjørn's brother
Callan	*the last Emperor of the West, Gwenna's grandfather*
Casyn	*the first Princip of Ésparias, Callan's brother*
Cenko	Berian innkeeper
Cillian	*senior prince of Ésparias; Comiádh, historian, diplomat*
Colm	*Callan's twin brother*
Colm	Gwenna's brother, physician and prince of Ésparias
Constyn	Faolyn & Siusàn's son, prince of Ésparias, cadet
Dagney	*Scáeli and Lady of the Ti'ach na Perras*
Daragh	Ruar's oldest son; heir presumptive to Linrathe
Decanius	*financial comptroller of Casil, advisor to Eudekia*
Dern	Commander of the Ésparian Fleet
Donnalch	*Teannasach of Linrathe, Ruar's father*
Druisius	Commander of the Ésparian Guard, Gwenna's spymaster
Duarte	Berian merchant
Eithnë	Lady of the Ti'ach na Barì
Eidyn	Captain of the Ésparian Guard
Ennaia	girlhood friend of Eudekia
Eudekia	Empress-Dowager of the East
Faolyn	*Princip of Ésparias, son to General Talyn*

Farry	Captain of Ésparias
Ferand	Lieutenant of the Ésparian Guard
Flynsà	Siusàn & Faolyn's daughter, princess of Ésparias
Finn	General of Ésparias, commanding the Eastern Fort
Fritjof	*King of Varsland in Empire's Hostage & Empire's Exile*
Garia	Major of Ésparias; Talyn's adjutant
Galen	Lena's father; Turlo's scout
Garth	Procurator of Leste; Maya's brother
Glynn	officer of Ésparias
Gnaius	*physician of Casil*
Gulian	officer of Ésparias
Gwenna	*Principe* of Ésparias
Gwyllar	Prince of Ésparias, son to Gwenna and Ruar
Hathus	*Prince of the Boranoi, married to Eudekia*
Helvi	*Ruar's wife, a Marai earl's daughter*
Irmgard	princess of Varsland, Bryngyl and Bjørn's mother
Isa	*housekeeper at the Ti'ach na Cillian*
Jordis	*a noblewoman of Linrathe*
Junia	Commander of the Horse Archers of Casil
Kira	Headwoman of Tirvan; Gwenna's aunt; midwife
Kyreth	Headwoman of Berge; midwife
Kúsi	*Comiádh* of the *Ti'ach na Kúsi*
Lairís	Sorley's niece
Lena	General of Ésparias; Gwenna & Colm's mother
Liam	*regent of Linrathe, Ruar's great-uncle*
Lianë	*Lena & Cillian's daughter, princess of Ésparias*
Lorcann	*Ruar's uncle, briefly Teannasach of Linrathe*
Lucian	*early Emperor of the West*
Lynthe	Major and princess of Ésparias; Gwenna's *quincala*
Maj	Sorley's stepmother
Marius	Druisius's brother, a merchant of Casil
Maya	Lena's lover in *Empire's Daughter;* headwoman of Tain
Muire	senior trade official for Ésparias
Narma	innkeeper in Beria
Nessus	son to the Procurator of Beria
Michan	*Major of Ésparias; senior trade envoy*
Oriacus	Procurator of Ésparias
Pallius	Governor of Ésparias
Perras	*Comiádh of the Ti'ach na Perras*
Philita	Princess of Casil, Alekos & Rosale's daughter
Philitòs	*Emperor of Casil, Eudekia's first husband; Alekos' father*

Quintus   *advisor to Eudekia, uncle to Decanius*
Reif   Major of Ésparias, Lena's adjutant
Rielo   Berian man, Nessus's bodyguard
Roghan   Sorley's brother, Lord of Gundarstorp
Rosale   Empress-Consort of Casil and the East
Ruar   *Teannasach* of Linrathe
Selekos   Prince of Casil, Alekos & Rosale's son
Siusàn   wife to Faolyn; Ruar's sister
Sorley   Lord Sorley of Gundarstorp, *scáeli* and diplomat
Tadius   Marius's younger son
Talyn   General of Ésparias; mother of Faolyn & Lynthe
Teárdh   Gwenna's cousin; son of her aunt Kira and a Marai man
Tevius   Berian landholder
Trostann   *sjaldr* of Varsland
Trygve   Prince of Varsland
Turlo   *General of the Ésparian army*
Ullach   Ruar's younger son by his wife Helvi
Valens   Marius's older son
Valle   Captain of the Ésparian Guard at the Eastern Fort
Vidar   Earl of Varsland
Vita   Marius's wife
Zinta   woman of Beria; Rielo's wife

Background characters with a historical counterpart:

Catilius   Marcus Aurelius

Peritas, Constyn's childhood dog, has the same name as Alexander the Great's dog.

Ladon, Lena's dog, has the same name as one of Acteon's hounds – and the dragon that guarded the golden apples in the Garden of the Hesperides.

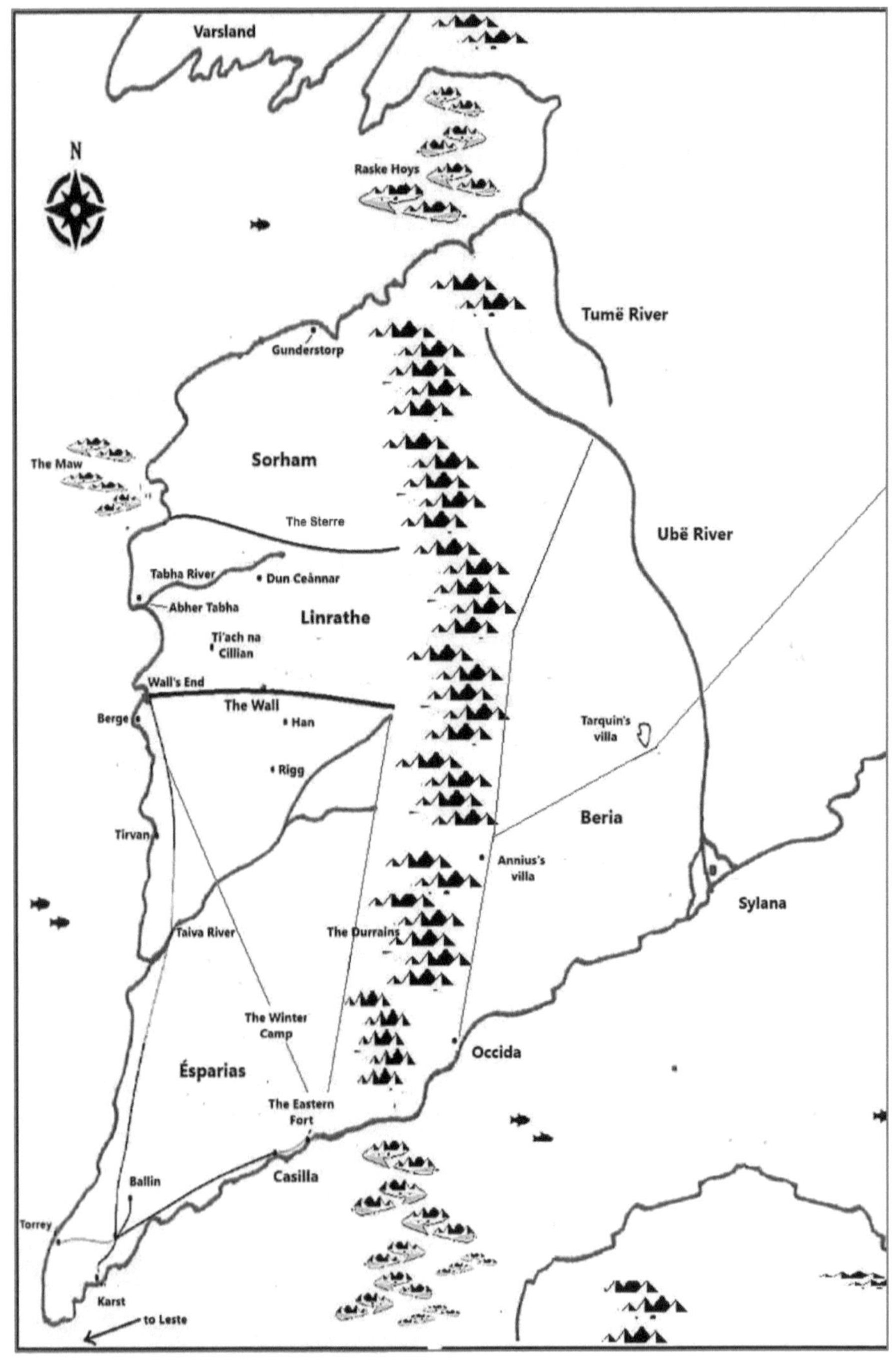
N
Varsland
Raske Hoys
Tumë River
Gunderstorp
The Maw
Sorham
Ubë River
The Sterre
Tabha River
Dun Ceànnar
Abher Tabha
Linrathe
Ti'ach na
Cillian
Wall's End
The Wall
Tarquin's
villa
Berge
Han
Rigg
Beria
Tirvan
Annius's
villa
Taiva River
Sylana
The Durrains
The Winter
Camp
Ésparias
Occida
The Eastern
Fort
Ballin
Casilla
Torrey
Karst
to Leste

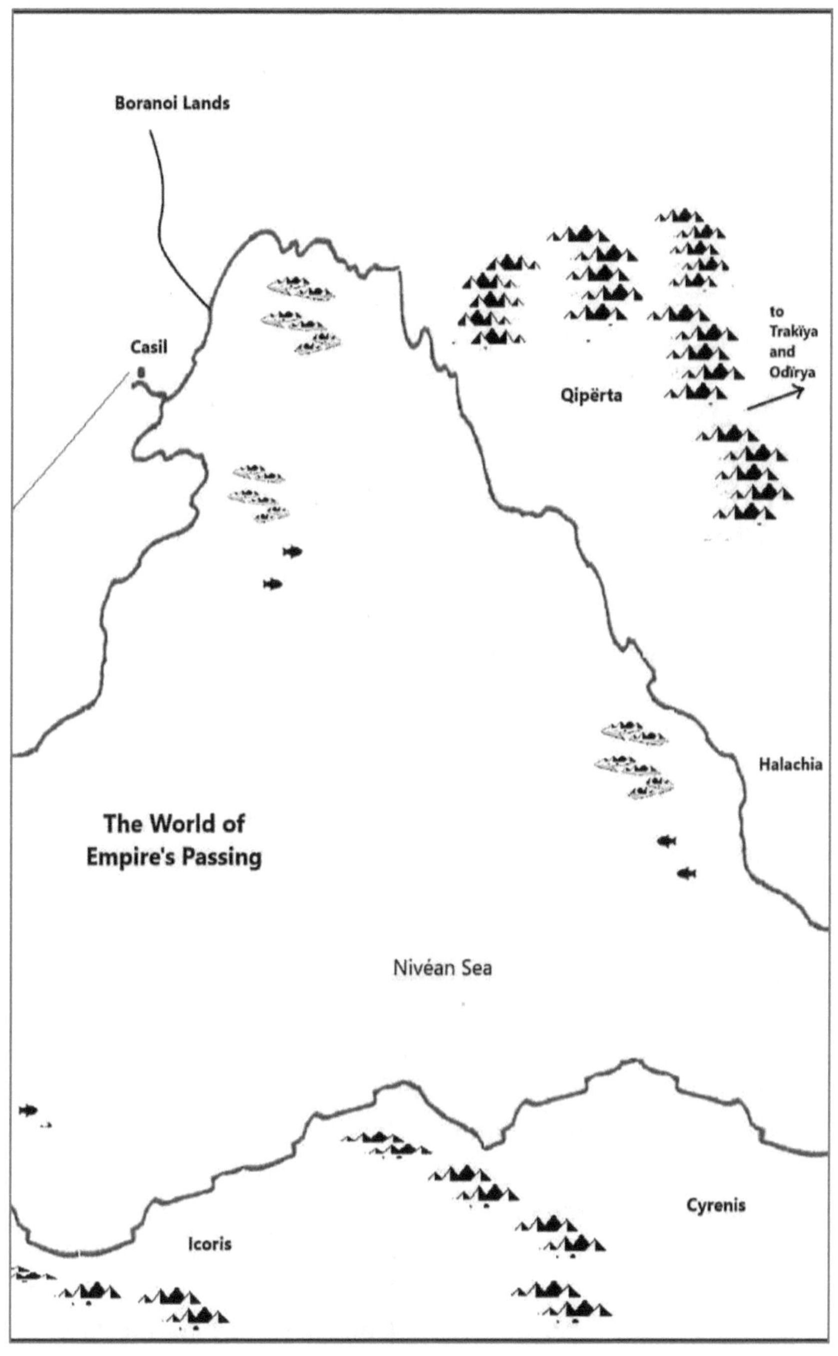
Boranoi Lands
Casil
Qipërta
to
Trakïya
and
Odïrya
The World of
Empire's Passing
Halachia
Nivéan Sea
Icoris
Cyrenis

Author's Note

Well. How do you say goodbye to characters that, in some cases, have been living in your head for twenty-five years? I began to write the story that became the first book of this series, *Empire's Daughter,* somewhere in the very late 1990s. I was forty, or thereabouts. My character Lena was almost eighteen. Now I'm sixty-five, and she's fifty-one. What a journey we've had!

As usual, there are so many people to thank: my Monday morning informal writing group; Guelph's Red Brick Café, for letting us sit and write all morning on the strength of a couple of cups of coffee; the virtual writing communities of various social media; friends and family for asking 'how's it going' occasionally; everyone who's asked for this book and promoted its predecessors through word of mouth and/or social media.

This may not have been an easy book to read; it wasn't easy to write. I read a lot of books on grief and mourning in a search for understanding of how, primarily, Lena and Sorley would react to loss. As Lena says, the path is different for everyone, but of all the books I read, Kat Lister's *The Elements: A Widowhood* was the most useful.

Music inspires my writing; there's almost always one or two songs that evoke scenes or themes in each book. This time, I was sitting in a lawn chair at an outdoor folk festival, late in an August afternoon, listening to Garnet Rogers. He sang his song *So Happy*—and all of a sudden I had an entire subplot and the final scene. (You can find it on YouTube and Bandcamp – just don't confuse it with *Oh How Happy*. I prefer the Bandcamp version.) Another song I played over and over again was Dougie McLean's *Caledonia.* You can find that on YouTube as well.

But that final scene also benefited from a song I found, also on Bandcamp, only as I read through the next-to-final proofs: the beautiful *Lost Words Blessing* on Spell Song's album *Gifts of Light.* Based on Jackie

Morris's and Robert MacFarlane's two books *The Lost Words* and *The Lost Spells*, the entire album felt like Sorley's music, the way I imagine it, but *Lost Words Blessing*, the last track, brought tears to my eyes. So I reflected just a tiny bit of that song in the last scene, because it fit.

Tony O'Brien, my cover designer, has again translated my ideas into reality, capturing the sense of the many endings that permeate the book. Thanks, Tony.

Two people deserve special mention: my friends and first readers Bjørn Larssen and Karen Heenan. Much of *Empire's Passing* was plotted on long walks in parks and wildlife refuges near Philadelphia with Karen, and not a day passed during the more than sixteen months the book took to write without discussion, critique, and/or encouragement from one or both. Having two good friends who know your characters and your world just about as well as you do is simply wonderful.

But as always, my deepest thanks are reserved for my husband, Brian Rennie. I'm not the only one who's lived with these characters for a long time! But especially this year, when family concerns meant we were apart for several months, his constant encouragement and belief that I *would* finish this book were invaluable. He also gave me the title—for that alone, he deserves a round of applause. *Thà mi air a bheth beànnaichte, kärestan.*